desert winter

NOVELS BY MICHAEL CRAFT

Rehearsing

The Mark Manning Series

Flight Dreams
Eye Contact
Body Language
Name Games
Boy Toy
Hot Spot

The Claire Gray Series

Desert Autumn
Desert Winter

www.michaelcraft.com

MICHAEL CRAFT

desert winter

st. martin's minotaur ✳ new york

121206

F
Cra

www.minotaurbooks.com

Library of Congress Cataloging-in-Publication Data

Craft, Michael, 1950–
    Desert winter / Michael Craft.—1st ed.
      p. cm.
    ISBN 0-312-30501-X
    1. Women theatrical producers and directors—Fiction.   2. Collectors and collecting—Fiction.   3. Women college teachers—Fiction.   4. Palm Springs (Calif.)—Fiction.
I. Title.

PS3553.R215 D475   2003
813'.54—dc21

                                  2002031891

First Edition: February 2003

10 9 8 7 6 5 4 3 2 1

Naturellement, numéro neuf
est encore pour Léon.

acknowledgments

The author wishes to thank Steve Morgan and Leigh Ellen Murphy for their generous assistance with various plot details. As before, Keith Kahla and Mitchell Waters provided the driving force that brings this series to print.

PART ONE

windfall

Stewart Chaffee heaved a derisive grunt. "*That's* no way to hide a murder weapon. How in hell are you supposed to disguise a sawed-off shotgun as a walking stick?"

"Precisely my point." I echoed his grunt, attempting to inflect it with a more ladylike lilt. "The walking stick seems implausible at best. But hiding the gun in a clock cabinet—*that* makes sense. And it's a handy setup that allows our killer to strike again."

A child-size papier-mâché cherub looked sternly down at us, suspended above a twelve-foot spruce that had been flocked a delicate pastel, an unlikely hue the color of champagne. The angel wore flowing but stiff brocade robes; her puffed cheeks and puckered lips tooted mute excelsis-deos from a long silver trumpet. She—like all the artful ornaments hanging from the tree and tucked among its branches—might have been pilfered from some forgotten storeroom at the Vatican. Without question, Stewart Chaffee's Christmas tree was the most tastefully exuberant specimen I'd ever seen.

Beyond the tree, huge glass doors were folded open to admit the warm, dry breeze of a late Saturday morning in early December. Fronds of date palms swayed along the perimeter of a vast lawn. The carpetlike turf—manicured bent grass—suggested a perfect, boundless putting green.

Indoors, in the lofty living room, sitting not three feet from me, Stewart drummed his fingers on the arm of his wheelchair, nodding. With a wheeze, he asked, "So you plan to adopt that detail—the clock—from the movie plot and use it in your stage production? Purists might object, Claire."

"It's worth the risk," I assured him. "When *Laura* was published in 1942, readers readily bought into the improbable melodrama of Waldo Lydecker's old, ornate walking stick serving as a devilishly disguised shotgun. Shortly after, when Vera Caspary's novel was adapted for the stage, the walking-stick gambit remained, and audiences ate it up. But when the movie appeared in 1944, at the height of the *film noir* period, the screenplay took a more realistic, hard-boiled approach: the shotgun was simply hidden by the conniving Waldo in the case of an antique pendulum clock in Laura's apartment, a clock that Waldo himself had given to the enigmatic young heroine."

I spoke of this history as if I remembered it firsthand, but in fact, it predated my birth by some five years. Stewart, however, at eighty-two, had already reached adulthood when *Laura* first captivated the masses and became an enduring masterpiece of the American suspense genre.

Leaning toward me, Stewart raised a thinning eyebrow, gray gone white. Behind him, occupying most of a wall, hung an oil painting of heroic scale depicting the rape of the Sabine women. Yellowed by passing centuries and obscured by cracked varnish, the plump, coy beauties looked more titillated than frightened by the armored warriors on their rearing steeds. Incongruously, the picture's grotesque Baroque frame bore festive holiday swags of pine entwined with pink velvet ribbons. Stewart observed flatly, "You've come to borrow a clock."

Before I could reply, Grant Knoll admitted, "That was *my* idea, Stewart. I seem to recall a marvelous Austrian case clock in your collection. Claire is now in the final week of rehearsal for her first main-stage production at Desert Arts College. I needn't tell you how fortunate we are to have a director of Claire Gray's caliber here in our midst. It's only fitting that every aspect of *Laura* should be perfect. Your clock would be the crown jewel in the setting of Laura's apartment." Grant winked at me.

I laughed at my accommodating neighbor, who had driven me to Stewart's estate that morning from our relatively humble condominiums, where we lived only steps apart, across a shared courtyard. "God, Grant, you sound as if I'd coached you."

He leaned from the sofa where we both sat, telling Stewart in a stage whisper, "In truth, milady *did* coach me, all the way over here in my car."

"This visit was *your* idea," I reminded him.

"Oh? Guess it was." Grant smoothed the sleeves of an elegant, lightweight sweater he wore that morning. He then returned his attention to Stewart. "I saw a rehearsal the other night. The set is wonderful, and the production is first-class, but there's a *hideous* old cabinet standing in as the clock. Claire told me roughly what she had in mind, and of *course* I thought of your antique Austrian pendulum clock. It's a whimsical little piece, if I'm not mistaken, not five feet high, with a vaguely oriental motif to the painted decoration of the case. I told Claire, 'Let's go right to the source and ask him.' Really, Stewart, who else but the king of Palm Springs decorators would be in a better position to supply the finishing touch to a perfect production?"

Lamely, I added, "We'd be delighted to give you printed recognition in the program," as if Stewart Chaffee's reputation could be aggrandized by a squib in my play's production credits. Though he'd retired from decorating years earlier, Stewart was now recognized as one of the preeminent art-and-antiques collectors in Southern California.

"It'll take me a day to get it out of storage," he was saying, twirling a hand, as if searching for lost details, past memories. "Pea should be able to track it down." From a black-and-white pony-skin saddlebag that hung from the arm of his wheelchair, Stewart fished a pad of paper and a pencil, then scribbled himself a note.

"Wonderful," said Grant. "If we pick it up tomorrow morning, Claire and I can get it to the theater in time for the Sunday-afternoon rehearsal."

"Tech rehearsal," I elaborated. "It'll be a long afternoon, and I'd really hoped to have everything in place by then, so I can't thank you enough."

Stewart gave me a wary grin, confused by my chatter, as if he'd already forgotten what we were talking about. Then he snapped his fingers—"That reminds me, Grant. Have you finished with my Biedermeier desk?"

It was now I who was confused.

"Later today," said Grant. "The designer showhouse closes this afternoon. I'll pick up the desk and return it tomorrow when I drive back with Claire."

I must have still looked confused.

Grant explained, "It's a lovely little Biedermeier piece, a diminutive writing desk. It'll fit in the car. That's how I moved it before."

I now recalled why Grant had suggested Stewart as a source for my clock in the first place: Grant, a high-end real-estate broker, had occasionally borrowed from Stewart exceptional pieces of furniture or art to outfit decorator showhouses for charity events.

Stewart tittered, telling my affable neighbor, "Be careful schlepping that furniture, cupcake. You wouldn't want to chip a nail. Let me send Pea over to help with the toting and hauling."

"Now, *that* would be a sight," Grant camped. "Pea with a tool belt and a dolly. Can't you just *see* him sporting big suede work gloves?"

Both men—gay, of course—shrieked with laughter. Though separated by more than thirty years, they shared a brotherhood transcending the age, race, faith, or station of its members. As for Pea, the name was unknown to me.

Wiping a milky eye, composing himself, Stewart asked, "You know the security code, don't you?"

Grant reminded him, "We got in this morning."

"Yes, yes, but on Sunday morning I'm not sure who'll be around the house to answer the intercom and buzz you in. Just use the keypad at the gate." And he told Grant a four-digit code, not a very clever one, by my reckoning. It wouldn't take a cryptographer to decipher that the gate code was the year of Stewart's birth.

"Mr. Chaffee?"

I turned at the sound of the voice, which I recognized as that of Bonnie Bahr, Stewart's at-home nurse, who had earlier admitted us.

She stepped farther into the room. "Mr. Lloyd is here to see you. Shall I have him wait?" She folded her hands in front of her white polyester uniform. A big woman with muscled arms (more muscled than those of any man in the room), she wore her lifeless blond hair cropped short and serviceable. In contrast to this inelegant image, her pleasant voice lent a note of femininity.

Grant said, "Please, Stewart, don't detain your guest on our account. Claire and I won't take any more of your time." He pulled his weight to the edge of the sofa, as if to rise.

"Bah," said Stewart, "stay put. Lloyd's here so often, he hardly qualifies as a guest." Then Stewart turned to his nurse. "Hey, you. Show him in, piglet."

Aghast as I was by his manner of addressing his buxom caregiver, I was even less prepared for her response. She lobbed the insult right back at him: "You crippled old goat—someone ought to put you out of your misery." Bonnie turned on her heel, marching out of the room.

Grant was no less appalled than I was by this exchange. Taken aback, we both sat stiff and silent on the sofa, not daring to let our eyes meet. Even the cherub, assisted by a fortuitous draft, turned her back on the embarrassing scene. One of the Sabine women, with the back of her hand frozen to her forehead in overwrought horror, silently gasped.

But Stewart roared with laughter. Was the verbal sparring with his nurse merely a well-practiced routine he enjoyed? Or did his laughter signal a callous disregard not only for their acrimony, but also for the discomfort of his guests?

"Stewart!" said a man in his late fifties, presumably Mr. Lloyd, striding into the room. He wore a dark business suit, looking too formal for the desert, especially on Saturday morning. He was followed by Bonnie and by another woman, younger, still in her twenties, also dressed for business, whose ruddy hair, clipped in a severe china-doll coiffure—very Sassoon—gave her a quiet air of urban sophistication. Mr. Lloyd stepped up to Stewart, shaking hands. "Hope I'm not intruding. Have time for a bit of banking?"

Grant and I stood. Stewart remained anchored to the wheelchair.

He told the visitor, "Always time for banking, Merrit. Always. In fact, there's something I've been meaning to give you." He ferreted in his saddlebag.

There was an awkward silence as Stewart continued to rummage, so the visitor turned to me and introduced himself. "I'm Merrit Lloyd, vice president for client services at Indian Wells Bank and Trust. It's my pleasure to serve as Stewart's personal banker. He's a very special customer."

Grant, who apparently knew the banker, said, "Merrit, it's *my* pleasure to introduce Claire Gray, one of the American theater's most illustrious talents."

Merrit gave my hand a gentle shake, holding it for a moment. "I'm honored, Miss Gray. I hope you're finding desert life agreeable." In a word, the man struck me as clean—nice features, perfectly groomed, well mannered. And his touch conveyed that he was not a member of Grant and Stewart's fraternity.

"On a spectacular day like this," I bantered, gesturing toward the idyllic setting beyond the Christmas tree, "my only regret is not having moved here years ago." I'd arrived in the Sonoran Desert just three months earlier, leaving my professional career on Broadway to chair the theater department at the new arts college. "Please do call me Claire. After a certain age, 'Miss' has deadly overtones." I primped.

"Claire," he obliged, "I'd like you to meet my assistant, Robin Jones."

The young woman stepped forward, smiled, set down a briefcase, and shook my hand. "Actually," she noted wryly, "I'm Merrit's secretary. 'Assistant' is overly generous, if politically correct. Welcome to California, Claire."

"Thank you, Robin."

Stewart slipped a plain white envelope out of his pony-skin bag and set it in his lap. "Robin runs the whole show," he told me. "Merrit couldn't get a damn thing done without her."

With a good-natured shrug, Merrit admitted, "He's right."

"*Bonnie*," barked Stewart, "where are your manners? We have guests. I think everyone might enjoy some pink fluff."

Bonnie told the rest of us, "And I thought I was his *nurse,* not a waitress."

"Quitcher whinin'," Stewart snapped at her. "Pink fluff!"

I had no idea what he was talking about.

"I already told you, goat man, it's *gone.*"

Stewart fumed at her. "Wait till Pea gets home . . ."

"Oh, yeah? What's *he* gonna do about it?" Bonnie planted her hefty hands on her hips. "He's worthless in the kitchen. So you'll just have to wait till I have a chance to whip up a fresh batch." Her humor lightened. "I'll try to make some at home tonight—on my own time." She turned to the rest of us, explaining through a modest grin, "He laps it up as fast as I can make it." Then she offered, "Can I get you something else, though? Maybe something to drink?"

We all declined.

Judiciously, Merrit changed the topic from refreshments, telling Grant, "I understand congratulations are in order, Mr. President."

Grant looked momentarily befuddled, then laughed. "Thanks, but the title doesn't mean much—it's more like a second job." He explained to the others, "I've just begun serving a term as president of the board of directors at DMSA, the Desert Museum of Southwestern Arts."

"Thatta boy, Grant," said Stewart, thwacking his palm on the arm of his chair. "It's a fine museum with a worthy collection. They've always struggled, but now, *you* can help. You've got a shrewd business sense, and more important, no one in the valley is better connected with the 'right' social contacts."

Deflecting this flattery, Grant assured Stewart, "I'll help any way I can. Truth is, though, the museum *isn't* struggling anymore. Now that it's been brought under the wing of Desert Arts College, its future is secure. Glenn Yeats has not only endowed DMSA in perpetuity; he's built the museum a brand-new facility on the campus of his college."

Merrit said, "Mr. Yeats is exceedingly generous."

Stewart wasn't quite so complimentary. "With *that* man's wealth, it's *easy* to be generous."

"But he's more than magnanimous," I said. "The man has vision."

We were speaking of D. Glenn Yeats, the computer-software ty-coon, the multibillionaire with a soft spot for the arts who had de-cided to "give back" to society by building, from the sand up, a world-class arts college right there in the Coachella Valley. Yeats now devoted his energies to serving as president of the college, and it was he who had recruited me—personally, with lavish offers I could not ultimately refuse—to leave my career in New York and join his faculty.

"There's wealth," said the banker, "and then there's *wealth*." He sighed. Glenn Yeats's fortune far outweighed that of any client at Indian Wells Bank and Trust. In fact, Yeats's assets surely dwarfed those of the bank itself.

As our wistful conversation paid homage to the benevolent power of cash, Robin quietly prepared for business. On a low table near the sofa, she opened the fat briefcase, which I now realized belonged to Merrit, not her, and began to remove its contents. She arranged accounts, contracts, files, and other paperwork in neat stacks on the table. Checking to see that a pen was working, she set it atop one of the piles; I presumed Stewart's signature was needed. Robin also inventoried and tidied items belonging to Merrit—his cell phone, his car keys, his calendar. Stewart's earlier comment was apt. Merrit was clearly dependent upon his secretary's efficient services.

Merrit and Stewart got to work, with Merrit explaining the need for various disbursements, Stewart signing checks and other docu-ments. Their discussion covered household bills, tax payments, art acquisitions—everything. Merrit's assistance went well beyond matters of banking; he was both a personal and a financial spaniel to his client. Robin remained in the background throughout these deal-ings, handing documents to her boss, filing others when Stewart had signed them, maintaining a checklist of the morning's transactions.

While they worked, Grant and I felt free to wander about the living room. He described a few antiques and works of art, all of it museum-quality, adding, "That's just the tip of the iceberg. Stewart's collection is so vast, most of it's in storage." He paused to admire the shell-and-ivory marquetry of a Louis Something sideboard.

Ambling away from Grant, toward the Christmas tree, I studied it up close, amazed by the intricacy of its ornaments and the quality of its curios, many of which struck me as miniature objets d'art worthy of being displayed on a mantel or a pedestal—not stuck in a flocked tree.

"It's pretty, isn't it?"

Focused on the tree, I hadn't noticed Stewart's nurse step up beside me. Her strong features beamed a childlike joy as she stared at a svelte crystal ballerina that dangled and spun from a nearby branch. I answered her question through a breathy gasp, "I've never seen anything like it. The lights must be magnificent. Have you seen it at night, Bonnie?"

She nodded. "Many times. It's almost overwhelming, and the grounds are a real fairyland. Oops." She touched her fingers to her lips. "I didn't mean that the way it sounded."

I laughed quietly. "I understand."

"Mr. Chaffee can seem sorta gruff at times, with the name-calling and such, but underneath, there's a wonderful sense of humor. And it goes without saying, no one alive has a finer appreciation for everything beautiful." She glanced about our surroundings.

"You seem to enjoy working for him."

"Who wouldn't?" She again paused to give the opulent digs an appreciative glance.

My gaze was drawn to a grand piano, less than six inches long, hanging near the ballerina. The piano's inlaid lid was propped open, revealing eighty-eight taut golden strings within. Mulling Bonnie's enthusiasm for her job, I said, "I couldn't help thinking that Stewart might be difficult to work for."

"I'm a nurse," Bonnie reminded me with a thin smile and evident pride. "I'm used to dealing with people at their worst."

Having spent a lifetime in the theater, I'd become a student of character—all types—and Bonnie suddenly fascinated me. I wanted to know more. "May I ask how long you've worked here?"

"Mr. Chaffee suffered a stroke about two years ago, and that's when my duties here began. It wasn't that serious, and he's recovered nicely, but at eighty-two, he needs help. Even before the stroke, he was dealing with congestive heart disease. That's why he uses the wheelchair—it's easier for him to get around."

"Then he's not . . . ?" I whirled a hand, searching for a genteel euphemism for *crippled*.

Bonnie suggested, "Disabled?"

This struck me as entirely too vague; I was expecting something more along the lines of *ambulatorily impaired*. Just to make sure we were on the same page, I rephrased my question: "He can walk, then?"

"Yes, Miss Gray. With difficulty. Gosh, you must think I'm awful." She clasped her hands in front of her stout, white-clad bosom. "I would *never* tease him about being a 'crippled old goat' if in fact he was . . ."

I supplied the evasive word. "Disabled."

With downcast eyes, she mumbled, "Exactly, Miss Gray."

"Enough!" Stewart bleated (the old goat). "The rest of this hoo-ha will have to wait. I'm not a well man, remember." And with that, he shifted his weight to one hip and blew a hefty fart. From the sound of it, he could have ripped the leather seat of his wheelchair.

"Oh, my!" said Bonnie, oddly pleased by her patient's anal out-burst. Like a doting mommy, she told us, "His fleshy trumpet seems to be in fine tune this morning."

Grant and I caught each other's glance and struggled not to laugh.

Merrit and Robin proceeded with their paper pushing as though nothing had happened; perhaps they'd heard previous trumpet re-citals. Glancing at a file and handing it to Robin, Merrit told his client, "I can return with the rest early Monday. No problem." He turned to Grant and me, adding, "Many days, I'm here more than once."

"Maybe by then," said Stewart to his banker, "by Monday, you'll know if that collector in Boston is ready to sell. I want that Winslow Homer seascape."

Merrit jogged another stack of papers. "Your last offer caught his interest, all right. I think he'll bite. Meanwhile, Robin has been verifying the painting's provenance."

Stewart grunted his approval.

I must have looked confused. Grant, standing near me, explained, "A provenance is the documentation of an artwork's authenticity, as established by its history of ownership."

"Ah."

Merrit assured all of us, "Robin is a first-rate researcher. Our clients' interests are well protected."

"Thank you, sir," she said, allowing a smile.

"Speaking of research," Stewart addressed the young woman, "have you had any success in setting up that appointment for Monday?"

Robin nodded. "Everything's taken care of, Mr. Chaffee. I tracked down the gallery in Santa Barbara, and your meeting is booked as requested."

Merrit asked, "Is there anything else, Stewart? I didn't intend to rob you of so much time with your guests," meaning Grant and me.

"Actually"—Stewart paused, heaving a sigh—"there *is* something else." He lifted from his lap the envelope that he'd retrieved from his saddlebag. "This is important. I want you to place it in my safe-deposit box at the bank."

"Certainly, Stewart. My pleasure." Merrit took the ordinary white envelope, examined it briefly (it didn't seem to contain much, perhaps a page or two), then handed it to Robin, who placed it in a folder, which in turn went into the briefcase.

Robin said, "I notice the envelope has no markings, Mr. Chaffee. Are there any special instructions?"

"There are." Stewart turned from the secretary to the banker. "Merrit, I trust you. You've had complete access to my affairs for many years now. I think of you not only as my banker, but also as my friend. When I die, I want you to go to my safe-deposit box and open that envelope. It will make my wishes plain enough."

"Stewart, I really think it would be more appropriate for—"

Bonnie interrupted. "No, Mr. Chaffee. This isn't necessary, not yet. Your condition is difficult, I know, but it's not life-threatening. You're in no immediate danger. Please, try not to think such morbid thoughts."

The old man gave his nurse a get-real stare. "Bonnie, I'm eighty-two—with a stroke and a heart condition. I'm not being morbid, just realistic."

"But, Stewart," said his banker, "I've told you before: you need a good lawyer, an estate planner, to assist you with these matters. Your holdings are far too vast to be settled by a simple letter of intent. Your entire estate could be held up in probate for years, and your final wishes could end up unfulfilled. It's complicated, but—"

"It's *not* complicated," Stewart insisted. "In fact, it's perfectly straightforward. As for lawyers, you know how I've always felt about them—I just don't trust them. And I'm not about to *start* trusting them *now.*" Harrumph.

"A homemade letter of intent, which lawyers would call a holographic will, is a risky instrument at best. As your financial adviser, I strongly recommend—"

"I didn't ask for your advice, Merrit. I asked you to keep the envelope for me and to open it when I'm gone."

With a weary nod, the banker said, "Yes, Stewart, of course I'll do that. But in the meantime, give some thought to your family, your loved ones."

With a sarcastic snort, Stewart said, "All these years, there's been nothing but bad blood between me and the rest of my family— what's left of it. So it's time to get things settled." He jerked his head toward the briefcase that now contained his envelope.

Then he repeated, "That will make my wishes plain enough," punctuating the statement with another toot of his fleshy trumpet.

Overhead, the papier-mâché cherub still puffed into her long silver trumpet, but sounded not a note.

2

Grant Knoll phoned from his car and checked in with Tracie, receptionist at the Nirvana sales office, where Grant was the principal broker. An exclusive, gated development of mountainside homes, Nirvana was also the site of a dramatically modern estate built by D. Glenn Yeats, the computer tycoon. When I had agreed to join Yeats's faculty at Desert Arts College, he had put me in touch with Grant to assist in finding housing for me. Grant would become not only my neighbor, but my new best friend.

Tracie told Grant that it had been a quiet Saturday morning and there were no appointments for him that afternoon, so Grant suggested I join him for lunch at his condo. This had become something of a weekend ritual for us, and I happily accepted.

Lush landscaping whisked past the car as we passed through Rancho Mirage, headed home toward Palm Desert. Driving away from Stewart Chaffee's estate, I noticed that it was located near that of the late Walter Annenberg, where sprawling grounds within the landmark pink walls included both a golf course and a mausoleum—talk about covering your bases.

"For a struggling decorator," I thought aloud, "Stewart didn't do too badly. This must be one of the priciest neighborhoods in the valley."

With eyes on the road, Grant told me, "Stewart never struggled. He was in the right place at the right time—and he was good. A society decorator during one of the desert's early boom periods, he established a prosperous career, and his fortunes snowballed. He eventually outgrew his original quarters in old Palm Springs and moved down valley to a choice tract of land here in Rancho."

"Needed a bit of elbow room, eh?"

"Yup. As his decorating career waned, he got more involved as a serious collector, so the space has served him well."

Mulling the events of that morning, I couldn't help observing, "It's hard to imagine that he ever ran a thriving business. I mean, he's cantankerous and self-centered. He refuses to deal with lawyers. In a word, he's eccentric."

Turning onto Highway One-Eleven, the main route through the string of desert cities, Grant told me, "Some of Stewart's edginess came with age. He wasn't always a curmudgeon; he was known to be quite charming. Besides, top-end clients are willing to put up with a measure of attitude from their decorator. In fact," Grant added with a knowing laugh, "they'd feel cheated without some of that posturing, better known as flair."

Quietly, I noted, "It's a different world out here." I was still adjusting to life in California. Not that New Yorkers couldn't hold their own when it came to edginess and posturing, but there was a distinct mind-set here on the opposite coast, and I was not yet fully attuned to it.

"In spite of Stewart's cranky nature," Grant said, "he's always been philanthropic with his wealth. He's played a substantial role in helping to establish a vibrant arts scene throughout the valley."

"Then I guess we can forgive his eccentricities." I chortled. I was a fine one to talk of others' foibles.

We gabbed in this agreeable manner until reaching Villa Paseo, a six-unit condominium complex that we both called home. Some ten years earlier, Grant had been a partner in designing and building the charming development, which resembled a fanciful, tile-roofed stage setting for some merry operetta—replete with fountains, wrought-iron balconies entwined with bougainvillea, and staggered, white-washed chimneys.

Grant parked in his garage; then we crossed the center courtyard together, approaching his unit, which was located in a prime location adjacent to the common pool. I asked, "Do you need some time to yourself first?"

"Nah. Come on in." He opened the iron gate to his entry court. "We can gossip while I throw lunch together." As he opened his front door, the security system beeped, and he entered a code to shut it down.

I asked, "It's just us?"

"Kane doesn't seem to be home yet." Grant led me inside. "But I'm sure he'll appear by the time we're ready to eat."

"Such a dear boy."

With a licentious growl, Grant agreed, "Isn't he?"

It was something of a slip, referring to Kane Richter as a boy; he was twenty-one. Grant, at forty-nine, was old enough to be his father, but the age difference didn't faze them in the least. Since meeting in September, neither man had ever seemed happier.

"Make yourself comfortable," said Grant as he tossed his keys into a little basket on the hall table, then stepped into the kitchen and checked the phone for messages. Finding none, he pulled the refrigerator open. "Wine?"

"Not yet, thanks," I called from the living room. "Maybe with lunch."

Surveying the room, I noted that Grant had not yet decorated for Christmas, but I assumed this was a task he would soon undertake with relish. After all, these tasteful quarters were now home to two men, not one. Most of the room's artwork was the same; it had been displayed there since my arrival in the desert. And Grant's collection of old mercury glass still filled the space with sparkle. But many of the framed photos had been changed. Before, I had noted that most of these snapshots were of Grant on his travels—solo—or escorting dowagers and socialites to charity balls. Now, photos of Grant and Kane—together—beamed infectious, loving smiles from every corner of the room. They posed together on their first "real" date, dinner at the Regal Palms Hotel. There were framed mementos of their tram ride to Mount San Jacinto and quick weekend trips to Las Vegas and Los Angeles. And on and on. Their whirlwind courtship had been well documented, and there was no end in sight.

I strolled to the kitchen, where Grant was working up a bountiful luncheon salad for us. I told him, "You're a changed man."

"Don't I know it, doll." He continued whisking his vinaigrette without missing a beat. "I thought it would never happen, but it was love at first sight."

I could well recall the moment when they'd met. Grant and I had driven into Palm Springs for dinner at a trendy new restaurant, Fusión, and Kane was working there that night as a parking valet. At first glance, he was just another college kid in tennis shorts with a fetching smile, great tan, and a body in its prime. Now, in retrospect, what followed seemed inevitable. "You two didn't waste any time."

"Why should we?" Grant glanced over his shoulder at me. "Kane and I were right for each other—we *are* right for each other. It's not just lust, Claire. It's commitment. It's real."

"I can tell." I crossed to the refrigerator, opened it, and retrieved the wine Grant had offered. "You and Kane strike me as the most settled, 'normal' couple I know."

"Despite our age difference? And our same sex? I'll take that as a compliment."

"It was meant as a compliment. Mind if I help myself? Care for some?"

"Please." Grant's hands were busy with something in the big ceramic salad bowl, so he jerked his head toward the breakfast table, where he'd set out some wineglasses, three.

Filling two of them, I asked, "Can I assume you've adjusted to couplehood? You'd been on your own quite a while, Grant."

"I'm amazed at how smoothly we've both adapted. I can't imagine what I was thinking all those years."

"You were waiting for the right man to come along, remember?" Grant laughed. "He came along, all right. Thank God." Then, as though he'd overlooked some niggling detail, he added, "Oh. Did I tell you we're getting married?"

Dumbstruck, I set down the wine bottle.

"Well," Grant explained, "not in the official, *legal* sense, of course. What I mean is, Kane and I are planning, in effect, to *contractually* marry. I'm going to set up a meeting with my lawyer; then we can draw up reciprocal wills and exchange powers of attorney. We want to be fully responsible for each other. We'll also register as domestic partners with the California secretary of state's office. It's as close to marriage as the law allows."

I had to ask, "Aren't you moving awfully fast with this?"

He allowed, "I know it's been only three months. Maybe I ought to have my head examined—"

"Maybe you ought to be kidnapped and deprogrammed." I was kidding, sort of.

"Living together was my idea. Marriage was Kane's."

"Aha."

"But I'm all for it. All in due time, that is. Kane is more than ready to make everything official—right now—but I think we need a few more months before we tie any knots."

"Good idea."

"Not that anything could change my mind."

"Of course not. Will there be a ceremony of some kind?"

"Maybe. If there is, you'll be the first to be invited."

I stepped to my neighbor and wrapped him in a hug. "Congratulations, Grant. I wish you and Kane every happiness together. What a pity that gay marriage is still such a sticky issue, that our society refuses to recognize what you're doing."

"All in due time. The day will come."

I stepped back, studying him. "Your patience and optimism are commendable, but if I were in your shoes, I'd be itching for some validation."

Wryly, he reminded me, "You're *not* in my shoes. There's nothing standing in *your* way. You can have all the validation you want. What's milady waiting for?"

I froze. I'd unintentionally steered our conversation in a direction I was unwilling to travel. Struggling for words, I was saved by the sound of the front door opening.

"Hey, who's here? Oh, hi, Claire," said Kane Richter as he walked into the kitchen. "Hope I'm not interrupting anything."

"Nothing at all," I assured the pleasant young man as he paused to greet his partner with a kiss, a long one, not a peck. No doubt about it—they were in love. Kane didn't look like a kid anymore, though he wore shorts and a T-shirt. And Grant looked far younger than his years, though he was impeccably dressed from his morning of casual business meetings. In spite of the two men's seeming incongruity, they were a perfect match.

"You're just in time for lunch," said Grant.

"Glad I didn't stop for a burger on the way home. I had a hunch you might be up to something." Kane turned to me, grinning. "The guy even *cooks*. How lucky is that?"

Grant dismissed the flattery. "Not much cooking today, I'm afraid. It's just a salad." His words were too humble. The various ingredients—the greens, the fluted mushrooms, the grilled chicken—had taken a considerable amount of advance preparation.

"Perfect," said Kane. "I'll help with the table. Outdoors?"

Silly question. It was a pristine early-winter day in the desert. By now, the temperature had nudged seventy. From the terrace by the pool, the peaks of the surrounding mountain ranges—the Santa Rosas, San Jacintos, and San Bernardinos—looked close enough to touch, like artful but artificial backdrops constructed for the stage.

Within minutes, we had settled around the glass-topped table under an arbor near the pool. A distant mockingbird's melodic drill drifted on a dry breeze spiced with citrus and oleander. The setting, far more intoxicating than the chardonnay I sipped, still seemed unreal to me. I was tempted to pinch myself, as it did not seem possible to think of paradise as home.

We gabbed as we ate, speaking of Stewart Chaffee's quirky behavior, regaling Kane with our tale of Stewart's friendly feud with his full-figured nurse, capping our story with the ill-mannered incident of the fleshy trumpet.

Predictably, Kane found this uproarious. He leaned back in his chair, cupping his hands and applauding slowly as he laughed—when did the younger generation begin doing that? Where on earth did they pick up this odd, pervasive habit? I blinked away the image of Kane as a trained seal with a ruffle around its neck, clapping its flippers and barking. At the same time, I studied Kane's technique, knowing I could put it to use in some future production that might feature a contemporary twenty-something male.

Kane wiped an eye, sat forward again, and asked, "Why were you with this guy in the first place?"

Grant explained that I needed a particular sort of clock for the *Laura* set. "It's like a grandfather clock, but smaller. Stewart has a wonderful example in his collection—Austrian, eighteenth-century. Claire and I will be returning tomorrow morning to pick it up. Maybe you could ride along to help with the lifting."

"Sure, happy to." Then Kane turned to me. "The play opens next week, doesn't it?"

"Friday night." A knot gripped my stomach as I set down my wineglass. Though I'd directed hundreds of plays in a career spanning three decades, the prospect of an opening night still brought butterflies. This healthy apprehension served to remind me that my work was soon to be judged, that I could never let down my guard. "The show's in great shape," I told Kane blithely (I was acting). "My work is all but done. The last week of production always feels like automatic pilot."

Grant shook his head, laughing softly. "I'm amazed you're so calm about it, doll. The whole valley is abuzz. Did you see the headline of today's feature in the *Desert Sun*? It blared, CLAIRE GRAY'S LOCAL DEBUT AN INSTANT SELLOUT. Ever since your arrival at Desert Arts College, people have been looking forward to Friday's opening with *breathless* anticipation."

"Well, then," I responded with a carefree flip of my hands, "it's time to deliver." My easy smile concealed mild panic. As if to reassure myself, I noted, "The theater itself is magnificent. The set and costumes are first-rate. And I've never seen a finer student cast."

Graciously, Grant reminded me, "No student cast has ever been taught by a finer director."

"Oh, shush. I'm sure that's an exaggeration." I loved it.

"You haven't said much about Tanner lately. Has he lived up to your expectations in his role?"

I paused, then said in earnest, "My instincts about Tanner were dead-on. He's a born actor, a natural talent. In fact, I chose *Laura* as DAC's premier production specifically so I could cast him as the leading man, McPherson, the detective. Prepare to be wowed."

Grant chortled. "Tanner wouldn't even need to open his mouth to wow an audience. Christ, what a looker."

"*I'll* say." Kane twitched his brows.

We were speaking of Tanner Griffin, a heartthrob I'd discovered working in a body shop shortly before classes started. At twenty-six, he'd yet to follow his dream of entering acting school. As director of a fledgling theater program, I'd seen at once that he could add an important dimension of maturity to my young troupe. So at my invitation, he'd enrolled at DAC.

With a wistful sigh, Grant said, "Would that he liked boys."

With smug certainty, I assured my neighbor, "He doesn't. Pity for you."

"Alas. Even so, Kane and I wouldn't *think* of missing the big night."

Kane added, "Thanks for the tickets, Claire. I hear they're hard to get. Some of the staff at the museum were complaining that they had to settle for the show's second weekend."

I set down my fork. "I'm sorry, Kane. I've been so busy with the production, I'd forgotten about your internship at the museum. How's the new job going?"

"Great. I love it—it sure beats parking cars. And it's already been helpful, getting some actual working experience in design. Lots of other students wanted that internship."

I grinned. "Guess you got lucky." Truth is, Kane had connections. Strings had been pulled.

Shortly after he and Grant had met, I learned that Kane was studying graphic design at a local community college and hoped to further his studies at a four-year school. Since Desert Arts College had just opened its doors and I was on the faculty—wielding considerable clout with the school's founder and president—I had no trouble pulling some strings, and Kane was admitted to the design program as a late transfer a few weeks into the semester.

Meanwhile, the Desert Museum of Southwestern Arts was moving into its new facility on campus, and Grant, who had long served as one of its directors, was elected president of the board. The college was funding a new assistantship at the museum for a graphic-design intern who would work in the office and help with publicity projects. So Grant pulled some strings. And Kane was sitting pretty.

He was telling me, "Grant helped me set up a home studio in our second bedroom. Pretty cool."

"Bringing your work home?"

"Some. But mainly it's for assignments for design class. I could use the computer lab on campus, but it seems to be most crowded when you need it most. So Grant gave up the extra bedroom."

"Small sacrifice," said Grant. "I've never much cared for houseguests anyway."

Kane asked, "Wanna see it, Claire?" He was practically out of his seat.

"Sure. Right after lunch."

Right after lunch, we all cleared the table, Grant began tidying up the kitchen, and Kane led me down the hall, turning into the guest room, now his at-home studio.

I paused in the doorway, both impressed and surprised. I'm not sure what I'd expected, having no practical knowledge of the graphic-design trade or its tools, but I hadn't realized that the field was now essentially electronic. There was no drafting table, easel, or any of the other appurtenances I might have guessed I would find.

"Since the era of desktop publishing," Kane was explaining, "computers have completely replaced mechanical art, or pasteups. And pre-press rarely involves film anymore; a print job will generally go direct-to-plate from my electronic file."

I nodded knowledgeably, but had no idea what he was talking about.

Kane added some gibberish about his computer, its extralarge monitor, two printers (high-resolution laser, four-color ink-jet), and flatbed scanner. "Grant didn't skimp on anything. The whole setup is professional-grade."

I posited, "Since you aim to enter the profession, you need the right tools."

Kane smiled. "That's just what Grant said."

"Did I hear my name?" said Grant, entering the room as he finished wiping his hands with a striped dish towel.

"Yes," I said, "your name was on our lips—most of it favorable."

Grant gestured at the array of new equipment. "Can you believe it? Things have sure changed since *I* was in art school." To Kane, he added, "Way back then, we used to etch bison on stone tablets. I was considered quite good."

Kane laughed, sat down at his desk, and flipped a master switch. Something bleeped.

I crossed my arms, thinking. "Did I know you were an art student, Grant?"

"Not sure we've ever discussed it. There's *plenty* we haven't covered, doll." He gave me a lewd wink.

"I mean," I rambled, "I *know* you're artistic, but I assumed that just went with the territory, so to speak."

He tisked. "The gay part is genetic—I'm reasonably sure of that—but the artsy part is acquired. It has to be learned. No one's *born* with fabulous taste."

"Ah." I was still learning.

"And that's why I majored in painting and drawing." To Kane, he emphasized, "Painting and drawing—that's what they call 'fine art,' muffin. Design, architecture, and such—those are all 'applied arts.' When we fine artists weren't busy sketching bison, we used to swap designer jokes. 'How many graphic designers does it take to sharpen a pencil?' That sort of thing."

"And now you're practically married to one," the kid reminded him, looking up from his computer screen. "Wonders never cease."

"So why," I asked Grant, "did you end up a businessman?"

"To accommodate my expensive tastes. Let's face it—for many of us, college is a holding pattern. I had no idea what I wanted to do with my life, so I majored in something I liked. I'm still grateful for the art background, but Lord knows, I couldn't make a *career* out of it."

"Yeah," said Kane, under his breath, "especially when all the bison died off."

"Exactly. So I found my niche in real estate. It's not an art, I admit, but I think I've succeeded in bringing an element of art *to* it."

"Well said," I told him, though he doubtless had meant his assertion to be more poetic than earnest.

Kane swiveled his chair to face us. "Bottom line: Grant was great to set this up for me. Someday, I'll try to pay him back."

Grant stepped over to his young lover and hugged his shoulders. "You've already repaid me in a million ways, every day. Besides, it was time to get modern. This place needed a dedicated workstation for a computer. I use it too."

"For Internet access," said Kane, "but you could handle that with a laptop." He returned his attention to the screen, clicking on icons for various programs, which opened in layers. Whatever he was doing, he seemed adept and intent at it.

I laughed at a fleeting thought.

"Yes?" asked Grant. "Milady is amused?"

"Somehow, I just can't picture you as an artist—an *artiste*—with a beret, a palette, and a billowing, flouncy smock."

"Oh, really?" he grumbled, tossing down his towel. "A flouncy smock wouldn't suit me? Truth is, back in my college days, you were more likely to find me in tattered jeans and a military-surplus work shirt."

"Impossible." I shook my head decisively. "You're making this up."

"None of it. In fact"—he crossed the room and opened the double doors of a closet—"herein lie the remains of my four years in art school."

I stepped near him and peered inside. I saw no denim bell-bottoms, but I did see stacks of canvases, some dozen large, zippered portfolios, oversize pads of newsprint, and piles of spiral-bound sketchbooks. My eye rested curiously on a big beat-up tackle box, virtually covered with paint smudges.

"My oils and brushes," Grant explained, "now dried out and worthless, I'm sure." As if to prove his point, he pulled the case out of the closet, snapped open its locks, and raised the lid. Crusty old tubes of paint lay curled together like colorful little corpses. He lifted a bunch of artist's brushes, bound with a brittle rubber band that crumbled at his touch. He shrugged. "Dead. That's what happens after nearly thirty years of disuse."

I sniffed something pleasant. "*That's* still alive. What is that?"

"Linseed oil. Isn't it great? I love that smell." He opened a compartment beneath the tray of brushes. "At least the pencils are still good. And the charcoal will last forever. I always liked working in charcoal—it's so spontaneous and expressive. But the beauty of it is, you can rework the drawing with your hands, smudging and toning it with your fingers." He displayed his perfectly manicured hands. "You wouldn't believe the mess."

"Can you show me some drawings?"

"Thought you'd never ask." He pulled out one of the large pads. "These are just sketches," he explained, flipping past the cover, "quick studies that were done at the start of a life-drawing class. Warm-up exercises."

"They're *wonderful*," I gushed as he turned page after page. The incomplete drawings showed varied poses of the same nude model, sometimes focusing on a detail that had caught Grant's young eye— the crook of an elbow, the drooping fingers of a relaxed hand, the firm muscles of someone's beefy buttocks.

He laughed at that last one—"I couldn't resist, even then." He turned a few more sketches. Then the rest of the pages were blank. "I kept different sketchbooks for each class. Many aren't filled, but I saved everything."

"I don't blame you. You have such a distinct, sensitive style."

"I'm nothing if not sensitive." He smirked.

"And if I'm not mistaken, one of those lovely framed drawings in the living room is *yours*." It was not a mere sketch, but a finished, fully rendered drawing of a Gothic church in deep shadow. Perhaps he'd spent one of his college years abroad.

"Guilty. I've always been fond of that one, but I never even signed it. Hell, I don't qualify as an artist—maybe when I was in school, but certainly not now."

Kane peeped up at us from his computer. "He's fishing, Claire."

I asked, "Have you seen these drawings, Kane?"

"The whole collection," the kid assured me. "They're great. I keep telling Grant that we should frame a few more."

"Nope," Grant said flatly. "That discussion is closed." Then he closed the pad of sketches, closed the tackle box, returned everything to the closet, and closed the doors.

I squeezed his arm. "You're too modest. I appreciate the private showing."

He sauntered away from the closet, eager to change the topic. "Any plans tonight?"

"Nothing special. There's no rehearsal. I want everyone well rested for tomorrow afternoon's tech rehearsal, which may be grueling."

Grant reminded me, "It's Saturday night. No point in wasting it. Kane and I will be going out to dinner, not sure where. Why don't you join us?" Meaningfully, he added, "You and a guest."

Brightly, Kane seconded, "*Yeah*. Table for four. Somewhere nice."

I was tempted, but hesitated, then declined. "Things have been awfully hectic lately, and next week will be no better. I've been needing an evening home alone. I'd better take advantage of it."

"Aww," Grant clucked. "Home alone. How pathetic."

"That's right," I said coyly. "Home alone."

3

Both Grant and Kane understood that when I spoke of needing an evening home alone, I meant home alone with Tanner Griffin. Though Tanner and I were not living together, not exactly, he had indeed moved "a few things" into my condominium at Villa Paseo—things like clothing and toiletries, as opposed to furniture or mail delivery. This was ultimately a matter of common sense. My place was much nearer the campus of Desert Arts College, where he was enrolled in my theater program. More to the point, we now enjoyed spending frequent nights together.

I offer no excuse for this unlikely relationship other than our shared magnetism, which neither of us felt inclined to resist. Yes, the ethics of our intimacy were dubious; society frowns on the coupling of mentors with protégés. If I were able to view my own actions more objectively, I would doubtless join in the jowl-wagging.

At fifty-four, however, I have ceased caring about the approbation of others—or the lack of it—with regard to my perceived morals. If Tanner Griffin could look beyond our teacher-student relationship, to say nothing of the difference in our years, then so could I. He was flat-out handsome, certainly, but even more appealing was his mature charm, his youthful drive and innocence, and his deep commitment to building a career on the stage. He was *solid*—the word always sprang to mind when I thought of him.

For reasons I could still not fully fathom, he found this attraction mutual.

I have never tried to fool myself into thinking myself beautiful, not in the conventional sense. Much to my good fortune, Tanner claimed to evaluate the "whole person"—his words—so I must have passed muster. I had no doubt that my status in the theater world accounted for some measure of my allure, which some might judge as opportunistic on Tanner's part. On the other hand, I could not expect Tanner to distinguish between me and my career, since I myself was unable to draw such a line. I was therefore content to judge his doting both profound and guileless.

I was also content to spend the evening home alone with him, sans neighbors.

"Rare?" he asked, heading out the French doors to the back terrace, ready to grill a pair of plump steaks he hoisted on a plate.

"Bloody," I affirmed.

It was just past six. Though our Saturday dinner seemed oafishly early, the sun had set and night had fallen, so we decided to get on with it, enjoying a bottle of good cabernet while preparing a leisurely meal. Besides, we both faced a long day and an important rehearsal at the theater on Sunday, so there would be no late-night reveling.

He returned from the terrace, minus the meat. Closing the door behind him, he hugged himself. "It's getting chilly. How about a fire?"

"Delightful idea. Could you take care of it?" I was far too busy lolling with my wine, watching him, to be bothered with household chores.

He mimicked an elaborate bow to the sultan, then crossed the room to the fireplace. His corduroy pants, the dusty color of sage, swooshed softly as the legs scissored past me. Hunkering at the hearth, he began crumpling newspapers beneath the kindling, treating me to a fine view of his backside. As he fussed with the logs, his shoulder muscles rolled and flexed beneath the white waffle-weave undershirt he wore like a form-fitting sweater; its sleeves were shoved up past the elbows, where they bunched beneath his biceps. Completing this hunky picture, tan work shoes coordinated nicely with his thick, flaxen mop of hair.

I was tempted, then and there, to set down my glass, pussyfoot across the room, and mount him from behind. Shame on me—that could wait. Nestled in a corner of the sofa, I had my feet pulled up, toes wedged into the crack between the cushions, cozy as could be. I pondered for a moment my dismal lack of Christmas decorations, not even a limp string of lights swagged from the mantel. Would this be the year, I wondered, when I would finally get around to putting up a tree? Perhaps, after the play opened, Tanner could help. Just us. We could string popcorn, deck the halls, boil some glogg or whatever—

"So you got the clock?" he asked over his shoulder, interrupting my musing, continuing a conversation we'd begun earlier. He struck a match and held it under the grate.

"We got Stewart Chaffee's promise to *lend* us the clock, but I haven't seen it yet. Grant says it's perfect, which is good enough for me. We're returning tomorrow morning for it. With any luck, we'll be rehearsing on a finished stage tomorrow."

Tanner stood as the papers caught fire, burning bright yellow for a few moments. "The painting too?" He was asking about the portrait of Laura that, in the play, would inspire his character's love for a woman thought to be dead.

"Hope so. We should have had the painting on Friday, but it needed more time to dry." Swirling the wine in my glass, I wondered what other loose ends still needed tying up. "Lance Caldwell will be there tomorrow as well."

"From the music faculty?"

I nodded. "He composed and recorded the incidental music. It was finished last week, and I'm dying to hear it, but he wants to 'unveil' it for the whole cast and crew on Sunday."

"Then he must be pleased with it." Tanner checked his hands, brushing grime from his fingers.

Wryly, I noted, "Maestro Caldwell is generally pleased with himself." The kindling popped, as if adding an exclamation point to my remark.

Tanner crossed to the dining table, where he'd set down his glass before taking the meat to the grill. His first sip of wine had been perfunctory, a quick toast before heading outdoors, but now he lifted the glass and gave it a slow, attentive tasting. Swallowing, he let out a rapturous moan.

I'd heard *that* before. My mind danced with still-fresh memories of our adventurous, evolving intimacy.

"Wow." He reached for the bottle and studied the label. "Easy to guess where *this* came from."

I challenged, "So guess."

"Not that I find anything lacking in your usual wine selections, Claire, but I have a hunch this bottle was sprung from the cellar of D. Glenn Yeats."

I shrugged. "Yes, the wine was a gift from our college president." I had no idea what it was worth—surely hundreds of dollars.

Tanner set the bottle down. "Nothing but the best for Glenn."

"Thank you." My tone was matter-of-fact. "According to Glenn, that's why I'm here. He *had* to have me on his faculty."

"Good for him. I'm glad he got his way." Tanner moved to the sofa and sat near my feet. Looking me in the eye, he added quietly, "Glenn's a powerful man. He deserves to get his way. But not in everything."

Three months earlier, just before the start of classes, Glenn had stunned me one evening during a party at his home, taking me aside to tell me that he had loved me from afar, wondering if some sort of relationship might be possible between us. He made it sufficiently clear that his goal was marriage; the man was serious.

It was common knowledge that Glenn had left two failed marriages in the wake of building his computer empire. It was also common knowledge that marriage was a gambit I had never tried, so I felt on an unequal footing with my would-be suitor. Needless to say, I had been unable to answer him that night, not only because his overture had been so sudden, but also because of Tanner.

Since first meeting Tanner, there had been an element of flirtation to our encounters. Then, on the day before Glenn would make his unexpected declaration to me, Tanner and I had given in to the irresistible chemistry of an opportune moment in an empty theater.

As for Glenn, he was realistic enough to understand that I had never thought of him romantically. He understood that I needed time to weigh his advance and, he hoped, find the spark of reciprocal attraction. He also understood that I had taken a special interest in

Tanner Griffin, an acting student whose innate star quality promised to add luster to our school's fledgling theater program.

Glenn did not understand, however, that I had essentially left his profession of love "on hold" while I explored my passions for the young man who now sat next to me on the sofa.

Tanner was well aware of my awkward position, understanding that our relationship, while not quite clandestine, was simply not a matter of public discourse. My neighbor friends had the whole picture. Lord knows, my housekeeper, Oralia, did as well. But as far as anyone at Desert Arts College was concerned—including Glenn— the lust shared by Tanner and me was limited to our ardor for the art of Thespis.

Tanner touched my arm. I blinked. A log shifted in the grate, bringing me back to the moment.

"I didn't mean to upset you," said Tanner.

Was I upset?

He pulled me toward him on the sofa, wrapping an arm around me. "I shouldn't talk about Glenn that way. He's been great to both of us."

With a wan smile, I agreed, "He's been truly generous. I admire his technical brilliance, his dedication to the arts, his awesome wealth. But, Tanner, I just don't think I could ever love him."

"Good." He said the word with no hint of rivalry or triumph, but with simple satisfaction. As he said the word, he smiled.

God, what a smile. It was the smile that had left my knees weak on that morning when I met him at the body shop he managed on the outskirts of Palm Springs. It was the smile that later nourished me on mornings when I awoke with him, that left me hungering on mornings when I did not. It was the smile that would soon brighten my stage, the smile that could catapult a lad like Tanner to bona fide stardom. My time with him, I sensed, was limited.

During our time together, we often spoke of Glenn Yeats. He was such a magnified presence in our lives, it was only natural that he should pop into our conversations, whether trivial or profound. None of these discussions were more profound than those that brushed upon the topic of love.

Glenn had spoken of love on the night when he'd revealed his feelings for me. I myself had spoken of love just now when telling Tanner how I felt—or more precisely, how I *didn't* feel—about Glenn. But the word never seemed to come up when Tanner and I spoke of our feelings for each other. Tanner's reticence didn't concern me, but my own did. Love, I feared, was fraught with danger.

When Tanner and I weren't talking about Glenn, we usually spoke of theater. "So tell me," he said, rising from the sofa, "are you happy with the production? I mean, tech issues aside, how's the acting shaping up?" He reached for the wine bottle and refreshed my glass.

"You're angling for a compliment, Tanner. But I don't mind. You're fabulous."

He put the wine back on the table. "Sorry, that really came out wrong." He scratched behind his head, looking adorably sheepish. "I meant the whole cast, the ensemble. How do you feel about printing your name on the program?"

"I couldn't be prouder. When you consider that everyone involved with this production had never worked together or even met until September, it's remarkable how quickly we've formed a cohesive, professional-caliber troupe. Cyndy, for example, has made great strides in growing into the role of Laura. And Scott's just wonderful as the effete Waldo Lydecker, a perfect foil to your hard-boiled but sensitive portrayal of Detective McPherson. Even Thad—hailing from Nowhere, Wisconsin—gosh, he's taken the minor role of Danny and polished it into one of the show's special highlights."

Tanner agreed, "That kid's got a *lot* of promise."

Speaking from the side of my mouth, I confided, "Don't spread this through the cast, but I've been sufficiently pleased with rehearsals to invite several prominent critics and talent scouts to Friday's opening."

Tanner arched one brow. "Any names I'd know?"

"*All* of them."

"Think they'll come?"

I chortled knowingly. "They'll come."

Tanner's brow suddenly furrowed. He sniffed the air.

I did likewise. "God, I just assumed that was the fireplace."

"No"—Tanner was already darting through the French doors—"it's the meat."

Laughing, I called after him, "No need to turn the steaks. At least *one* side will be rare."

4

Sunday morning dawned clear and cool. I greeted the day feeling rested and fully energized. Good thing, as I had a busy schedule ahead of me. That afternoon's tech rehearsal could run well into the evening—taxing enough—but first, I needed to return to Stewart Chaffee's estate, pick up his antique Austrian case clock, and haul it over to campus.

Tanner and I awoke early, taking some time to indulge our fantasies between the sheets before rising, then sharing coffee together and perusing the morning papers. The *Desert Sun* had landed at my door, as it did every morning, and Tanner slipped out while the coffee brewed, fetching a copy of the Sunday *New York Times* from a nearby convenience store (I had yet to grow curious about the Los Angeles paper). When we were both up to speed on world events, Tanner gave me a kiss, gulped the last of a thick protein concoction, and headed out to the gym—bodies like his don't just happen. I spent another half hour reading the various arts sections.

Eventually I had showered and dressed, and by ten-thirty, I heard Grant and Kane cross the courtyard and open the iron gate to my entry court. "Ready, doll?" called Grant, rapping at my door. A minute later, I had locked up, and the three of us stepped around to the garage.

Grant's car, a great beast of a white Mercedes, was already loaded with the pretty little Biedermeier desk he was returning from a designer showhouse. The desk was wrapped and padded with a mover's blanket, lying on its back side in the trunk, which was held almost closed by stretchy cords looped from the lid to the bumper. Grant drove, and Kane insisted that I take the front seat while he sat in back with a few of the drawers that had been removed from the desk.

As we pulled out of the garage, I asked, "Will the clock fit in the trunk?" Having never seen the clock, I wasn't sure of its height.

"Probably," said Grant. "If not, we can just slide it into the backseat."

"But what about Kane?"

Kane leaned forward, resting his arm on the back of my seat. "Not a problem," he told me, grinning. "I'm agile."

Grant snorted. "*I'll* tell the world."

The trip to neighboring Rancho Mirage was brief, with little traffic along Highway One-Eleven to impede us. Heading northwest, I noted that the peak of Mount San Jacinto now sported a snowy cap above its granite slopes.

Along the way, we spoke of our plans for the day: I was eager to begin the final week of production with that afternoon's technical rehearsal. Grant would spend some time at the Nirvana sales office, checking on anything he'd missed during his absence on Saturday. Kane planned to spend the afternoon at the Desert Museum of Southwestern Arts; he didn't normally work on Sundays, but the campus museum was mounting an elaborate exhibit of kachina dolls to coincide with my play's opening, and the publicity office was putting in some extra hours.

Driving toward the gate to Stewart's estate, Grant lowered his window and slowed the car. Unlike many of the desert's wealthy residents, Stewart did not live in a walled community with a guardhouse. Rather, his expansive property was equipped with a sophisticated security system of its own, as evidenced by a keypad at the motorized gate, an ever-watchful video camera, and a sign notifying would-be intruders that the perimeter was protected by a laser shield—whatever that meant.

Instead of using the intercom at the gate, Grant simply punched in the code that Stewart had given him on Saturday. His finger barely left the keypad, and the barred gate rolled aside, admitting us.

As we entered the grounds, Grant pointed out some of the estate's features to Kane, who had never been there.

Though Grant was speaking clearly, his words seemed unintelligible to me, as I felt suddenly preoccupied by an inexplicable sense of dread. Chiding myself, I dismissed this uneasiness as melodramatic nonsense. My foreboding was utterly irrational. It was a beautiful, cloudless day, after all, and the purpose of this visit was to add a crowning touch to my debut production at the college. All was well. Was I simply spooked by the queerness of our previous visit, by the grim artwork, by Stewart's self-indulgent behavior, by his fleshy trumpet?

As we drove near the house, I was distracted from these thoughts by the appearance of a man at the front door. An odd little guy of wiry build, he was dressed casually that morning in black jeans and turtleneck. Rushing toward the car, flailing his arms, he directed us with broad gestures to drive around to the side of the house. Instantly, my apprehension was supplanted by amused curiosity.

Turning the wheel, Grant told us, "That's Pea. Guess he wants us to unload at the garage."

"Pea?" asked Kane. "Too weird. Who *is* he?"

"If I recall correctly, his real name is Makepeace. He's Stewart's majordomo."

"Ah," I said.

"Huh?" asked Kane.

"Sort of a butler. He runs the household."

At the moment, he was running behind the car as we drove around the house toward the attached garage and a back entrance, presumably the kitchen. We were well out of view of the street when Grant stopped the car in a parking court and set the brake. We all got out.

"Morning, Pea," Grant greeted the little man.

Pea nodded, but made no move to shake hands or return the greeting. "Stewart said you'd be returning the desk. 'Bout time, too." His words carried the hint of a drawl that he'd mostly lost—along with his manners.

Grant took over, making a proper round of introductions. I

learned that the houseman's full name was Makepeace Fertig.

"But everyone's called me Pea since I was a kid. Just sorta stuck." Despite his diminutive stature, he seemed athletic and fit for his years, which I judged to be in the midforties. His attitude warmed some as he explained, "We can put the desk in the garage. I'll help you unload it."

So I watched Pea, Grant, and Kane hoist the desk out of the trunk and trundle it toward the open garage. A vintage Rolls-Royce was parked inside, along with a new Cadillac, both white. There in the parking court, near Grant's car, was a powdery blue Korean compact. At the moment, though, I had little interest in cars. I wanted to see the clock, and owing to the clutter in the shadows of the garage, I couldn't tell if it was there.

"The drawers," said Pea, a touch of panic coloring his voice as they removed the padding from the desk. "Where are the drawers?"

"In the car." Grant explained, "It was easier to move the desk without the drawers in it, and I didn't want to risk having any of them fall out."

"I'll get them," said Kane, trotting off to the car. He opened the back door and leaned inside. Pea's stern features lightened as he eyed the young man's rump.

Strolling over to Kane, I volunteered, "Can I help?" The drawers didn't look heavy, but as there were four or five of them, it would have been awkward for Kane to carry them all.

"Sure, Claire, thanks." He handed me a couple.

As we carried them back to the garage, Pea fretted, "I hope you know how to get everything back in the right place . . ."

"Would you *relax?*" said Grant with an exasperated laugh.

Pea fussed, "Do you have *any* idea what this desk is worth?"

"Of *course* I do. For God's sake, each drawer is a different size. Any two-year-old could match up the holes." Proving his point, Grant took the drawers from Kane and me, sliding each into its appropriate opening. Everything fit perfectly on the first try. He told Pea, "Duly delivered, all in one piece. Now stop being such a nervous Nellie."

Pea heaved a put-upon sigh. "Well . . ." He squatted to examine the little writing desk, running his fingers across its inlaid blond-and-black finish. "Yes, everything seems to be in order." Then he gasped. "Where's the *key?* The key is missing!" He stood, looking steamed, all five-foot-six of him. "The drawers have an original, antique key. It's irreplaceable. Where *is* it?"

Grant checked his pockets, then snapped his fingers. "Sorry. I left it at home. I know exactly where it is—on the kitchen counter. It has a green silk tassel."

"Stewart will be *furious,*" warned Pea.

"I highly doubt that," Grant told him calmly. "If it's that important, I'll go back for it right now."

"You better *believe* it's important. Why, if—"

"What's going on out here?" a voice interrupted. It was Stewart Chaffee himself, seated in his wheelchair, calling from the back door of the house, which he had opened.

The four of us emerged from the adjacent garage into the full sunlight. "Morning, Stewart," said Grant. "We've returned the Biedermeier desk, but—"

"But he lost the damn key," sniped Pea. "Really, Stewart, you should have second thoughts about lending that clock."

"The key isn't *lost,*" Grant assured Stewart, then explained where it was, offering to get it immediately.

Stewart wasn't listening. He'd just noticed Kane among us and seemed far more intrigued by the studly college kid than by the trumped-up mystery of the missing key. When Pea finally managed to convey to Stewart the reason for his fuming, Stewart dismissed the calamity with a derisive laugh. "Grant can return the key anytime. What's the difference?"

Pea stamped one of his loafers and spun away from us in a huff.

"Morning, Claire!" barked Stewart, looking decidedly jolly in a red velvet dressing gown that reminded me of a choir robe. "I presume you've come to collect my Austrian clock. Marvelous piece, marvelous."

"I've been *dying* to see it. Did you manage to get it out of storage for me?"

"Yes, Claire, of course. Anything for the arts, you know."

Enough of this chitchat. I wanted to ask, Then where the hell is it?

He must have read my thoughts. "It's here in the great room. Won't you come in, all of you?" And he backed his chair into the house.

Without hesitation, I hustled toward the door. Grant followed, but without my sense of urgency. Kane sauntered with Grant. Pea, though still miffed, turned and brought up the rear, doubtless fearing he might miss something.

Entering the house a few steps, I was blocked by Stewart's wheelchair in a kitchen aisle. He was bubbling something about theater, someone he'd once met, but I wasn't listening; I was looking about for the clock. It wasn't in the kitchen, naturally, but the room opened at its other end to a large space for casual living, sort of a family room. I didn't see the clock, but then, my view of the space was mostly blocked, as was the kitchen aisle where Stewart sat and prattled while riffling for something in his pony-skin saddlebag.

The kitchen, I noted, had a dated, midcentury-modern look, which I assumed was studied and intentional rather than leftover, outmoded decorating. The old white appliances, all top-line, were of rounded, streamlined design, laden with heavy chrome hardware and fittings. Pink Formica countertops were trimmed with stainless-steel edging. Pink and gray tiles formed a checkerboard on the floor.

Stewart gabbed nonstop as I observed all this, causing a backup in the doorway as the others entered behind me. When Kane had worked his way into the hall, Stewart's monologue ceased as he openly ogled the young man. Cocking his head, he asked, "What did you say your name was?"

"It's Kane, sir."

Grant added, "Kane and I are now living together, Stewart."

From the side of his mouth, the old man told Grant, "Good for you, cupcake. Not bad. If you ever grow tired of him . . ." He trailed off suggestively.

With surprising composure, Grant told him, "Never, Stewart. It's far more likely that Kane would tire of *me*."

Kane assured Grant, "That is *not* gonna happen."

Stewart persisted, "You never know with the young ones. Right, Pea?" He sniggered merrily, but no one else found humor in the comment.

Pea didn't answer the question. He simply gave Grant a knowing glance, then said to anyone, "I believe you came for a clock?"

"Yes," I said, happy to be back on track. "It's here?" I glanced about.

"Here in the great room," said Stewart, at last wheeling out of the aisle, allowing the rest of us to move.

We followed as he rolled from the kitchen to the airy, comfortable room, less formal than the living room I'd visited on Saturday. While the appointments of the entire house seemed equally luxe, the tone of this room was friendlier, less pretentious, with furniture that invited relaxation. I noticed a computer and printer at a corner desk, messy from use. Christmas decorations were less churchy than those in the living room, and the artwork here was more modern and blithe, some of it simply propped against the walls or displayed on easels, as if it was frequently rotated from storage. Glass doors along the far wall opened to a terrace and swimming pool.

Although there was plenty to look at, my gaze quickly settled on the Austrian pendulum clock, which I spotted near the desk. Grant's description, while enthusiastic, had not given me an accurate mental picture of the clock, but I now understood what he had meant when calling it "a whimsical little piece with a vaguely oriental motif." To my eye, it was a mishmash of styles, yet clearly of antique pedigree, pleasantly bizarre. Most important, it struck me as exactly the sort of cockeyed gift that Waldo Lydecker might give to an unsuspecting Laura—then hide his shotgun in it.

"Oh, dear," said Grant, strolling over to the clock. "I think it's too big."

I came up behind him. "Nonsense. It's wonderful. It'll look perfect on the set." Stepping to the clock, I ran my fingers along its painted cabinet. Opening the glass door that protected the pendulum, I was satisfied that the space within could conceal Waldo's murder weapon.

"I mean," Grant explained, "I think it's too big for the car."

"Oh." I stepped back half a pace, sizing it up. It was substantially smaller than a conventional grandfather's clock, but Grant had a point—I doubted that it would fit into the trunk of his car, and I wasn't too sure about the backseat either.

Grant asked Stewart, "Does the finial come off?"

Stewart instructed his majordomo, "Try it, Pea."

So Pea stood on a chair near the desk, fiddled with a fanciful spindle atop the clock, and sure enough, it popped right out, reducing the height by a few inches.

"That's better . . . ," said Grant, rubbing his chin. "I still have my doubts, though. Got a tape measure?"

Stewart and Pea searched a few drawers, carping at each other but managing to find a tape measure among some picture-hanging tools. Kane stepped forward, volunteering to measure the clock. Then he trotted outdoors to check the space available in the car. Moments later, he darted back inside. "Sorry. Not even close."

"Oh . . . *shoot*," I said, minding my manners. "I had *so* wanted to have a finished set this afternoon." I slumped onto the broad arm of a nearby sofa.

Kane suggested, "Maybe we could get the school to send a truck over."

But it was Sunday, and discussing the logistics of various options, we realized that my chances of getting the clock to the theater in time for rehearsal were slim.

My trouper instincts, my show-must-go-on mentality, then kicked in. "Well," I said, standing, "it's no disaster. Quite the contrary— the clock is marvelous. I'll just have to wait another day to get it onstage." Reviewing everyone's schedules, I decided to return on Monday afternoon, sometime after lunch, with Tanner's open Jeep. "The clock will fit easily, standing upright, and I'm sure that Tanner will be available to help." To Grant, I added, "I've already wasted too much of your time."

He dismissed my implied apology, but conceded that his Monday schedule was already heavily booked.

At some point during this conversation, Stewart's nurse, Bonnie Bahr, bustled into the room and reminded her charge that he was due for medication, which, out of sheer contrariness, he resisted. Clearly, she'd had prior experience enduring his obstinacy, as well as his insults, showing the patience of a mother with a sickly child. She managed to get a variety of pills down him, watching like a warden as he gulped a glass of water.

"*There,*" he said, handing her the empty glass, "are you satisfied, piglet?"

I'd have slapped him then and there. But I wanted his clock.

He looked up at his nurse with a sly grin. "Don't you think I deserve a treat?"

She crossed her beefy arms. "Like what?"

"Pink fluff!" He started wheeling himself toward the refrigerator.

"I *told* you, you old goat: there *isn't* any."

Having heard this conversation before, I wondered about Stewart's sudden mood swings. At one moment, he could discuss art or theater with keen insight, and the next moment, he sounded like a rude child on the verge of a tantrum. I knew of his heart condition and his stroke. Was he also bedeviled by encroaching Alzheimer's?

Pea spoke up to Bonnie, "How *dare* you address Stewart like that!"

She blasted back, "Pipe down, you little worm."

"I want pink fluff," Stewart whined, "and *you* said you'd get me some." He punctuated his demand with a fart—a gaseous variant of Tourette's, perhaps?

"On my *time off,*" Bonnie reminded him. "That means tomorrow. I couldn't get to it last night, so I'll make a batch tonight and bring it over in the morning."

I was reluctant to ask, so I was relieved when Grant finally did: "What on earth is pink fluff?"

"Stewart just loves it," Bonnie gushed, hand to bosom. "Nothing complicated," she added in a whisper, as if imparting a secret recipe. "It's red Jell-O mixed with Cool Whip." She licked her lips.

"A pedestrian concoction," Pea said with a sniff.

Bonnie turned on him, flashing daggers. "If it's so damn easy, you might try making some for Stewart now and then." While it seemed that Bonnie and Stewart's sparring amounted to nothing more than gaming, it was only too apparent that the hostility between Bonnie and Pea was deep and genuine.

While the big woman in white volleyed more insults with the little man in black, Stewart wheeled into the kitchen and planted his chair in front of the refrigerator. Reaching up, he grabbed the handle and began to tug. A collection of vintage chrome cocktail shakers displayed on top of the refrigerator wobbled and clattered as Stewart's tugging became more insistent. Soon, he was rising from the seat of his chair.

Seeing this, Bonnie abruptly ended her sniping with Pea—she flipped him the finger—then rushed to assist Stewart. Getting him seated again and wheeling him back a few feet, she said, "There's no pink fluff, but let's see what else we can find." And she swung the door wide open.

Stewart wheeled himself forward, examining the shelves.

"There's some nice, fresh melba sauce," Bonnie told him. "That's red, like Jell-O. Want some on ice cream?"

Stewart shook his head. Spotting something, he shrieked, *"Krispies!"*

"Oh!" Bonnie echoed his shriek. "I forgot we had these." She handled the plate like hidden treasure, removing it from the refrigerator and setting it on the counter. "Would anyone care for a Rice Krispies square?" Stewart had already grabbed one and was gnawing away at it like a dog with a bone.

Grant and I mumbled no-thank-yous. The silence that followed was broken only by Stewart's crunching. Then that stopped.

Stewart looked up from his chair, as if waking from a dream. "No takers?" he asked, sounding mature and cordial. "They're really quite good. How about the young man? Kane, wouldn't you like one?" Stewart lifted the plate from the counter, heaped with a pyramid of the gooey treats, and proffered it to Kane.

Kane smiled uncertainly. "Well . . . , *yeah.* Thanks." And he reached for one.

"Do take two," Stewart insisted, leaning forward in his red robe, conjuring the disparate image of a licentious elf. "They're small. And

I'm sure you need all the energy you can get." He gave Grant a canny wink.

Grant rolled his eyes as Kane wolfed down the first of the two bricks of cereal. He sounded as if he was eating Styrofoam. Bonnie returned the plate to the refrigerator, shutting the door with a solid thud.

"Oh," said Stewart, wheeling close to Grant and nabbing his arm, "I nearly forgot. I haven't shown you my most recent acquisition, have I?"

Grant laughed. "It's impossible to keep up with *your* acquisitions, Stewart."

The old man led Grant back into the great room, saying how proud he was to have landed an entire collection of works by an overlooked Swedish artist. I followed with the others and couldn't help marveling at how quickly Stewart's behavior had been transformed after eating the Rice Krispies square. Maybe he'd needed sugar. Was he diabetic too? Bonnie, I mused, really had her hands full.

The easels I'd noted earlier displayed the paintings, some dozen of them, all smallish landscapes, scattered about the room. The compositions were all of the same general style, pleasant and colorful, but one in particular caught my eye. Stepping nearer to scrutinize it, I saw that it depicted an old-fashioned drawbridge, a crude wooden structure at the edge of a placid stream. A few cows grazed nearby. Spectacular clouds roiled overhead in a palette suggesting sunset.

"Isn't it delightful?" gushed Stewart, wheeling next to me. "Such mood and vibrancy. Per-Olof Östman deserves far greater recognition. Though a minor master from the relatively obscure Swedish neo-impressionist school, his pointillist style is among the finest, most precious I've seen."

I asked, "When were these painted, Stewart?"

"They all date from the 1890s, at the height of the neo-impressionist movement. I'm sure Östman's work would be better known if this entire series hadn't been in the hands of a private collector for more than a century. We tracked it down in Stockholm, and according to the certified provenance, these little masterpieces have never been publicly exhibited."

"Nor will they be," Grant noted.

Stewart's gaze turned from the paintings to Grant. "Why do you say that?"

With a shrug, Grant explained, "Because they've been acquired by another private collector. They're all yours, Stewart, yours to enjoy."

"For a while, yes."

Grant's expression said that he didn't understand Stewart's meaning. Neither did I.

"I'm *old*," Stewart reminded us. "Art endures, but I, alas, will not."

Bonnie rushed to his wheelchair. "Now, now, Mr. Chaffee. That's no way to talk. You have many good years ahead of you. I'll see to *that*."

Pea also flitted to his side, kneeling face-to-face. "Stewart, honey, don't say such things. We're all here for you. You have *friends*."

"And family," I added, trying to be helpful. But in the next instant, I recalled that Stewart had commented on Saturday about "bad blood" between himself and his family.

Stewart quickly set me straight. "I have little family left, thank God. When I went *my* way, they went *theirs*. They have never been supportive, and I have no intention of turning to them now. They can *all* go to hell."

The room fell silent. In a limited sense, I could connect with Stewart's sentiments, as I felt highly conflicted with regard to my own familial ties, particularly my relationship with my mother, who, like Stewart, had seen her better years. Still, Stewart's open contempt for his family was shamefully harsh. I ventured, "I'm sure you don't mean that. There must be *someone* you relate to—emotionally, as well as by blood."

He sighed. "I had a niece, Dawn, who showed the most promise. From what I understand, she became something of an art scholar in her own right. We have that much in common, but nothing else."

"You 'had' a niece?" I asked, having found his wording ambiguous. Was Dawn dead or alive?

He clarified, "Dawn lives in Santa Barbara, I'm told, but I haven't seen her in nearly forty years. She was a toddler at the time."

"Then perhaps it's time to reach out to her."

"Bah! She never once 'reached out' to me. Why in hell should I open a door that's best left shut?" With a disgusted shake of his head, he wheeled away from his circle of listeners, parking himself near the kitchen, alone.

As we murmured some comments about the sad consequences of his bitterness, I recalled that Stewart had also mentioned Santa Barbara on Saturday. He'd asked his banker's secretary about a Monday appointment with someone from that city. Whoever he was planning to meet, it was surely not his niece.

Sounding a brighter note, Stewart spun in his chair, telling us, "I think young Kane might enjoy another Rice Krispies square."

"Thank you, sir, but no, I've had enough."

Stewart leaned toward him, stretching his neck. "You're quite sure?" I'd swear his eyes twinkled.

"Quite sure. Thanks anyway."

Stewart rolled his chair toward the refrigerator, apparently deciding that he himself needed another treat, even if Kane didn't want one.

Pea cruised over to his master. "Really, Stewart," he said under his breath. "Trying to lure children with candy—has it come to that?"

"Whatever it takes!" Stewart roared with laughter. Pea joined him.

The rest of us remained silent. Then Grant suggested, "We'd better be going."

Stewart asked him, "But you're coming back tomorrow for the clock?"

"Claire will arrange to pick it up in the afternoon, but I won't be with her."

Pea reminded him, with a testy edge to his voice, "You need to return that key. When will we have it?"

Since I would be returning anyway, I was about to offer to bring the key with me, when Kane volunteered, "I'll be going to campus early tomorrow. I can drop it off on my way. You'll have it first thing in the morning."

Pea gave a curt nod; the plan apparently satisfied him.

"How too very *kind* of you," Stewart told Kane, imagining God knows what.

We said our good-byes, moving toward the back door. Before leaving, Grant took Kane aside and playfully cautioned him, "Watch out for Stewart. I think he's interested in you."

"Don't worry," Kane replied through a grin. "If he tries anything, I ought to be able to fight him off."

We again exchanged a few parting pleasantries, then headed out.

Glancing back, I saw Stewart tugging at the door of the refrigerator.

Up above, the chrome cocktail shakers wobbled and clattered.

5

D. Glenn Yeats had dangled many carrots during his campaign to recruit me to his faculty at Desert Arts College. He offered a generous, steady income, complete artistic freedom, and the opportunity to help shape the next generation of American actors. The most appealing of Glenn's carrots, however, the one I could simply not resist, was the theater he built for me. It was a true playhouse, as opposed to a concert hall or a musical theater, accommodating an audience of some five hundred, neither too large nor too small, with acoustics specifically designed for the spoken word. It featured a proscenium stage and seats of crimson velvet—very traditional—while at the same time employing state-of-the-art stage hydraulics and fully computerized lighting and sound systems. The building itself was designed, with my input and ultimate approval, by I. T. Dirkman, the same world-renowned architect who developed the master plan for the entire school. My theater figured prominently in the overall scheme, with its dramatic facade providing the visual focal point for College Circle, a huge public terrace at the center of campus.

How could I resist so magnanimous a gesture on Glenn's part? This was no mere promise. This wasn't lip service. This was steel and concrete and glass.

When I arrived at one o'clock that afternoon and entered through a stage door near the parking structure, most of the technical staff was already hard at it. Some of them, I knew, had worked late yesterday and again this morning, aiming lights, programming circuits, rehearsing cross-fades. The cast was straggling in, ready for a long haul. They were already capable of running through the whole show, focusing on timing, interpretation, and delivery. But today they would, in effect, take a step backwards. At this afternoon's tech rehearsal, the focus would be on lighting, sound, and costumes; the actors would frequently be forced to stop, wait, and repeat while the show's various technical aspects were cued and tweaked.

Fortunately, the technical demands of the *Laura* script were not complex. We were dealing with a single interior, with only a few special effects. But this was the college's premier production, the one that people had been buzzing about for over a year, since I had first agreed to leave New York and join the faculty, so everything had to be perfect. I had a reputation to uphold—my own.

Crossing the stage toward the auditorium, I paused to admire the set. No question, it was a stunner, heavily influenced by the film's setting of the successful young businesswoman's fashionable New York apartment. For the fabrics, furnishings, and even the costumes, we'd limited the palette to a muted, nearly monochromatic range, intended to give the audience the impression of watching the play in black and white—until Laura's unexpected entrance at the end of act one. Once it's known that Laura is alive, color is introduced to the costuming. Not too subtle, I admit. But dramatically effective.

Tanner spotted me onstage and called from the auditorium, "Well, where's the clock?"

I descended the rehearsal stairs at the stage apron and met him near the first row of seats. "It's perfect, but we couldn't fit it into the car." With an impish pout, I added, "Can I impose upon you to help me get it tomorrow afternoon? After lunch, in your Jeep."

"Of course," he said, giving me a little hug. "Anything to help." He was already in full makeup, but not in costume, wearing a pair of baggy shorts and an old white shirt, sleeves rolled up, collar turned in and under—his makeup smock.

Overhearing us, the stage manager asked, "No clock, huh? I'll find our understudy."

I laughed. "Thanks, Tony. We'll have to make do with that awful old cabinet—just one more time."

From behind, someone asked, "Will you need an extra hand to-morrow?"

"Hi, Thad," Tanner greeted his fellow cast member. Turning to me, Tanner asked, "What do you think? Is the clock heavy?"

"Not sure. More awkward than heavy, I imagine. One thing's certain: it's delicate. We could probably use some help. Thanks for offering, Thad."

Thad and Tanner conversed a bit, ironing out the logistics of our excursion to the Chaffee estate. Watching them, I noted that they represented the two extremes of my new theater program. Tanner Griffin, at twenty-six, was my oldest student and my most seasoned actor; Thad Quatrain, the kid from Wisconsin, was among the youngest, a freshman, just out of high school. They were equally committed, however, not only to their intended careers, but also to the needs of our opening production, both of them putting in long hours at the theater in addition to their rehearsal schedule.

"Miss Gray?" said Thad. I'd invited everyone in the production to address me as Claire, but he was characteristically polite and seemed more comfortable maintaining a traditional, respectful distinction between students and teachers. Needless to say, this was one aspect in which he and Tanner differed greatly.

"Yes, Thad?"

"My uncle Mark asked me to say hello for him. He's driving my car out here and should arrive sometime tomorrow." Thad was referring to his guardian, Mark Manning, an investigative journalist of considerable renown, whom I'd met in Chicago. He had since moved to a small town in Wisconsin, where he was now publisher of the local paper.

"Wonderful!" I said. "How long is he staying? He'll be here for Friday's opening, won't he?"

"Sure. He wouldn't miss *that*. Neil is flying out to join him later in the week." Thad's uncle was gay; Neil, an architect, was his partner. I knew through highly reliable sources—production scuttlebutt—that Thad himself was straight.

I told him, "I hope your uncle plans to save a bit of time for me."

"Yeah. He wants to see you. So I was wondering—well, I know it's against policy, Miss Gray—but would you mind if Mark came to rehearsal with me tomorrow night?"

I frowned, then broke into a grin. "I'd be happy to make an exception for the illustrious Mark Manning. Sure, bring him along."

Glenn Yeats strolled into our circle of conversation. "Making exceptions, Claire? For the illustrious who?"

"Hi, Glenn." I stepped to him and offered a friendly hug. There was nothing unusual about the computer tycoon's appearance at our rehearsal that afternoon. The cast and crew had grown used to having him around; on several occasions, he'd even rolled up his silk sleeves to help with lugging this or that. Throughout his career, Glenn's approach to any project, including his newly built arts college, had been strictly hands-on. He'd avowed a special interest in theater— as well as in me—so it came as no surprise that he'd taken such an active interest in *Laura*, awaiting my first full-scale production at DAC like a nervous mother hen. Answering his question, I explained, "We were talking about Thad's uncle, Mark Manning."

Glenn thought for a moment, then something clicked. "The reporter?"

"That's the one, except he's now turned his hand to publishing."

Thad elaborated, "He bought the *Dumont Daily Register* three years ago."

"Aha," said Glenn. "I wondered why I hadn't heard the name of late." The name Mark Manning had become a household word as the result of several high-profile stories he'd reported during his days at the *Chicago Journal*. "I'd enjoy meeting him."

"You're in luck," I said. "Mark is arriving from Wisconsin tomorrow. Thad's bringing him to rehearsal."

"Great." Glenn hardly needed to add, "I'll be here."

A couple of stagehands appeared from the wings, hauling a tall, old cabinet onto the set.

Glenn grimaced. "*That* won't do."

I told him, "I tried, but I won't have the clock till tomorrow."

Tanner related to Glenn our intention to pick up the clock and transport it in Tanner's Jeep. Glenn offered to send a truck, but Tanner assured him that the plan was set.

As they spoke, it was difficult for me not to compare the two men. At fifty-one, Glenn was nearly twice Tanner's age, but still three years younger than I. No doubt about it—my romantic prospects had improved considerably since my move from New York, where the closest I'd come to any sort of protracted relationship had been with Hector Bosch, the noted theater critic for the *New York Weekly Review.* I was attracted to both Glenn and Tanner, but for different reasons.

Glenn offered wealth and power—heady enticements—as well as his open affection and his eagerness to woo me. He was gentlemanly, and I enjoyed his company. But I felt no spark. In spite of his vast accomplishments, Glenn was essentially a dressed-up techie, a nerd in designer clothing. What's more, I had lingering fears that this captain of e-industry harbored some ingrained control issues, and I had always cherished my independence.

As for Tanner—oh, God, the sparks. I had never been driven much by sexual quests, but Tanner had changed that the first time we touched. I couldn't get enough of him. Similarly, remarkably, his appetite for me seemed forever unsatisfied. Most attractive, though, was his sheer potential as both an actor and a mature human being. He was right there, on the verge, on the brink, of shooting to stardom—under my direction. What an aphrodisiac! But the difference in our ages—was I crazy?

Glenn was asking Tanner, "And where exactly *is* the clock?"

"It belongs to someone in Rancho Mirage."

I told Glenn, "The clock is from Stewart Chaffee's collection. We're picking it up at his estate. He was a hotshot society decorator, but now he's elderly and concentrates on collecting art and antiques."

"Sure, I know Stewart. Back in his prime, he was the most highly regarded decorator in the valley, and with good reason. His interiors speak for themselves; they're timeless." Glenn paused, then shook his head, adding, "But I have to wonder if Stewart's years aren't catching up with him."

I admitted, "He has some health problems," an understatement.

"I mean, up here"—Glenn tapped his noggin. "I've seen much of Stewart's collection, and frankly, I feel he's lost his ability to discern between fine art and the merely mediocre."

I grinned. "I'm sure that's an exaggeration, Glenn." More to the point, I was sure it was sour grapes. Glenn himself had become an avid art collector, with virtually unlimited funds for the pursuit of his genteel pastime. His background in the arts, however, was relatively recent, while Stewart Chaffee's knowledge had a pedigree—a provenance—stemming from his long career.

"Costume parade! Ten minutes!" Kiki Jasper-Plunkett whooshed down the aisle, rattling two armloads of bracelets as she called to the cast.

Tanner and Thad darted off.

From the side of his mouth, Glenn asked, "Costume parade?"

I explained, "It's a final review of all the costumes for the show, onstage, with full lights and makeup. We'll check to see that everything visual has gelled."

A tall woman of dramatic demeanor, Kiki jangled over to us. "It's *so* exciting, isn't it? I *love* this moment—assuming I *don't* discover that it's back to the ol' drawing board." She laughed too loudly, a touch of hysteria coloring her voice.

I assured her, "Everything will be gorgeous, Kiki. You've outdone yourself, as usual." Kiki was my oldest friend, having attended theater school with me more than thirty years earlier. Her career path had led to costuming, mine to directing. Glenn had recruited her to his faculty ahead of me, assuming correctly that her presence at DAC would further entice me to make the move. Now Kiki and I were neighbors, living in the same condominium complex as Grant Knoll.

"Madam Director," bellowed a voice from the back of the hall.

All heads turned.

"Maestro Caldwell," I answered. "Have you come to deliver your new opus?"

"I have," he intoned, "I have." His voice filled the auditorium as he bounded down the stairs. Our sound technician, noting the composer's arrival, followed.

Caldwell was on the school's music faculty. Glenn greeted him, "Hi, Lance."

"Glenn," Caldwell acknowledged our employer, then returned his attention to me. "Yes, Claire, it's ready. I think you'll be *very* pleased. And I think you should know how *proud* I am to be a part of this project." With a flourish, he produced a CD from the inside breast pocket of his nubby tweed sport coat.

"Stan," I told the soundman, "let's cue this up and take a listen."

Stan snatched it from Caldwell's fingers and rushed back to the control booth.

The composer was explaining, "Once I hit upon the central theme, the rest just flowed. It *flowed*. There's a longish prelude or overture, to be played prior to curtain, then the two entr'actes, as well as incidental music for key scenes throughout. I decided on a synthesized performance, not only because it allowed me complete control, but because it has a certain 'detached' quality that seems to fit the mood of the script. Then I burned everything onto a CD, which should facilitate cuing."

Stan's voice came over a loudspeaker: "Ready, Miss Gray."

Shielding my eyes with my hand, I looked up toward the booth, calling, "Let's dim the houselights to half—better to set the mood—then go." Turning toward stage, I called, "Quiet, everyone, please."

Instantly, a hush came over the auditorium as the houselights began to fade. Caldwell, Glenn, and I took seats in the fifth row, center, waiting for the sound to wash over us. I held my breath. I'd had lengthy discussions with the composer regarding the tone I wished to establish with his music, but I had yet to hear even a theme, a phrase, a note, so I had no idea what to expect from an artist known for his ego as much as for his skill.

Then, out of silence, it began. By the second measure, I knew that Caldwell had truly delivered. It was impossible not to compare his music to David Raksin's sumptuous film score, and it proved a worthy rival. Plus, it was original. It was ours.

Sitting next to the composer, I put my hand over his and gave it a grasp of thanks. Without question, his music would add an important dimension to the production, a dimension that I hadn't even realized, till now, had been lacking.

After a few minutes, the introductory music had finished, and the remaining sections proved to be variations on the same wonderful theme. I began an animated discussion of the music with both Caldwell and Glenn, and sensing that my demand for silence had expired, the cast and crew broke into discussion as well. Someone was humming the infectious melody, and I became ever more confident that our show would be a smash.

When the houselights ramped up again, Kiki clapped her hands for attention. "Costume parade! All actors onstage, please." And within a minute or two, my cast of eight young charges had entered from the wings, modeling their finery for my scrutiny as well as Kiki's. We had taken a straightforward, realistic approach in designing all of the costumes, which were stylish street wear of the 1940s.

Tanner was predictably handsome in his wide-lapeled suit as Lieutenant McPherson. Thad was drop-dead endearing as Danny Dorgan, the nineteen-year-old son of the superintendent of Laura's apartment building, a small role, but the first to speak. And then, of course, there was Laura herself, played by the beautiful Cynthia Pryor— remember that name. She, as well as several other cast members, had a number of costume changes, so the parade took a bit of time, as each costume needed to be viewed in combination with other characters. Before long, Kiki herself had climbed the stairs to the stage, poufing dresses, adjusting seams, and fussing with jewelry while dictating notes to an assistant.

During all this hubbub, a backstage door opened, admitting a shaft of daylight. I heard voices raised in greeting while something big was hauled inside. The heavy door closed with a reverberant thump, and moments later, from the wing, a man, fifty-something, strutted onstage as if he owned it, parting the cast like the waters of the Red Sea.

"Atticus!" Glenn hailed him from the auditorium. "You've brought the painting?"

Good God. In the hectic to-and-fro, I'd forgotten that we did not yet have one all-important set piece, the portrait of Laura. The bare wall above the fireplace awaited the painting that would inspire our intrepid detective's obsession with a woman thought murdered. Atticus Jones, from the school's painting faculty, had been chosen to produce the portrait, which needed to readily resemble the young actress playing the role.

I was skeptical. Atticus—professionally, he went by the single name—was renowned for an abstract, violently expressionistic style of painting. This was totally at odds with the haunting, romantic style appropriate to the script, which specified that the portrait had been painted by Stuart Jacoby, a fictitious imitator of American artist Eugene Speicher. But Glenn had assured me that he had recruited the talented Atticus because he was a master of many styles, a flexibility that served him well as a teacher. "Having Atticus is like having a painting faculty of six, all in one," Glenn had told me.

I was not inclined to second-guess Glenn, but the moment of truth had arrived.

"Yes," Atticus was saying from the stage, "the canvas has dried. Your portrait is ready, and it is, I must say, magnificent. Shall we take a look?" And with that, he clapped his hands sharply, twice, as if summoning slaves. He backed up a step and waited. Clearly, the painter's ego was an easy match for that of composer Lance Caldwell.

Two stagehands entered with the painting, still enticingly veiled. Another stagehand positioned a ladder at the fireplace and climbed a few steps. The crew of three raised the covered portrait into position and secured it to the wall. Then Atticus stepped to the fireplace and, with a snap of his fingers, dismissed the crew, which fled.

"I give you . . . ," he said, pausing to reach for the veil, "Laura!" And the covering fell, revealing the framed portrait.

There was a moment's silence, then a collective gasp.

"Jesus," said Glenn standing next to me, fingers to his mouth.

The cast members stood agog, some of them pointing to the picture.

Cynthia Pryor, Laura in the flesh, dropped her jaw upon seeing Laura in oil.

"Atticus," I called to him, "I'm stunned. It *is* magnificent!"

And everyone broke into applause.

I should never have doubted Glenn. Atticus had delivered an enchanting portrait, lovingly rendered, easily recognizable as the actress performing the role. What's more, Atticus had tuned in to the precise aesthetic of the setting, costumes, and period of the production. As far as I was concerned, his posturing and fanfare were now fully justified.

"You like?" he asked, begging for more adulation.

"I *love* it, Atticus. Bravo. And thank you."

To the continued applause of cast and crew, he swirled his hand in a sort of farewell salute, turned, and left the stage.

"Well, now," I told everyone, "we're off to an auspicious start. This production is pulling together beautifully, and I'm proud of all of you. But our work today has only begun; we've got a long rehearsal ahead of us. Let's try to remember everything we've learned, then take it to the next level. I'll have notes, as usual, afterward. Places, please."

The cast and crew scattered backstage.

"Tony," I told the stage manager, "give me one minute, then cue the music and start the show."

I settled at my director's table near the middle row of seats, and Glenn slid in next to me, as was his habit. Kiki and Lance Caldwell settled elsewhere in the auditorium to watch, as did the set designer and some of the crew. I jogged my notes into a single pile, grabbed my reading glasses, uncapped a pen, and checked the time. When the music began, the houselights started their slow fade.

"Claire," Glenn said softly, leaning close to me, "are you happy?"

I could honestly tell him, "I don't remember being happier. I can't thank you enough for making this possible."

"My pleasure." He meant it. After a moment's hesitation, he added, "I'm not sure how to broach this, but I couldn't help wondering: Have you warmed at all to the possibility of a future . . . for us?"

I patted his hand. "Forgive me, Glenn, but the time's not right for that discussion. My mind is elsewhere."

"I understand. Of course, dear."

As the houselights went black, I sighed. Everything was perfect.

All that was lacking was Stewart Chaffee's clock.

6

Our Sunday rehearsal was an unqualified success, so Monday found me in an upbeat mood, almost celebratory. Though my chickens were not yet hatched, I felt no qualms about counting them.

Tanner had a class on campus that morning, leaving early, but I stayed at home, following up with a few phone calls to special guests—critics—who I hoped would attend that Friday night's opening of *Laura*. I had a quiet lunch, snacking on whatever I could find. Then, sometime after twelve-thirty, Tanner called on his cell phone to say that he and Thad Quatrain were on their way to pick me up. We had a clock to fetch.

A few minutes later, I was waiting on the street in front of Villa Paseo when the spotless black Jeep pulled up the block and stopped at the curb. Thad jumped in back, hoisting himself under the roll bar, so I could take the front seat. With a few cheery greetings, we were off, heading up valley toward Rancho Mirage. The noontide sun had crept as high as it would get in the December sky, warming my face in the cool breeze. Overnight, I noticed, the snow on Mount San Jacinto had spread lower from its peak, but down here on the desert floor, the temperature felt like a perfect seventy-two.

In Rancho Mirage, I directed Tanner to turn off the highway. We drove north into the valley, past the Annenbergs' pink, guarded walls, slowing as we approached Stewart Chaffee's gate. "Try the intercom," I said. Tanner braked the Jeep and pressed the button.

We waited for a response, but after a full minute we had heard nothing but birdsong from the riotous flowering foliage that covered the walls at the entrance. I checked my watch; it was just past one.

Drumming my fingers on the top edge of the door, I said, "Stewart told Grant that if no one answered the intercom, we could use a code to get in." I gave Tanner the four digits that signified Stewart's birth eighty-two years earlier.

Tanner punched in the code, and instantly, the gate rolled open, just as it had done for Grant on the previous morning. "We're in," said Tanner, as if launching a commando mission, throwing the Jeep into gear and lurching past the gate onto the grounds of the estate.

Driving to the house, I half expected Pea to bolt from the front door, waving his arms as he had done yesterday. Though I'd found him in general to be an annoying little man, I now would have welcomed any sort of greeting, even one of Pea's bossy performances as the household's put-upon majordomo. But when we had rolled to a stop at the entrance to the house, all was quiet—the birds seemed to pause in their chatter—so I stepped down from the Jeep, walked to the door, and rang the bell, whose faint chime sounded from far within.

The door was hung with an oversize wreath of pine sprigs flocked the hue of champagne, like the tree I'd seen in the living room on Saturday. Dangling from the wreath were wide velvet ribbons, not red, but burgundy, almost brown, looking more somber than merry. While I waited, a wave of anxiety washed over me, the same nebulous sense of dread I had felt yesterday when Grant had driven me here. Though yesterday's foreboding had been proven irrational and groundless, today's uneasiness sprang from a pragmatic, specific worry that grew more real by the second. What if no one was home? What if Stewart had forgotten, or reconsidered, his promise to give me the clock?

"What'll we do?" asked Tanner. The idling Jeep sputtered with an uncertainty that mirrored my own.

Mustering a show of determination, I answered, "Let's go around back. That's probably where we'll load up." And I hopped into the Jeep, directing Tanner around the house, away from the street, toward the garage.

"Wow," said Thad from behind me, "a Rolls." The garage door was wide-open, with the vintage car parked in the same space where it had been the day before. The white Cadillac was gone, however, and there were no other cars, such as yesterday's Korean compact, outside in the parking court.

I suggested, "Maybe they left the clock in the garage for us."

Tanner asked, "It's valuable, isn't it? Do you think they'd leave it out like that?"

I shrugged. "The grounds are gated."

"True." Tanner cut the engine.

We all got out of the Jeep, walked toward the cluttered garage, and snooped. Thad's investigation was limited to the Rolls-Royce—not many in Wisconsin, I reasoned. But I could tell at a glance that the distinctive Austrian clock was not there. I told the others, "I'll try the kitchen door."

I left the garage, stepping to the nearby back entrance to the house. Standing in the shade of a date palm, I pressed the doorbell, hearing it chime within. Again, I felt a ripple of apprehension pass through me as I waited. Again, there was no answer. So I gave a yoo-hoo. Still nothing. I called, "Anyone home?"

Tanner and Thad stood watching from the garage, wondering, I'm sure, if I had dragged them on a wild-goose chase.

I peered through the door's window, but it was partially curtained, and the glare of sunshine made it impossible to see inside. Plucking up my resolve, I reached for the knob and gave it a turn.

But it was locked.

"Miss Gray?" said Thad. "There's another door in here." He pointed past the Rolls to a door in the garage wall common to the house.

I had assumed since yesterday that the opulent old car belonged to Stewart, so it was reasonable to conclude that Stewart was at home. Perhaps he was napping. If so, I didn't like the idea of waking an elderly, ailing man, but still, I was expected. This had all been prearranged. It was my third visit, and I did not intend to leave without that clock. Eyeing the door discovered by Thad, I figured, "Worth a try."

So I entered the garage again, stepped between Thad and Tanner, and approached the door. There was no bell, no window. I knocked.

Doing so, I found that the door had not been tightly closed; it inched open at my touch. I yoo-hooed through the crack, calling, "Stewart? Pea? Bonnie? Is anyone there?"

Hearing no answer, hearing nothing at all, I opened the door wider, poking my head inside.

I gasped, losing my breath for a moment. Then I swung the door wide and rushed inside. I heard Tanner's and Thad's footfalls as they bounded through the door from the garage, stopping behind me. But my eyes were fixed on what I saw ahead.

There on the kitchen floor lay Stewart Chaffee, crushed beneath the refrigerator, which had toppled onto him, covering his lower torso. The scene was a grisly mess, with Stewart pinned in the mangled metal frame of his wheelchair. The refrigerator was still running, its condenser humming, its door flung open. Foodstuffs were scattered everywhere, including a large bowlful of pink fluff, which had oozed across Stewart's chest and spread to the floor. His head was shmooshed against the black-and-white pony skin of his saddlebag. From his mouth, blood had streamed and begun to coagulate, puddling on the floor with melba sauce, forming a horrific red-and-pink swirl with his favorite treat. Strewn about the tile floor, in addition to the dishes, bowls, and bottles that had been dumped there, was the collection of cocktail shakers that I'd seen displayed atop the refrigerator. Stylized chrome penguins, zeppelins, barbells, and fireplugs now littered the farthest corners of the room, where they had bounced and clanged.

Absorbing it all, I was struck speechless. We all were.

Thad broke the silence—"We've got to *help* him"—and he darted around me toward Stewart.

"No," I commanded. Then I issued the obligatory warning: "Don't touch *anything*." Had I thought there was any chance of saving a life, I'd have rushed with Thad toward the body on the floor. But it was only too evident that Stewart's body was already a corpse.

Tanner said, "I'll call nine-one-one." He unsnapped the cell phone from a holster on his belt.

"Wait," I said. "Stewart is clearly beyond helping. We don't need an ambulance, but the police. May I?"

Tanner handed me his phone. "Do you remember the number?"

I eyed him askance, as if to ask, Are you kidding? Though it had been three months, I had no trouble recalling the number I tapped into the phone.

"Yes," I said when someone answered, "may I speak to Detective Larry Knoll, please? Tell him it's Claire Gray. And it's an emergency."

Half an hour later, just past one-thirty, the grounds of the estate were cluttered with various police vehicles from the Riverside County sheriff's department. The house itself, particularly the kitchen, was a beehive of commotion as investigators began trying to piece together the unknown circumstances that had led to the death of the king of Palm Springs decorators. Larry Knoll, the detective in charge, sat in the great room with Tanner, Thad, and me, taking notes while we recounted how we'd happened on the scene.

One of the uniformed deputies interrupted us, telling the plain-clothes detective, "We've searched the entire premises. There's no one else here."

I quickly added, "We'd reached that conclusion ourselves, or we wouldn't have entered the house." I explained our arrangements to pick up the clock, which I needed for the set of our play.

Larry's eyes slid to the clock; the swing of its long, delicate pendulum marked a few passing seconds. He loosened his tie, asking me, "Any tickets left for opening night?"

"Long sold out." I grinned. "Sure, Larry, I'll find you a pair of comps."

"Is Grant going that night?" He was referring to his brother, Grant Knoll, my neighbor. Larry, at forty-six, was three years younger than Grant.

Shortly after I'd moved to the desert, the week before classes were to begin, I'd picked up a fellow faculty member at the airport one morning, driving him home. Entering the house together, we'd discovered his wife's dead body. Grant had then put me in touch with his brother, a sheriff's detective who would become involved with the investigation; eventually, so would I.

"Yes," I told Larry, "Grant and Kane will be there on Friday. Would you and your wife care to sit with them?"

"If you can arrange it, great. But I'll be happy with anything available."

"Consider it done."

In the kitchen, cameras were flashing. Several deputies grunted and scuffled, trying to right the refrigerator.

Larry looked over his notebook, spread open on a coffee table. Tanner, Thad, and I sat across from him on a leather sofa. He asked me, "So the three of you entered from the garage and found the scene exactly as it was when I arrived, correct?"

"Correct."

Tanner added, "Claire made sure we didn't touch anything."

Through a wary smile, Larry said to me, "Most professional. You don't intend to make a habit of this, I hope."

"Of course not." Perish the thought.

With a heave, the deputies in the kitchen got the refrigerator standing upright. It slammed against the wall before resting on its feet.

"Detective Knoll?" asked Thad, wide-eyed. "Do you know what happened? I mean, did someone *murder* him?"

"Too early to tell. The victim may have simply had the misfortune of tipping the refrigerator over—onto himself."

Tanner said, "An accident? That seems unlikely. Too fluky." He and the detective were already well acquainted from my previous foray into crime solving.

Larry scratched behind an ear. "The circumstances of Chaffee's death aren't really so freakish as they seem. The AMA reports, for instance, that over a thousand teenagers have been killed by Coke machines."

"Huh?" I asked skeptically. From the corner of my eye, I watched the awful spectacle of Stewart's body being disentangled from the crumpled wheelchair.

Larry elaborated, "Man against machine. Fights over lost quarters."

Thad admitted, "I've seen *that* often enough. But I've never seen a Coke machine fall."

"It happens," Larry assured us.

The medical examiner and an assistant now hovered over the body on the floor, trying to assess the injuries and their causes.

I recalled, "And just yesterday, I saw Stewart sitting in front of the refrigerator, tugging at the handle—twice. Those cocktail shakers were ready to take a dive even then. Too bad there was no one around this morning to help him. Poor guy. What an awful way to go."

"Detective?" An evidence technician had popped in from the kitchen. "We've dusted the refrigerator handle for prints. *Nada.*"

"Nothing at all?" asked Larry, hand to chin.

The tech shook his head. "Clean as a whistle."

"Be sure to dust the knobs of all the exterior doors, inside and out."

The tech nodded and returned to his work.

Larry recited while making note of it, "Fridge handle, clean."

Eyeing him, I prompted, "Which means . . ."

"Which means, foul play is now apparent. That door didn't open itself; *someone* had to touch the handle. I doubt if Mr. Chaffee accidentally pinned himself beneath the refrigerator, then, as his dying act, polished the hardware."

Following his line of reason, I added, "And whoever *did* polish the handle eventually left the house, which is why you're checking all the doorknobs."

Larry nodded. "Maybe someone got careless. So we'll need to take prints of everyone who's been here, hoping to zero in on a set that's unaccounted for."

"Foul play," repeated Thad. "That's like, murder, right?"

Larry raised a finger. "Maybe. For now, I'm treating it as a suspicious death."

Tanner agreed, "Plenty suspicious."

The medical examiner stepped into the great room. Eyeing Larry, he jerked his head toward the kitchen, wanting to talk.

Larry excused himself and stepped a few yards away from us. I had no trouble hearing him ask the examiner, "What do you know?"

"This is preliminary, of course, but the victim clearly died of severe hemorrhaging caused by traumatic injuries to his lower torso, beginning just beneath the rib cage."

Larry grimaced. "Did he go fast?"

"The direct injuries involved neither the heart nor the brain, so I doubt if he died instantly. There may have been time to save him, but whoever was responsible left him to die."

"When did it happen?"

"It's going to be difficult to establish the exact time of death because the refrigerator had been pumping cold air over the corpse since falling. A complete medical-legal autopsy will be required. With any luck, we'll sort this out."

Larry persisted, "Give me your best guess."

The medical examiner checked his watch. "It happened a few hours ago; I can't be more specific. It was definitely this morning, probably later rather than earlier. Let's say sometime after ten."

Larry nodded, thinking.

As the medical examiner returned to his crew in the kitchen, two sheriff's deputies lined up to speak to Larry. One of them said, "We did a quick check with the DMV, and the Rolls in the garage is registered to the victim, Stewart Chaffee."

Larry thanked him, and he left.

The other deputy said, "We may have some evidence, Detective." He held out two plastic bags.

"Over here," said Larry, returning to the coffee table—affording me a fine view. "What have you got?"

The cop turned over the first bag, containing a piece of paper. "This was found in the victim's lap, stuck there by the mess from the refrigerator."

Larry smoothed it on the table. Inside was a handwritten note, smeared with a mixture of blood, Jell-O, and Cool Whip. Tanner and Thad leaned, trying to see it, but it was upside down.

I didn't horse around. Rising, I stepped to Larry's side and read the note aloud: " 'Pink fluff in the fridge. Go ahead—pig out, you old goat.' " I explained to the others, "That has to be from Bonnie Bahr, Stewart's nurse."

Larry sat down and turned to a new page of notes. Clicking his pen, he asked, "What do you know about her?"

I filled him in.

Larry scribbled details. "She sounds like a real Nurse Ratched."

I tisked. "Hardly. What makes you say that?"

"Well, that note," he blustered. "The tone of it—'pig out, you old goat'—not very professional. Insubordinate. And just possibly sadistic."

"Possibly," I allowed, "but my instincts suggest otherwise. After all, she made him a batch of pink fluff and brought it over on her day off. I've watched them interact. They sniped, but it struck me as gaming and ultimately good-natured."

Larry looked up from his notes. "For her sake, I hope you're right."

The deputy held out the second plastic bag. "We found this in the victim's breast pocket. Pretty fancy. Something valuable? Theft maybe?"

Larry examined the bag. It contained an old, ornate key with a green silk tassel. Though I had never before seen it, I knew exactly what it was. "Yeah," said Larry, holding it up to the light, "theft. A good possibility for a motive. If we can find out what this key unlocks—a jewelry box, a silver chest—we could be halfway home to solving this."

I hesitated. "Sorry, Larry. That key has nothing to do with stolen goods."

He plopped the bagged key onto the table. "And how do you know *that?*"

"The key fits the drawers of an antique Biedermeier writing desk that Grant had borrowed for a designer showhouse. We returned the desk yesterday; it should still be in the garage. But we forgot to return the key. So Kane brought it over here this morning."

Larry blinked. "*Grant's* Kane?" What he meant to ask was, My brother's boyfriend? But the words were unnatural to him. The two brothers lived in different worlds.

"Yes," I answered, "Kane Richter was here with us yesterday, and he offered to drop off the key this morning on his way to campus. Obviously, he did just that, and then Stewart pocketed the key before . . ."

"Before what?"

I tossed my hands. "Before . . . whatever happened. I distinctly recall that Kane planned to come here early, and the medical examiner just said that Stewart was killed after ten. I'm sure there's no connection whatever."

We heard a commotion in the garage. Then one of the officers rushed in. "Detective Knoll? This gentleman says he lives here."

"What do you *mean*, there's been an accident? What in God's name—" Pea burst into the kitchen from behind the officer, then froze in his tracks, seeing Stewart on the floor. "I . . . I . . ." A clutch of shopping bags dropped from his hands—Saks, Brooks Brothers, Banana Republic. "Stewart?" he asked quietly, inching a step forward. "Oh, *God,* Stewart, what's happened?" And he darted toward the body.

Two deputies restrained him before he could touch the corpse. Pea was now kneeling within a yard of Stewart, with his dressy tan slacks hopelessly stained by the sanguine mess on the tile floor. Looking to the ceiling, he heaved a painful sigh, then fell forward and began to sob, mumbling Stewart's name.

Everyone observed a respectful moment of silence while Pea vented the initial shock of his loss. Even the medical examiner's team, jaded by countless scenes of unexpected death, seemed moved by Pea's display of raw grief. Naturally, I felt sympathy for the man, whom I barely knew. At the same time, I couldn't help wondering if perhaps, just maybe, this scene had been rehearsed. I'd seen a lot of theater in my years. Was I being shamefully cynical—or justifiably suspicious?

Larry leaned to ask me, "Who is he, do you know?"

I whispered, "He runs the household, sort of a secretary-butler. I think the name is Makepeace Fertig, but he goes by Pea."

Hearing the odd moniker, Larry gave me a squint. "Were they, uh . . . ?"

"Lovers? Not to my knowledge." I'd never even considered that possibility, as Pea and Stewart must have been separated by some forty years.

Larry stepped over to the pitiful scene in the kitchen. He asked gently, "Mr. Fertig, is it?"

Pea's tear-streaked face turned up. "Yes?"

"I'm sorry, sir. I can see what a terrible shock this has been for you. Do you think you need a doctor?"

"Uh, no." Pea shook his head, composing himself. "I'm fine, I think." He tried getting up, but had to steady himself with a hand on the floor, so one of the latex-gloved deputies helped him to his feet. Not only his slacks, but also his white tennis sweater was smeared with spilled food and blood.

"Do you feel up to a few questions? I'm Larry Knoll, the sheriff's detective in charge of the case."

Pea absentmindedly wiped his hands on his thighs. "Of course, Detective. Anything to help. Let me just . . ." He stepped to the sink, rinsed his hands, dried them, and shook hands with Larry, who was taller by a head. Pea looked up to tell him, "Thanks for being here."

"We'll be more comfortable in the other room," said Larry, leading Pea from the kitchen.

Tanner and Thad, who had risen from the sofa in the great room during Pea's dramatic entrance from the garage, now gathered with me, standing near the Austrian clock, while Larry returned to his notes at the coffee table. Larry took his previous chair, and Pea sat across from him, perching on the edge of the leather sofa's center cushion, where I had been.

"Tanner," I said quietly, "why don't you and Thad go relax outdoors? The grounds are beautiful."

Tanner nodded; he understood that I didn't want to expose young Thad to more of these proceedings than I had already inadvertently done. "Sure. Let us know when things wrap up, and we'll get that clock loaded." They headed out through the glass doors toward the pool.

A new worry: With Stewart gone, would I still get the clock?

Larry had begun his routine questioning, which first covered Pea's name, established his age as forty-five, and confirmed that he resided at the estate. "And how long have you lived here, Mr. Fertig?"

"Years. Forever." He focused his thoughts, then elaborated, "It's been about twenty years, since Stewart moved from his place in Palm Springs."

"And what was your relationship to the victim?"

"Household help. Stewart and I would joke about it, calling me his majordomo. But there really isn't a staff, at least no other live-ins. We have part-time help for cleaning, gardening, pool mainte-nance. The list goes on and on."

"What about the nurse?" Larry checked his notes. "Bonnie Bahr, right?"

"That's her name. She's full-time, but she doesn't live here."

"Where is she right now?"

"Monday is her day off. No idea what she does with her own time."

Larry added a line to his notes. He paused before asking, "Aside from your household duties, did you also have a personal relationship with Mr. Chaffee?"

Pea choked up. "We were . . . *friends,* sure. But nothing more." Then, as if the question had only now occurred to him, Pea asked, "What happened, Detective?" He gestured toward the kitchen.

"There's no quick answer, I'm afraid. At first glance, this appears to be a dreadful accident. I'm really very sorry."

While Larry and Pea exchanged a few words lamenting the trag-edy, I wondered why Larry had not shared with Pea his suspicions of foul play. Was Pea already on the suspect list?

Larry returned to his notes. "I need to begin constructing a chro-nology, a timetable, of everything that happened here at the house this morning. I hope you can help me."

"I wish I could, but I wasn't here."

"Where were you?"

"I left the house early, around seven-thirty, for my daily workout, over at Decathlon Gym."

Larry made note of the gym. "Do you routinely sign in there?"

"Yeah, but why? You don't think I had something to do with this, do you?"

"Not at all. I simply need to establish who was and wasn't here this morning, and when. So how long were you at the gym?"

"About an hour and a half, maybe longer. I had errands to run afterward, but since it's Bonnie's day off, I thought I should stop back here and check in on Stewart, which I did. I returned to the house at nine-thirty; I recall checking the time because I wanted to plan the rest of the morning. I found Stewart sleeping peacefully in his wheelchair, positioned near a sunny window in the living room."

"Here?" asked Larry, pointing toward the doors to the pool terrace.

"No," Pea explained, "the living room is near the center of the house, just off the main hall. Stewart was resting and seemed comfortable, so I didn't wake him. I left within fifteen minutes."

"Where did you go?"

Pea exhaled noisily, flapping his lips. "Gosh, all over. Shopping, mostly. The stores open at ten, and I hit quite a few. Clothes—it was time for some new duds."

"Do you have receipts?"

"Sure. That's a good idea; we can figure out when I was at each store. By the time I was finished, it was after twelve, so I had lunch at a nice little place on El Paseo. Then I came home. When I saw the gate open, I wondered if something was wrong. When I saw all the police cars, I sorta panicked. That's when I ran in from the garage." His eyes got glassy as he recalled what he'd seen in the kitchen.

"Mr. Fertig," said Larry, lifting one of the plastic bags from the table, "do you recognize this?"

Pea gave a decisive nod. "That's the key to Stewart's Biedermeier desk, which someone borrowed. When they returned it, they forgot to—" Pea stopped short. Something had clicked. He asked, "*What's your name, Detective?*"

"Knoll." Larry smiled. "Grant is my brother."

"Well, I'll be damned. You two sure don't dress alike, but yeah, I can see the resemblance. What a coincidence that you should end up *here.*"

Butting in, I explained, "Truth is, Pea, it's not a coincidence. I'm the common link. Grant is my neighbor, and he introduced me to Larry. When I found Stewart this afternoon, the first thing I did was phone Larry."

"Ah." Pea's tone was colored by a lingering shade of confusion.

Getting back on track, Larry said to Pea, "So Grant borrowed the desk, and when he returned it yesterday, he forgot the key. Claire tells me that Grant's friend Kane volunteered to bring the key back this morning."

"I do recall that." Pea tapped the bagged key. "So the kid must have been here."

"Did you happen to see him, or maybe his car, when you came home at nine-thirty to check on Stewart?"

"No, there was no one here. Stewart was alone."

"How about the key? Did you notice it? We found it in Stewart's breast pocket."

With a tiny sigh, Pea said, "Sorry."

Larry flipped back through his pad. "All right. The note from the nurse, Bonnie Bahr." He showed it to Pea. "Does this look like her writing?"

"Well, that *snip,*" said Pea, indignant, hand to hip. "I *warned* her about her abusive manner with Stewart, and here she is, at it again, calling him an old goat. Really!" He shoved the note aside. "That's Bonnie, all right."

"I understand she routinely made pink fluff for Stewart."

Pea stuck a finger down his throat.

I reminded him, "Stewart seemed to enjoy it."

"Yes," Pea conceded, "Stewart loved the stuff. Poor Stewart. I suppose I should thank Bonnie. Unless . . ." He trailed off suggestively.

Larry asked, "Unless what?"

"Unless Bonnie used the pink fluff as . . . as *bait,* as an excuse to see him alone today."

I asked, "Why would she do that?"

Pea shrugged. "It's as good a theory as any."

Larry reminded him, "But I'm assuming that Stewart's death was an accident. Are you suggesting otherwise?"

"Uh . . . well, no, of course not." Pea fell awkwardly silent. Glancing down, he noticed the mess on his clothes. His eyes bulged, as if he didn't remember groveling in the kitchen.

The coroner's crew had arrived, wheeling a gurney in from the garage.

Larry continued, "Then it's safe to say that when you returned home at nine-thirty, you didn't see Bonnie."

Pea repeated, "There was no one here. Stewart was alone."

Larry summarized, "Stewart was here all morning. You came and went. And it's reasonable to conclude that both Bonnie Bahr and Kane Richter were here at some point. Do you know of anyone else who might have come to the house today?"

Pea shook his head. "Mondays are generally quiet. The pool boy comes later this afternoon, but otherwise, no other help."

"The gate is electronically monitored, right?"

Pea snapped his fingers. "Of course! I forgot. We've never had trouble in the past, so I hardly give the security system a second thought. But sure, there's a camera at the gate, and it records a time-stamped video photo of the license plate of every car that enters."

"And when they exit?"

"I don't think so. Whoever designed this setup must have figured that since there's only one entrance, that's the only exit too."

"Makes sense. Those videos will go a long way toward establishing the exact sequence of events here this morning. Can I get the tape?"

"Absolutely. I'll phone the monitoring service and let them know you need it."

Larry seemed satisfied with this, making a last note before returning the book to his pocket. Then he rose from the chair, stepped to the kitchen, and huddled in conversation with some of the investigators.

The medical examiner had just finished up, and the coroner's crew had moved Stewart's body to their gurney. Zipping his remains inside the long, black bag, they began wheeling the fallen king of decorators from the house. Pea slumped forward, elbows on his knees, wearied by the frightful turn of events.

When Larry glanced back in my direction, I made a show of checking my watch. He walked over and told me, "If you need to be going, that's fine. But we need to take fingerprints from you and your friends, and I'll probably have to follow up with you later."

"Whenever you need me," I offered—too eagerly.

With an amiable frown, he reminded me, "You've got a play to keep you busy."

"Do I ever."

"So *you* focus on theater, and *I'll* focus on homicide."

"Yes, sir." Wryly, I reminded him, "You just told Pea this was an accident."

"Leave the strategizing to me, Claire."

"You're right, Larry. Sorry." Then I remembered, "Oh, hell. I need that clock. But now?"

Larry rubbed the nape of his neck. "How badly do you need it? Can't it wait?"

"We're going into our last three rehearsals," I blabbered, "and we open on Friday. The set is otherwise finished, and the cast needs to work with real props and furnishings. Besides, I'm afraid if I leave here today without the clock, I'll never get it. Who knows what the next few days will bring?" With a pout of defeat, I slumped.

"Let's see what we can do." Jerking his head toward the sofa, Larry signaled me to follow him.

Pea saw us coming. He stood, looking bedraggled, needing a hot shower, a change of clothes, and probably a good stiff drink. He asked Larry, "Do you mind if I . . . ?"

"Not at all, Mr. Fertig. Get yourself cleaned up, and get some rest. We can finish here on our own. But we'd like to get your fingerprints first, and I'll need to talk to you again, probably tomorrow."

"Of course." He stepped away from us, intending to leave the room.

"Just one other thing. I'm sure you'll recall that the reason Miss Gray came over this afternoon was to borrow a clock—that one—to use in her play."

Pea eyed the clock, then me. His features twisted in thought as he reminded us of the obvious: "The clock is Stewart's, but Stewart is dead."

Feeling somewhat childish, I reminded Pea, "He said I could use it."

Pea repeated, "But Stewart is dead."

"Mr. Fertig," said Larry, "it would be very helpful if Miss Gray could take the clock today."

"If you're asking *permission*," said Pea, starting to sound belligerent, "I say no. But then, who's to say? Whose clock is it—now?"

Larry acknowledged, "Your point is well taken. It's not yet clear where authority rests with regard to Mr. Chaffee's property. But he did intend to lend the clock to Miss Gray, and she only wants to borrow it, not keep it. I know Miss Gray, and I'm willing to vouch for her. The clock will be in good hands."

Pea hesitated, tantalizing me. Huffily, he said, "*Well!* I see it hasn't taken long for the buzzards to circle the carcass."

With greater self-control than I could have summoned, Larry said, "This is a stressful situation, I understand, but I'm sure you don't mean to imply anything unflattering by that remark."

Pea's spine stiffened. "Detective Knoll, I'm not sure *what* I mean to imply. But if you intend to get that clock by bullying or by force, then take it. There's no one to stand in your way." And with that, Pea turned on his heel and left the room, retreating to the other end of the house.

Larry shook his head wearily.

I rounded up Tanner and Thad.

We gave our fingerprints.

Then we took the clock.

7

Stewart Chaffee's Austrian pendulum clock was a sensational addition to the *Laura* set. It was, as Grant Knoll had predicted, a perfect finishing touch to our production, an exotic visual counterpoint to the feminine surroundings of the three-walled apartment created onstage. At rehearsal on Monday night, the clock proved sensational not only because of its inherent aesthetics, but also because word had spread among the cast and crew that the clock belonged to a man whom I'd found gruesomely killed that very afternoon.

"It's all too delicious," said my friend Kiki, the costumer, watching as Tanner helped a couple of stagehands cart the clock from the wings and install it on the set. "*Laura* is such a dark script—what an opportune publicity angle for the show."

I dismissed this suggestion, telling Kiki dryly, "I think we're better off promoting the production on its own merits. Besides, we don't want to draw undue attention to the clock; it's pivotal to the plot."

Kiki was unconvinced. "You know the old advertising adage: sell the sizzle, not the steak."

"Trust me, Kiki." Mine was the voice of integrity. "We've got sizzle galore. There's no need to resort to ghoulish tabloid tactics."

With a shrug, she sauntered from the auditorium to check the backstage wardrobe, pausing on the set to take a closer look at the clock. She wasn't the only one. A small crowd had gathered, admiring the clock with awed reverence, fascinated by its morbid overtones.

"Crushed by a refrigerator," said someone.

"And the clock was there in the same room," someone else elaborated.

"Can you imagine?"

"Too cool." And on and on.

Needless to say, I did not share in this giddiness, and neither did Tanner or Thad. We'd witnessed the aftermath of Stewart Chaffee's painful annihilation, and there was nothing cool about it. While Tanner was mature enough to put the troubling afternoon in perspective and to focus on the task at hand—rehearsal—Thad had become noticeably shaken, and I worried that his performance might suffer that night. I could only hope that he was sufficiently experienced to put the real world aside while creating another reality onstage.

What's more, Thad was in a spin that evening because of the expected arrival of his uncle. I do not, as a rule, approve of the presence of visitors, especially family of the cast. Work, not socializing, is the purpose of rehearsals, and visitors invariably prove distracting. Mark Manning, however, was an easy exception to my rule. Knowing the importance of his role in Thad's life, I could not, in good conscience, have barred him from the theater that evening. I'd already, in a sense, been responsible for their past three months of separation.

More to the point, I myself was eager to see Mark again. We were little more than acquaintances, and it had been nearly four years since our last encounter, but we had a lasting affinity; we had clicked. On top of which, few journalists, let alone cops, were more adept than Mark at untangling riddles of mysterious death. That evening, I had just such a death on my mind.

"Miss Gray?" said someone from behind, nipping my thoughts. I turned to find Thad standing in the aisle near the front row of seats. He was already in costume as a New York kid from the 1940s, wearing argyle sweater, baggy pants, and black canvas high-tops. Beaming proudly, he said, "Sorry to interrupt, but my uncle wanted—"

"Mark!" I said, opening my arms for a hug. "Welcome to paradise." I'd already adopted the locals' stock greeting, though tonight it had an off ring.

"Thank you, Claire." After an affectionate embrace, he held me at arm's length. "You look wonderful. Desert life obviously agrees with you."

I grinned. "I think it does, yes. And you, Mark—handsome as ever. It's been a long time, but I must say, you're wearing the years well." It was no idle compliment. While gabbing these pleasantries, I noted that Mark's hair was showing more gray—he was now in his midforties—but he looked even more vital and dashing than before. Men. How do they do that?

As we spoke, he stood by Thad with an arm draped around the kid's shoulder. Mark had never looked happier; his eyes, so arrestingly green, spoke volumes. Was it just the flush of their reunion, or was it deeper? I told him, "It seems you've adapted well to the unexpected role of fatherhood."

"Who'd have thought?" Mark mussed Thad's hair. "Yeah, it's worked out just fine, though Neil and I have had a rough time adapting to our latest role, empty-nesters. I'm starting to feel *old*."

Thad cuffed his uncle's arm. "*That'll* be the day."

I checked my watch—a quarter till seven. Asking Mark to excuse me for a moment, I stepped to the front of the auditorium, in front of the stage. "Attention, everyone." I clapped my hands. "We'll begin at seven sharp tonight, but otherwise, everything will be identical to Friday's eight o'clock curtain. We have but three rehearsals remaining, and we'll treat them as actual performances. No stopping, no matter what."

Standing just offstage, Tanner asked, "Does that mean you're finished giving notes?" He was kidding.

I chortled. "Fat chance." There was a round of disappointed awwws. "Notes, as usual, at the end. Also, we'll begin practicing curtain call tonight." This, predictably, elicited a brighter response from the cast.

"So, then, the house is now open. The seats are beginning to fill with an expectant audience, a capacity crowd in the mood for magic. You've worked hard, and now it's time to summon that extra measure of focus and concentration that will truly breathe life into our theatrical artifice. I know you're up to the challenge." I gave everyone a thumbs-up. "Tony, drop the curtain. Places, everyone, please. Silence backstage. And break a leg."

As instructed, actors and crew disappeared. The curtain fell. The houselights rose to full level, allowing my imaginary audience to read their programs.

Clipboard in hand, I started up the aisle, pausing as I approached Mark.

He offered, "Would it be better if I left? I know directors can be sort of touchy about—"

"Nonsense. I'm glad you're here."

"So am I." He sighed through a smile. "You'll probably find this hard to understand, but I've actually been looking *forward* to driving Thad's car out here. It's a two-thousand-mile haul."

I squeezed Mark's arm. "I understand. You have every right to be proud of Thad. He's a delightful young man and a valuable member of our troupe."

"He's okay, then?"

"Okay? He's an extraordinarily promising actor. Wait till you see what he does with the role of Danny. It's the smallest part in the play, but he does big things with it. Rest assured, I'll put him to better use in the *next* production."

Mark grinned. "I appreciate hearing that, but I meant to ask if he's okay with everything in general—his move away from home, adjusting to college, new friends, and all. Does he seem happy?"

"Very." Then I recalled that afternoon and gestured for Mark to sit. We took two seats on the aisle. "Did Thad tell you what happened today?"

"He said something about an accident, sort of laughed it off. Were you there?"

I gathered my thoughts, then recounted our excursion to the Chaffee estate, concluding, "So we all got fingerprinted, including Thad. Sorry."

Mark asked, "Do the police suspect foul play?"

"They do. I'm sure the whole episode upset Thad. It upset *me*."

Mark shook his head pensively. "Thad lost his mother to violent death, so he's dealt with it before."

"Good heavens, I had no idea. This time, at least, he has no ties to the victim. Still, I'm glad you'll be around for a few days."

"Me too. Plus, Thad has the play to think about. That should be more than enough to keep his mind off murder."

I felt it unwise to point out just then that *Laura* was a play about a particularly heinous crime—a shotgun blast, close range, to a woman's face. Glossing past this, I suggested, "Care to sit with me while I take notes? We'll begin soon."

"I'd be honored to observe the legendary director at work."

Little did he know that I hoped, in the near future, to observe *him* at work. I stood, saying, "Follow me." Then I led him up the aisle, turning into the row where my table was set up.

As we settled in, I noticed Glenn enter the auditorium, trotting down an aisle toward us. I asked Mark, "Have you met Glenn Yeats? He's taken a keen interest in the theater program, attending most rehearsals."

Mark reflexively stood again, doubtless in deference to the vast wealth represented by Glenn and his software empire. They greeted each other from opposite sides of the table, reaching in front of me to shake hands, each sounding downright starstruck in making the other's acquaintance. After a round of mutual kowtowing, they sat, Glenn to the left of me, Mark to my right.

The tycoon asked the journalist, "Where are you staying?"

"The Regal Palms Hotel. Nice place. Great views. It's halfway up a mountain."

"I know it well." Glenn laughed.

I explained, "Glenn's home is in Nirvana, the development farther up the hill from the Regal Palms."

"Ah," said Mark. "I'd expect no less." He told Glenn, "I admire your taste, by the way. The campus is magnificent. My partner is an architect, and he's been following the project in the trade journals— no lack of publicity."

Sell the sizzle, I thought.

"I'm pleased with it," Glenn allowed humbly. "I hope you'll also get a chance to see my home during your stay. The vistas are magnificent."

The houselights dimmed slightly, and Lance Caldwell's recorded music began to play in the auditorium. The curtain would rise in precisely three minutes. I organized my notes and readied my pen.

Glenn and Mark continued to converse, instinctively hushing their tone as the lights dimmed. Switching on a desk lamp and reviewing a checklist I'd written after Sunday's tech rehearsal, I caught snatches of their discussion.

Mark was saying, "I'm planning to visit the *Desert Sun* and meet with its management. I'm always on the lookout for ways to improve my own paper."

"I know the publisher." Glenn offered, "Would you like an introduction?"

"Thanks, but they've already rolled out the welcome mat."

Before long, Glenn was inviting Mark to his home, wanting to throw a cocktail party in honor of the esteemed visiting journalist. Dates were bantered about. I was consulted. From my perspective, the best time would have been Thursday, the evening before opening, when I traditionally gave my cast and crew a night of rest. But Mark had already planned to spend that evening with Thad, catching up, and their time together was sacrosanct. So Glenn settled on Wednesday, the night of my final rehearsal.

Since many of the prospective guests would also be involved in the play production, Glenn revised the concept of his party. It would no longer be a cocktail bash, but a brief, early reception featuring a light buffet supper prior to dress rehearsal. "Actually," he said, "that works out all the better. The winter sun sets early, and there'll still be some light for the evening views."

"Okay, now. Hush," I said playfully, but meaning it. "It's show-time."

Caldwell's music sounded its closing chord as the houselights faded to black. A moment later, the curtain rose in unison with the stage lights. Suddenly, there before our eyes was Laura Hunt's lovely apartment, replete with its fanciful Austrian case clock, a gift from the scheming Waldo Lydecker.

"*Gorgeous* set," Mark leaned to whisper in my right ear.

Glenn squeezed my left hand. "You've done us proud, Claire."

They were right. I couldn't recall reigning over a more polished production. I made a note to have the clock's face lightly soaped; the convex glass produced a lot of glare, and the time shown by the hands was clearly visible, an intrusive reality.

The scene had begun, and Mark was now glued to his nephew's performance as Danny, playing against Tanner as Detective Mc-Pherson.

Glenn whispered, "I see you got the clock."

"Yes, thank God, but it wasn't easy. Did you hear what happened?"

"No. What?"

"Later. Long story."

"I must admit, the clock is superb." With a snort, Glenn added, "I had my doubts." And at last he fell quiet, listening to the dialogue.

I wondered if his condescending attitude toward Stewart Chaffee would remain so smug after he learned that the rival collector had been killed that afternoon, crushed by a refrigerator.

Then I cleared my mind, suspended disbelief, and crossed the invisible fourth wall.

Tuesday morning, Tanner and I lounged with coffee and newspapers on the terrace near the pool at Villa Paseo. Having spent a late night at the theater, we took our time rising that morning. Though it was well past nine, an overnight chill still clung to the valley, so we'd donned comfy, bulky sweaters and lit the firepot on the terrace near our table. An unimaginative cook at best, I'd managed to butter a stack of toast, which we now nibbled at, sharing from a common plate.

Sitting across from me at the round table, Tanner poured me a fresh cup of coffee, drizzling it in a long stream from the pot. Its steam dazzled in the desert sunshine, then vanished in the clear morning air. Reaching for the cup, I set aside the Palm Springs paper. Its headline announced the demise of the king of decorators, a longtime figure on the local social scene. The story gave no details as to how Stewart Chaffee had died; it merely referred to an accident at home that police were still investigating. Quotes from all manner of high-profile acquaintances mourned the loss.

"Two more rehearsals," I told Tanner, affecting a breezy tone, trying to push the murder from my mind. "We're almost there. Isn't it thrilling?"

"It is for *me*." Tanner lolled back in his chair, smiling—God, that smile. "But I can't imagine that *you* find this production all that thrilling. I mean, you've directed some of the finest theatrical talent in the English-speaking world. Let's face it: this is a glorified school play."

"Don't sell yourself short." I winked astutely. "With Glenn Yeats's backing, the technical aspects of this show rival the best professional productions anywhere. As to the acting talent, well, it's my job to raise the bar and set new standards."

"Have we lived up to them?" asked Tanner, referring to the whole cast.

I answered with a question of my own. "Do you think I'd invite the New York press—to say nothing of prominent talent scouts—to Friday's opening if I were less than confident of delivering top-notch theater?"

"Guess not."

"Oh, sure," I continued, "we still have work to do. There were a few lighting glitches last night, but we'll get them ironed out. There's always room to improve the acting, naturally, and—"

"You gave enough *notes* last night."

"Of course I did. But what did the notes focus on? Not flubbed lines, missed entrances, or sloppy cues. No, we're down to the nitty-gritty, the meat of acting—interpretation, pacing, and cohesive ensemble skills. Trust me, Tanner. We're very, very close."

Had I been totally honest, I would have confided to Tanner that Monday's rehearsal had, in my judgment, slipped some from our previous efforts. But I attributed this to the hoo-ha generated by the murder, and I was confident that the distraction would quickly pass—by that evening, I hoped.

Tanner paused in thought, holding his coffee mug with both hands, then slurped from it, exhaling steam. He looked up. "Critics and talent scouts—you've mentioned them before. It's unlike you to be so coy, Claire. What are you up to?"

I grinned. "I'm not being coy. Hardly. It's just that I have reason to believe there will be some very big names in the audience on Friday night. If a buzz gets going among the cast, it could be counterproductive. Besides, the spotlight belongs on the stage, not on the auditorium."

Tanner leaned forward, set his coffee down, and fixed me in his stare. With a tone of mock threat, he demanded, "I want names, Claire."

How could I refuse him? *Who* could refuse him? "Very well. You understand, though, this is for your ears only, not backstage gossip."

"Got it." He mimed zipping his lips. Lord, those lips.

"I've invited a number of theater writers, but the most prominent of these"—I paused for effect—"is Hector Bosch, critic at large for the *New York Weekly Review.*"

"I'm impressed."

"We're old friends."

"He's tough, though."

I shrugged. "He's a *critic*. Get used to it."

Tanner considered this for a moment, then asked, "Who else?"

"All right." I cleared my throat. "Don't read too much into this. I haven't called in any 'talent scouts' as such, but since we're so near to LA, I thought I'd invite a couple of film producers whom I've met in the past. They're always on the lookout for new talent, and they've accepted."

"Who?"

"One you wouldn't know. The other is Spencer Wallace."

I'd expected Tanner to be surprised, but not dumbstruck. His jaw actually dropped. With a choked cough, he finally found his voice. "You have *got* to be kidding. Spencer Wallace? The mega-producer supreme? Mr. Blockbuster?"

"The same."

"Wallace will be in *our* audience on Friday?"

I laughed. "Let's hope he doesn't whisk you away when the show closes. This is our first production, an auspicious start, but I need to build a whole department, a lasting program." I spoke of this concern blithely, as if Hollywood never beckoned so quickly, only in fairy tales. In truth, I already dreaded losing Tanner, whether sooner or later.

It was Tanner's turn to laugh. "Not to worry, Claire. I'll do my best to deliver a great show to Wallace and Bosch and anyone else you've invited, but I have no delusions about overnight stardom. I'm quite content to pay my dues for a while—and to learn my craft from you."

Was it any mystery that I found him so infatuating?

"Morning, doll!" said my neighbor, Grant Knoll, strolling out to the terrace, coffee in one hand, newspaper in the other. "You too, Claire."

"Morning, Grant," said Tanner.

"Hello, Grant." I offered my cheek, which he obligingly kissed.

He told us, "I spotted you from the kitchen window. Mind some company?"

"Of course not," we said. "Have a seat." Which he did, sitting between us, flopping the paper on the table.

I said, "I see you've read the news. I'm sorry about your friend. The paper didn't go into much detail, but I was *there*. So was Tanner. You'll never believe—"

"I've heard *all* about it," he assured me. "My brother Larry paid a call last night, needing to clarify the particulars of Kane's visit with Stewart yesterday morning."

"Ah. Of course."

"Here he is now," said Grant. He called, "Over here, Kane. Join us."

And Grant's young lover walked out from their living room, dressed for a day of classes, looking every inch the college kid. He carried a banana. "Hi, guys," he greeted all of us, approaching the table.

We greeted him in turn as he sat in the fourth chair, across from Grant. Peeling his banana, he spotted the newspapers. "Man, how 'bout that? I was *there* yesterday, returning the desk key."

Tanner told him, "Claire and I were there in the afternoon. We *found* him."

Kane nodded. "Larry told us what happened. He even took my fingerprints—pretty cool!" Kane bit off the end of the banana, chewed, and swallowed. Then his features turned more serious. "It must've been awful, finding the old guy like that. He was sure alive when I was there."

"Oh?" I sensed that Kane had more to tell. "What time was that?"

Wryly, Grant noted, "You sound like my brother—the cop. Milady isn't wheedling her way into another murder investigation, is she?"

I shushed him. "Don't be ridiculous."

Kane answered my question. "I stopped there on my way to campus. I left here around eight and arrived at DAC by eight-thirty, so I must have dropped off the key around eight-fifteen. That's what I told Larry last night."

"How long were you there? Did you talk to anyone?"

Kane laughed. "That's what *Larry* asked."

From the corner of his mouth, Grant said, "I rest my case. Madam is sleuthing again."

"I wasn't there long," said Kane, "no more than five minutes. I rang the intercom at the gate, and someone buzzed me in. When the gate opened, I drove in and went up to the front door. The old guy answered it himself. It took him a while; he was in his wheelchair. He asked me to come in, saying he had more 'treats' for me." Kane rolled his eyes. "I knew better than *that,* so I just handed him the key, thanked him, and left. That's all there was to it."

I asked, "And there was no one else around?"

"Nope. Not that I could tell." Kane ate more of his banana.

I recalled the previous afternoon, when Larry had questioned Pea Fertig about his whereabouts that morning. Pea had said he'd left the house for the gym at seven-thirty, then checked back on Stewart at nine-thirty. Kane's brief visit had been squarely in the middle of Pea's absence, leaving a lot of time unaccounted for.

Grant asked me, "Bottom line—did you get Stewart's clock for your set?"

I nodded. "Larry convinced Pea to let me take it. I can't thank you enough, Grant, for suggesting it. The clock is perfect; the set's a knockout."

"Can't wait to see it." And we gabbed about the play.

Still, the murder was like a cloud intruding on the bright morning, and our conversation kept drifting back to it. We all agreed that while Stewart's death was not exactly untimely—he was eighty-two—it was nonetheless an ugly injustice. What's more, it was baffling. Larry had already ruled out the possibility that Stewart had died of a self-inflicted accident. Someone had killed him, but why? Though Stewart had been a wealthy man, there was not yet an apparent, specific motive for anyone to want him dead.

Grant checked his watch, downed the last of his coffee, and set the mug on the table. "It's after ten already. I can't linger."

I asked, "Busy day ahead at the Nirvana office?" I myself looked forward to a day of leisure. After Monday night's rehearsal, I'd cancelled my only Tuesday class, an advanced acting workshop. Most of my students were involved with the play. Why waste their energies on class when they'd be doing the real thing again that night?

"No," said Grant, "there's nothing going on at the office this morning, but I have an appointment to meet Stewart's banker, Merrit Lloyd, in Indian Wells."

I was suddenly on high alert. "Oh?"

Grant grinned, delighted that he had tantalized me so easily. "Merrit phoned me at home last night, shortly after my brother left. He's planning to open Stewart's safe-deposit box this morning and examine its contents. He recalled that Stewart had given him some minor item a few years ago, asking him to place it in the vault and telling him that it should be given to the Desert Museum of Southwestern Arts. Since I'm now president of the museum's board, Merrit thought I might want to be present when the box is opened. So I need to head over to Indian Wells Bank and Trust." Grant pushed back his chair.

Hoping to delay his departure, I asked, "Did Merrit give you any idea of what Stewart had left for the museum? Something highly valuable?"

Tanner cleared his throat, a suggestion that I should mind my own business.

Grant shook his head. "I got the impression it was an Indian artifact of some kind. As to what else he kept in the bank vault—who knows?"

I reminded him, "We know there's a plain white envelope in there. Stewart gave it to Merrit on Saturday. From the tenor of their conversation that day, the envelope contained a homemade will." I twitched my brow as if to ask, Get it?

Grant eyed me with suspicion. "What conceivable interest does milady have in Stewart Chaffee's will?"

With an exasperated grumble, I explained, "The *murder*. Stewart didn't trust lawyers, so he wrote himself a will and delivered it to his banker. Two days later, Stewart was dead."

Kane set down his banana peel. "Maybe someone was after an inheritance."

"I have to admit," said Tanner, "it's not far-fetched."

"No," I stressed the obvious, "it's *not* far-fetched." Turning to Grant, I added, "That's why I'd like to go with you this morning."

"*What?*"

"Maybe Merrit will open the will."

"Maybe," Grant conceded, "but the contents of that letter concern only Stewart and his heirs."

"And possibly the police."

Grant sat back in his chair. "How, pray tell, does any of this involve you?"

I paused, collecting my thoughts. "You're quite correct," I told him calmly. "The investigation is—and belongs—in your brother's capable hands. But I'm *already* involved. After all, I discovered the body, so by any logical reasoning, I'm a suspect."

Grant tisked. "Don't be nuts. Larry wouldn't suspect you for even a minute."

Preposterously, I asked, "Why not? I took the victim's clock, didn't I?"

"For God's sake."

"Hold on," said Tanner, only half-joking. "I was there too. And Thad Quatrain. Don't implicate *us*."

Calming down, I flashed Tanner a soft smile. "No, of course not. Never." Then I turned to Grant, admitting, "Let's just say I've developed an obsessive interest in Stewart Chaffee since discovering his body—and the hideous circumstances of his death. Who wouldn't? Yesterday, throughout rehearsal, I had to struggle to keep my mind on the show because my eye kept wandering back to that damn clock. Call me nosy. Call me theatrical, but I sniff a nicely twisted plot here, and I'm itching for some resolution."

Grant turned to Tanner. "If I take her to the bank, will I regret it?"

Tanner blew a low whistle. "More likely, you'll regret it if you don't."

Grant gave me a blank look, then smiled. "All right, doll."

"Wonderful." I pushed my chair back.

He stared at me aghast.

"What's wrong?"

"Well, you can't go like *that.*"

I glanced down. No, my breakfast grubs would not be deemed presentable in the rarefied environs of Indian Wells. "Give me five minutes. Kane and Tanner can keep you company." I stood.

Kane, sitting next to me, stood as well. "Actually, I need to run, or I'll be late for class." He told Grant, "I'll take our stuff back to the kitchen." He picked up the remains of his banana, crumpled a paper napkin, then reached in front of me for Grant's empty coffee mug.

As he did so, I noticed a nasty bruise on his upper arm. "Oooh, poor Kane." I turned an accusing eye to Grant. "Don't tell me you've been beating this dear child."

Grant instantly paled. "*Claire.*" he said, both astonished and defensive, "how could you say such a thing? I'd *never*—"

"I'm *kidding*, Grant." Laughing, I picked up my coffee and the plate of cold toast.

Kane also laughed. Twisting his arm to examine it, he explained, "I was unloading some groceries from the car when I got home yesterday, and the door jabbed me. No big deal."

"See?" said Grant, mustering his usual humor. "I may be many unsavory things, but I am *not* a wife beater."

Kane quipped, "I thought *you* were the wife."

"That's on Mondays and Wednesdays, pumpkin, but today is Tuesday."

"Oops. My mistake." Kane stepped around the table, gave his lover a peck, then went indoors.

9

Grant looked over at me from the wheel of his car. "You look fabulous, doll. It takes *me* two hours to get out of the house. Shaving alone takes twenty minutes; I'm serious. I don't know how you manage to put yourself together so quickly."

"Just a knack, I guess." Truth is, my speedy makeover was hardly adroit. Even though I'd taken ten minutes instead of the promised five, I still felt as if I'd just rolled out of bed. Finding a presentable outfit was little challenge—red always projects self-confidence, and besides, it was December. One glance in the mirror, however, had told me my hair was beyond easy redemption, so I'd wrapped it in a festive green silk scarf. I hoped to God this didn't give me the appearance of a chili pepper in heels, but once I'd conjured that image, I found it hard to shake.

"I just had a thought," said Grant.

"So did I." I assumed he was still talking about his lengthy routine of grooming and dressing. "Perhaps if you shaved before going to bed, you could save yourself some time in the morning."

His face wrinkled. "And start the day with stubble? I think *not.*" He swiped his fingertips over his chin, just checking.

We were driving down valley through Palm Desert on Highway One-Eleven, headed toward Indian Wells, considered by many to be the area's best address. To my eye, it was expensive real estate with little sense of community. It had no schools, no downtown, not even a library. But it did have banks.

"So," I asked, "what was your thought?"

"I was thinking about Tanner and you—and Kane and me—

sitting on the terrace together this morning. Don't you see the parallel?"

Perhaps I hadn't had enough coffee. "You mean, you met Kane around the same time I met Tanner three months ago."

"That's part of it . . ."

I tried another angle. "You and I are both attached to younger men."

"*Much* younger men. Kane is twenty-one, and I'm forty-nine, so I'm twenty-eight years his senior."

"Cradle robber."

"And if I'm not mistaken, Tanner is twenty-six, right?"

I nearly choked. "Stop right there. No more math, please." I'd just figured out that I too was twenty-eight years older than my live-in.

"By rights," Grant continued, "Kane and Tanner might be better off together."

"Nothing against Kane, but I'm afraid that *he'd* enjoy such a setup more than Tanner would."

Grant considered this obstacle to his theory, drumming his fingers on the steering wheel. "Tanner would adjust. I'm sure milady has taught him a lesson or two in versatility."

I conceded, "He's an apt pupil. But I'd describe Tanner's technique as more agile than versatile. Then again, his appetites are voracious."

"See?" Then Grant's smile fell; his brow wrinkled. "Of course, if *they* clicked, that would leave *us* together."

I laughed. "Now, *there's* an unlikely union."

He shrugged a why-not. "A few years down the road, we could change each other's diapers."

"An attractive prospect. But first"—I pointed to a building on the next corner—"I believe we have some banking matters to attend to."

Grant pulled into the neatly landscaped parking lot adjacent to Indian Wells Bank and Trust. His white Mercedes glided into a spot between a white Bentley and a white BMW roadster—basic transportation in these parts, where the only concession to practicality in the choice of vehicles is the overwhelming popularity of white or silver, colors that absorb less heat during the more torrid months.

I opened my door, but Grant was quick and chivalrous, trotting around the back of the car to assist me out, closing the door behind me. I carried an everyday handbag; Grant had his slim, handsome briefcase. As we walked together toward the entrance of the bank, Grant nodded toward a row of employee's vehicles. "This must be the place," he said, referring to a sign on the wall identifying a parking space reserved for Merrit Lloyd, Vice President, Client Services. A muscular-looking silver Mercedes was nosed to the wall, a newer model than Grant's. Recession? Never heard of it.

Escorting me indoors, Grant paused to tell a receptionist that he was expected by Mr. Lloyd. I looked about, absorbing my surroundings. The lobby was cool and hushed, starkly contemporary. Floors of polished black granite bespoke permanence and solidity, while white marble walls, soaring ceilings, and overscale artwork, sleek and modern, spoke a language well understood by the institution's wealthy clientele.

Within moments, the quiet lobby resounded with the peck of heels on the stone floor as Robin, Merrit's secretary, strode forward, greeting us by name. The severe, coppery bangs of her china-doll haircut bobbed as she shook hands with both of us, lamenting the terrible circumstances of Stewart Chaffee's sudden death.

Since I had not been expected, Grant began to account for my presence, but Robin dismissed any need for explanation, making me feel perfectly welcome. "Before we go in," she offered, "may I get you something to drink?" I had no idea whether she was referring to water or a highball, but I had no need for the former and it was too early for the latter, so I declined, as did Grant.

Robin led us through a series of offices and consulting rooms that bore no resemblance to a conventional bank. Conspicuously, there were no tellers; all business here was conducted by appointment, one-on-one. "Here we are," she said, stepping aside to admit us, then following us in.

"Grant!" said Merrit, rising from his chair. "And Claire too—what a pleasant surprise—even under such unpleasant circumstances." He stepped around his desk to shake hands with us.

The desk, I noted, was not the sort that one would expect in a banker's office—no carved walnut panels, brass lamp, or leather-edged blotter. Rather, the desk consisted of a polished concrete slab supported by rusted steel trestles. Its top was neat and clutter-free, bearing a phone, a photo of his family (himself, his wife, and a son of about Kane's age, but not nearly so good-looking), and a single, slim file folder, bright red. A long credenza behind the desk was similarly spare, but it had drawers and doors that presumably concealed additional files, his computer, and the day-to-day whatnot of business.

Above the credenza was displayed not a portrait of Washington or the bank's founder, but a large minimalist painting, some ten feet by four, entirely black, with the exception of a chrome-yellow squiggle running through the middle, suggesting a horizon. Its only other detail was the artist's signature. Though I could not make it out, I had no doubt that the scrawl marked a modern masterpiece worth several times the price of my home.

"I didn't mean to intrude on your day," Merrit was telling Grant, "but Stewart had given me explicit verbal instructions to donate the ring to the museum's collection. Since he eschewed professional es-tate planning, probate may get sticky. I thought I'd just give you the ring and be done with it."

"That's good of you," said Grant. "You've certainly piqued my curiosity. Stewart's taste didn't focus much on Southwestern arts and crafts."

So I'd noticed. Stewart's taste had leaned more toward Louis This and Louis That.

Merrit reminded us, "His collection was highly eclectic. It's been quite a while since I've seen inside his safe-deposit box, but I do recall the large ring he asked me to place there some two or three years ago. It's in a velvet pouch, and the ring itself is clearly of Native American origin—not sure what tribe."

"Well, then," said Grant, "suppose we have a look."

"Of course." Merrit turned to his secretary. "Do you have Mr. Chaffee's key?"

"It's at my desk. Let me get it for you." Robin left the office.

Merrit told us, "If you'll follow me, I'll take you to the vault." Leading us out of his office, he paused at Robin's desk, where she handed him a small key. He thanked her, palmed the key, then guided Grant and me down a central hall. "Once Stewart's estate is settled, it won't seem quite natural not having him on our roster of clients."

Grant asked, "How long has he done business with the bank?"

"Twenty-three years," Merrit answered without pausing to calculate. "Stewart brought his business to us the day these facilities opened. He said he admired the architecture."

"As good a reason as any," I quipped. I was tempted to add that I'd once opened an account at a bank that had enticed me with a toaster, but I feared this would be judged not only lowbrow, but vulgar.

"Needless to say," Merrit continued, "we were gratified to welcome such a gifted—and influential—client, and we were more than eager to please him, even after learning his somewhat eccentric views with regard to lawyers and conventional banking practices."

I recalled, "I know he didn't trust lawyers, but how did he feel about bankers?"

"As far as I know, he had no quibble with bankers—he was always cordial to *me*—but on the day he walked through our doors, he made it clear that he'd have no relationship with a banking institution that insisted on holding a master key to its safe-deposit boxes. He wanted complete privacy in the vault, with the assurance that there were no master keys in circulation. Since he was our first important customer, we tailored our policies to suit him, and they remain in effect even today."

Grant laughed. "Stewart certainly had moxie."

"Indeed he did. Ironically, within a few weeks of opening the account with us, he asked me to hold a copy of his key for him." Pausing outside the vault, Merrit tossed the key in his palm, telling us, "Here we are."

Now, at last, our surroundings did indeed look like a bank. The vault door, some two feet thick, stood open for the day's business, with an armed guard seated behind a small desk near the door. The guard exchanged a nod with Merrit, who turned to Grant and me, then flourished an arm, bidding us to enter before him.

Though the vault was large, its interior felt compressed and claustrophobic. Indirect lighting emanated from the low ceiling with unnatural whiteness; ventilated air swirled through the space, feeling chilled and artificial; the acoustics were utterly dead. The place reminded me of a tomb, an image made all the more vivid by the safe-deposit boxes lining the walls—like locked drawers for the deceased in a mausoleum. At the room's center, an oblong table, chest high, took on the morbid shape of a sarcophagus. Grant plopped his briefcase on top of it.

Merrit stepped around to the other side of the table. "Stewart is right over here," he said, presumably meaning Stewart's box, not his remains. Merrit unlocked one of the bigger boxes and slid it out of the wall.

"My," said Grant, "a double-wide, and in a prime location, no less."

With a grunt, Merrit placed the long, heavy box on the table. He tapped an engraved plate on the face of it, telling us, "Vault box number one."

Grant acknowledged, "Stewart always did have a nose for real estate."

As Merrit lifted the lid, Grant and I gathered near him at the table. I held my breath, uncertain of what I'd see inside. Bones, perhaps? Spiderwebs, gold bullion, a stash of uncut jewels? I chided myself for such foolish melodrama when I saw that the interior of Stewart's safe-deposit box contained nothing more malign than the messy miscellany I'd tossed into the bottom drawer of my own office desk. Odd-sized papers and envelopes defied tidy filing, while an assortment of small objects had settled in the corners, reminding me of so many spent ballpoint pens and pencil stubs that I ought to have thrown away.

Merrit began removing items from the box, describing them as he placed them on the table: "Insurance policies, car titles, deeds to his home and other real property, a bundled stack of old family photos, and files relating to his art collection—receipts and provenances." Among the paperwork he inventoried, I noticed a plain, white business envelope, surely the one I'd seen Stewart hand to his banker three days earlier.

Merrit continued plucking things from the box. "Stewart also kept a few of the smaller, more valuable items from his collection here at the bank." Displayed on the table now was an assortment of jewelry and tiny antique curios. "Ah, here we are," said Merrit, reaching for a small blue velvet bag. "This is the ring that Stewart asked me to donate to the museum in his name." Untying a cord at the neck of the bag, he emptied it into his palm, then handed a thick silver ring to Grant.

Playfully, Grant slipped it on, held the ring up to the light, and glanced at me. "It's fabulous, doll, but is it 'me'?" The oversize ring—perhaps designed for some ceremonial purpose—was encrusted with a setting of quartz crystals and turquoise.

"If anyone could pull it off, Grant, *you* could." My features pinched. "But Cartier is more your style."

"Yes"—he squinted at the ring, scowling—"you're right." Then, seriously, he told Merrit, "On behalf of the Desert Museum of Southwestern Arts, I can't thank you enough. And Stewart too, of course. This is a charming piece. I'll be sure that it's added to DMSA's permanent display of primitive crafts." Grant dropped the ring into the velvet bag, then slipped the bag into his briefcase.

"There," said Merrit with a nod, "my duty has been done. I'm glad the ring will now have a home where it's appreciated." He began to reload the safe-deposit box with items from the table.

I coughed, catching Grant's eye.

"What?" he asked.

With a jerk of my head, I indicated the box.

Seeing this, Merrit asked, "Is something wrong?"

"Well, no," I explained clumsily, "but we were wondering when you intend to open the letter." I tapped the plain white envelope, conspicuous among other, larger, labeled ones on the table.

"Ahhh." He paused, raising a hand to his chin. "Stewart did want me to open it, didn't he?"

I recalled, "His very words were 'When I die, I want you to go to my safe-deposit box and open that envelope.' "

Grant explained to Merrit, "Claire's theatrical training has given her an uncanny memory for dialogue and detail."

Checking my watch, I reminded Merrit, "Stewart has now been dead for some twenty-four hours. I can't help feeling that his letter may shed some light on his death."

Grant again explained on my behalf, "Claire discovered the body, as you know, and my brother is the detective in charge of the investigation. Unless I'm mistaken, Claire has taken something of a personal interest in the case."

I exhaled a loud sigh, admitting, "Perhaps I have. Regardless, the letter should be opened, as Stewart instructed."

"You're right, Claire," said Merrit. "I have no objection to opening it now. In fact, I'm glad you reminded me." He picked up the envelope, held it up to the light from the ceiling, and turned it in his hand. "No markings or notation whatever." He paused. "Hngh. Interesting."

"What?" I asked.

"I'd assumed there was a letter inside, but whatever it is, it looks sort of yellow."

Grant suggested, "Ivory stationery?"

I prodded them along: "One way to find out."

"True enough." Merrit set down the letter, opened a shallow drawer near the top of the table, and peered inside. "Oh, dear. No letter opener."

For God's sake, just *rip* it. I smiled patiently.

"I have a pocketknife," said Grant, offering the elegant little gold tool from his key chain.

"Splendid. How resourceful." Merrit fidgeted with the tiny knife, at last getting it to flip open.

"Uh, no," said Grant, wagging a finger, "that's the nail file."

"Ah, so it is. How clever." He closed the knife and tried again.

By now, I'd reassessed my original assumption that Merrit Lloyd was straight. Still, I'd just seen that family photo on his desk. Were the wife and kid actually a sister and nephew, or were all bankers, like accountants, compulsively anal?

I asked sweetly, "Need some help?"

"Thanks, but—*there*," he said. "Got it." He hoisted the one-inch blade in triumph, then brandished it like a buccaneer—a buccaneer in a button-down, pin-striped, French-cuffed shirt—before setting to work on the envelope, slitting it open with surgical precision.

"Well done," said Grant.

"Thank you, sir." Merrit gave a little bow, returning Grant's knife.

"What a handy little gadget. Do you recall where you got it?"

"Sorry, it was a gift. But it may have come from Tiffany's."

"Really? I'll have Robin check for me."

"Gentlemen," I reminded them soberly, "we were about to exhume a man's dying wishes."

"Oops," said Grant, "milady is getting antsy."

Merrit said, "Of course, Claire. Let's take a look at what Stewart left for us." And he slid a folded piece of paper out of the envelope. "Hngh," he said, opening it with care, "it's not a letter at all, but an old newspaper clipping."

Grant wondered aloud, "What's that supposed to tell us?"

"It appears to be an interview with Stewart. Ah. Look," said Merrit, pointing to the margin of the fragile newsprint. "Stewart wrote something along the side: 'This will make my wishes plain enough.'"

I noted, "Those were his words when he gave you the envelope on Saturday."

Merrit added, "He signed his name, dating it three days ago—Saturday."

I asked, "Can you verify the signature?"

"Certainly. We can check it against his signature on file, but I'd know Stewart's handwriting anywhere. It's his, all right."

"Well?" asked Grant. "What's in the article?"

"Interesting." Merrit pointed to the top margin of the page. "This was clipped from the *Palm Springs Herald,* an issue dated 1954, nearly fifty years ago, when Stewart was in his early thirties."

"The *Herald*?" I asked.

Grant explained, "A former competitor of the *Desert Sun*."

"Long defunct," Merrit added. Then he began skimming the article, summarizing as he read. "It's basically a personality profile. Stewart's star was already rising by the time he'd reached thirty, and the story notes some of the high-profile decorating projects he'd recently completed. A few celebrities of the day are quoted, praising his talents—it's quite a valentine. Here we go. Near the end, the reporter, noting that Stewart wasn't married and had no children, asks about his long-term intentions for the art collection he was already beginning to amass. Oh, my." Merrit looked up from the article with an expression of blank astonishment.

"Yes?" we prompted. "What does it say?"

Merrit held up the clipping and read, " 'The flamboyant Mr. Chaffee turned momentarily serious, responding with earnest, "Everything I own is to be my legacy to the Southwest Museum. We have a heritage here, and after I'm gone, I want to be a part of it." ' "

Grant looked stunned. "Good God."

"Huh?" I asked stupidly, though I had an inkling.

Setting down the clipping, Merrit explained, "Unless I'm mistaken, the Southwest Museum eventually became the Desert Museum of Southwestern Arts."

Grant verified, "DMSA was known in its early days as the Southwest Museum. The name change occurred years ago, long before the museum's recent affiliation with Desert Arts College. In any event, it has remained the same corporate entity since its inception."

"Well, then," said Merrit, smiling broadly and patting Grant on the back, "it appears that the museum, while under your able watch, has just inherited a windfall. Congratulations." He shook Grant's hand.

Still befuddled by this turn of events, Grant gestured to the shred of old newsprint on the table. "Will *that* stand up in court?"

"I'm no lawyer, but the bank has probate attorneys on staff, so I'll refer the legalities to them. In *my* opinion, however, this clipping should qualify as a holographic will."

Knowing little of such matters, I ventured, "Doesn't a holographic will have to be handwritten?"

"Traditionally, yes, but in recent years, the courts have been inclined to grant some leeway. Increasingly now, their prime criterion has become whether or not the deceased has clearly and verifiably communicated his or her wishes. In this case, even though Stewart's intentions are stated in the printed text of the article, his handwritten marginalia—signed and dated—are explicit."

"And," I recalled, "he verbally reiterated those intentions in front of all of us on Saturday when he handed you the envelope."

Merrit tapped the clipping on the table. "It's a very strong case."

Still in a daze, Grant said, "How incredibly ironic—that I should happen to be present when Stewart gave this document to Merrit."

I patted Grant's hand. "Somehow, I doubt that the timing was coincidental. Stewart knew that both you and Merrit were coming to the house that morning. Maybe it was his way of acknowledging your recent leadership at the museum. He made a point of complimenting your business sense and your social contacts. Remember?"

"True."

Merrit agreed, "Claire's right. I'll bet Stewart meant to telegraph his intentions to all of us that morning. He had such a colorful personality—always did have that streak of gaming. Still, I feel it would be prudent for us to take a few precautions." He stepped to a wall phone, picked up the receiver, and punched in a number. "Robin, could you join us in the vault, please? And bring along our file copy of Stewart Chaffee's signature."

Waiting for Robin, Merrit voiced some other probate issues, telling Grant that he hoped they could forestall any contesting claims to the estate.

While they spoke, I picked up the clipping, examined it, and found it unquestionably genuine. The paper was brittle and yellow, attesting to its age. I read through the entire interview, then glanced at the back side, where I found part of an ad for a Nash dealer with a four-digit phone number. Its headline trumpeted THE HOTTEST DEALS IN THE DESERT. The more things changed, it seemed, the more they stayed the same.

"Thank you, Robin," said Merrit as his secretary entered the vault and handed him Stewart's signature card. Holding the card beneath the signature on the clipping, he asked Robin to examine both. "Are they a satisfactory match?"

"No doubt whatever," she said at a glance. "May I ask the nature of the document?"

"Of course." Merrit apprised Robin of the clipping's significance, concluding, "The disbursement of a multimillion-dollar estate rests on this scrap of paper."

She nodded. "Then authentication is a top priority."

"Precisely. So there are several things I'd like for you to do, please. First, make several photocopies of the clipping for our own use and files, returning the original to Mr. Knoll."

"Me?" asked Grant.

"You represent the museum, and the museum is the sole beneficiary. You have the greatest interest in the integrity of the original."

"Wouldn't it be safer here, at your bank?"

"That might be seen as a conflict of interest, insofar as you are now the claimant against the deceased's estate." Merrit turned to his secretary. "Robin, be sure to find a protective sleeve for the newsprint; it should not be folded or handled any more than necessary."

"Yes, sir."

"Then do some library research to verify that the interview was actually published by the *Herald* in 1954. The clipping is clearly genuine—one look makes it self-evident—but with so much at stake, the authenticity could be routinely challenged by contesting claims on the estate. So let's do our homework up front."

"I'll get right on it. There should be microfilm in Palm Springs." Robin lifted the old clipping from the table, touching only the top corners. "Anything else, sir?"

"Uh . . ." Merrit glanced about. "Oh, yes. Here's an old stack of family photos that was among Mr. Chaffee's effects. I suppose they should go to his niece in Santa Barbara. You know how to reach her, don't you?"

"Yes, sir. We were in touch last week. I'll take care of it." Robin set the clipping on top of the photos, lifted the bundle, and left the vault.

Merrit turned to Grant. "Well, now," he said with a quiet laugh, "it seems you got more than you bargained for this morning."

Grant peered into his briefcase. "I was happy to get the *ring* . . ."

"And you got the whole shooting match."

I told Grant, "I hate to think of Stewart's death as having a silver lining, but I guess it did. It was a windfall for the arts."

Grant nodded. Pensively, he told us, "In a sense, I ought to be thrilled, but the truth is, it's a pointless sort of windfall."

Merrit and I exchanged a quizzical glance.

Grant elaborated, "For years, the museum struggled financially, but now that D. Glenn Yeats has brought it under his wing, built it a new facility, and affiliated it with Desert Arts College, the museum finds itself in the enviable position of not having a financial worry in the world."

Merrit shrugged. "And now you've got a 'little something' extra. A nice cushion. Think of it as an endowment."

"But most of Stewart's wealth was tied up in his collection, I assume."

"Yes, that's largely true."

"So the museum has inherited a vast collection of art and antiques."

I asked Grant wryly, "Something wrong with that?"

"Nothing at all. It's a wonderful, generous bequest. Except, most of Stewart's collection is not even remotely connected to Southwestern arts. It doesn't fit our artistic mission."

Merrit suggested the obvious: "So sell off the non-Southwestern pieces."

Grant brightened at the thought. Then he noticed my scowl. "What's wrong?"

"Sorry, gentlemen, but I don't think that idea will fly. Read the entire interview. In the paragraph after Stewart's statement about everything going to the Southwest Museum, he stipulates that nothing may be sold."

Merrit sighed. "That's a fairly typical restriction in bequests such as this."

"Which means," said Grant, "DMSA has just inherited a windfall with some very sticky strings attached."

"All that beautiful stuff . . ." I shook my head. "If you don't want to display it, and you can't sell it, what do you do with it?"

Grant tossed his hands. "Put it in storage."

PART TWO

duplicity

10

Climbing the mountainside toward Nirvana, I asked, "Are you sure I'm dressed for this?"

Grant glanced over at me, grinning. "You look spectacular, doll. I'm honored to escort you *anywhere.*"

"I mean, don't you think this is a tad Christmassy?" Seated next to him in the Mercedes, I swept a hand from my red dress to my green turban.

He paused. "It's December."

"Somehow, the suave crowd at the Regal Palms strikes me as more sophisticated—and less thematic."

"Shush. They're just people, mere *tourists*. Milady is a star. She's entitled to make a statement. Here we are." He turned off the steep road that continued up to the gated Nirvana housing development, swinging into the driveway of the Regal Palms Hotel.

By the time we had finished our dealings with Merrit Lloyd at the bank, it was nearly noon, and Grant was still reeling from having learned the unexpected disposition of Stewart Chaffee's estate. So he'd phoned from the car to reserve a terrace table at the hotel, where we could discuss that morning's events in relaxed, genteel surroundings.

"Ah," said Grant, peering ahead through the windshield, "Larry's here."

We had decided that the developments regarding Chaffee's fortune would be found equally intriguing by Grant's brother, Detective Larry Knoll, so we had phoned him as well, telling him what we'd learned. Since he happened to be driving down valley from Palm

Springs, we invited him to join us for lunch. He readily agreed, saying there was something important he needed to discuss with Grant.

Larry had arrived first and now stood under the huge portico at the hotel's entrance, eyes closed, face aimed toward the sun, soaking up a few mild winter rays. In the glare, he didn't notice Grant's car pull up.

A pair of uniformed parking valets stepped to the car, opening both front doors. Getting out, grabbing his briefcase from the back-seat, Grant said, "We're just staying for lunch."

Hearing this, Larry snapped out of his trance and greeted us, adding, "What took you so long?"

Grant reminded Larry, "I don't have the option of stopping traffic and running red lights when I'm late for a rendezvous."

"I would *never* do that." The brothers shook hands.

"Hi, Larry." I gave the detective a hug.

"Nice to see you again, Claire—under considerably more pleasant circumstances than yesterday."

I nodded. "The circumstances are different, but the topic's the same."

Grant suggested, "Shall we continue this inside? I've booked a fabulous table."

Walking us to the entrance, Larry told his gay brother, "I'd expect nothing less than 'fabulous' from you, Grant."

Crossing the lobby toward the dining room, Grant was saying, "It pays to have pull—"

"Claire!" someone interrupted. "Of all people."

Several guests milled nearby, so it took me a moment to spot Mark Manning striding toward us. He wore a crisp khaki business suit. "Mark!" I hailed, stopping under an expansive chandelier.

"I was just on my way out. What a nice surprise." He kissed my cheek.

"I forgot you were staying here. Everything to your liking?"

He made a gesture encompassing the graceful room. "What's not to like?"

Remembering my manners, I turned to introduce the brothers

Knoll and saw at once that Grant had a hungry interest in Mark. So I saved that introduction—the better to tantalize my neighbor—telling Larry, "This is Mark Manning, a journalist from the Midwest. His nephew is my student Thad Quatrain, who was with me yesterday at the Chaffee home."

Larry shook hands. "He seems like a great kid, Mark. Sorry he had to witness something like that." Then he explained, "I'm Larry Knoll, the detective in charge of the case."

I let them banter some, knowing that Grant was now all the more eager to meet my handsome, green-eyed friend. He was surely aware that Mark was not only a star journalist, but openly gay.

"Grant," I said at last, "do you know Mark Manning?"

"By reputation, of course. My pleasure, Mark." Grant beamed, shaking hands. "I'm Claire's neighbor—and Larry's brother." When all the pleasantries had been dispatched, Grant added, "Won't you join us for lunch? We'd *love* to have you."

At first, Grant's suggestion struck me as ill timed, motivated by shallow attraction when we had a deeper matter, murder, to discuss. Then I recalled that Mark had solved many such crimes during his investigative career, so I hoped he would accept Grant's invitation.

"Thanks, but I have plans"—Mark checked his watch—"and I'm running late. I have a lunch meeting with the publisher of the *Desert Sun.* Then I'm touring their offices and printing plant."

I joshed, "A working vacation . . ."

"Yeah, I guess." Mark laughed. "The fourth estate—ever vigilant." Then, after a quick round of farewells, he dashed out the front door.

Grant turned to watch him leave.

I said, "You're almost 'married,' remember."

"And blissfully so. But I'll never stop looking."

I singsonged, "Look but don't touch."

"*Gawd,* you're square." He tisked, then abruptly changed gears, asking, "Lunchtime?" And he escorted us to the dining room.

Grant had not exaggerated. His table was indeed "fabulous." As we settled on the back terrace and unfurled our heavy linen napkins, I gazed across the Coachella Valley, which spread out beneath us and disappeared through the San Gorgonio Pass. Overhead, palms rustled in a languid breeze.

A waiter offered drinks. Out of deference to Larry, who was on duty, we all opted for iced tea. "It's quite delectable," Grant told me, whirling a hand. "They infuse it with mango or . . . or *some* manner of exotic sapor."

Larry squinted. " 'Sapor'?"

"Flavoring. Really, Larry."

"Sorry. Once a philistine . . ."

Waiting for our tea to arrive, we moved quickly to our intended topic. "So," asked Larry, "Chaffee left everything to the museum?"

Grant lifted his briefcase from the limestone floor, set it in his lap, wedged it open, and peeped inside. "It was the damnedest thing. Merrit Lloyd had called me down to the bank because Stewart had left a turquoise ring to the museum, but I left with, in his words, 'the whole shooting match.' " Grant plucked from his case the plastic sleeve that now held the old newspaper clipping. "If you ask me, this is a highly peculiar last will and testament, but Merrit thinks it'll stand up."

I added, "The banker said it should qualify as a holographic will because of Stewart's handwritten note in the margin."

Larry took the clipping from Grant and skimmed through it. "I'm no legal genius, but the intentions of the deceased do seem perfectly clear." He set the printed interview aside.

Our tea arrived just then, and we raised our glasses in a toast to the Desert Museum of Southwestern Arts. Grant added, "And to Stewart Chaffee's memory, of course."

"Of course." We clinked glasses and sipped. Guava, perhaps.

Pausing in thought, Grant then told Larry, "The odd thing is, from the museum's standpoint, there's very little to celebrate."

"Why not? It's a windfall."

"That word keeps popping up." Grant went on to explain the double irony: Chaffee's art collection was largely inappropriate to DMSA's artistic mission, and the museum was no longer in financial need, thanks to Glenn Yeats's generosity in bringing it under the stewardship of Desert Arts College. "What's more," Grant noted, "we won't be able to *sell* the collection, so we'll be faced with the trouble—and expense—of storing it."

Menus were presented, which we perused briefly before ordering light lunches—twenty-dollar hotel salads. Grant reminded us, "This one's on me." He removed the newspaper clipping from the table and returned it to his briefcase on the floor.

When our waiter had left, I leaned into the table, asking Larry, "Well? Anything to report?"

Grant roared with laughter, drawing glances from several nearby tables.

Larry asked me, "Do I detect an inordinate note of interest in this investigation? Don't tell me you've developed an appetite for police work—again."

Grant cracked, "I thought you'd come to appreciate Claire's 'theatrical perspective' on crime solving."

"Actually," said Larry, sitting back, "I have. I admit, when Claire got involved in the case of the sculptor's wife, I was skeptical. But I found that her years in the theater have indeed imbued her with a keen understanding of plotting, motivation, and character. Plus, I've rarely known anyone with a sharper memory for detail."

I suggested, "That's because you've never memorized a three-hour Shakespearean script." With a sharp nod, I added, "Verbatim."

"No, I've never done that, and I doubt that I could. Plus, I don't have Claire's firsthand knowledge of the interaction, prior to yesterday, between Stewart Chaffee, the victim; Bonnie Bahr, the nurse; and Pea Fertig, the houseman. I'm man enough to admit it—I could use Claire's help."

I showed Grant the tip of my tongue, then turned to his brother. "I'll be happy to help any way I can."

Grant reminded me, "You've got a *show* to put on."

"Yes," I conceded, "that's my top priority. But we're into production week now, and the show has its own momentum. What's more, my theatrical duties are at night." Glancing at my watch, I grinned. "It's barely past noon."

"Oh, Lord." Grant sat back, crowing. "Milady's a sidekick again."

Shushing him, I turned to Larry and repeated my original question. "Well? Anything to report?"

The detective pulled a notebook from his pocket and opened it on the table. "Here's where we are. First, as established yesterday at the crime scene, the lack of fingerprints on the refrigerator handle points convincingly to foul play."

"Meaning," I clarified, "murder."

"Yes. Further, when the refrigerator fell on Chaffee, crushing him, the door was splayed wide open."

"Right," I recalled. "That's why there was such a mess."

"Yes, but think about it. The logistics are inconsistent with how the refrigerator would have fallen if Chaffee *himself* had accidentally toppled it while trying to pull the door open. If the door had already opened wide enough to clear him, he would have stopped pulling. No, someone *else* opened the door, then easily overturned the refrigerator by using the leverage provided by the door. The culprit stayed only long enough to remove the fingerprints, then left Chaffee to die a horrible, painful death."

"Poor Stewart," said Grant, ditching his glib manner. "I wasn't aware of the details. What a vile way to kill a helpless old man."

Larry said, "The coroner has not ruled out the possibility that the 'accident' was staged to mask some other murder method, such as drug overdose or poisoning. Toxicology tests have been ordered, but those results can take days, even weeks, depending on the caseload."

Grant suggested, "If it turns out that Stewart did have a drug overdose, that would point to the nurse, wouldn't it?"

"On the surface," I thought aloud. "But anyone with access to Stewart and his prescriptions might have given him an overdose to make it *appear* that Bonnie had done it."

"Someone like Pea?"

I shrugged. "They seem to despise each other." Turning to Larry, I said, "So toxicology is a big 'if.' Meanwhile, what has the coroner definitely established?"

Larry tapped his notebook. "Time of death. The autopsy itself is complete, and the coroner has fixed the time of Chaffee's death sometime between ten-thirty and eleven-thirty on Monday morning. I'd prefer a tighter window, of course, but the time can't be fixed more precisely because it's impossible to calculate the effect of the refrigerator upon the victim's loss of body temperature."

"Still," I noted, "that narrows it down to an hour. What about the security tape of cars entering the gate? That should tell you plenty."

"It does."

"Huh?" asked Grant, going pale.

Had he choked on a guava seed? Concerned, I asked, "Is something wrong?"

"Security tape?"

Larry explained to his brother, "The gate at Chaffee's estate is equipped with a security system that shoots time-stamped photos of the rear bumper of every vehicle entering the grounds. There was a fair amount of traffic there yesterday morning. We had no trouble tracing all the plates."

Grant weighed this news before saying, awkwardly, "Then I guess I understand why you were so quick to meet us for lunch. You said there was something important you needed to discuss."

If there was caffeine in my tea, it hadn't kicked in yet. Dense me. I asked, "What are you talking about?"

Grant slumped forward, bracing himself on his elbows. "I drove out to the estate yesterday morning." With a sigh, he added, "It was sometime after eleven. Yes, I was there."

I saved Larry the trouble of asking, "What for?"

Grant told both of us, "I was driving through the vicinity on an errand, and I wanted to make sure that Stewart had gotten the desk key, as promised. That's all there was to it. When I pulled up to the gate and used the intercom, no one answered, so I punched in the code, which Stewart himself had given me. I went to the front door, rang the bell several times, but no one answered. So I left."

Larry asked, "You were never inside the house?"

"No, not yesterday. Since no one seemed to be home, I left within a minute or two after I arrived." Grant's face brightened with a thought. "I'm sure the tapes will verify that."

"I'm sure they would," said the detective with a soft laugh, "but unfortunately, the system isn't set up to record exiting vehicles."

"Peachy." Grant grimaced. "As far as anyone knows, I was there for *hours*, engaged in all manner of devilry."

"Don't be silly." I patted his arm. "I arrived shortly after one o'clock with Tanner and Thad. You weren't there *then*, so you couldn't have been there for more than, say, an hour and a half."

"Thanks a heap."

Larry prompted his brother, "I assume you had lunch somewhere yesterday."

Grant sniffed haughtily. "Have you *ever* seen me brown-bag it? I always dine out, and I generally have witnesses. In fact, I was right here yesterday, with a client, at this very table."

Larry took notes. "What time?"

Grant fudged, "Noonish."

I slid an accusing eye in his direction. "Which left you a whole hour for mischief." I thought I'd better add, "Just kidding. Why would anyone suspect *you*, even remotely, of harboring motives to harm Stewart? You two were old friends."

Larry suggested, "What about the windfall for the museum?" Though I assumed he wasn't serious, I couldn't be sure.

"Larry," said Grant, "I've already told you—that 'windfall' is of very little use to DMSA, and it presents the museum with an enormous storage problem."

"Relax," said the cop. "I don't suspect you any more than Claire does, but you *were* there yesterday, so I need to get you crossed off my list."

"Good. How do we accomplish that?"

"For starters"—Larry hesitated—"you could volunteer a set of your fingerprints."

Grant gasped. "You can't be serious."

"Sorry, I am."

"Then you won't need all ten, just the right index finger." Grant displayed the digit. "The only thing I touched was the doorbell."

Larry explained, "It's a process of elimination. If we can match prints found at the property with people known to be there, people

whose presence we can explain, we then stand a chance of identifying any unaccountable set of prints."

"Mystery prints . . . ," I called them.

"Killer's prints," said Larry.

"Very *well*," said Grant, sounding put-upon. "If you want my
prints, you can certainly have them. What do I have to do—go
down to the cop shop in shackles?"

Larry allowed a laugh. "Of course not. When we leave here, I
can take care of it at my car. It won't take half a minute."

"Oh." Grant lost his attitude. "Fine. No problem."

I asked Larry, "Yesterday at the crime scene, you instructed a
deputy to check the exterior doors for prints. I take it you found
some."

"Sure. Doorknobs are fingerprint *magnets,* so there were plenty.
But because the refrigerator door handle had been wiped clean, I
thought the killer might have cleaned the doorknobs as well."

"And?"

The detective grinned. "Someone got sloppy—or rushed. They
polished the inside knob of the front door before leaving, but neglected to clean the outside knob."

I suggested, "Maybe they pulled the door closed by handling its
edge with a cloth."

"Entirely possible. But I doubt if they *entered* the house that way."

"Aha."

Grant leaned across the table, eyeing his brother's notebook.

"Yes?" asked Larry.

"I believe you mentioned something about crossing me off your
list."

With a comical flourish of his pen, Larry did so.

Visibly relieved, Grant took a long swallow of his iced tea. Relieved *for* him, I did likewise. Still, I couldn't shake the uneasy feeling
that Grant's reason for visiting the estate—checking on the key—
had been lame. His young partner, Kane, had taken responsibility
for returning the key. Why would Grant have given a second
thought to so simple a mission? Watching Larry scribble notes, I
wondered if he had questioned this as well.

Grant set down his glass. "You mentioned tracing the plates of quite a few cars that visited the estate yesterday. Might I ask who else was there?"

I seconded, "Good question."

"Sure," said Larry, "let's run through the list. Feel free to share your thoughts about any of this. The first car entering through the gate yesterday morning was a Mercedes-Benz belonging to Merrit Lloyd, the victim's banker. It was early, about a quarter to eight."

I recalled, "When I first met Merrit at the estate on Saturday, he mentioned that he would return with some paperwork early Monday, on his way into the office, I presume. I got the impression his services extended well beyond the normal bounds of banking. He said, 'Many days, I'm here more than once.'"

"That checks out." Larry tapped his pen on the pad. "Merrit showed up twice that morning."

Grant sighed. "Ah, the privileged lifestyle of the wealthy few."

I asked Larry, "Who arrived next?"

"Kane Richter. The tape shows that he drove past the gate at eight-fifteen, exactly as he told me last night. He returned the key to Stewart and left immediately."

Grant added, "Kane said he didn't see anyone else around, so Merrit Lloyd must have left by then, within a half hour after he arrived. He probably just needed a few signatures."

"I'll check it out," said Larry, "but sure, that would make sense."

I prodded, "Next?"

"The nurse, Bonnie Bahr, entered the grounds at nine on the nose."

"Delivering the pink fluff," I surmised.

"Yeah, that's what she told me when I reached her by phone last night. She sounded pretty distraught about Chaffee's death, so I didn't press for details. I've arranged to meet her after lunch."

"Not that I actively suspect Bonnie," I said, "but that meeting should be informative. She was probably as close to Stewart as anyone was during his latter days, with total access to the house and complete knowledge of his various medical conditions. If she's willing to open up, she could tell us plenty."

"Us?" asked Larry.

"Well, I meant 'us' in the general sense of the investigation." I sipped my tea.

Larry tapped his notes again. "Now we come to the houseman, Pea Fertig. This one is an intriguing character, if you'll pardon the understatement."

Grant said, "He's been with Stewart forever. Frankly, I've never known what to make of Pea." Grant paused before acknowledging, "He *is* odd."

Larry continued, "He drove through the gate around nine-thirty."

I recalled, "That's what he told us yesterday afternoon. He said he'd gone out to a gym at seven-thirty and decided to check on Stewart briefly before going on his shopping spree."

"Right. But remember, we have no way of verifying either the time he departed for the gym or the time he left to go shopping. And even though he said there seemed to be no one else at the house while he was there, we don't know for a fact when Bonnie left."

Grant asked, "Meaning, she could have been hiding, lurking, waiting?"

"Please," I told him, "spare us the melodrama."

"Anything's possible," Larry acknowledged, "especially when you consider that my time line is approaching the window established by the coroner for Chaffee's death. This is where it starts to get interesting—and confusing."

Grant cracked, "I must be having a blond day, but *I've* been confused since we sat down."

A waiter—not the one who took our order, but a younger, beefier one who happened to be blond—appeared with our salads and circled the table, serving us. Grant and I were both mesmerized by the lad's posterior, which, level with our eyes, alternately clenched and flexed as he stepped and reached, providing a momentary but welcome distraction from the headier theme of murder.

Larry set his notebook to the side as his salad landed in front of him. Oblivious to our ogling, he asked, "Do you mind if we continue to discuss business while we eat? I'm sorry the topic is so unappetizing."

"No problem," we assured him. The waiter had disappeared. "Please, go on."

Larry glanced at his notes. "The next person to arrive, at ten-fifteen, was Merrit Lloyd—his second visit that morning."

I considered the timing of Merrit's return while forking a plump shrimp from the delicate, oily greens on my plate. "It was a workday, so I imagine Merrit's second visit, like his first, was brief. He was probably gone by ten-thirty, the earliest that Stewart could have died."

"Probably," repeated Larry. "Now, here's where I really need some help: Do either of you know anything about a Dawn Chaffee-Tucker? I got the ID on her car just as I was arriving here at the hotel. It's registered in Santa Barbara, but there was some confusion as to whether it was hers or her husband's, so the report took longer than it should have."

Grant looked at me, then blinked. "On Sunday, when we returned the desk, didn't Stewart mention a niece named Dawn from Santa Barbara?"

"He did. But he flatly rejected my suggestion that he should 'reach out' to her. Earlier, on Saturday, he confirmed with Merrit's secretary that a Monday meeting had been set up with someone from a gallery in Santa Barbara. Sunday, he made such disparaging remarks about his niece, I assumed that the meeting was with someone *else* from Santa Barbara."

Grant nodded. "Then, this morning, Merrit asked his secretary to send the bundle of old photos from Stewart's safe-deposit box to the niece."

"No way around it," said Larry. "The niece from Santa Barbara and the person who Stewart planned to meet were clearly one and the same—Dawn Chaffee-Tucker."

"Clearly," I agreed. "But I don't get it. Why would Stewart confirm the meeting on Saturday, disavow any interest in his niece on Sunday, then meet with her on Monday?"

"Hard to say. Maybe *she* can tell us."

Grant asked, "What time did she arrive yesterday?"

"Eleven sharp, top of the hour, right on time for an appointment."

"And right in the middle," I noted, "of the time frame in which Stewart died."

Larry swirled a strip of chicken in a glistening puddle of vinaigrette. "I've already instructed the department to contact her. The timing of her visit is suspicious, certainly, but if, as you say, Chaffee himself called the meeting, the agenda was his, not hers." He paused in thought. "I need to talk to her." Then he ate the chicken.

Grant hesitated. "I hate to ask, but who's next on the list?"

"You, O brother mine. You opened the gate at eleven-twenty."

I asked Grant, "Doesn't it give you a nice, secure feeling to know that someone's looking after you?"

"And *you*, Claire," said Larry, "arrived in Tanner's Jeep at eight minutes past one." He frowned, looking down at his plate. "Could stand some pepper."

I passed it to him. "So we have a detailed record of everyone entering the grounds of the estate yesterday."

"And what we *don't* have is any verifiable means of determining how long each of those visitors stayed. We have their own accounts, as well as each successive visitor's report that no one else was there."

I paused while he peppered, then asked, "What's next?"

"Meet with them. Talk to them. Start examining motives, means, and opportunities. And hope that something clicks—or someone slips."

I reminded him, "I'm free all afternoon."

With only a moment's hesitation, Larry said, "Not anymore, you're not."

Grant gave me a canny grin, but didn't say a word.

Finishing our meal, Grant, Larry, and I rose from the table, paused to savor a last look across the valley, then left the terrace together, walking back through the dining room toward the hotel lobby.

The lunch crowd had swelled since our arrival, and the room now seemed inelegantly noisy with the chatter of patrons and clatter of plates. Several tables were turning, with a flurry of guests both arriving and departing. We got caught in this tangle near the door, pausing to let others pass as they entered.

Just as we were leaving, I happened to notice, from the corner of my eye, a couple being seated at a banquette along the wall. They were partly obscured by a waiter who adjusted the table as they settled side by side on the upholstered bench, but there was something familiar about them, so I lingered for a moment to watch. They leaned together and shared a kiss of easy intimacy; then the waiter handed them their menus and stepped away.

"What the—" I mumbled.

"Hmm?" asked Grant, wondering why I tarried.

"Look," I said, "it's Robin. With Atticus."

"Who?"

"Robin," I repeated, "Merrit Lloyd's secretary."

"I *know* Robin," Grant reminded me, "but who—or what—is Atticus?"

By now, Larry was also sufficiently intrigued to join us in ogling the couple in the booth.

I explained, "Atticus is a colleague of mine at DAC, a painter. In fact, he did a marvelous portrait of Laura for our stage setting."

"Oh?" asked Grant. "I'm eager to see it."

"Soon enough. But meanwhile, what are *they* doing *here?*"

"Having lunch, I imagine."

"I mean, what are they doing here *together?*"

At that moment, Robin placed her fingertips on Atticus's forearm, looked into his eyes, and spoke to him with quiet intensity.

Larry cleared his throat. "I'd say it's fairly obvious why they're together." With a laugh, he added, "That dog—he must be a good twenty years older than she is."

Grant tisked. "I can't imagine what she sees in *him*. Of course, they both have red hair."

Though I'd grown accustomed to Grant's non sequiturs, I had to ask, "What does that have to do with anything?"

"Red hair?" He whirled a hand. "It's a mutant strain, you know, a freakish hiccup of genetics. So they're *drawn* to each other. Survival of the species—it has an irresistible allure."

"You are *so* full of crap." I was not amused. My ill humor, however, had nothing to do with Grant's slant on Darwin. Rather, I was still stuck on Larry's candid observation that Robin and Atticus were mismatched by age. He was right. They made a dreadful-looking couple. Did total strangers similarly recoil at the sight of me with Tanner?

Just then, Robin caught sight of us gawking. Following her eyes, Atticus turned to see us as well. Recognizing me through the crowd, he stood, doffed an imaginary hat, and greeted my little group with a supercilious bow. Knowing the man's ego, I did not find it surprising that he took apparent pride in being discovered at lunch with a fashionable young girlfriend.

Robin, on the other hand, looked mortified.

11

Larry Knoll discreetly took a set of his brother's fingerprints in the shadows of the hotel portico, then drove me from the Regal Palms in his anonymous-looking county-issue sedan. The souped-up cruiser resembled Grant's car in only one respect: it was white. We snaked down the mountain roadway from the hotel, then headed up valley along Highway One-Eleven, passing out of ritzy Rancho Mirage and into working-class Cathedral City.

"By my count," I summarized, "there were six people at the Stewart Chaffee estate yesterday morning—Merrit Lloyd, Kane Richter, Bonnie Bahr, Pea Fertig, Dawn Chaffee-Tucker, and Grant—plus Stewart himself, of course."

"Correct. And of those, I'm willing to assume, for now, that three are above suspicion. Either timing or circumstances seem to clear Merrit Lloyd, Kane, and Grant. On the other hand, there's still plenty to sort out regarding the nurse, the houseman, and the niece."

The first of those suspects, nurse Bonnie Bahr, lived on a quiet side street off the main highway in Cathedral City, a few blocks from the new city hall and its surrounding downtown redevelopment. Larry coasted to the curb in front of a modest but tidy stucco house. Its garage faced the street; parked in the driveway was the powdery blue Korean compact I'd seen on Sunday at Chaffee's estate. Larry pulled out his notebook to double-check the address. I told him, "This is the place. That's Bonnie's car."

We got out of the unmarked sedan and stepped along the short, curving walk to the front door. "I'm eager to meet this gal," Larry told me as he rang the bell.

Recalling that he'd characterized Bonnie as a Nurse Ratched, I assured him, "She's not what you think."

We waited a few moments, but no one answered, so Larry pushed the doorbell again. I asked, "We *are* expected, right?"

"You're not, but I am." He checked his watch.

Then the door opened. "Gosh," Bonnie told Larry, "I hope you weren't waiting long. I had the TV on—must've been sorta loud." Spotting me, she said, "Why, Miss Gray, what a nice surprise."

Larry introduced himself, adding, "It was good of you, Miss Bahr, to make time for me today. And I understand you were most cooperative in providing my deputy with fingerprints this morning. This has surely been difficult for you. I hope you don't mind that I brought Claire along. As you may know, she's the one who discovered what happened yesterday."

"Oh, you poor dear," cooed Bonnie. "Of course you're welcome. I'm glad you're here. Please, won't you come in? No point in standing outdoors."

Truth is, it was a spectacular afternoon, and I would have enjoyed having our discussion on a little patio somewhere—Bonnie's home probably had one in back—but she waved us through the front door, which opened directly into a small, dark living room, its curtains drawn against the midday sun. A large, ungainly television hunkered in one corner. A ceramic Christmas tree, about a foot high with a light in it, doubtless the handiwork of some crafts class, was perched atop the cabinet, placed off to the side like an afterthought. The TV sound was muted, but the screen flashed the opening credits of the soap opera *Passions*.

Bonnie wore white slacks—surely part of a nursing uniform, not flattering on a big woman—along with a rumpled top in a colorful print that looked more dingy than joyful in the shadowy room. Clearly, she was out of sorts. Unless she had killed Stewart Chaffee, she had not expected to be home today. She offered, "Can I get you something?"

"No, thanks," we answered. "Just came from lunch."

"Then, please, have a seat. Make yourselves comfortable."

Larry and I both sat on a nubby green couch flanked by end tables holding lamps with huge white silk shades, grossly out of proportion with the room. One of the lamps was within reach of me, and I was tempted to switch it on, as my eyes had not yet fully adjusted from the daylight. Bonnie sat in a recliner, apparently "her" chair, placed at an angle to the couch, facing the TV, which flickered at the corner of my vision.

Larry flipped open his notebook and clicked a ballpoint pen. "If you don't mind, Miss Bahr, I'd like to run through a few routine questions establishing your background."

"Certainly, Detective." She affirmed her name and address and gave her age as thirty-four. While detailing her education and early nursing career, she kept glancing from Larry to the television. Pausing to watch for a moment, she said, "Isn't that cute?"

I turned to look at the screen. Juliet Mills, playing a dotty witch done up in a hairdo that made her look like a refugee from *Cats,* was sipping a pink cocktail while conversing with a floating head. With a forced laugh, I agreed, "Cute."

Larry cleared his throat. "You're single, correct, Miss Bahr?"

Her wan smile faded as she shifted her focus from the witch in the soap opera to the detective in her living room. "Yes," she said, "single. Never married. Grew up in the Midwest, so I have no family out here. In a sense, I guess you could say I'm alone in the world."

I would have found her self-profile disarmingly pitiable were it not for my own circumstances, which were remarkably similar to hers—except that I'd never been happier. Bonnie, on the other hand, had just suffered an unexpected death in her life, and I could not yet judge the depth of her relationship to the deceased.

"Don't get me wrong," she continued. "Just because I'm alone doesn't mean I feel unneeded or useless. I'm a nurse—a caregiver, as they like to say. It may sound sorta cliché, but I'm wed to my career."

Larry gave her a soft smile. "I'm sure it's satisfying work."

"It *can* be." Her expression went hard. "The nursing field has changed a lot, even in the ten years or so that I've been at it. Hospital nursing isn't nearly so noble as I thought it would be when I was a kid. It's constant paperwork, impossible hours, and inflexible regulation. It got to the point where I couldn't stand it, so I bowed out and found a different calling—private-duty nursing."

"When did you make this transition?"

"Two years ago." She thought a moment. "Two years, two months. I had just resigned from my hospital position when Stewart suffered his stroke, requiring full-time at-home nursing and rehab. Not to sound opportunist, but I guess you could say I was in the right place at the right time. I've been employed in his household ever since." She bowed her head, adding, "Till yesterday, of course."

I told her, "I'm a little surprised you're at home today."

She gave me a strange look. "My patient has expired. And so has my job."

"I understand. But in the aftermath of Stewart's sudden death, I should think you'd be needed at the estate—at least for a little while—sorting through things, helping out."

"You'd think so, wouldn't you?" She shook her head with disgust, getting agitated. "Pea, that weasel, seems to think he's ruling the roost now. The little shit has actually *barred* me from returning to the house." She swiped up a remote control and jabbed one of its buttons, which blackened the television. The room now seemed eerily dark, with searing streaks of sunlight leaking in from the slits and edges of the curtains.

Larry asked, "In what sense did Pea 'bar' your return?"

"Said he'd call the *cops,* that bitchy little mother—" She stopped herself.

"I can't imagine why," said Larry. "Under the circumstances, I doubt if the police would act on his complaint. As far as we know, he has no authority there. He's out of work too."

"Tell *him* that."

"I just may. I'm meeting with him later this afternoon."

A vindictive grin turned Bonnie's mouth.

Larry continued, "We could use your help in sorting through Stewart's medications. I understand there were quite a few."

She reminded him, "They had to hire a *nurse* to deal with it all. There was *plenty* to keep track of." She got up from her chair, crossed the room to a window, and drew the curtains open, admitting a blast of light.

Larry squinted. "Can you recall any of them?"

"Sure. All of them." And Bonnie proceeded to list well over a dozen prescription medicines that had sustained Stewart during his latter days. Larry took notes as Bonnie described each drug's purpose and detailed its dosage.

"In addition to the medications," said Larry, "Stewart needed rehab, correct?"

Nodding, Bonnie moved from the window to the sofa, standing squarely before Larry and me. "After the stroke, Stewart couldn't walk, lost the use of one arm, and needed speech therapy. Gradually, with a lot of work, everything improved. Even though he felt he still needed the wheelchair, his arm and his speech recovered completely. It was gratifying to see him come back physically and emerge from his aphasia. Because I hadn't known the man *before* his stroke, it was almost like witnessing his birth."

As Bonnie detailed the regimens of physical therapy she had provided, it was easy to imagine her hoisting the ill, stretching sluggish muscles, pummeling away pain. This benign image was countered by a more sinister one—Bonnie toppling a refrigerator with the effortless nudge of a well-trained arm.

"Miss Bahr," said Larry, "I never had the pleasure of meeting Mr. Chaffee, but I certainly knew *of* him; everyone in the valley did. What was he like?"

With a sheepish smile, Bonnie said, "I'm sorta reluctant to talk about him, now that he's gone."

I leaned forward, telling her, "I think what Larry is asking is, what was it like, working for Stewart? How would you describe your relationship?"

Larry gave me a discreet, grateful wink.

Bonnie reminded us, "I never knew him in his prime, but from everything I've heard, he was always quite a character." She sat again in the recliner, knees together, hands folded, looking suddenly dainty, an improbable image. "Stewart had a quirky personality, that's for sure, and he was difficult to work for at times—but he was sick, and that's why I was there. Sometimes his mind wasn't right, and those were the most difficult times, but he always snapped out of it. He could be charming and gracious. I think *that* was his true nature, believe it or not."

I nodded, admitting, "I could see that in him, easily. Still, during my visits, his manner was generally gruff and unpredictable. At times, Bonnie, his treatment of *you* verged on abusive."

She shook her head, telling us flatly, "That wasn't the real Stewart Chaffee. It's unfair to judge him for his name-calling. There's a special relationship between a patient and a long-term caregiver that's difficult for an outsider to understand. Good Lord, I helped *bathe* the man; he depended on me. And sure, I depended on him; he paid me well. So our barking back and forth didn't mean anything. Really. Not a thing."

Larry asked, "Is it safe to say, then, that you were not only Mr. Chaffee's nurse, but also his companion?"

She gave the detective an odd look. "Well, sort of. When Pea wasn't around."

Larry flashed me a quizzical glance. I shrugged an I-dunno. He asked Bonnie, "You served as Mr. Chaffee's companion when the houseman wasn't around?"

"I never thought of Pea as the 'houseman.' He was more of a secretary. You know—he scheduled things, ran errands, and such."

"Okay," said Larry, amending his notes. "But Pea was also Mr. Chaffee's companion?"

"Maybe I'm behind the times." Bonnie blew an exasperated sigh. "I'm not sure *what* they call themselves these days."

Larry scratched behind an ear. "You're not sure what *who* call themselves?"

She blurted, "*Gay* people."

Larry still looked confused. "Everyone's aware that Stewart Chaffee was gay. And I got the impression that Pea Fertig is also. Are you now telling me that Stewart and Pea were . . . gay *together?*"

I translated: "Bonnie, were Pea and Stewart lovers?"

"Well, they weren't *sleeping* together, if that's what you mean. But I'm pretty sure they used to."

"How long ago?"

"Beats me. *Long* time ago. I'm not even sure how long those two had been together, but it must've been decades. Cripes, I wonder what Stewart ever saw in *him*."

"For one thing," I suggested, "Pea was thirty-some years younger. Chances are, Stewart found that *highly* attractive."

Bonnie's face wrinkled. "That's disgusting."

In light of my relationship with Tanner, I was tempted to take offense. Instead, I countered, "It sounds to me as if they were loving and loyal. Sex had withered from their relationship, but Pea, still in his best years, held on. He remained 'there' for Stewart because he was needed."

Bonnie corrected me, "He remained 'there' for Stewart because he was *paid*. And don't kid yourself—Pea resented it."

"How could you tell?"

"His behavior, of course. He's a nasty little bastard. But think about it. How would *you* feel? You used to be this rich, important guy's 'wife,' and now here you are, reduced to nothing more than paid domestic help."

Bonnie had made a good point. Both Larry and I recognized it. He asked her, "What sort of services did Pea perform in the household?"

Bonnie began to speak, then hesitated. "I'm not entirely sure. Maybe you should ask him about that. To my way of thinking, he wasn't very useful at all. One thing's for sure—he couldn't cook."

"And you *can*," I said brightly, shifting the topic.

Modestly, she allowed, "I get by in the kitchen, but nothing fancy. On my day shifts at the estate, I always made lunch for Stewart. Simple stuff—soup and sandwiches."

Larry asked, "Who fixed dinner?"

"There was part-time help who came in for that. Or Pea would bring meals home from various restaurants that Stewart liked."

I reminded her, "You also made pink fluff."

She smiled sweetly. "Sure. Rice Krispies squares, too. They're easy to make, and he enjoyed them so. Considering his refined tastes and cultured past, I don't know why he took such a liking to such childish foods. His favorite lunch was canned spaghetti."

"Sometimes," I ventured, "as we grow older, our tastes change. And it's often been observed that the elderly seem to revert to childhood—playing with dolls, for instance, or collecting stuffed toys." As another example of age reversion, I recalled Grant joking with me, that very morning, about changing each other's diapers. In the interest of decorum, however, I kept the thought to myself.

"It's true," said Bonnie. "In health care, we see it every day. As death approaches, it often brings with it a second infancy."

Finding Bonnie's observation both sensitive and poetic, I was glad I hadn't mentioned diapers.

Getting us back on track, Larry asked the nurse, "This pink fluff—you brought some to Stewart yesterday morning, correct?"

She nodded. "He'd been asking for it for several days, so I made a batch of it here at home on Sunday night."

Larry turned a page of his notebook. "Please tell me everything you can remember about going to the estate yesterday."

Bonnie paused, closing her eyes, gathering her thoughts. With a blink, she began, "Monday is my day off. I had the pink fluff in a large green Tupperware bowl. I left here sometime before nine and drove over to the estate, arriving a few minutes later. I let myself in through the front gate, using the entry code. Then I drove up to the house and went inside, using my key."

I asked, "Where did you park? Which door did you use."

"I parked around back, in the courtyard by the garage, as usual. Then I entered through the kitchen door, as usual."

Larry asked, "Did you need to disarm the security system at the door?"

"No, it was activated only at night. During the day, the gate security was sufficient to keep out salesmen or snoops."

"Tell us about entering the house."

"There's nothing much to tell. Passing through the kitchen, I put the pink fluff in the fridge, then went to find Mr. Chaffee. I wanted to tell him that I'd brought the fluff, but I also wanted to check on him and see if there was anything he needed."

"Did you call his name?"

"No. He sleeps at all hours, so I didn't want to risk waking him. I began walking through the house and quickly found him—in the living room, asleep in his wheelchair, taking some sun through the window. I went back to the kitchen and wrote him a note about the fluff. I put the note in his lap, where he'd be sure to find it, and then I left."

Everything she said was consistent with the story Pea had told us after he'd returned to the estate on Monday afternoon. Her estimated arrival time was consistent with the evidence of the video camera.

Larry asked, "While you were there, did you see anyone besides Mr. Chaffee?"

"The house sure *seemed* empty, but I didn't make a point of checking. None of the service people would be there at that hour, and I assumed Pea had gone to the gym, which he often does in the morning. The garage door was closed, so I don't know for a fact if his car was there or not."

Larry was making detailed notes. "Thank you, Miss Bahr. This is helpful. Where did you go after leaving the estate?"

"It was a beautiful day—we've been having such delightful weather, with winter setting in. Since I'd never been to the Living Desert Reserve, I decided to check it out."

I asked, "Living Desert?"

Larry explained, "It's a popular botanical park on the outskirts of Palm Desert, up in the foothills on Portola Avenue."

Bonnie added, "They've got all the indigenous plants, plus an exhibit of palms of the world, not to mention the *animals*."

"Snakes?" I asked feebly.

"They keep those separate," she assured me, "in another building."

"How sensible. A snakehouse."

"But most of the other critters are right out in the open. You should see the meerkats. They're adorable."

Trying to sound interested, I asked, "Are they some sort of wildcat?"

"No, they're not cats at all. They sorta look like prairie dogs, but they're part of the mongoose family."

This too struck me as sensible—in case of a breach at the snakehouse.

Larry asked, "How long were you there?"

"Till well past one. I had lunch there. It was okay, but they were slow. It's crowded this time of year."

"Did you get an entry ticket, maybe a stub?"

"I think they gave me a receipt when I paid, but I probably tossed it." Then she thought of something. "I got a pamphlet, though. Would you like to see it?" And she rose from her chair, went to a table near the door, and brought back a brochure about the park.

"Thank you," said Larry, glancing at it, handing it to me.

"Those are the meerkats," said Bonnie, pointing to a photo on the cover. "Don't they look like they're smiling?" In fact, they did.

While Larry continued to question Bonnie about the remainder of her Monday afternoon, I idly paged through the brochure. It told me that, in all likelihood, Bonnie had visited the park, but it didn't tell me when. If, as she claimed, she was there on Monday from midmorning through noon, she would be held above suspicion in Chaffee's murder.

On the other hand, because she seemed unable to verify her alibi of visiting the crowded tourist attraction, alone, at the time of Chaffee's death, it was conceivable that she had not left the estate after writing the note that morning. She could have hidden in the house during the succession of later visitors, lured her elderly patient to the refrigerator, using pink fluff as bait, then toppled the refrigerator, crushing him. The note may have been an afterthought, planted on his dead or dying body to help exonerate her.

In other words, Bonnie Bahr had had the means and possibly the opportunity to kill Stewart Chaffee. But did she have a motive? Seemingly, she had none at all.

Larry was wrapping up his questions, thanking her for her cooperation, when she asked, "Exactly what happened, Detective? The newspaper didn't give much information, and when Pea called to inform me that my services were no longer needed, he mentioned something about the kitchen, but told me no more. How did Stewart die?" She sat again, looking somber and concerned.

Larry hesitated, then said, "Mr. Chaffee was found in the kitchen, crushed in his wheelchair by the refrigerator, which had fallen over. It may have been an accident, but some of the circumstances suggest foul play." He was being as vague about his suspicions, I noted, as he had been yesterday while talking with Pea at the crime scene.

Bonnie had gone pale. "My God," she whispered, lifting both hands to her face, "Stewart must've been after the pink fluff." She began to cry, telling us through her tears, "I shouldn't have left that note for him. I should have woken him up and given him his treat. He always had trouble opening the fridge door."

With a sob, she whined, "I should've stayed to *help* him."

12

Pulling up to the gate outside the Chaffee estate, Larry Knoll reached from the window of his car and pressed the intercom button. No one answered, so he punched in the keypad code. When the gate slid open, he drove onto the grounds, telling me, "Pea said I should check for him by the garage."

"What's he doing, working on his car? He doesn't strike me as the type."

As soon as we had pulled around to the side of the house, I had my answer. Though Pea's Cadillac was visible inside the open garage, next to Stewart's orphaned Rolls, neither car was the object of Pea's attention. Rather, he was directing a crew of helpers, workers in tan jumpsuits who were sorting and packing some of the clutter that had accumulated in the garage.

While Larry parked, I watched Pea strut about with a clipboard, nosing into cartons, pointing this way and that, hoisting a few things the workers had missed. He wore black nylon shorts, a pink tank top, and white tennis shoes with bulky gray socks. Though the day was barely warm, not hot, he'd worked up a sweat, which soaked his skimpy shirt with red splotches. It was clear at a glance that his time at the gym had been spent not lounging in a whirlpool, but engaged in obsessive physical training. For a short, middle-aged man, he had a great body. Though I admired the apparent determination with which he had compensated for his diminutive stature, I couldn't help also thinking that Pea Fertig would have no difficulty whatever toppling a heavy refrigerator.

As Larry and I got out of the car, Pea spotted us, crossing the courtyard to meet us. "Afternoon, Detective. Hello, Miss Gray." His tone was neither cheery nor defensive, but flat and neutral, as if numbed by the events of the previous day. If he was surprised to find me in Larry's company, he didn't express it.

Larry said, "Thanks for making some time for me today." They shook hands.

I offered mine. "I'm so sorry about everything. In addition to your loss, it seems you're swamped by the aftermath."

"It helps to keep busy," he said, accepting my hand, shaking it without interest. "Besides, someone has to do it."

A large panel truck backed into the courtyard, bleeping its warning signal as workers cleared a path through the cartons.

Larry suggested, "Perhaps we could go inside. It'll be easier to talk."

"Sure." Pea led us across the courtyard to the kitchen door, opened it, and stepped aside so we could enter.

I half expected to find other helpers at work inside, but no. The quiet of the house stood in eerie contrast to the bustle and noise outside the garage.

"In here okay?" asked Pea, directing us toward the great room.

"Fine, thanks." Larry followed him through the kitchen.

I paused to look at the spot where Stewart had been killed. The refrigerator had been righted, of course, but the collection of cocktail shakers, some of them now chipped and dented, had been shoved haphazardly into a corner of the countertop. There was no sign of Stewart's crumpled wheelchair, surely taken as evidence. The mess of foodstuffs—and blood—had been cleaned up, but I noticed with a wave of repugnance that in front of the refrigerator door, the cracks between the floor tiles were stained brown.

"Uh, Claire?" From the great room, Larry saw me staring at the kitchen floor. "Are you coming?"

I looked from Larry to the floor and back to Larry again. Then I mustered a weak smile, left the kitchen, and joined Larry with Pea in the great room. The space was much as it had been on the previous afternoon, except that some of the artwork had been taken from the walls and propped on the floor. The collection of paintings by Per-Olof Östman had been removed from the easels and stacked against a wall, draped with sheets. The room was still festooned, however, with its Christmas decorations, which looked insanely mal-apropos, their cheeriness mocking the grim mood that now shrouded the dead man's home.

Pea had settled on the leather sofa, using a towel he'd grabbed in the kitchen to blot perspiration from his face and chest. Larry sat across from him, at the coffee table, as the day before, reviewing his notes. I remained standing, drawn to the glass doors that looked over the terrace to the pool.

Pea glanced in my direction, asking, "The clock—you transported it safely?"

"Yes, thank you. It's ticking away onstage, even as we speak." I felt it wise not to mention that we'd soaped its face, as Pea was such a fussbudget.

Larry seconded, "Yes, thank you for allowing Claire to take it yesterday. I'm sure Mr. Chaffee would be highly pleased, knowing the clock makes such an important contribution to her play."

Pea responded with a cynical smile. He still wasn't happy that I'd gotten the clock. Did he feel it was rightfully his? Or did he simply feel loyal to his deceased employer and protective of his property?

Larry continued, "I notice you've moved some of the paintings." He gestured toward the stack of draped canvases. "May I ask what you intend to do with them?"

Pea snapped, "Well, I don't intend to *steal* them."

"Sorry. I didn't mean to imply anything."

Pea exhaled. "I'm sorry too. I didn't get much sleep last night, and I've been on edge all day." Referring to the stack of paintings, he explained, "I have no idea what's to become of everything, but I thought I should start getting things organized for the bank."

"Then you've spoken to Merrit Lloyd?"

"Yes, he phoned to explain about the old clipping. The courts will probably appoint him the estate's executor while everything grinds through probate. Fine by me—I wouldn't know where to begin."

I noted, "Things look fairly well organized out in the courtyard."

"I called in a crew this morning, before I'd heard from Merrit. The garage was a mess; most of it's my own stuff. Not sure where to send it, but I want to be ready."

I crossed to the sofa and sat, separated from Pea by the middle cushion. With a tone of concern as well as curiosity, I asked, "But didn't you expect to remain here at the house?"

His features twisted. "Why would I?" He tossed the damp towel on the floor. "It was Stewart's house, and now he's gone."

I glanced at Larry, unsure how to respond. The day before, Pea had told us that he and Stewart had been friends and nothing more. "Pea," I said, "weren't you and Stewart a couple?"

"Why would you ask such a thing?" His tone suggested that I had accused him of something unseemly.

"Intuition." I shrugged, letting him know that I found their relationship unremarkable.

He paused, then turned to face me on the sofa. His bare leg squeaked on the leather cushion. "Well, actually, yes, Stewart and I went way back together. There was a time when we were intimate, but that was long ago." With a snort, he added, "Longer ago than I'd care to admit." Pea's head bowed.

Larry assured him, "We don't mean to pry, and I certainly don't mean to judge. After all, my own brother's gay. But your background with Stewart could be helpful to our investigation. We all share the same goal—we want to figure out who killed your friend."

Pea looked up. "Then it wasn't an accident?"

Larry leveled, "We believe Stewart was murdered." He explained how the refrigerator door handle had been cleaned of all fingerprints.

"Yesterday," said Pea, "the police were also checking the doors and knobs for fingerprints, right?"

"Right. We found traces of your prints on all the doorknobs— front, back, and garage. Since you live here, that's exactly what we'd expect. What's most telling is that the inside knob of the front door had been wiped clean. The killer must have been flustered or in a hurry. We have a lot to sort through."

"Who could do such a thing? And why?"

"At the moment, I don't know."

I added, "That's why we need your help, Pea. You knew Stewart better than anyone, I gather. Please, tell us how you came to know him."

With a faint laugh, he told us, "It's a long story."

Larry sat back, resting an ankle on the opposite knee. "I've got plenty of time."

Pea nodded. "Okay." He collected his thoughts. "I should back up—before I came to California."

Larry turned a page of his notebook. "Where did you grow up?"

"Born and raised in Charlotte. In the proper Southern tradition, my parents were both literary types, and I was named after William Makepeace Thackeray. From the start, everyone called me Pea, which I really resented, since it was only a breath away from Peewee. But the name stuck, and eventually I grew to like it. I mean, it's different. And it sure as hell beats Makepeace."

I laughed. "I'm inclined to agree with you."

"In college, I majored in English. My parents thoroughly approved, but careerwise, the degree prepared me for nothing. By the time I graduated, I'd 'found' myself—sexually, I mean—so I moved to California for the freer lifestyle."

"What'd your parents think of *that?*"

"Not much. But then, I didn't tell them much. After all, that was almost twenty-five years ago—those times were still fairly closeted, even after Stonewall. So I settled in LA for a while, hoping to blend into the counterculture. One weekend, I visited Palm Springs with friends, and it was a real eye-opener. It was early spring, so the weather was spectacular—and so were the guys. That weekend was one long party, and sure enough, at a bar on Saturday night, I met Stewart. We shared an instant, mutual attraction."

I said, "Do you mind if I ask how old you were then?"

"Not at all. That was just over twenty years ago. I was twenty-four; Stewart was sixty-one." He smiled at the memory.

In spite of my relationship with Tanner Griffin, or perhaps because of it, I had to ask, "Didn't the age difference present some . . . obstacles?"

"Like what?" Either Pea had been truly infatuated, or he was very naive.

I tried explaining, "You were nearly forty years apart, and—"

"Miss Gray," he interrupted, "I have always had a thing for older men. It's not that unusual. Wealth is an amazing turn-on, and Stewart offered fame as well; those are two qualities than can override all manner of shortcomings. Besides, guys never really lose the urge, regardless of age. Stewart didn't. Of course, his tastes were the opposite of mine. Till the day he died, he was always partial to *younger* men—and lots of them—for all the obvious reasons."

"Sounds like a match made in heaven," I said, attempting to inflect my words with a tone other than cynicism.

"It was, at least at first."

Larry got curious. "What went wrong?"

"What *usually* goes wrong? One of us got bored. After three or four years as lovers—and we really did love each other, emotionally as well as physically—Stewart's eye began to wander. What can I say? He lost interest in me. He liked to screw around. As angry as that made me, I was in no position to object—or leave. Like it or not, I'd built a comfortable life with Stewart, and I wasn't inclined to walk away from it in a fit of jealous pique. So Stewart kept me on as his secretary. I'd fallen a notch from lady of the manor, but my life was no less cushy, and truth is, the job suited me."

"What were your duties?"

"You name it. I generally ran the estate, coordinating the schedules of all the part-time help. Stewart knew he could trust me, so he eventually put me in charge of the household accounts, paying bills and such. I also took care of his social correspondence; there was a lot of it." He gestured toward the desk there in the great room. "We finally got a computer a few years ago, and it's really helped. Stewart never quite got the hang of it, but I've found it a godsend, especially for accounting and correspondence."

Larry noted, "So this room has been your home office."

"I suppose you could call it that. Comfortable surroundings, eh? Stewart even built me a nice workout room here on the estate. He converted one of the guesthouses."

Through a squint I asked, "Then why did you go out to Decath-lon Gym yesterday morning?"

"You *would* ask," said Pea, almost blushing, as if I'd caught him in a fib. I hoped I had. The murder investigation would take on sudden life if we were about to learn that he'd fabricated yesterday's story about being away from the house that morning. But no. Pea continued, "The workout room here at home is great; I really ap-preciate that Stewart went to the trouble of installing it. But it's *too* convenient. I found I missed the discipline of actually *going* some-where for my workout—more like keeping an appointment. And that's not all." He paused, twitching a brow. "The scenery is far better at Decathlon. So without fail, I head over there every morn-ing, promptly at seven-thirty."

Stupidly, I said, "I find it hard to imagine that the views at your gym are any better than those here at the estate." I gestured toward the glass doors and the mountainous vista beyond.

"I'm talking about the *guys* there," he explained. "The locker room at Decathlon is spectacular. There's *plenty* to look at. Here, it's just little ol' me."

"Oh."

Larry indulged in a good laugh. He wasn't quite so square as I'd judged him.

"So basically," I summarized, "your relationship with Stewart had evolved from that of lovers to that of trusted friends."

"Yeah, I guess. But after his health went bad, even our friendship was strained. In the end, we were little more than boss and em-ployee." Bitterly, he added, "The terms of that half-assed 'will' make it pretty clear how little he thought of me."

I reminded him, "That interview was printed nearly fifty years ago. His intentions predated your arrival on the scene."

"But I *did* arrive on the scene. I was with him for *twenty-one* years, through thick and thin. I hate to sound like some floozy, but I gave that man the best years of my life. He had so much—wouldn't you think he'd leave me *something?*"

I had to admit, "It does seem insensitive." I thought of my neigh-bor Grant and his young lover, Kane, who were demonstrating the foresight to arrange a contractual "marriage." How modern of them—and wise. Trying to console Pea, I ventured, "Stewart wasn't himself in his latter years. It was apparent even to me, during two brief visits, that his mind wasn't quite right. Try not to blame him for what he'd become. Curse the illness, not the man."

"Like 'hate the sin, love the sinner'?"

Though the parallel was apt, I found myself silenced by it, unable to respond. I recognized that the aphorism Pea had quoted was often a condescending crumb of tolerance tendered to the gay community by the religiously inclined.

Larry picked up the conversation, telling Pea, "According to that old clipping, Mr. Chaffee intended, all along, to leave everything to the Desert Museum of Southwestern Arts. Are you tempted to contest the museum's claim against the estate?"

Frustrated, Pea stood. "I just find it hard to believe that a scrap of newsprint, half a century old, could be used as evidence of *anyone's* intentions."

"But," I told him, "Stewart recently wrote in the margin, 'This will make my wishes plain enough.' What's more, he said those very words when he handed the envelope to Merrit Lloyd on Saturday. I was there, in the living room." Pea had not been present that morning; I had met him later, on Sunday.

Pea paced in front of the glass doors. "Still, it's a *clipping,* for God's sake. I know Stewart didn't trust lawyers—neither do I—but why wouldn't he write his intentions, explicitly, in a letter of some kind?"

I admitted, "That's what I *assumed* was in the envelope. I think we all did."

"Well, what's done is done." He stopped pacing, then faced us squarely. With a snide laugh, he added, "At least *she* didn't get anything."

"Who?" asked Larry and I in unison.

"Bonnie, of course. Who'd you think?"

Truth is, my first reaction was that Pea had been referring to Stewart's niece, whom Stewart had derided in Pea's presence on Sunday morning. But I decided not to share this notion, which would only heighten Pea's paranoia of circling buzzards, the metaphor he had invoked on Monday afternoon.

Larry asked him, "Did Bonnie expect to be included in the will?"

"Ask *her*. Though I'm sure you wouldn't get an honest answer."

"Why do you say that?"

Pea paused. "Isn't it self-evident, Detective? Don't try to tell me you haven't seen this sort of thing before. Bonnie Bahr is the classic 'healing angel,' a Florence Nightingale who tends to the infirm and the dying. She waltzes into someone's life at the last minute, so to speak, and ingratiates herself as the only one who truly cares. She feeds, bathes, and pampers her wealthy victim, knowing it will soon be over—and hoping for a big, fat remembrance, a hefty gratuity from the otherworld."

"Isn't that a tad harsh?" I asked. "We just visited Bonnie. She's *grieving*, Pea."

"Practice makes perfect. She's walked many a geriatric to the grave, I'm sure. You're a director, Miss Gray. You might want to take notes from the charming and talented Miss Bahr. She's an *actrice extraordinaire*."

I shook my head. "She struck me as guileless. She finds soap operas 'cute' and thinks meerkats are 'adorable.' "

"What's a meerkat?"

Larry volunteered, "A member of the mongoose family."

Pea looked momentarily befuddled.

I told him, "I know there's been some hostility between you and Bonnie. You're welcome to think what you will of her. But did you really feel she should be barred from returning to the house?"

"You bet. She's done enough damage already."

Larry asked, "What sort of damage?"

"For starters"—Pea looked the cop in the eye—"she killed Stewart. She crushed an old man under a goddamn refrigerator. Isn't that damage *enough?*"

With flat inflection, Larry said, "You seriously suspect her."

"*Yes.*" Pea returned to the sofa, sitting not at the end as before, but in the middle, next to me, almost touching knees, directly across from Larry. Lowering his voice, he told both of us, "I've suspected Bonnie of plotting to profit from Stewart's death since the day she entered this house. I know this sounds unwarranted, as if I'm jumping to conclusions, but think about it. We *know* she was here yesterday morning. We *know* she brought the pink fluff and left the note for Stewart. We *know* he was killed while trying to get the pink fluff from the refrigerator. Christ. Connect the dots."

Larry conceded, "It's a reasonable theory, yes."

"But it's also an obvious theory," I added. "Too obvious."

Pea persisted, "I assume the security photos showed Bonnie entering the estate yesterday."

"They did," said Larry. "She arrived at nine o'clock, well before you returned from the gym. She found Stewart sleeping in the living room, as you did, so she decided not to wake him and left him the note. She says she left within a few minutes. And you said there was no one here when you arrived at nine-thirty. Your stories seem to validate each other."

"But the *point,*" said Pea, "is that you have no way of knowing when Bonnie actually left. All you've got is her word on it."

I touched Pea's arm. "I don't mean to insinuate anything, but we have no way of verifying when *you* left, either. All we know for sure is that, later that morning, after both you and Bonnie claim to have left the house, Stewart was killed."

With greater composure than I expected, Pea conceded, "Fine. But I had no *reason* to kill Stewart. I loved him."

Larry reminded him, "Not ten minutes ago, you expressed dismay that Stewart left you nothing after you'd given him the best years of your life. In other words, you expected an inheritance; you claim Bonnie did as well. On the surface, that's a feasible motive for either of you. An expected inheritance makes a nice, tidy motive when *any* wealthy person dies of sudden, unnatural causes. But I'll need more than that to name Stewart Chaffee's killer."

"Then try this on for size." Pea paused for effect. "Mercy killing."

Larry and I exchanged a wary glance. He told Pea, "That's a serious accusation. If it's no more than wild speculation—"

Pea raised his hands in a calming gesture. "It's speculation, I admit, but it's anything but wild. Did Bonnie happen to tell you about her career in hospital nursing?"

"Yes, in detail."

"Did she tell you why she left it?"

Larry glanced back through his notes. "She told us that hospital nursing had changed a lot, that she grew tired of the paperwork, regulations, and hours. So she bowed out and entered private-duty nursing."

"Mm-hmm. That's essentially what she told me when we interviewed her to care for Stewart. She had just left her hospital career, saying it had become a bureaucratic nightmare."

"So?" I asked. "Same story. Perfectly consistent."

"But later," said Pea, leaning forward, as if to huddle with us, "I began to hear *other* stories. The scuttlebutt is that Bonnie did *not* bow out of hospital nursing. No, she was *drummed* out when it was discovered that she had been writing anonymous letters to the local paper in support of euthanasia. Yes, this is hearsay, but where there's smoke . . ."

"Really now, Pea." I flumped back in my seat. "I doubt if Larry can book the woman on the basis of bad gossip."

"Well, I'm sorry, but that's all I have. Check it out."

"I intend to," Larry assured him.

"Besides," said Pea, "it all fits. Two years ago, when Stewart suffered his stroke, it was clear that we'd need help at home when he returned from the rehab ward. Everyone warned me how tremendously difficult it is to find good long-term home-nursing help. I heard some real horror stories. But lo and behold, just when we needed her, there was Bonnie. She was highly qualified and eager to work for us, saying she'd had it with hospitals. I recall thinking that the timing of her career shift seemed too good to be true—lucky us. Later, when I got drift of the rumors, I realized that maybe Bonnie *was* too good to be true."

Larry asked, "Who told you about these letters to the editor?"

"I know this sounds lame, but I don't even remember. It was a friend-of-a-friend kind of deal. Someone at a party. Or the gym. It's popped up more than once."

I asked, "If you had these awful suspicions, why didn't you confront Bonnie with them?"

He shook his head. "I should have. But, like you, I recognized these stories as mere gossip. Besides, she did her job, we needed her, and Stewart seemed to like her. It may have been a horrible mistake, but I didn't want to rock the boat."

"These letters," said Larry, "were they supposedly published around the time you retained Bonnie?"

"I think so, yes, but I'm not sure how long it had been going on." Pea continued to detail for Larry the chronology of Bonnie's employment at the estate.

But I had tuned out, recalling the morning, three days earlier, when I'd met Stewart Chaffee's nurse. Among the many unexpected turns of that first visit was an exchange between the eccentric decorator and his caregiver that now stood out in bold relief:

When Merrit Lloyd and his secretary had arrived, Stewart had told his buxom nurse, "Hey, you. Show him in, piglet." Undaunted, Bonnie had lobbed back, "You crippled old goat—someone ought to put you out of your misery."

Now Pea had raised the specter of mercy killing.

It seemed far-fetched.

But I had to wonder.

13

Wednesday morning, I sat alone in my theater, writing notes at Laura's desk.

The previous night's rehearsal had been, in a word, disappointing. Though the cast's performance had been technically proficient, they had lost some of the focus they'd attained prior to that week. This was due in part to the approach of Friday's opening, which brought with it an air of excitement and predictable jitters.

More serious was the disquieting stir caused by Stewart Chaffee's murder and fueled by the presence of the dead man's clock on the set. On Tuesday, I had assured myself that this buzz would quickly dissipate, but to my chagrin, it had not; it had grown. I had already put my reputation on the line by inviting to the play's opening, among others, Hector Bosch and Spencer Wallace, whose objectivity would not be clouded by friendship if my efforts failed to deliver. Now, I realized, an unsolved murder, that of a man I barely knew, was jeopardizing not only the quality of the school's first main-stage production and not only my own professional credibility, but also the dreams and ego of D. Glenn Yeats, who had committed several years' work, not to mention hundreds of millions of dollars, to launching a fledgling arts college that had been built around a world-class theater program and the director he had wooed to chair it— me.

I had made a habit of writing memos to my student cast, critiquing past efforts and suggesting improvements. That night, Wednesday, would be our final rehearsal, so I could not afford to miss this last opportunity to polish the production, nudge the cast onward, and refocus our efforts.

The scratch of my pen on the yellow legal pad seemed amplified in the well-tuned acoustics of the auditorium. As I wrote, I searched for precise, concrete phrases to express the intangibles of acting—characterization, motivation, interpretation, timing, delivery, and on and on. So much of an actor's craft is intuitive, I found it a struggle to communicate my directions in words and commit them to paper. But I'd been hired to teach, and teach I would.

I'd chosen to sit onstage, in the make-believe world of Laura's living room, the better to absorb the ambiance of the script and inspire my writing. I found, however, that the play's sinister mood, to say nothing of the heinous shotgun violence it sought to untangle, kept tugging my mind from my mission and forcing me to contemplate the real-life murder that had increasingly dominated my thoughts and my time.

Compounding this distraction was the ornate Austrian clock that stood downstage right, peering over the auditorium like a blinded, one-eyed oracle. The convex glass of its round face, now soaped, had looked over Stewart Chaffee's kitchen on Monday morning, witnessing the who and the how of his agonized last moments. I opened my mouth, preparing to speak to the clock, beseeching answers, then quickly reconsidered, chiding myself for such lunacy. Duly self-chastised, I hunkered down and wrote my notes.

After filling several pages, I read them from the start, did some quick editing, then judged them worthy of transcription. I would walk them over to my office, then have the department secretary type them up and place copies in the cast members' mail slots. So I switched on a single work light, shut down the stage circuits, and left the theater through the auditorium.

Emerging from the dim lobby into the full sun of College Circle, I crossed the plaza with my notes, headed toward the administration building. The sky was cloudless, the morning serene. It was the middle of a class period, so there was no rush of students crisscrossing the pavement. In fact, I was alone in the vast courtyard with its fountains and palms, a setting that invited introspection.

My pace slowed. Once again, my mind was drawn to the riddle of Stewart Chaffee's death. I was tempted to weigh my emerging suspicions of both Bonnie Bahr and Pea Fertig, but dismissed this notion as useless conjecture. The investigation was still young.

So I glanced at my notes, studying them as I continued toward the offices. I'd written tips for each member of the cast, including Tanner Griffin and Thad Quatrain. At the sight of Thad's name, written in my own hand, my thoughts drifted to his journalist uncle, Mark Manning, renowned for his investigative skills. He already had a passing interest in Chaffee's murder—his nephew had been with me when I discovered the body. If the investigation could be speeded along, I reasoned, Thad, Tanner, the rest of the cast, and I would all be able to focus more on the play and less on the crime.

I knew that Detective Larry Knoll would hardly welcome the involvement of yet another amateur crime solver, let alone that of an out-of-towner with no working knowledge of the turf or the victim. Still, I had an inkling that Mark's distance and objectivity could prove helpful in unexpected ways. I was reluctant to actively recruit his help, but wondered if there wasn't some way to lure him into the investigation, if only tangentially, and with Larry's blessing. A tall order.

Then I blinked. That very evening, D. Glenn Yeats would host a reception at his Nirvana home for Mark. I would be there, of course. Grant Knoll, who often arranged at-home entertaining for Nirvana residents, would surely be there as well. So why not Grant's brother, Larry? What's one more face in the crowd? Deciding to ask Glenn if I might extend an invitation to Detective Knoll on his behalf, I altered my course across the plaza, heading not toward the theater department's offices, but toward another door, that leading to the suite of presidential offices.

The administration building, indeed the entire campus, was circular in design, with Glenn's lavish suite at the epicenter. While its symbolism was strong and the concept had doubtless looked great on paper, the finished effect of this plan was to befuddle newcomers with curved hallways, abstruse signage, and a numbering system that lacked the essential logic of a grid. It had taken me weeks of practice to find my own office without retracing my steps, but by now the pecking order of concentric orbits had become second nature to me, and I located without difficulty the entrance to Glenn's lair.

It was hard to miss. The twin doors of polished mahogany bore no resemblance to the plain white slabs leading to the offices of Glenn's minions. Stepping inside, I found the sleek reception room empty, its carpet-muffled silence broken only by the gentle, plasticky tapping of a keyboard in the next room.

The typing stopped, and a moment later, a tall, muscular black woman in a Band-Aid of a leather miniskirt appeared in the doorway. "Oh, good morning, Ms. Gray," she said through a resonant purr. "How can I help you?" Glenn Yeats's secretary was about the same age, not quite thirty, as Merrit Lloyd's secretary, Robin. What's more, they both struck me as efficient and loyal to their respective bosses. Otherwise, they could have been creatures from two different planets.

"Morning, Tide," I returned her greeting, stepping toward her office. "Is Glenn available?" I looked beyond her desk to the doors of the inner sanctum.

"I'm sorry, no, he went over to the gallery. Shall I phone him for you?"

"Thanks, but I'll just walk over and find him. It's nothing urgent. I was wondering if I might invite an extra guest to his reception for Mr. Manning this evening."

Tide gave me a sisterly wink. "I'm keeper of the guest list. I'm sure he wouldn't mind." We'd done this before.

I was tempted by her offer. Through a chortle, I declined, "I'd better ask."

"As if there's anything he'd refuse you."

"You're probably right," I said, sounding bored by the doting of a billionaire. "Still, it's only polite. I just need to have these notes typed up"—I wagged my sheaf of scrawlings—"then I'll go over to the museum and find Glenn."

Extending an athletic arm, she offered, "Let *me* take care of that for you."

It would save me a trip through the circular maze. "But then," I pouted, "the notes need to be distributed to the students' mailboxes."

She insisted with a smile, "I can handle it, Ms. Gray."

So I gave her the papers with my profuse thanks, left the office, and headed outdoors, crossing College Circle again.

Although my theater, with its soaring flies, was the dominant feature of the architectural landscape, the new home of the Desert Museum of Southwestern Arts was no less dramatic. In designing the structure, I. T. Dirkman had found inspiration in the organic forms and muted palette of the desert, taking further cues from the primitive aesthetics of the collection that the building was meant to house. The new museum, therefore, was as simple and austere as my theater was fanciful and lyric.

On that Wednesday morning, workmen traipsed about scaffolding in front of the wide, glass-walled lobby, installing and testing lighting fixtures that would accent the building against the night sky. The rush was on. DMSA's inaugural exhibit of kachina dolls would open to the public on Friday evening, timed to the premiere of my play, the better to capitalize on publicity and crowds.

Stepping inside from the warm plaza, I was engulfed by the cool, filtered, processed air that would preserve ancient artifacts while numbing visitors with goose bumps and shivers. Most of the workmen inside the lobby, including the more brutish among them, wore jackets. Their din and babble reverberated against the glass and stone surfaces of the bright, airy room.

Beyond the lobby were galleries for both the permanent collection and temporary exhibits. A gift shop and a trendy little restaurant were being readied to indulge the art-weary. Another concourse led to storage vaults and offices. I assumed that I would find Glenn in the museum director's office, so I headed in that direction. Passing the entrance to the main gallery, though, I noticed a flurry of activity within, and at the center of this vortex stood the college founder and president.

"We can group the photographers over here," he was saying as I entered. "That'll be a great angle, and they won't be looking into the glare of the lights." He gestured about the large bare room with its pale gray walls.

"Good thinking, Glenn" said Iesha Birch, an exotic woman in her late thirties, the museum's new executive director. Scribbling on her clipboard, she asked, "Do you want to do an actual unveiling?"

"No, no, no"—he shook his head, as if the answer were self-evident—"it'll be an unveiling in only the *figurative* sense. The reception will be held in the outer lobby; then, when the doors to the main gallery are opened with a bit of fanfare, the entire *collection* will be, in a sense, unveiled." He prattled on.

Just then I noticed my neighbors, Grant and his young partner, Kane, standing off to the side, speaking to each other. Though I hadn't expected to see them, their presence came as no surprise. Grant, after all, was president of the museum board, and Kane was a design intern in the museum's publicity office, so if Glenn Yeats called a meeting, they were apt to attend. As I approached, they spotted me, each giving a friendly wave.

"What's the big powwow?" I asked.

Grant jerked his head toward the lobby, where we could talk without interrupting the meeting, even though it appeared to be breaking up.

As we emerged into the late-morning dazzle of the glass-fronted lobby, workers were hanging huge banners promoting the opening exhibit. The images of kachina dolls, some ten feet tall, looked like fearsome, prehistoric astronauts. Kane told me, "Mr. Yeats decided to throw a press conference."

"To announce the doll exhibit?"

Grant shook his head. "That's already been publicized. No, Glenn wants to make a big deal out of Stewart's bequest, inviting the press for the surprise announcement. He feels it's a good publicity angle for the opening of DMSA's new facility here on campus."

I shrugged. "He's right."

Grant nodded. "But it's all rather rushed, and I hope it doesn't come across as slipshod. Image is everything, you know."

"Tell me," I agreed. We weren't being shallow; we were simply acknowledging that the arts are built on artifice.

"So the Regal Palms will cater. They're expensive, but dependable."

"It's only money." I was tempted to add, Glenn will never miss it. But that was presumptuous, and my point was already made. I asked, "When is it?"

"*Tomorrow.* Tomorrow evening."

"God, that is short notice."

"Fret not," said the e-titan himself, striding from the gallery, looking dweebishly Californian in a silk shirt, linen slacks, low-slung loafers, and no socks. "We've got *the* best staff in the world. Everything will come off without a hitch."

"We'll do our very best," said Iesha, underscoring something on her clipboard with a determined slash. Her movement caused an oversize necklace of painted bones and gilded shells to clatter against her chest. Then she paused to adjust the pareu that was knotted around her waist. Underneath the colorful, makeshift skirt, she wore black tights, from the ends of which popped white feet sporting acid-green chef's clogs.

I asked Glenn, "Why the big hurry?"

"This is *news*. Bequests such as this will help put Desert Arts College on the map. Besides, it's only fitting that we pay tribute to our benefactor and his unexpected gift."

I wondered if Glenn was being facetious. Chaffee's bequest, while generous, was nothing compared to the fortune already donated by Glenn himself toward building the campus. What's more, only days earlier, Glenn had not bothered to conceal his skepticism regarding the quality of Chaffee's collection, a disdain that I had interpreted as sour grapes. Why the sudden interest in extolling a gift that the museum didn't much need or want?

As if reading my mind, Glenn explained, "This is spin, pure and simple. When someone leaves a gift of that magnitude to an institution, the public is bound to view it as a testament to the institution's mission and worthiness."

"Makes sense. But," I repeated, "why the big hurry?"

Before Glenn could respond, Grant blurted, "This is *your* doing, doll."

"Mine?"

"Your play," Glenn elaborated. "Once your play opens on Friday, that's where I'll want to focus our publicity. And if we wait till next week for the press conference, the bequest will be old news. I'd like to do it *tonight*, but that would be pushing things."

I reminded him, "You've already invited a crowd to your house tonight."

"Precisely. Which leaves tomorrow evening, Thursday, for the event here at the museum."

His mind was made up, and I had no reason to dissuade him, but still, the whole notion struck me as off-putting—not exactly crass, but certainly opportunistic. Glenn Yeats, however, had never been criticized for lack of savvy in achieving his goals, so I could only conclude that his plan would in fact enhance the prestige of the college.

Grant was telling me, "On behalf of the museum board, I'll make a little speech out here in the lobby during the cocktail reception, greeting the press and other invited guests. Then, after the doors to the main gallery are opened, Glenn himself will announce the bequest."

Glenn added, "I'm hoping we can get a few pieces from Chaffee's collection to use as a backdrop for the announcement. The press would eat it up, and we'd get far better photo coverage. I realize the estate may be tied up in probate for a while, but I'm sure *something* can be arranged. With all the extra publicity, we should devote the main gallery to the Chaffee collection for the first few weeks."

Kane asked, "Mr. Yeats, will we need a new set of posters and banners?"

"You bet. Can they be ready by tomorrow night?"

"Yes, sir. No problem—if I can authorize a rush with the supplier."

"Do it."

Iesha asked, "What about the kachinas? Are we postponing the exhibit?"

"Heavens, no," said Glenn. "We'll run the two exhibits concurrently—the more noise the better. But since the main gallery will now be devoted to Chaffee, we'll have to move the kachinas to one of the temporary galleries."

"Got it." Iesha's pen scratched at her clipboard.

Kane asked, "And what about the history display?"

Glenn looked blankly to Iesha, who turned to Grant, who asked Kane, "What history display?"

"Museum history. I thought the opening of the new museum was going to include an exhibit pertaining to its history."

"Not a bad idea," said Iesha, "but it's news to me."

"First I've heard of it," said Glenn. "Good concept, but let's save it, maybe use it for the first anniversary of the new facility. I think we've got enough on our plates right now."

Iesha wrote another note, looking relieved that she wasn't required to research and mount a history exhibit by the next evening. She told Glenn, "If there's nothing else, I need to get cracking."

"Me too," said Kane. "Posters, banners, press release."

"In wording the release," Glenn instructed, "make it clear that the evening is a tribute to the late Stewart Chaffee. Also indicate that the press is being invited to hear an important announcement regarding the estate of the deceased. They'll put two and two together; we'll have a mob on our hands."

Iesha suggested, "We should probably have some sort of printed program. Perhaps a handout regarding Mr. Chaffee and his collection."

With an eager nod, Kane agreed, "Sounds good. If someone can supply the copy, I'll set the type, lay it out, and make sure it's printed on time."

Glenn offered, "Feel free to use my office in any way that's needed. We probably have that background on file. And Tide can help you get word out to the press. She's been working with them a lot lately."

"Thanks," said Iesha, grinning, "we just may take you up on that." Then she and Kane excused themselves and left the lobby together, heading down the corridor toward the museum offices.

Watching them leave, it took me a moment to notice that Glenn's gaze was fixed squarely on me. Reading something in my face, he seemed concerned. "I hope you don't mind, Claire." Stepping near, he gave me an apologetic hug.

Though I enjoyed the manifest affection of my employer, I was mystified by both his words and his action. Patting his back, I looked over his shoulder at Grant, who appeared as bewildered as I was. I asked, "You hope I don't mind what, Glenn?"

He held me at arm's length. "This last-minute hullabaloo over Chaffee's bequest—I hope you don't feel it's stealing thunder from your play."

Now that he mentioned it, maybe I did have reason to be irked. What had started out as a quest for an oddball piece of set dressing, the Austrian case clock, had evolved into a perplexing murder that threatened the concentration of my student actors. Now the propitious fallout of that murder, the museum's windfall, had inspired a misdirected media circus that ought, by rights, to be focused on the opening of *Laura*.

"Don't be ridiculous," I assured him. "Image is everything. The announcement of the bequest will be good for the school. And the extra media attention will only heighten the public's interest in the play." This, I recognized, was a stretch of logic, but the wheels were already in motion for the press reception, so I thought it prudent to convince myself, as well as Glenn, that the tribute to Chaffee was a dandy idea.

What's more, I appreciated that Glenn was sensitive enough to care about my feelings on the matter. His aspirations for the success of the play were as lofty and intense as my own. His dedication to the theater program had been unwavering. I would appear petty indeed if I now begrudged the museum a few moments in the limelight.

Glenn continued to eye me with concern. "It's just that you seem preoccupied. Is something troubling you? How can I make it right?"

Standing behind Glenn, Grant gave me a goofy, bored look.

"Glenn"—I laughed softly—"you amaze me sometimes. You're far too caring."

"How could I not care about *you?*" He pecked the side of my mouth.

I pecked back. The exchange was hardly passionate, but it carried genuine fondness. What's more, I realized with a spark of revelation that these warm feelings were mutual; I really did care about the man. Since Glenn had first made his affections known to me three months earlier, I had shied from considering that I might find in his overture any appeal beyond its obvious material implications. Glenn understood this, but he had shown patience, taking no apparent umbrage in my need to think things through and to examine my heart— a process, a window, that also allowed me to bed Tanner Griffin with indulgent regularity. Glenn simply hoped that, in time, I would come around. Was I now, in fact, doing just that?

"So?" He repeated, "Is something troubling you?"

My two-timing was troubling me, but that's not what he had read in my face. I explained, "It's the murder."

"Ahhh," said Glenn, wrapping me in another hug, but this time it felt more paternal than romantic. "It's disturbing, I know, but don't worry yourself with it. The investigation is in good hands."

"My brother's hands," Grant reminded me. His grin conveyed knowledge that I had already wheedled my way into Larry Knoll's investigation. It also conveyed knowledge that Glenn did not approve.

My comforting employer clucked into my ear, "The police know what they're doing, Claire. They're trained to deal with these matters—and to minimize the risks, the inherent dangers of nosing into homicide."

I pulled away from him. "Glenn, *please* don't be patronizing."

"Sorry." He raised his hands in a gesture of backing off.

We'd been through this before, and I was now clearly reminded of why I'd "needed time" to weigh his earlier profession of love. It wasn't only that I found Tanner so achingly attractive; it was Glenn's condescending presumption that I needed his protection and mothering.

Calming myself (there was no point in berating the man while preparing to ask him a favor), I hedged, "This has nothing to do with any personal interest I've taken in Chaffee's murder. Having discovered the body, however, I *am* involved, and it occurs to me that Detective Knoll's investigation might be helped along if he were invited to the party at your home tomorrow evening."

"Fine." Glenn blinked. "But why?"

"To observe people. The ebb and flow of conversation could help—"

Suddenly enlightened, Glenn interrupted, "It's Mark Manning, isn't it?"

The name caught Grant's attention, fast. "Oh? What about Mark Manning?" Though Grant was coordinating the catering and other hotel services that would be needed the next night at Glenn's home, he apparently had not been informed of the party's purpose.

I explained, "Mark will be the guest of honor."

"Do tell?" Grant looked downright bubbly at the prospects of rubbing elbows with the famed journalist.

Glenn continued, "And you're speculating, Claire, that Manning may have a few useful ideas for the investigation."

Lamely, I admitted, "Two heads are better than one," though I didn't specify to whom the other head belonged.

"Fine," Glenn repeated. "Detective Knoll is more than welcome. Shall I have Tide phone him?"

I shook my head. "I'll be in touch with him, I'm sure." Then I had another thought. "Besides the press, who else will be invited to tomorrow's event here at the museum?"

"Anyone who's interested. After all, the reception is being billed as a tribute to Stewart Chaffee—not quite a memorial, but ostensibly, he's the focus. Family, friends, business associates, they're all welcome. Why?"

"Well, think about it. Such an event might very well have overtones for the murder investigation."

Facetiously, Glenn asked, "A killer in the crowd?"

With a quiet laugh, I allowed, "Maybe I *am* being melodramatic, but I think Larry will want to be here."

"Then ask him."

Grant pulled a cell phone from the pocket of his camel-hair blazer. "Be my guest," he said, offering me the phone and reminding me of his brother's programmed number.

"Thanks, Grant." I glanced about the high-ceilinged lobby and wrinkled my face in response to its harsh acoustics. "I think I'll phone him from outside. Less noise." I also wanted to escape the air-conditioning.

"As milady pleases." Grant gave me a deft bow, then turned to Glenn and began discussing some matter of museum policy. I was already headed for the door.

The warmth of the plaza felt therapeutic as I crossed to a bench near a clump of palms and sat facing the sun. I opened Grant's phone, punched in Larry's code, and within a few seconds, he was on the line.

"Morning, Claire. Always a pleasure to hear from you. What's up?"

I told him about Thursday's press conference, and he readily agreed that he should be there, thanking me for the tip. But when I also suggested that he attend the party at Glenn Yeats's home tonight, he asked, "What's the point?"

I was not inclined to tell him that a visitor from Wisconsin might be able to help with his investigation. Instead, I explained, "The guest of honor is Mark Manning—you met him in the hotel lobby yesterday on our way to lunch. Mark is gay and a prominent professional, as was Stewart. I'm not sure of Glenn's guest list, but it's apt to include a few A-gays. Maybe someone will know something. Maybe something will be said."

"Worth a shot," Larry conceded. "What time?"

I gave him the particulars.

"I'll be there. But I'm betting that Thursday's news conference holds greater promise for developments. You never know."

"You never know," I echoed, watching a roadrunner scamper

across College Circle and hop to the top of a low hedge of oleander, from which it surveyed the quiet plaza with random jerks of its head. Recalling Glenn's statement that Chaffee's friends and family would be welcome at the museum press conference, I said into the phone, "I wonder about Dawn, Stewart's niece from Santa Barbara. Perhaps she should be notified. After all, the reception is a tribute to her late uncle."

"I spoke to Dawn Chaffee-Tucker by phone late yesterday," Larry told me. "The department had already informed her of her uncle's death, and she readily admitted having visited the estate on Monday morning, claiming to have been summoned to an eleven o'clock meeting by Chaffee's banker."

I noted, "That's consistent with Monday's security tape and with the discussion I heard on Saturday at Chaffee's estate. How did Dawn take the news?"

"When I myself spoke to her, she seemed unemotional about it. Of course, she'd already heard the news from one of my deputies, so the shock, if there was any, had worn off. I will say this: she was extremely cooperative. I asked if she would mind having a set of fingerprints made by the Santa Barbara police, and she did it as soon as we hung up. They've already been sent to me."

"And?" Our discussion of fingers had led me to examine my own. With my free hand, I picked the dried little hook of a hangnail.

"And they don't match any that we found at the crime scene."

"She's in the clear, then?"

"Not necessarily. She admits being there." Larry asked rhetorically, "Why no prints?"

"Have you asked her about that?" My cuticle began to bleed, so I stopped toying with it.

"I intend to. Turns out, she's driving back to the valley today. As Chaffee's next of kin, she's meeting with Merrit Lloyd at Indian Wells Bank and Trust to discuss the disposition of her uncle's estate. I need to question both the banker *and* the niece, so I plan to join their meeting at two o'clock."

"One-stop shopping," I joshed tritely.

"Yup," he agreed, "two birds with one stone."

14

My exploits with Larry Knoll had evolved to the point where I barely needed to beg to accompany him that afternoon on his visit to the bank. When I asked, he paused and grumbled—out of sheer principle. Then I pleaded sweetly, explaining that I should be there, on behalf of the college, to invite Dawn to her uncle's tribute at the museum. Satisfied, Larry relented. Our routine was well practiced by now, and I found that I needed to offer only minimal justification for tagging along with him.

We drove our own cars, meeting at the bank. At a minute or so before two, I pulled my Beetle into the parking lot, noting that Larry had already arrived and sat waiting for me. When I got out of my car, he got out of his. "Right on time," he said, walking in my direction.

Meeting him halfway, I offered a hug, noting, "I'm compulsively prompt. Guess it's to compensate for a fear of being late. I'm always having dreams about missing tests. Do you suppose that signals some deep-seated psychopathy?"

"God, I hope not." Larry eyed me with concern.

"Sorry. I was oversharing." The California vocabulary had already become second nature to me.

Walking me toward the building, he said, "I wonder if the niece was equally prompt."

I looked around the parking lot, but would not have known her car if I'd seen it. "Not sure about Dawn, but Merrit Lloyd is here." I pointed to his big silver Mercedes; it hunkered like a tank in the blue shadow of the building.

Larry nodded. He'd seen the rear bumper in Monday's security photos from the estate.

As we entered the bank lobby, I noticed that it had been decked out with a few seasonal touches since the previous morning. In keeping with the severe, minimalist style of the building and its furnishings, the Christmas decorations consisted of nothing more than a bowl of silver balls on the receptionist's desk, a few crystal icicles hung from the overhead light fixture, and a strand of clear lights spiraling around the trunk of a potted palm. Happy holidays.

Larry introduced himself, the receptionist recognized me from Tuesday, and a moment later, Merrit Lloyd's secretary came out to greet us. "Good afternoon," said Robin, heels snapping at the granite floor.

We stepped forward, greeting her in turn. Was it my imagination, or had something changed in Robin's manner since our sighting yesterday at lunch? Though she had never been the vivacious sort, she now seemed downright mousy, as if I'd caught her in a compromising position—keeping company with an older man. Who was I, after all, to judge the May-December thing? With Tanner and me, the sexes and ages were reversed, but otherwise, we were in the same brow-raising boat as Robin and Atticus.

"Mr. Lloyd is expecting you," she told Larry. If she found anything unusual in my presence, she didn't voice it. "I understand you also wish to meet with Dawn Chaffee-Tucker, Mr. Chaffee's niece."

"Yes, has she arrived?"

"Some time ago. She and Mr. Lloyd have wrapped up their business and are ready to see you. This way, please."

Larry and I followed Robin toward the back of the bank, past her own desk, and into Merrit Lloyd's office. "Detective Knoll and Miss Gray," she announced us, then left the room.

Merrit stood to greet us, as did Dawn. Though the banker had not expected to see me, he welcomed me warmly and introduced me to Dawn as a recent acquaintance of her late uncle, adding, "Stewart graciously lent Claire a clock from his collection, to be used on the set of her play at Desert Arts College."

Dawn blinked. "Claire Gray? The director?"

"Guilty," I admitted. It was an insipid acknowledgment, but seemed to fit the tone of our conversation, which was curiously light. Larry brought it down a notch, telling Dawn, "I'm so very sorry for your loss." He shook her hand.

"Ah"—the woman nodded—"Stewart's death did come as a surprise. And from what I understand, he died under the most lamentable circumstances. But the truth is, I hardly knew him. We were never close."

I studied her as she spoke. Dawn looked some ten years younger than me, in her early forties. She stood with perfect composure and spoke with quiet, unemotional precision. I knew from previous discussions that she had a background in the arts and ran a gallery in Santa Barbara, which brought to mind the role of Iesha Birch at DMSA. But the two women bore no resemblance to each other. While Iesha projected the image of a free-spirited bohemian, Dawn looked every inch the businesswoman. Her skirt and jacket were finely tailored, probably Chanel, accented with a single strand of gray pearls. She even wore a hat, a pert pillbox, lacking only gloves to complete the Jackie-esque picture. Her handbag was indeed Chanel—no mistaking the large gold clasp—with a long gold chain instead of a strap. She was an articulate, educated woman of refined bearing and classic good taste. I liked her.

"I met Stewart only once," she was saying, "when I was very young. I don't think I was walking yet; I don't even remember the encounter. I was always *told* I'd met my uncle, and the family lore stuck."

"Just last Sunday," I said, "your uncle recounted the same story. Yes, you'd met. It was forty years ago, when you were a toddler."

Confirmation of this detail from Dawn's early life cast a pensive pall over her features. The room was momentarily silent.

Breaking the lull, Merrit suggested, "Let's all sit down." He gestured toward a round conference table occupying the side of his office away from the brutally chic concrete desk. Conveniently, the table was surrounded by four chairs; disquietingly, each of the chairs sprouted three legs. We settled in.

Larry began, "Mrs. Chaffee-Tucker—"

"Please, Detective, call me Dawn. The hyphenated name once seemed so important to me. Now it's just cumbersome."

Larry grinned. "You're welcome to call me Larry, as well. First, Dawn, I want to thank you for being so cooperative with the investigation. It was good of you to supply your fingerprints so quickly."

With a soft shake of her head, she said, "Just trying to be a good citizen." The words seemed stale, but their tone was sincere.

"The prints were sent to us from Santa Barbara, and there was no match with any found at the crime scene." Larry, I noted, told these findings without suggesting their significance, which we had found uncertain.

But the meaning of these findings was clear in Dawn's mind. With the slightest shrug, she said, "I wouldn't *expect* you to find my fingerprints at the crime scene."

I asked, "But you were *at* Stewart's estate on Monday morning, right?"

"Yes, I was there, but I didn't go inside the house."

"Let's back up," said Larry. "Tell us what led up to your visit that morning."

"This." Dawn snapped open her purse and took out an envelope. "I received a letter from Uncle Stewart about two weeks ago, saying that he would like to see me again. My first reaction was that it was some sort of hoax, a cruel joke." She handed the letter to Larry.

At first glance, the detective's face wrinkled. He blurted, "What a mess."

Curious, I leaned past his arm to look at the letter. It was word-processed and laser-printed, but typed without skill and clumsily formatted. The column of type sat tight against the right edge, some lines running off the paper, with an overly wide margin on the left. The sloppy, unprofessional appearance conveyed that little or no care had been lavished on this missive, which purported to bring important tidings from Dawn's past. The opening sentence made reference to Stewart and Dawn's "shared love of the visual arts."

Merrit, who had already seen the letter, conjectured, "Stewart wasn't much of a typist. I guess that's why he had a secretary. The signature is authentic, by the way. I'd know it anywhere."

I recalled, "When Larry and I spoke with Pea yesterday, he mentioned that Stewart 'never quite got the hang' of using their home computer. This letter bears that out. Clearly, he wrote it without Pea's assistance." As an afterthought, I explained to Dawn, "Pea was your uncle's live-in secretary and houseman."

"Then why," asked Dawn, "didn't the secretary help Stewart with the letter?"

Merrit explained, "Stewart didn't want Pea to know that he was meeting you. He specifically asked my office to set up the appointment on a Monday morning, when there would be no one else at the house. Stewart felt that Pea might find the meeting upsetting for some reason, though I don't know the underlying reason."

I did. Suddenly, a lot made sense. For example, Stewart had made disparaging remarks about Dawn during my visit on Sunday, when Grant and I returned the desk. Pea was present that day, whereas he had not been present on Saturday, when I'd heard Stewart confirm with Robin that a meeting with Dawn had been arranged. Stewart's underlying reason for this subterfuge, I now understood, was that he didn't want to alert his ex-lover, Pea, that he was considering a rapprochement with his next of kin, Dawn. Stewart was doubtless aware that Pea entertained expectations of a substantial inheritance.

Larry had taken out his notebook and had begun writing. He asked Dawn, "If you thought the letter was a hoax, why did you act on it?"

"The tone seemed genuinely conciliatory, and Stewart concluded by telling me to expect a call from his banker's office for the purpose of setting up an appointment. Not long after, I did hear from the bank, and Robin booked the meeting."

"Tell me about your visit that morning."

"We were scheduled to meet at my uncle's estate at eleven o'clock. It's about a four-hour drive from Santa Barbara, depending on traffic, so I started out early and arrived early in the valley. I stopped somewhere for coffee, freshened up a bit, then drove over to my uncle's, pulling up to the gate at eleven on the dot."

Larry looked up from his notes. "Are you always so punctual?"

She allowed, "More or less. Well, no, not always. But this meeting seemed important to my uncle, so I wanted to play by the rules, as it were. There'd already been enough bad blood in the family. I didn't want to contribute to it with the implied disrespect of tardiness."

"Bad blood," I repeated. "Your uncle used those very words. What was the source of all that enmity?"

Dawn shook her head feebly. "I never knew for sure. As I said, I had never really known my uncle. I'd only heard *about* him, and it was never very flattering. My father—he's been dead nearly ten years—was Stewart's older brother. Even as a child, I was aware of deep-seated resentment between Stewart and the entire family, but I was never sure of its roots. Now, so many years later, I suspect it was the gay issue, which doesn't concern me in the least."

Getting back on track, Larry said, "So you arrived at the estate at eleven, expecting some sort of reconciliation."

"I assumed that was the point of the meeting, yes. So I pulled up to the gate and tried the intercom, but got no response. Robin had told me I might need to let myself in, so I punched in the code. The gate opened, and I drove to the front door. I got out of the car and rang the doorbell, but no one answered. I tried once or twice again. After waiting several minutes, I left."

I said, "But you'd driven so far. Didn't you try phoning the bank?"

Dawn shook her head. "To be honest, I was angry by then. Waiting at the door, it was apparent that no one was home, or at least that no one intended to answer. I quickly concluded that my original inclination was correct—I'd been set up for a cruel ruse. I left feeling hurt and victimized." Wistfully, she added, "Little did I know that my uncle Stewart was the actual victim."

Larry asked, "How long, in total, were you there?"

"It seemed like forever standing at the door, but it was less than five minutes. Probably less than two."

"Did you notice anyone else on the premises?"

"No. I'd have asked a few questions if I'd spotted anyone."

"How about cars? Did you see any other vehicles on the grounds?"

"Not in front of the house. I didn't look in back. I just left."

Larry tapped his pen on the pad. "And you didn't touch anything—other than the keypad at the gate and the doorbell button. You didn't try the door handle?"

"Certainly not," she said as if the suggestion were unthinkable. "I wouldn't have entered someone's home without being admitted. Other than a common thief, who would?"

I felt myself slumping in my three-legged chair.

Larry deduced, "And because you didn't touch anything, that's why you assumed we wouldn't find your fingerprints at the scene."

"I suppose. But more to the point, I was wearing gloves."

My earlier observation about her attire now seemed premature. Larry's brow wrinkled. "Do you often wear gloves?"

"When I drive, I do." She snapped open her purse again and extracted a limp, skintight pair of perforated doeskin driving gloves, plopping them on the table. She concluded, "And I drove straight back to Santa Barbara. I hadn't a clue that anything was wrong till yesterday afternoon, when I heard from the sheriff's department here in Riverside County."

Larry asked Merrit, "Have you and Dawn discussed Mr. Chaffee's bequest to the museum?"

"Yes," said the banker, "we discussed it thoroughly before you arrived. I gave Dawn a copy of the interview from the *Herald*."

Obliquely, Larry asked Dawn, "What did you think?"

With a nascent laugh, she said, "I think my uncle chose a peculiar way to make his intentions known." More seriously, she added, "I admire his philanthropy. I share his interest in art, and this is a marvelous final gesture. If you're wondering if I feel slighted, no, I don't. Given the history of friction in my father's family, I never expected to inherit a thing from my uncle. Although I must say, his holographic will is bizarre."

Merrit cleared his throat, assuring Dawn, "The bank's probate team is studying the whole matter, but there appears to be no reason to suspect that the old newspaper clipping is other than what it appears to be, a statement of Stewart's last wishes."

I recalled, from our meeting at the bank on Tuesday, "Wasn't Robin going to do some research in that regard?"

"She was, and she did. In fact—well, let's have Robin tell you what she found." Merrit rose from the table, crossed to the door, and asked Robin to step inside.

"Yes, sir?" she asked as they approached our table together.

"The others were wondering about your library research."

"Ah." Robin turned to us. "Yesterday afternoon, I went out to the Palm Springs Library Center on Sunrise Way, which has extensive records of local periodicals on microfilm and microfiche. The *Desert Sun,* for instance, goes back to 1934. The *Palm Springs Herald,* however, maintained its own archives for the several decades of its existence, which were always a struggle against the larger paper. The *Herald* folded during the sixties, and its archives suffered some damage when a water line burst in their warehouse shortly after publication had ceased. A few years later, the archives were acquired by the local library, which has done a superb job of cataloging and preserving them. However, due to the warehouse flood, there are a number of gaps in the collection where issues were destroyed or missing. Unfortunately, one of these gaps spans several months in 1954, when the Chaffee interview was published."

Larry asked, "So there's no way to verify, absolutely, that the clipping is genuine?"

"Short of recovering a complete issue of that day's *Herald,* I suppose not."

"Thank you," Merrit dismissed his secretary; she left. Sitting again at the table with us, the banker told Larry, "The original clipping, now in your brother's possession, certainly *appears* to be genuine, and I believe it would stand up as evidence if the disposition of the estate were to be contested."

Dawn touched his arm, assuring him, "It won't come to that. I wouldn't dream of contesting my uncle's estate. Why would I?"

"As next of kin," Merrit reminded her, "many would-be heirs

would find ample reason to contest such a will. I'm highly relieved, of course, that you're able to weigh the situation so philosophically."

"I'm not all that noble," she told him with a wry grin. "If I were starving or destitute, I'd probably take an altogether different tack. But my circumstances are more than comfortable."

Larry asked, "Would you mind giving us some details of those circumstances—a bit of your personal background?"

"Not at all. What would you like to know?"

Larry prompted, "You're married, correct?"

"Yes. My husband is Dr. Troy Chaffee-Tucker, a dermatologist with an established practice in Santa Barbara. We were married nineteen years ago, when he was finishing medical school. You'll notice he took the same hyphenated name; he's a remarkably supportive man. Our daughter came along a year after we were married. Joconda is eighteen now, in her first year of college." Dawn took her wallet from her purse and slid a photo from one of the plastic sleeves. "This was taken last summer on a sailing trip to Catalina." Proudly, she tendered the photo to Larry and me.

Larry made some approving comment about the boat. I focused on doctor Troy and daughter Joconda. He was handsome, toothy, blond, and wind-tossed. She, poor dear, had inherited none of her parents' good looks. Perhaps she had yet to flower out of a gawky adolescence. I told Joconda's mother, "She has such beautiful skin," faint praise for a dermatologist's kid.

"Thank you." Dawn gave me an appreciative nod and returned the photo to her wallet.

Larry asked her, "You run a museum, correct?"

"No, not a museum. It's a small, commercial gallery—I sell art. I have a doctorate in art history, and twelve years ago, after Joconda started school, I decided to put the degree to use, opening the gallery as something of a lark. To the astonishment of both Troy and myself, the business has thrived from the outset. I represent some top contemporary talent, but my specialty has always been the work of earlier masters."

I said, "Then I can understand why your uncle sensed an affinity with you. He'd followed your career from a distance and clearly approved. What a shame the two of you never connected, talked, and explored your common interests."

"And we nearly did," she lamented. "Our timing was regrettably poor."

Their timing was worse than poor, I mused. The coroner had determined that Chaffee had died between ten-thirty and eleven-thirty on Monday morning. Dawn had arrived at eleven. They could not have missed meeting by more than a few minutes—a nanosecond in the context of Chaffee's eighty-two years.

Dawn continued, "There might have been so much family history for us to cover together, and now there's nothing. I have no memories of the man."

"What a shame." Then I recalled, "The reason I'm here today, Dawn, is to invite you to attend a reception tomorrow evening at the Desert Museum of Southwestern Arts. The press has been invited, and Glenn Yeats himself will announce the bequest, but the event is essentially a tribute to your late uncle. We thought you might want to be there."

She paused, considering this, then said with resolve, "I *would* like to be there. I feel so awful about . . . missing him on Monday. The least I can do is represent his family at the memorial service."

It would hardly be a "memorial service," not with the full glare of the media and with Glenn Yeats posturing and crowing on behalf of the college, but I was not inclined to disabuse Dawn of her quaint notion. So I simply told her, "The reception begins at seven at the museum's new facility on campus."

"Excuse me," said Robin, appearing in the doorway again, holding a tray. "Your meeting seemed to be running long, so I thought you might like some water."

"Thank you, Robin," said Merrit, waving her in, "most thoughtful of you."

Robin entered with the tray, which bore several bottles of mineral water, a dainty ice bucket and tongs, and four crystal goblets. Placing the tray in the center of the table, she distributed the glasses and twisted the lids from the bottles. Merrit poured for Dawn, Larry for me. I drank, but no one else seemed interested. Setting down my glass in a shaft of sunlight that crossed the table, I noted that I'd left a pristine set of fingerprints on the surface of the crystal.

Offhandedly, Dawn mentioned to Merrit, "It's a long way back and forth to Santa Barbara. Since I'll need to be here again tomorrow, perhaps I should spend the night."

"Good idea." The banker turned to his secretary. "Robin, could you give the Regal Palms a call? Mrs. Chaffee-Tucker will need a suite for tonight and perhaps tomorrow as well. Please ask them to bill it to the bank's account."

"Certainly." With a deferential bob, Robin slipped out to her desk.

Dawn told Merrit, "I *really* don't expect that."

"Nonsense," the banker insisted. "Your uncle was one of our oldest and most valued clients. We think of you as family."

"You've been exceptionally kind. I can well understand my uncle's loyalty."

Merrit beamed.

Dawn plucked her driving gloves off the table, wriggled her hands into them, and fastened the snaps at her wrists. She stood.

The rest of us stood with her, recapping our condolences and our thanks for each other's cooperation in attempting to resolve the mystery of her uncle's death.

Robin popped back into the room, carrying a folder. She told Dawn, "Everything is set at the Regal Palms. Do you need directions?"

"Thank you, but I know the way."

Robin stepped forward with the folder. "These are the photos I told you about—from your uncle's safe-deposit box."

"Ahhh," said Dawn, taking the folder, peeking inside, "a glimpse into my family's forgotten past. It seems I have a nostalgic evening ahead of me." With a sigh, she picked up her purse and tucked the photos under her arm. Then she reached with her free hand for the glass of water and swallowed a few sips. When she set down the goblet,

I noticed that her gloved fingers had left smudges, but no prints. "I really should be going. Thank you, Merrit, you've been wonderful."

After a round of farewells, Dawn swept out the door, followed by Robin.

Larry told Merrit, "I appreciate all the time you've given us."

"It's the least I can do. I only hope it's been helpful. Please, do let me know if I can be of any further assistance to the investigation."

"Actually," said Larry, "if you could spare a few more minutes, I'm confused about a particular matter that I hope you can clarify."

"I'll try, certainly." He gestured toward the table, and all three of us resumed our former seats.

Larry flipped a few pages back in his notebook. "Thank you for being so forthright about your visit to the Chaffee estate on Monday morning. We also appreciated your willingness to supply a set of fingerprints when my deputy called on you yesterday."

"I assume you found a match for mine—probably many—at the house." Merrit's voice carried no inflection of wariness. "I've been there so often, I've surely left paw marks everywhere."

"Not in the kitchen," Larry told him, "but yes, we did find traces of your prints on the front-door handle."

"Makes sense." Merrit shrugged. "I always used the front door. That's how I entered—and left—on Monday morning."

"And what time was that?"

"Early. Before eight o'clock, on my way to the office. I needed a signature or two, so I wasn't there more than a few minutes. Such visits were frequent."

"Sometimes more than once a day?"

"Sometimes, yes."

Larry asked, "So it wasn't unusual that you went to the Chaffee estate twice on Monday?"

Merrit paused. With a trace of confusion he asked, "I did? Is that what I told your deputy yesterday?"

"No. You said that you had been there early, before eight. You didn't mention a return visit, but the security tapes recorded a second visit at a quarter past ten."

"Really?" He shook his head as if to clear his thinking. He didn't seem to be squirming, merely befuddled. With an apologetic laugh, he said, "It's entirely *possible* that I returned on Monday. It wouldn't be unusual, but that's not my recollection. Unless I'm mistaken, I had a long meeting at ten that morning with the bank's auditing team; it ran into lunch."

I suggested, "Why don't you check."

"Of course." Merrit rose from the table and stepped to his desk. It's immaculate surface contained nothing so trivial as an appointment book, so he pressed a button on the phone and asked his secretary to come in.

"Yes, Mr. Lloyd," said Robin as she entered the office.

"Could you check my schedule for Monday, Robin? That auditors' meeting, it began at ten, right?"

The secretary scrunched her features. Rather than contradict her boss, she said, "Let me get your book." A moment later she returned with a gilt-edged day planner. "No, Mr. Lloyd. The auditors' meeting began at eleven."

Merrit told Larry, "Then I *was* mistaken. Sorry for the misinformation. Sometimes, one day just blurs into another—the perils of middle age."

Larry made note of the second meeting, closed his pad, and joked with Merrit about the early onset of senility.

But I was troubled.

Chaffee had died sometime after ten-thirty on Monday, and Merrit Lloyd, banker of the deceased, could not quite explain—or even recall—why he had arrived at the estate at ten-fifteen that morning.

15

Kiki Jasper-Plunkett and I hadn't seen as much of each other in recent weeks as we would have liked. We'd been closest friends in college; then, over the subsequent decades, we'd maintained that friendship from a distance. Now, having both moved to the desert a few months earlier, living in condominiums only steps apart, we'd assumed we'd be thick again. But maybe it's true—maybe there's no going back. While I loved my old chum and everything we'd shared, our new lives in California had brought new passions and priorities.

Kiki's interests had always been chameleonlike, shifting almost as frequently as she changed clothes—several times daily.

As for me, my life had been steered by a steady rudder, a myopic absorption with my career, but now, at fifty-four, I felt reborn. My days were filled with my work at Desert Arts College, where I believed, perhaps pretentiously, that I could shape a new generation of American actors. My nights were filled with Tanner Griffin; enough said. More often than not, my idle hours, my social times, were spent with Grant Knoll, a new neighbor whose friendship had proven instant and solid. What's more, I'd somehow managed to become involved in a murder investigation, my second in three months. So I hadn't found much time for Kiki.

Wednesday evening presented a good opportunity for us to make up for lost time together. The reception for Mark Manning at the Nirvana home of Glenn Yeats was scheduled to begin early, around five, because so many of the guests, including myself, would be busy later that evening with the full, final dress rehearsal of *Laura*. I often rode to such events with Grant, but he was helping coordinate staff and services for the party; he would arrive early. Tanner had errands to run up valley in Palm Springs; he would arrive later, alone, in his Jeep. So I had asked Kiki if she needed a ride. Now, in the slanting light of dusk, I drove her up the mountain in my silver Beetle.

"Are we allowed to drink?" she asked, checking her lips in a mirror behind the visor.

With eyes on the road, I reminded her, "It's a party. I'm sure the bar will be open." As I rounded a final curve, the angular structure of Glenn's home came into view, jutting dramatically against an indigo sky.

Kiki's bracelets jangled as she primped. "I *mean,* dare we drink before rehearsal?" Turning to me, she raised a single, inquiring brow.

"Our work is done. The show is now in the hands of cast and crew. *They're* on the wagon till curtain call. If *you* care to imbibe this evening—within moderation, of course—I'll doubtless join you."

"Within moderation, of course," she repeated with a wink in her voice. Then her tone turned serious. "Tanner will be here tonight, I assume."

"Later, yes."

"Claire, *darling,*" she gasped, "don't you find it a bit awkward, juggling two suitors in the same room?"

"They're not 'suitors,' " I demurred. "You make it sound so Victorian."

"Victorian? Hardly. I think it's terribly modern, even commendable—*if* you can get away with it." She gave me an envious scowl.

I was tempted to defend myself, but I found it difficult to argue with her. This reticence, I realized, was itself a point that bore discussing. Now, though, was simply not the time to analyze my romantic exploits or my deeper attitudes toward them. I had a play to open. And a murder to solve.

The Beetle groaned as I steered it up the sharp incline of Glenn's driveway, which led to an entry court behind the house. Several other cars had already arrived, and a pair of valets scurried to greet guests, whisking their vehicles to some hidden parking facility. When

Kiki and I got out of the car, it sputtered in the cool evening air like a puppy left whimpering in the night.

We crossed the courtyard to the house, its walls of stone and glass washed by soft lighting that seemed to emanate from nowhere. Following a granite walkway, edged on one side by precious sago palms and on the other by a shallow, black reflecting pool, we passed under a huge cantilever extending from the house in utter defiance of gravity. No apparent doorway separated outside from in; the transition to interior space was subtle and artful. Yet, there we were, in a sprawling lobby that dwarfed the mingling crowd, reverberating with party chat and the bouncy strains of a distant piano.

"Ms. Gray, Ms. Jasper-Plunkett," said Tide Arden, Glenn's executive secretary, stalking toward us on those long, muscular legs, "so happy to have you with us." She made two check marks on a list attached to her acrylic clipboard. "Mr. Yeats was asking if you'd arrived." Her wispy voice and pleasant words flowed in stark contrast to her fierce appearance. "Can we get you a drink?"

Before Kiki or I could answer, Tide snapped her strong black fingers—a sound that could crack glass—at a passing tuxedoed waiter, who froze. "These ladies need drinks," she informed him, somehow managing to glare at him while smiling at us.

A bone-dry martini, brimming with shaved ice, would have suited both my uncertain mood and the sophisticated surroundings to a tee, but I had a working evening ahead of me, so I opted for something less potent, ordering kir. Kiki, who generally marches to a different drum, its beat heard only by herself, surprised me by telling the young man, "Make it two."

"Claire! There you are!" Glenn Yeats, the amiable billionaire himself, bustled through the shifting crowd to greet me under the daggerlike prisms of a modern, asymmetrical chandelier. Like everything in his home, the fixture was of heroic scale. Though it appeared ephemeral, a mere bauble in the soaring heights beneath the distant ceiling, it surely weighed tons.

"Glenn"—I leaned to kiss his cheek—"you've outdone yourself, as usual."

With a modest shrug, he reminded me, "I have help."

"I thought we'd be early, but things seem to be rolling already."

"With so many of you due at the theater by seven, there seemed to be little interest in arriving fashionably late." He gestured toward a buffet table at the far end of the hall, where a goodly number of my troupe already grazed on chilled shrimp and rare tenderloin, juggling their plates with glasses of amber-colored bubbly that I hoped was ginger ale. Among them was Thad Quatrain.

I asked, "Has our guest of honor arrived?"

"Indeed, just minutes ago, with his nephew. Mark is on the terrace, I believe. Grant zipped him outdoors to catch the view by twilight."

"I'll bet he did," I mused with a dry chortle.

Kiki had a taste for meat, so she excused herself as Glenn escorted me through the living room toward the open wall to the terrace. Along the way, we stopped to chat briefly here and there. Guests drifted back and forth from the living room to the terrace, which was getting chilly in the night air. A pair of gargantuan fireplaces, festooned with pine swags, were ablaze for warmth and for seasonal effect—indoors and out.

Near the gleaming grand piano, I noticed Atticus, the painter, and Lance Caldwell, the composer, huddled in animated conversation, thumping their chests and gesticulating broadly. Like most of the faculty present, they both wore basic, arty black. The firelight picked out and magnified the red in Atticus's graying hair, giving the little man a tempestuous look that matched the bravado of his body language. Caldwell, lean and catlike, arched his spine, hissing something about music theory. Iesha Birch, the museum director, joined them and sided with Atticus, launching into a defense of the "plastic and graphic arts."

"Let's find Mark," I told Glenn, winking—meaning, Get me out of here.

With easy affection, he looped an arm through mine and guided me through the invisible wall. Again, the transition from indoors to out was subtle and seamless. In an instant, the air turned cooler, the light dimmed, and the party noise seemed quiet and distant, overlaid now by the echo of a coyote's howl. Across the pool, at the far side of the terrace, clumps of guests gathered near a stone parapet, gazing out over craggy arroyos to the valley floor some thousand feet below. The day's last light defined peaks of a western mountain range. The purple horizon faded to black in a riot of stars overhead.

Even in the twilight, I had no difficulty spotting Mark Manning, whose crisp tan suit defined a striking silhouette against the encroaching night. Grant Knoll stood beside him, pointing across the valley toward the lights of the main runway at the airport. Glenn and I stepped up behind them. I asked, "Does it remind you of December in Wisconsin?"

Mark laughed, still facing the serene, dusky vista. "Not even remotely." Then he turned to greet me with a kiss. "Good evening, Claire."

I returned the kiss. "Grant, I see, is giving you the grand tour."

"He's been an attentive guide. Thank you, Grant."

"My pleasure." Grant's eyes slid to mine. He twitched his brows.

I couldn't resist asking him, "Where's Kane tonight?"

"Nose to the grindstone, working on the program for tomorrow's event at the museum."

Mark turned to tell our host, "I'm at a loss for words, Glenn—everything's spectacular. I can't thank you enough for inviting me up tonight."

Dismissing the flattery and thanks, Glenn gestured toward our rarefied surroundings. "If it can't be shared, it's worth very little."

Continuing in this gracious vein, we were soon interrupted by the arrival of a waiter with a tray who, serving double duty, also escorted Detective Larry Knoll to the terrace.

Glenn stepped forward, extending his hand. "Good evening, Detective. Welcome."

"Thanks for asking me. Nice to be back." The last time Larry had visited Nirvana, he'd capped the evening with an arrest.

"Since you're not working tonight," said Glenn, "won't you have a drink?"

Larry hesitated. "Maybe I will." And he asked the waiter for bourbon, neat.

The waiter's tray contained my kir and Mark's iced vodka, which was garnished with a pungent twist of orange peel; its fragrance seemed magnified in the still, chilly night. Grant already carried a flute of champagne. Glenn wasn't drinking. As the waiter retreated to the house for Larry's bourbon, the three of us with glasses skoaled and sipped.

Instinctively, we drew near the open hearth of the overscale fireplace that blazed near the pool. Reflected flames skipped and twirled on the black surface of the water. Huddling against the night, we drank and talked. Larry's whiskey arrived, smelling warm and wintry. Before long, we spoke of murder.

Glenn asked, "You've ruled out the possibility that Stewart Chaffee's death was accidental?"

Larry glanced at me. He surely had reservations about discussing details of an investigation at a cocktail party—in the presence of a high-profile journalist, no less. Still, he'd come to this gathering to observe interactions and explore possible leads, so there was nothing to be gained by holding back. What's more, grouped near the fire, we were secluded from the party's to-and-fro, so he could speak in reasonable confidence.

Larry answered Glenn, "All the evidence points to foul play. I'm treating Chaffee's death as a homicide." He told about the absence of fingerprints on the refrigerator handle and the efficient leverage the wide-open door had provided.

Mark swirled the vodka in his glass. "Who are the heirs?" He didn't need to elaborate that he was curious about the most obvious of possible motives.

Grant spoke up. "In a sense, I am." He explained his position as president of the board of the museum that had received the unexpected bequest.

I told Mark about Chaffee's next of kin, his niece, Dawn. "She never really knew her uncle and had no expectations of an inheritance. Even though Stewart's will is bizarre at best, she has no intention of contesting it." I gave details of the 1954 interview from the defunct *Palm Springs Herald* and Stewart's handwritten marginalia.

Mark sipped his drink, thinking, following along. "If the niece wasn't expecting a windfall, was anyone else?"

I glanced at Larry. He gave me the slightest nod of permission to proceed. I explained, "There's a houseman, who's the former lover of the deceased. There's also a nurse who cared for Stewart at home full-time during the last two years of his life. It's reasonable to assume they both expected something."

"And now they're bitter," Mark reasoned.

"The houseman is, without question. The nurse is harder to read."

Glenn shook his head. "It all seems so . . . pointless." Responding to our quizzical looks, he expounded, "There may be people who *wanted* to inherit something from Stewart, and there may even be people who *deserved* to, but his gift to the museum, while generous, is ultimately pointless. The Desert Museum of Southwestern Arts has a relatively narrow artistic mission—and no interest in the vast majority of pieces from Stewart's collection."

"We can't even sell off the unwanted pieces," Grant added. "We'll end up storing them."

Glenn summed up, "It's an albatross. Honest to God, if I didn't know better, I'd swear Stewart was trying to one-up me. He knew only too well that I had already richly endowed DMSA and secured its future through its affiliation with the college. I can't imagine what he was thinking—unless, of course, he did this as a last, feeble attempt to add some luster to his collection, which had always, frankly, struck me as second-rate." Harrumph.

This ungracious pronouncement painted its speaker as more than a tad swellheaded. But that was Glenn. If the others were put off by the billionaire's puffery, they didn't let on. Whether this could be attributed to good manners or to bootlicking, I couldn't say. For that matter, I was unable to identify the root of my own acquiescence to Glenn's fragile, though enormous, ego.

I simply said, "Stewart's death was tragic enough. It's a shame his legacy hasn't brought more happiness to his survivors."

Focusing on the death, not the legacy, Mark noted, "The motive seems muddled. And the means are no mystery—virtually anyone could have toppled the refrigerator. But what about opportunity? Do you know who was there in the house that morning?"

"Indeed we do," said Larry. "The problem is verifying who *wasn't* there at the time of the victim's death." He explained about the security camera at the gate, which left a time-stamped record of those entering but not exiting the estate.

"Excuse me, Glenn?"

We turned. Iesha Birch had joined our group by the fire. Pulling a saffron-colored silk shawl over her bare shoulders, she told Glenn, "Tide and I were reviewing details of tomorrow's press reception, and there's some confusion about the question-and-answer period. Did you have a particular protocol in mind?"

Glenn raised a finger, preparing to give instructions, then reconsidered. "Perhaps we should go inside and have Tide take notes. Tomorrow's event is important. I want it to run like clockwork."

"Yes, sir. Very good."

Glenn turned to the rest of us. "If you'll excuse me?"

"Of course," we effused. "By all means." And he left the terrace with Iesha.

From the side of my mouth, I told Mark, "From all the scraping and bowing, you'd think *he* was the star attraction at this party."

Mark grinned. "D. Glenn Yeats has a way of being the dominant presence at *any* gathering, I'm sure."

"Well, not tonight," said Grant, practically purring. "It's a *glorious* desert-winter evening. This is *your* party, Mark, and we've prattled entirely too much about homicide. So. Tell us. Enjoying your stay?"

"I am. I'd forgotten how peaceful it is here—in spite of all the growth."

In spite of the recent spate of slayings, I mused.

Grant prompted, "And what have you been up to . . . ?"

"Catching up with Thad. Relaxing. And yesterday I visited the *Desert Sun.*"

Grant clunked his forehead. "Silly me. You were on your way when we saw you at the Regal Palms."

"It's a fine paper. Impressive facilities, too." Mark shared with Grant a few particulars of his tour.

As they conversed, Larry turned to me and said privately, "That reminds me, I have a contact in editorial at the *Sun* who's trying to track down whether Bonnie Bahr wrote letters to the paper in support of mercy killing."

"Can't you just ask her about it?"

"I intend to. But when I ask the question, I want to already know the answer."

Mark was giving Grant some history of the local paper. "The *Sun* switched to offset in 1972. They've done a good job of keeping up with the technology curve, offering an on-line edition to complement their traditional hard copy."

Trying to focus on our guest's interests, I asked, "Offset?"

"Offset printing," he explained, "as opposed to letterpress printing. Letterpress, the older method, is essentially the technology Gutenberg used; a raised image is inked, then pressed against paper, transferring the ink from the plate to the paper. It's the same working principle as that of an ordinary rubber stamp. Technically, this is known as relief printing, the opposite of intaglio or engraving, in which the ink is pulled from an etched indentation *beneath* the surface of the plate."

I concluded, "So offset is engraving."

"No, sorry. Offset printing is a third, entirely different method known as planography, in which the image is transferred from a *flat* surface. In offset printing—more precisely, offset photolithography— the original image is transferred to a photographic emulsion on a flat printing plate. The exposed emulsion attracts ink, while the unexposed areas of the plate repel ink. This inked image is transferred, or offset, first to a rubber 'blanket,' then finally to the paper."

Grant whooped. "You've *got* to be kidding, Mark. That sounds like wizardry."

"I know it sounds crazy, but it works—and works very well. To the layman, the visual improvement of offset printing over letterpress may be difficult to detect, but to the trained eye, there's a world of difference, enough to justify the expense of switching."

I asked, "It's a costly conversion?"

"And how. The two technologies are so totally different, the conversion of a newspaper generally requires building a whole new printing plant and scrapping the old one—a tremendous investment. Many smaller papers, like the *Dumont Daily Register,* made the switch in the sixties and seventies, but the cost was so daunting for the big, old, established papers, many of them didn't convert to offset till the eighties and nineties. A few *still* haven't." Mark paused to sip the last of his drink. With a soft laugh, he said, "Pardon the lecture. You got far more information than you probably wanted."

"Nonsense," said Grant, enthralled by the handsome journalist's every word. As for myself, I was quickly losing interest, but Grant protracted the tech talk, asking Mark, "In 1954, the *Palm Springs Herald* would have been printed by letterpress, right?"

My interest was suddenly rekindled.

"Yes," Mark answered, "any newspaper from 1954 would almost certainly have been printed letterpress. That's conjecture; I could tell at a glance if I saw a sample of the paper."

"It just so happens," said Grant, "I have the original clipping of Stewart Chaffee's interview. It's still in my briefcase. Even I can tell it's *old,* but I wonder if you could point out how you can recognize the method of printing."

Mark eyed him wryly. "Boning up for future cocktail chat?"

"Exactly."

Larry coughed. "I wouldn't mind seeing that myself."

I raised my hand. "Count me in."

"Come on," said Grant, herding us from the terrace. "It's getting cold, and we need fresh drinks. My briefcase is in the library."

Passing through the invisible wall to the living room, we nabbed a waiter, ordered a round of drinks, and made our way across the room toward the library. I noticed that Tanner had just arrived, standing in the front hall gabbing with Kiki. Glenn was still huddled with Iesha and Tide, hammering out details for tomorrow's press conference. Mark waved at his nephew, Thad, still downing shrimp at the buffet table with other cast and crew members. The din of laughter and jabber now drowned out all but a few of the piano's higher trills.

"In here," said Grant, ushering us into the quiet of the library, closing the door behind us. This room, unlike Glenn Yeats's high-tech home office, was contemplative in mood and traditional in design. Bookcases lined the walls. Plump upholstered chairs invited reading. A handsome desk from the Directoire period was meant for letter writing, not word processing. Grant lifted his briefcase from the floor, opened it on the desk, and flipped through some files, extracting a plastic sleeve that held the old clipping.

"Careful," I reminded him as he slid the paper from its sleeve, "that's worth millions."

Grant handed the clipping to Mark, who held it carefully in his fingers, leaning to examine it under the electrified candles of an antique bouillotte lamp that stood near a corner of the desk. Larry, Grant, and I gathered near, peering at the paper over Mark's shoulders.

He stood motionless, saying nothing.

"Well," Grant finally asked, "was the *Herald* printed by letterpress?"

Mark set down the clipping and turned to face us. "I'm not sure how to tell you this"—he paused—"but something is very wrong. The clipping is a fraud."

At that moment, there was a rap at the door, which opened. A waiter entered bearing a tray. "Your drinks."

"Uh," said Grant, distracted, "just leave them, please."

The waiter nodded, placed the tray on a side table, and left, closing the door.

"What?" Grant asked Mark.

"Are you sure?" asked Larry.

"How can you tell?" I chimed.

Mark raised a hand, then stepped aside so the rest of us could better see the suspect shred of paper. "Obviously," he told us, "the newsprint is old—it's yellow and brittle—but the ink was not applied by letterpress *or* by offset. Letterpress printing leaves a slight impression in the paper, but this shows none at all. Even offset printing, with a flat plate, presses the ink into the fibers of the paper, but this shows no absorption, no show-through." He flipped to the back side, proving his point. "May I fold this?"

Grant shrugged. "Why not? If what you say is true, it's not worth *anything*."

Larry corrected his brother. "If what Mark says is true, our murder investigation has an important new lead."

Mark chose an area of the back-side advertisement that was heavy with black ink. He made a crease through it, then flattened the paper again. "Look," he said, tapping the crease, "the ink flakes off at the fold. Both letterpress and offset printing use wet, oily inks, but this was a dry-ink transfer. The pigment merely rests on the surface of the paper. No doubt about it—this was forged on a laser printer." Setting the clipping on the desk, he brushed the flaked ink from his fingers.

Larry asked Grant, "May I take this?"

"All yours." Grant slid the clipping back into its plastic sleeve, surrendering it as evidence to his brother.

Larry held it up at arm's length, pondering its significance to his investigation. "Name the forger," he said, "and we've probably named Stewart Chaffee's killer."

16

At Larry's urging, we decided, for the time being, to keep knowledge of the forged clipping hush-hush. Even though it was now highly questionable whether the museum was the true heir to Chaffee's estate, we would not alert Glenn Yeats, letting him proceed with Thursday night's press reception as planned. Larry's investigation had a promising new direction to explore, and he reasoned that going public with the faked interview would tip his hand to the killer.

So around six-thirty, I thanked Glenn for a splendid evening (he had no idea that it had proven not only entertaining, but informative), gathered my cast and crew, and left the party, heading over to the theater for our final rehearsal of *Laura*.

The memos I had written that morning helped. Almost any director would be thrilled with the level of polish my student cast had brought to the production, but still, I knew they were capable of better. I knew that the murder—and the victim's clock—had become a menacing distraction not only for Thad and Tanner, who had stumbled into the crime scene with me, but also for everyone else in the show. The buzz had proved infectious, the giddiness contagious. In the telling and retelling, Thad and Tanner's minimal contact with the crime, to say nothing of my own, had quickly swelled to mythic proportions.

While the gossip and excitement of an unsolved murder was seemingly harmless—no one's psyche would be permanently damaged—the distraction was sufficient to threaten the cohesiveness of Friday's opening performance, and I was worried. I had too much at stake. So did the college, and so did my students. When the curtain fell on Wednesday night's rehearsal, I understood that my opportunity to achieve true excellence through direction and teaching had ceased. The only way left to ensure the focus and concentration of my troupe was to solve the crime and get it behind us.

When Tanner and I left the theater and returned to my condo for the night, we were hyped by the rehearsal, by the knowledge that within forty-eight hours, our efforts would be judged by Spencer Wallace and Hector Bosch, among so many others. It would take a while to wind down for the night, so we sat up talking, sharing a drink or two.

I was tempted to bring Tanner up to date regarding the discovery of the forged clipping. It was intriguing news, and I had no doubt that I could trust him to keep it in confidence. Still, the last thing I wanted to do was contribute to the stir and ado of the murder, so I kept the topic off-limits. The only mystery we discussed that night was the scripted one we were preparing to enact onstage—more than enough to keep us up and gabbing till well past midnight.

When we finally went to bed, sleep, the gift of exhaustion, came quickly.

Thursday morning, I awoke to the sound of the shower. Rolling over, I squinted at the clock on a bedside table and saw that it was nearly nine, hours later than I typically rise. There was no need to rush—my only class that day was a late-afternoon seminar—but I was surprised that I'd slept so soundly. With rehearsals finished, perhaps my subconscious had temporarily set aside the pressures of my soon-to-open play. Stretching, kicking the bedclothes from one of my legs, sniffing coffee and shower steam and Tanner's shampoo, I felt wonderfully rested—and horny as hell.

The shower stopped running, and while the drain swallowed its last with a long gurgle, I heard Tanner toweling off, a treat for my mind's eye, which drank in the image of him bending and turning to blot and buff his wet body. Next he did some grooming; I heard the pop of plastic bottle caps, the clatter of a comb, the slapping of aftershave. Then he zipped up; he often wore a pair of shorts after his morning shower, before dressing for the day. I heard him pad through the hall and down the half flight of stairs to the kitchen.

Ceramic mugs, two of them, scraped the tile countertop. He poured the coffee in slow trickles, raising the pot high above each mug. He always poured that way, claiming the bubbles in the cup made the coffee taste better—something to do with aeration. I had no idea whether this was demonstrably true, but I could hardly argue the point, as any coffee, even instant swill, would taste better when served by the likes of Tanner Griffin topless.

The stairs creaked again, and in the next moment, he appeared in the bedroom. "Time to get up." He approached the bed with both mugs of coffee.

Good God, the sight of him. On the morning when I first saw him at a garage in Palm Springs, I knew at a glance that he had "leading man" writ large all over him. The magnetism, the star quality, radiated like a nimbus. If only he could act, I had mused. Now I knew that he could indeed act—superbly—and with very little luck, he might soon enjoy a Hollywood career.

For now, though, he was still a heartthrob in training, and there he was, standing near the side of my bed, smiling down upon me with a caring expression that made me go limp. Had I been standing, my knees would have buckled. He wore the same baggy pair of olive drab cargo shorts that he'd worn that morning at the garage—and nothing else. His mop of sandy blond hair was matched by a fleecy nap that twisted from his navel and disappeared beneath the loose waistband of his shorts.

"Still sleepy?" he asked. That face. That smile. God help me.

"Hardly." My shoulder blades dug at the mattress.

"Brought you some coffee." He set my cup on the bedside table, sipping from his own before setting it down as well.

"You're the perfect overnight guest, Tanner."

He laughed. "Is *that* what I am—a guest?"

"In a manner of speaking. Though you're welcome to stay as long as you like."

He glanced around the room. "In case you haven't noticed, I've been moving a few things in." The closet was jammed. The dresser drawers couldn't accommodate everything, so some of his clothes were still stored in boxes on the floor. "Sorry if I've crowded you."

"Have you heard me complaining?"

"No." With a grin, he leaned over the bed, planting his hands on the mattress to either side of my shoulders. I felt willingly trapped, deliciously caged by him. Hovering over me, he suggested, "If you *are* feeling cramped, maybe you should be looking for a bigger place."

"That's a thought." Reaching up, I traced a finger from his throat and down his chest, hooking it in his waistband where the hair disappeared.

"Oooh," he said softly, "I just got everything tucked in."

"Too bad," I said, undoing the metal button.

"I forgot to kiss you good-morning." And he lowered his head to deliver the dilatory greeting.

I tasted coffee on his tongue, parting my lips wider so he could probe deeper. With one hand, I raked my fingers through his still-damp hair. With the other, I unzipped him. As I took hold between his legs, he surfaced from my mouth to exhale a rapturous groan.

I whispered, "I love it when men do that."

As he nuzzled into my neck, I gave him ample motivation to groan all the louder, which seemed amplified as his mouth approached my ear. When he inserted his tongue, my moan bested his groan.

There was no turning back now—not that either of us was inclined to stop. He broke away for a moment to kick free of his shorts, then crawled onto the bed, straddling me. Our lovemaking always had an element of gaming to it; we had fun. The experience of my years, to say nothing of my innate creativity, was perfectly complemented by the vigor of his youth. I still had a few tricks to teach him, and he never tired of learning. That morning's lesson required a bit of contortion, which he handled with athletic aplomb, but eventually we got back to basics, and he was giving me the ride of my life.

I lost track of time. Whether mere moments flew or long minutes passed, I couldn't tell and didn't care. Tanner had found his rhythm—and how. Though not quite frenzied, he was clearly in the zone and seemed on the verge of driving it home, so to speak.

When there came a frantic pounding at the door.

"Huh?"

Tanner hadn't heard it, focused blindly on his studly mission. The knocking continued. Someone shouted my name.

"Tanner," I whispered. Did I really want him to stop? Hell, no.

The pounding—Tanner's *and* the door's—persisted. Whoever was on my stoop would have to wait. Tanner, I was certain, could not.

"*Claire!*" It was Grant, my neighbor. "Are you home, doll?"

Tanner froze, suddenly aware of what was happening. Bug-eyed, he whispered, "What was *that?*"

"I think it's Grant."

"What does he want?"

"I have no idea." Sharp raps of the door knocker made it apparent that Grant's visit was urgent.

In a sweat, Tanner slid out of me, uncertain what to do. Still rock-hard, he appeared to be on the brink of nuclear fission.

Poor baby, I couldn't leave him in the lurch like that, so I joined him in manipulating a quick, explosive orgasm. "God," I said, pecking his cheek, "I love it when men do that." As he slumped woozily onto his back, I hopped out of bed, slipped on my robe, and traipsed down the stairs to answer the door.

"Coming!" I called. The knocking stopped only when I opened the door, flinging it wide. "Good heavens, Grant, what's wrong?"

He rushed past me, beelining for the living room, where he turned back to me, ashen and shaken. "I was just getting ready to leave for the office, when I discovered something." His shoulders slumped. "Something dreadful."

I asked the logical question: "What did you find?"

"I'd rather show you. Can you come over to my place? Please?" He moved toward the door.

"Right *now?* Grant, I just rolled out of *bed.*" He, on the other hand, was preened for the day, impeccably dressed and groomed, fresh from his twenty-minute shave.

He flicked a wrist. "You always look spectacular, doll. I must say, you seem positively energized this morning."

"What's up, guys?" Tanner interrupted us, descending the stairs with the two full mugs of coffee. He'd thrown on a robe—one of mine, red silk.

"Oh, my," said Grant, fingers to mouth, absorbing the whole scene. "I hope I didn't interrupt something."

Tanner winked at me, telling Grant, "We managed to finish." Tanner gave me a kiss, then retreated to the kitchen, where he dumped the tepid coffee and poured two fresh cupfuls.

I told him, "No time for coffee, thanks. Something's come up, and Grant needs me next door."

Tanner peered out from the kitchen. Sizing me up, he grinned. "Better dress first." As I bounded upstairs, he asked, Grant, "What's wrong?"

I heard Grant explain that he'd found something, that he'd rather not say more about it, that he wanted me to have a look. Tanner offered him coffee, but he declined. Within a minute or so, I'd thrown on a shirt, khakis, and sandals.

"This better be good," I said, meeting Grant downstairs. The front door was still open, and the hall was now chilly.

"I'm afraid," said Grant with a perplexed sigh, "this is anything but good. It is, however, extraordinarily interesting. Milady will not regret this intrusion."

I mumbled, "That's easy for you to say," recalling Tanner's passion. I should have been lying upstairs now, sated, enjoying some rapturous afterglow—but here I was, half-dressed, looking like hell, being dragged out of my home by my hysterical neighbor for some impromptu show-and-tell. I blew Tanner a kiss, waggled my fingers, then went out the door, scurrying to follow Grant's lead.

"You *won't* believe this," he said, leading me across the courtyard, past the fountain, and through his gate and front door, both left wide open. "In here," he directed, striding through the hall to the spare bedroom, where Kane's home studio was set up.

The computer was up and running. I asked, "Is Kane here?"

Grant shook his head. "He left early. He put in some late hours here at home last night, working on material for tonight's press reception. I think he had to drop something off at the printer this morning on his way to the museum."

"He's very industrious. I'm sure you're proud of him."

Grant gave me a steely stare. "When he left the house this morning, I was fussing in the bathroom, and he asked if he should leave his computer booted up for me. I've been expecting an important e-mail relating to a land deal at Nirvana, so I asked him to leave it on so I could check before going to the office." With a flourish, Grant offered, "Have a seat, Claire."

Warily (this didn't sound good), I sat in the desk chair in front of the computer terminal. The monitor displayed some snappy, dancing graphics as well as the icons for dozens of programs, none of them familiar to me. I looked over my shoulder to ask Grant, "So what's the problem? Wrong response on that e-mail?"

"There was *no* response, but that's not the problem. See this?" He tapped his fingernail on a menu that ran down the side of the screen.

I squinted. "It looks like a listing of various categories of projects that Kane has been working on."

"Correct. You'll note that one of the menu items is labeled MUSEUM. Not finding my e-mail, I became idly curious about the materials Kane has been working on for DMSA, so I moused the cursor over MUSEUM and clicked on it. Try it, Claire."

As instructed, I clicked on MUSEUM. A submenu appeared beneath it.

"Most of the file names on this sublist made sense to me," said Grant, "except the one called HISTORY."

I inferred that I should click on it, so I did. The screen blanked for a moment before displaying a new image. When it did, I gasped.

There on the large, high-resolution monitor was Stewart Chaffee's bogus interview as it had supposedly appeared in the defunct *Palm Springs Herald*. Front and back were shown side by side on the screen, with the interview on one side and the car dealer's ad on the other. Peering close, I muttered, "What the hell?"

Grant was saying, "How stupid could I get? *There's* the layout, *here's* the laser printer"—he tapped the gizmo's plastic cabinet—"and right over *there*"—he pointed to the closet that contained the stored remnants of his art-school days—"there you'll find old sketch pads with page after page of blank, brittle, yellowed newsprint. Christ." He threw his hands in disgust.

Trying to stay objective, I asked, "Can you tell when Kane worked on this?"

Grant leaned over my shoulder, moused around the screen, then clicked open a directory. "The file was last edited on Sunday night. And Stewart—" He stopped himself, not needing to remind me that Stewart was killed on Monday morning.

Befuddled, I suggested, "There must be some reasonable explanation for this."

"You *bet* there is. There's no doubt whatever: Kane forged the goddamn clipping." He didn't need to remind me of his brother Larry's words from the previous evening, which now hung in the room as if freshly spoken: Name the forger, and we've probably named Stewart Chaffee's killer.

I shook my head, unwilling to accept the reality of the damning evidence displayed on the screen. "Why would Kane do such a thing? It doesn't add up."

"But there it is"—Grant pointed at the computer. "And to think I nearly made the biggest mistake of my life. I should have sensed it all along. It was too good to be true."

Either Grant was getting loopy, or I was too dense to follow. I asked. "What was too good to be true?"

"The *relationship*. The May-December thing. The hasty move-in. And the rush toward a contractual marriage." Grant muttered, "I *wondered* why he was pushing so hard."

Okay, I was attuned to Grant's logic now, though I found it specious. He was saying, in effect, that his young lover was possibly a scheming gold digger. It was an arguable assertion, yes, but it struck me as an overly convenient accusation, an easy way to lash out when confronted with the perplexing evidence of the forged clipping. I asked Grant, "What would Kane hope to gain from this—from either Chaffee *or* you?"

"And another thing," said Grant, on a roll, on a rant. "That bruise on Kane's arm—I was suspicious from the start. I find it hard to believe that he injured himself while unloading groceries from the car. He's hardly a klutz."

"No," I agreed, "he's not."

"*Ughh.* He said he loved me. It's the oldest trick in the book."

"Now, hold on," I told him, annoyed, standing. "That profession of love was mutual, Grant. You've been head over heels lately. You've had as much at stake in this relationship as Kane has. You said you've never been happier."

"That was true—at least I *thought* I'd found happiness."

"Then what, pray tell, compelled *you* to visit the Chaffee estate on Monday morning? You told Larry and me that you went there to make sure the desk key had been delivered, but come on, that's pretty lame." I crossed my arms, demanding, "What exactly were you up to?"

Grant eyed me defiantly for a moment, but then the fight—or the anger—drained from him. He hung his head, admitting, "Your skepticism is well warranted." Looking up, he explained, "You're right. I didn't drive out to Stewart's to check on the key. I went to check on Kane."

"Did you suspect him of something?"

"Of course not." With a sad laugh, he amplified, "I suspected *Stewart* of something—that lecherous old goat. I had misgivings from the start about letting Kane deliver the key. Stewart's interest in him was embarrassingly obvious."

"I noticed." Planting my rump on the edge of the desk, I asked, "So you . . . followed Kane?"

"No, no. Nothing like that. Kane drove over there early, remember, and I tried brushing it from my mind. By nine o'clock, though, I was getting curious, not concerned, so I called the museum to ask Kane how it went. The gal on the phone said that Kane hadn't come it yet, and that's when I started to worry. After checking several times and getting the same answer, I decided to drive over to the estate and check on things myself. As you already know, I arrived there sometime after eleven. There seemed to be no one there at all, which calmed my concerns, so I left."

I nodded. This all made sense, and it was basically consistent with what he had told us before. "But why," I asked, "weren't you more forthright about your motive for going there in the first place?"

Grant paused before explaining, "Because I didn't want Kane to feel I was being jealous, suspicious, or overprotective. But now?" Grant didn't finish his thought.

"Look," I said, trying to gather my own thoughts, "Kane clearly has some connection to the forged clipping, but we don't know the exact nature of his involvement, and we'd be foolish to jump to conclusions. Worst-case scenario: Kane killed Stewart. But why would he do that? More important, why would he *plot* to do that—forging the interview on Sunday and killing the victim on Monday? He stood nothing to gain by all this."

Calmer now, Grant agreed, "Good point. Kane couldn't have been motivated by greed, which leaves the flimsy speculation that he might have killed Stewart out of self-defense or revenge. But such a murder, a crime of passion, is generally spontaneous, which would provide no connection to the Sunday forgery. Hell, it's even conceivable that someone *planted* the interview on Kane's computer." In proposing this last possibility, Grant appeared much relieved. His voice softened; his mood lightened.

The notion that Kane had been set up, however, had the opposite effect on me. It was an appealing idea—that someone had planted the forgery to cast suspicion on Kane—but if this scenario were true, who would be in a better position to pull it off than Grant himself? After all, the net effect of the phony will had been to enrich the museum that Grant served as president. I was loath to ponder it, but I had to wonder: Was Grant's "discovery" of Kane's counterfeiting part of some elaborate, deadly scheme?

Unwilling to voice that possibility, I simply asked, "So what'll we do?"

"You mean, with regard to Kane?"

"I mean, with regard to your brother. Larry needs to know about this"—I gestured toward the fraudulent clipping displayed on Kane's monitor—"but when?"

Grant paused to weigh the implications of this question. "I'd prefer to get Kane's side of the story before reporting it to the police."

"I'm sure you would. So would I."

"But if we don't tell Larry, are we withholding evidence?"

Probably, I thought. "Who knows? We're not lawyers, Grant."

"Right." His voice took on a conspiratorial timbre. "We're only trying to help."

"Exactly."

The phone on the desk rang. I jumped to my feet as if it had snapped at my ass. Grant and I glanced at each other, bug-eyed, as if caught in some unseemly machination.

Grant reached for the receiver and answered on the second ring. "Hello? Oh, hi, Larry, we were just—" Grant's eyes slid to mine.

Good God. I'd known all along that Larry Knoll was a fine detective. Was he psychic too?

Grant said into the phone, "As a matter of fact, she's right here."

Uh-oh. Larry *was* psychic. And Grant and I were probably screwed.

Grant passed me the receiver, explaining, "He called you at home, and Tanner told him you were here."

"Ahhh." Not so psychic. I chirped into the phone, "Morning, Larry."

"Hi, Claire. Listen. I just heard back from that pal of mine at the *Desert Sun*. It seems Bonnie Bahr did indeed write a number of letters to the editor in support of euthanasia. They all appeared during the year prior to her leaving hospital nursing, just before she went to work at the Chaffee estate. It took a bit of digging to piece this together."

"Why? Sloppy records at the paper?"

"Not at all. Bonnie wrote the letters under a pseudonym—to protect her job, no doubt—which slipped past the editorial staff's verification process. She supplied her real address and phone number, so when the paper called to confirm her authorship, she simply answered to her pen name. In order to straighten this out, my contact in the editorial department had to research the letters by topic. When he found several relating to mercy killing, he dug into their files for addresses. Then it was easy to determine that the real writer had been one Bonnie Bahr of Cathedral City."

"How accommodating of them."

Larry laughed. "I'm a detective working on a murder case. Whatever the paper's policy, my contact had no qualms about opening their files for me."

"I presume you're ready to confront Bonnie with this."

"Correct. I'm in the car right now, driving over from Riverside. And that's why I'm calling, Claire. You and Bonnie sort of clicked. If you'd care to meet me at her house, I think the confrontation might be easier. She seems more willing to open up to you."

"She's a woman," I noted. "So am I."

"It's more than that. You're good at this."

It was an invitation I could hardly refuse. "How soon will you arrive?"

"I'm still on the interstate. Figure thirty minutes."

That would give me enough time to put myself together and make the short drive from Palm Desert. "I'll be there, Larry."

He thanked me, and we hung up.

Grant asked, "Yet another lead?"

"Suddenly, it seems, there's no shortage of suspects." I filled him in.

"Good," said Grant. "If Larry is preoccupied with the nurse, that buys us some time with Kane."

"But not much. We need to question him quickly. When I finish up with Larry, let's meet at the museum. Kane will be there, right?"

Grant nodded. "He works in the office on Thursday mornings. Shall we meet there at, say, ten-thirty?"

I checked my wrist, but in my rush to dress, I'd neglected to put on my watch. "That sounds fine, Grant. I'll see you later."

He gave me a kiss.

As I left the room, I turned to see him staring at Kane's computer.

17

When I pulled onto the unassuming side street in Cathedral City, I saw Larry Knoll's unmarked cruiser waiting at the curb a block ahead. Larry was still sitting inside, talking on the phone. As I parked behind him, he spotted me in his mirror and waved through the rear window. As before, Bonnie Bahr's Korean compact was parked in the driveway leading to her snug stucco home.

I got out of the Beetle and paused a moment to savor the brilliant blue sky, the cool morning sun. Not relishing my mission, but eager to resolve it, I dismissed the fine weather, gathered my thoughts, and stepped to Larry's car.

He opened the door and stepped into the street to greet me. "Thanks for coming, Claire. Hope I'm not messing up your day."

"Not at all. I enjoy being involved."

"Enjoy?" He eyed me skeptically.

"I mean, I want to see the crime solved, and I'm happy to help." I didn't explain that my baser motive was to get the murder behind us because the buzz and speculation threatened the performance of a school play. Our opening was now a scant thirty-some hours away.

Larry's mind was elsewhere. "You know," he said, shaking his head, "I usually look forward to confronting a suspect with a sticky piece of evidence. Those moments are rare and often mark the turning point in a case. But this business of mercy killing—it leaves me edgy."

"You've come face-to-face with far worse," I presumed.

"Sure, but I'm not talking about the *crime* of mercy killing. I'm talking about the psychology of it, the woman behind it."

Wryly, I asked, "Nurse Ratched? She was sadistic, yes, but I doubt that anyone would describe her as merciful."

"Good point. And that's exactly what makes this so . . . well, *eerie*. I've dealt with killers who've killed with hate or killed with greed, but none who've killed with kindness."

"It sounds as if you think she's guilty."

"At the moment, I have no better theory. Do you?"

"No." Nor could I think of any feasible connection between Bonnie Bahr and the fake newspaper clipping on Kane's computer, which was now clearly part of the riddle, one that Larry knew nothing about. If Bonnie had killed Stewart, was it mere coincidence that someone else had forged the clipping? This struck me as highly implausible.

As we walked up the driveway, brushing past Bonnie's parked car, I asked, "Is she expecting us?"

"Me, yes. You, no." The setup was the same as on Tuesday.

So was our reception. Bonnie answered the door, apologizing for having kept us waiting (which she hadn't) because the TV was too loud (which it was). She showed no surprise that I had tagged along again, extending a warm welcome. Turning to Larry, she said, "I'm at your service, Detective, but I must admit, I'm sorta curious about the return visit. You said it was urgent?"

Larry fudged, "Perhaps that was an overstatement. May we come in?"

"Certainly. Please." She ushered us through the door and into the living room, which was semidarkened, as before, for enhanced television viewing. A commercial for some hemorrhoid medication blared too cheerily from the big-screen behemoth in the corner. Bonnie switched it off before settling on her recliner. She wore white nurse's pants and duty shoes with another mismatched flouncy smock.

Larry and I sat, as before, on the nubby green couch, flanked by two huge table lamps. He took out his notebook, flipped it open, and reviewed a page for a moment. I studied the dreary quarters of a lonely woman who had lost her job—and had possibly slain her employer.

She ventured, "I assume you've made some discoveries, Detective."

Larry glanced up from his notes. "Why do you say that?"

She shrugged. "This meeting. When you left here on Tuesday, you seemed at a loss to explain Mr. Chaffee's death. But when you phoned this morning, you left the distinct impression that something had happened."

He confirmed, "There *has* been a new development, but I'm not sure what bearing it has on the case. It may mean nothing, or everything. Perhaps you can help me sort it out."

"I'll try."

Larry closed his notebook, recalling, "On Tuesday, you were telling us about the transition you made from hospital nursing to home care—two years ago, when you went to work at the Chaffee estate."

She nodded. "It was the best move I ever made in my life, a sound career decision. I'm at loose ends right now, but that's mostly due to the shock of how Stewart died."

I asked her, "Then you'll be seeking another position in home care?"

"Well, sure. I have to work. And I wouldn't go back to hospital nursing if you *paid* me." She laughed, a tad embarrassed. "I mean, of course they'd pay me, but I have no interest in it."

"We understand," said Larry. "Miss Bahr, I wonder if I might ask you, was there any other reason you made this career shift two years ago?"

Eyes to the ceiling, she recapped, ticking off on her fingers, "Impossible hours. Bureaucratic quagmire. Inflexible regulation." Her gaze returned to Larry. "What other reason would anyone *need*, Detective?"

He paused. "I'm not sure how to broach this, but it came to our attention that your departure from hospital nursing may not have been your own decision."

"That's plain silly—" she started to say. Then her face went hard. "Who told you this?"

"I'm not at liberty to say, but—"

She interrupted, sitting bolt upright. "It was Pea, wasn't it? That contemptible little pissant!"

"It's not important who said it."

"The *hell* it isn't. Don't you know mean-mouthed gossip when you hear it? Consider the source, Detective. What's *he* hiding, that he has to go spreading malicious hearsay?"

Calmly, Larry assured her, "If it were only hearsay, I wouldn't be here."

She sat back, asking through a wary squint, "What does that mean?"

Larry glanced at me with an expression suggesting that I was better suited to lay our cards on the table—woman to woman, I guess.

"Bonnie," I began, "it *was* a rumor, and secondhand at that. There was talk that you hadn't left hospital nursing because of the conditions, but because you were pressured to leave."

She insisted, "My record speaks for itself."

"It well may, but it seems your departure was negotiated off the record. The issue was"—I paused, I may have gulped—"euthanasia."

Larry added, "Mercy killing."

She shot at him, "I *know* the term."

"Apparently quite well," I said. "We heard that you'd written a number of letters to the editor of the local newspaper in support of mercy killing. This was two or three years ago. I imagine the debate was fueled when Dr. Kevorkian popped into the headlines again."

"But, Claire," she said, smiling, pleading to be believed, "that's nuts. I'm a *nurse*. I would never take such a stand—certainly not in print."

Larry told her, "Before you go too far with that denial, you should be aware that we've already looked into this. I checked with the *Desert Sun,* and they traced several published pro-euthanasia letters to this address and phone number." He checked his notes. "They were signed by a Marjorie Horne, but clearly, that was your pseudonym—unless someone else was living here two years ago."

She frowned, then heaved a sigh. "Oh, hell. Since you seem to know all about it, there's no point in saying it didn't happen. I must've been stupid."

I asked her quietly, "Why would you write such letters?"

Her tone was candid and direct. "Because I believed what I wrote."

Larry asked, "Do you still believe in mercy killing?"

"Look," she said, leaning forward, elbows to knees, "it's a *philosophy*, an idea. In my heart of hearts, yes, I support euthanasia—in principle. But I'm well aware it's against the law—in practice. I'm also well aware that mercy killing runs contrary to medical ethics, but honestly, I don't know how anyone who's seen what I've seen can possibly argue that it's noble or righteous to prolong a hopeless, painful, or vegetative life."

Larry posited, "And those views ended your hospital career."

"They sure did. Word got around about my letters—I still don't know how—and eventually the hospital administration confronted me with the rumor. They threatened a full-blown investigation and a much-publicized purge, offering me the alternative of a quiet resignation with an unblemished record. Easy choice, huh?"

I almost felt sorry for Bonnie. At the very least, I admired her integrity and sympathized with her dilemma, though I still had trouble with her underlying belief. I asked, "Have you ever had a terminally ill patient ask for assistance in ending his life?"

"No," she answered at once, "thank God. That really *would* be a pickle. But no, I've never faced such a decision."

Larry said, "Then you're telling us that you never even considered euthanizing Stewart Chaffee, correct?"

"*Detective,*" she said, aghast, splaying a hand on her chest, "you can't seriously think that *I* had anything to do with Stewart's death. He had some problems, sure—he was eighty-two, for God's sake. But he was *not* terminally ill, and he led a very comfortable life. What's more, he demonstrated a strong will to live. You should have seen the way he applied himself to physical therapy—this was *not* a man at the brink of the grave. Why, I doubt that Kevorkian himself would have judged Stewart a candidate for euthanasia. And besides"—Bonnie's tone turned huffy—"if I'd wanted to kill Stewart, I would have devised a means considerably more finessed than crushing him with a refrigerator!"

Larry reminded her, "But someone did precisely that."

"So you've said. But it wasn't me. Get this straight: Stewart Chaffee was alive and well, sleeping peacefully, when I left the estate on Monday morning."

"And when was that?" Larry had his notes open in front of him. He was doubtless checking whether her story would remain consistent.

"I arrived around nine and left within ten minutes." Bonnie's account of the events stayed the same, though we still had no way to verify her departure time.

Larry closed his notes. "Then we're left with a total mystery." His tone seemed to ask, Any suggestions?

Bonnie tisked. "Come now, Detective. If you need a suspect, he's been under your nose all along."

Larry arched his brows naively.

"Pea!" she blurted. "He and Stewart had a past. He resented that he'd been reduced to domestic help, and I'll bet he expected to inherit a fortune. If that's not a recipe for murder, I don't know what is." She ranted on, building her case against a scheming, nefarious little houseman. Though most of her accusations were emotional, even irrational, her basic argument was sound—Pea had harbored resentment and expectations.

What's more, Bonnie presumably didn't know that Pea had arrived at the house from the gym that morning at nine-thirty, after she claimed to have left. But Larry and I were privy to this detail, which lent credence to Bonnie's accusation. On the other hand, Bonnie and Pea's mutual hostility had been vented repeatedly, so her current denouncements could have been based on nothing more than spite.

"I don't know." Larry scratched behind an ear.

I echoed his skepticism, explaining to Bonnie, "Pea told us that he and Stewart were lovers for only a few years, early on. He was majordomo for nearly two *decades*. Sure, he may have felt downgraded by his menial circumstances, but he had plenty of time to get used to it. It seems to me that if he was going to turn vengeful, he'd have done it long ago. Even if he did have a general, gnawing sense of resentment, that alone wouldn't have provided a sufficient motive for murder."

Bonnie stood, paced once in front of the sofa, then faced us with resolve. "But there's more."

Larry and I exchanged a glance. He asked Bonnie, "There's something you haven't told us?"

She stood before us, nodding in such a way that her whole body wobbled. "This isn't the sort of thing I like talking about—it's downright indecent. And I hate to besmirch the memory of Mr. Chaffee. But the truth is, Pea had good reason to hate him, at least in his own mind." Bonnie bit her lower lip, hard, as if punishing herself for having said so much.

I asked gently, "What are you trying to say?"

She sniffed a short, sharp breath. "It started about a year ago. I'd already been working there for a year, so this was something new. It had *not* been going on for two decades; it was definitely a late addition to Pea's job description. If he resented his other duties, he *hated* this one."

Larry had opened his notebook again. "Tell us about it."

Bonnie turned from us, crossed to the window, and seemed to stare through the closed curtains. "During the last year, Pea began procuring for Stewart the services of young boys."

"Services?" asked Larry, though we both understood what she meant.

"Yes," said Bonnie, turning to us, "sexual services. Pea arranged for these visits with increasing regularity, sometimes while I was in the house, if you can believe it. Pea was embarrassed and angry, I could tell, but Stewart certainly enjoyed himself." With a note of disgust, she added, "The old goat."

I was tempted to ask her to be more explicit in describing these services—nosy me—but I refrained.

Larry asked, "When you say 'boys,' how old do you mean?"

"Too damn young for the likes of Mr. Chaffee!" She stepped to her lounger and tidied a few items on the end table, picking up the brochure from the Living Desert Reserve.

Larry persisted, "Are we talking, say, twelve, or more like twenty?"

Bonnie looked appalled. "Shame on you, Detective. They were *college* boys."

"I see." He scratched through something on his pad.

Listening to these revelations, I was struck by a different twist. "Bonnie, I can understand why these procurement duties might change Pea's attitude toward Stewart. Did Stewart's sexual peccadillos also sour your own attitude to him?"

"They didn't help," she admitted.

"Did you feel so strongly about the situation that you needed to stop it?"

Bonnie exhaled a long, low groan. She seemed to wilt before our eyes. "I know this may sound like a double standard—that it was wrong for Pea and okay for Stewart—but that *is* the way I felt. Stewart had little joy left in his life: paintings, fancy furniture, pink fluff, and these boys. He wasn't hurting anyone, and they got paid, so I guess it was a fair exchange. If I found it unseemly, too bad. Stewart didn't need my permission or approval. I was working for *him,* remember. He was generous and he was kind, at least when he wasn't crabbing. He let me into a world I'd never seen before." She glanced down at the brochure in her hands, at the smiling meerkats on the cover. With a whimper, she concluded, "I still miss him."

Softly, I said, "Of course you do. He's been gone just three days." I was about to add, Time heals all wounds, but I spared her the platitude.

"Perhaps you haven't heard," said Larry. "There's going to be a ceremony at the new art museum tomorrow night honoring Mr. Chaffee and his bequest. You might find it comforting to attend." It was a thoughtful suggestion on Larry's part, but I also understood that he was jockeying to bring all the possible suspects, including Bonnie, together at the event.

She brightened some. "Thank you, Detective. I *would* like to be there. It's the least I can do."

We rose, thanked her for her cooperation, wished her happier days, and left.

Walking to the street with me, Larry said, "The call boys—that's a whole new wrinkle. I like it."

I agreed, "It might have been enough to push Pea over the brink."

"I need to talk to him, and soon. Care to be in on it?"

I checked my watch; it was nearly ten-thirty. "I'd love to, Larry, but I'm due on campus for an important meeting."

"After lunch, then, at the estate. I'll set it up. One-thirty?"

"Perfect. See you then." I got into my car.

Before getting into his own car, Larry said brightly, "Don't work too hard." He assumed my meeting on campus related to classes or the play.

I waved and tootled off in the direction of Desert Arts College, where the true purpose of my meeting was to determine why the young lover of the detective's brother had created on his home computer a forged interview with a murder victim.

18

Shortly past ten-thirty, I had parked in my space in the faculty garage and was rushing across College Circle toward the Desert Museum of Southwestern Arts. The workers who, yesterday, had been installing lighting fixtures on the building's facade were occupied today with another task, mounting two long banners from the museum's cantilevered roof. Dangling on either side of the main entrance, one of the banners featured the huge, menacing image of a kachina from a distant galaxy, along with dates of the opening exhibit. The other simply proclaimed, in bold letters running vertically, THE CHAFFEE LEGACY, along with the years of his birth and death.

Entering the sun-filled lobby, I noted at once that the air-conditioning had been tweaked and now kept the space at a chilly but tolerable temperature. Yesterday's boisterous construction workers had been replaced by a stolid cleaning crew, mostly Latino women, who feverishly detailed the lobby's stone floor, massive windows, and gleaming chrome trim. Twins of the kachina and Chaffee banners hung from the ceiling, flanking the entrance to the main gallery, which appeared dark and empty.

Not sure whether Grant had yet arrived, I turned down the corridor that led to the museum offices, when I heard Grant call after me from the lobby. He had just entered the building and now rushed across the expansive, marble-paved room in my direction. "Sorry I'm late," he said as he neared. "I was tied up in a meeting at Nirvana. Have you seen Kane?"

"I was just going to look for him—and you. Are we expected?"

Grant nodded, catching his breath. "I called earlier, suggesting he have lunch with us, but he declined, saying he's too busy preparing for tonight's event. So I told him we'd drop by to say hello and have a look at everything."

"And everything's looking good." I nodded my approval.

Grant glanced about, agreeing, "Major strides since yesterday."

With a forbidding tone, I reminded him, "When D. Glenn Yeats sets deadlines, few dare fail."

Grant took my arm. "Let's find Kane." And he escorted me toward the suite of offices at the rear of the building.

The main office was bright, modern, and efficient, beautifully designed but more utilitarian than luxurious. A receptionist greeted Grant while fumbling with the new phone system. Losing a call, she mumbled an expletive deriding the march of technology. We waved to Iesha, who looked up briefly from a knot of staffers around her desk, returning the salute. Her huge, primitive pounded-brass necklace (it reminded me of a personal-size gong, decorated with multicolored glass dangles) banged and clattered as she leaned over the desk again. "In here," Grant told me, turning into a separate, smaller office, its door wide-open.

"Oh, hi!" said Kane, looking up from his computer terminal, smiling at the sight of Grant. His soft yellow polo shirt accentuated the deep tan of his face and arms, even under the sterile glare of fluorescent lights.

"You sound surprised to see us." Grant stepped to his young lover, who stood for a hug, a quick kiss.

"Just absorbed in one of these projects. Time really gets away from you." Then Kane acknowledged me, "Morning, Claire."

"Good morning, Kane. It looks as if everything is pulling together splendidly for tonight's big bash."

"It's what you *don't* see that has me worried." He began ticking through a list of unfinished projects, then stopped himself, telling us, "I'll spare you the lurid details."

Grant took a breath, paused, then asked, "Can you spare us a minute?"

There was something in the tone of the question that made Kane's face wrinkle. "Sure, Grant. For you and Claire, anytime. What's up?"

Grant hesitated, looking around. "Is there somewhere we could go to talk?" He added, "Somewhere more private."

Warily, Kane said, "This sounds serious." When we didn't respond, he suggested, "How about the main gallery. There's nothing cozy about it, but the workers are finished in there, for now, so we'll have the space to ourselves."

He led us out of the offices, returning to the lobby, then turning into the dark, gaping space of the gallery, where he switched on a few lights. "Will this be okay? Is something wrong?"

"This is fine," said Grant. "Let's sit down." There were a number of black boxes, display cubes, arranged throughout the space, but few of them held anything. There was a sparse arrangement of Indian artifacts in a Plexiglas case at the far side of the room, but otherwise, the gallery contained no art. Choosing a cluster of these vacant cubes near the center of the floor, Kane sat on one, and Grant and I faced him, sitting together on a larger one.

Kane repeated, "Is something wrong?"

Grant said, "I don't know. I hope not. But Claire and I discovered something this morning that's very disturbing."

Great, I thought. Pin it on me. The discovery was Grant's; he'd merely shared it with me.

Kane gave us a quizzical stare. If he felt guilt or panic at Grant's words, he hid it well. He simply looked confused, asking, "What did you find?"

Grant began, "After you left the house, I was on your computer—"

"Yeah. I left it on for you. Did you get that e-mail you needed?"

"Uh, no, it hadn't come in yet. So I was frustrated and a little bored. And I did a bit of browsing. I ended up going into some of your files."

"Okay . . ." Kane seemed neither surprised nor worried nor defensive. In fact, he pulled both feet up onto the cube, crossing his legs like a kindergartner (looking adorable, I must say—good for Grant). Kane asked, "And you found something . . . 'disturbing'?"

"Well, *yes,*" Grant answered, suddenly agitated. "For God's sake, Kane, I opened one of your museum files, the one labeled HISTORY, and it contained the interview with Stewart Chaffee that had *supposedly* appeared in a 1954 issue of the *Palm Springs Herald*." Grant crossed his arms, saying, in effect, that he'd said his fill.

But Kane's only reaction to this revelation was a continued look of confusion.

Perhaps, I thought, Kane's confusion stemmed from genuine lack of knowledge of the document that had been forged on his computer. Perhaps, as we had earlier speculated, someone else had planted it there, attempting to frame the kid for Chaffee's murder. I suggested, "You knew nothing about it?"

With a puzzled laugh, he blurted, "I know *everything* about it."

Grant and I looked at each other with blank, dumb astonishment.

Kane continued, "Of *course* I know about the Chaffee interview. I made it myself—on the computer in our spare bedroom." With a touch of pride, he fished, "Not bad, huh?"

"*Kane,*" said Grant, "do you have any idea of what you're saying—and implying? Don't you realize how serious this is?"

"Uh, no." The kid uncrossed his legs and sat up straight. "Sorry. What am I missing here?" He beaded Grant with an inquisitive stare.

Grant recited coldly, "You've just admitted forging an interview with Stewart Chaffee on your own computer. I checked the file and determined that you finished it on Sunday night. On Monday morning, you visited Stewart. He was found dead later that day, and on Tuesday, the fake clipping surfaced and was interpreted as Stewart's will, leaving a fortune to this museum—the same museum that *you* work for and *I* serve as board president. Don't you understand? Anyone might conclude that you and I plotted and executed this—and I know damn well that *I* did no such thing."

Kane now had a full grasp of the situation, insisting, "I had *nothing* to do with that old guy's death."

"And another thing," said Grant, reaching toward Kane, raising the sleeve of his polo shirt. "That bruise. How did it happen? Don't try to tell me the car door hit you—that's crap. And where were you for the rest of Monday morning? After you delivered the key to Stewart, I tried phoning you here at the museum, several times, and you hadn't arrived. What's going on, Kane?"

Rising from the cube where he'd been sitting, the college kid seemed both angered and amused. He told Grant, "You've asked me, like, about a dozen questions: Why was the clipping on my computer? How did I get the bruise? Where was I on Monday morning? What's going on?" Kane planted his hands on his hips. "Is there any particular order in which you'd like me to respond, Your Honor?"

"Don't get smart with me."

"Don't *you* play dad with *me*. You're my lover, not my parent. I want to 'marry' you, Grant. I love you. So you need to give me the benefit of the doubt sometimes. How could you possibly jump to such awful conclusions?"

Grant's mind was surely in a spin. The computer file was all but damning evidence against the young man Grant had brought into his home. Grant had understood, intellectually if not in his heart, that his attraction to Kane had been pure infatuation, but he'd thrown caution to the wind in merging their lives. Kane had recently been pressuring him to go a step further, to make their relationship contractually binding. Grant was now rudely sobered by that morning's discovery, forcing him to weigh their future prospects with a clearer head.

Still, Kane had just asked him for the benefit of the doubt, and based on their three months together, which had been totally loving—rapturous beyond Grant's jaded dreams—he was now inclined to suspend judgment and explore the situation rationally. He said softly, "Let's start with the clipping. What happened?"

"Okay," said Kane, gathering his thoughts. He began pacing as he spoke. "On Sunday afternoon, I was working here at the museum, putting in some extra hours. We were hustling to get the kachina exhibit ready for the museum's opening."

Grant nodded, recalling, "You helped Claire and me return the Biedermeier desk to the Chaffee estate that morning, and you said you'd be spending the rest of the day here."

"Right. And that's exactly what I did. There was a lot going on that afternoon, preparing both the building and the exhibit. I took a short break, and as I walked through the lobby, this guy asked to talk to me."

"Who?" both Grant and I asked.

"Someone from the school. I think he said he was Professor Eastman. He was involved with mounting a display that would chronicle the museum's history."

I recalled Kane mentioning a history display on Wednesday morning. "When you asked about it yesterday, Iesha said that no such exhibit had been planned."

"I know. But that's what the guy told me; someone must've been confused. Anyway, he explained that an important part of the museum's history was contained in a newspaper clipping, but that it was tattered with age and needed to remain safely in the school's files. So the museum needed a convincing reproduction for display purposes, and since they needed it fast, they'd pay some nice overtime. He gave me a few sheets of old newsprint, a photocopy of an old advertisement, and typewritten text of the interview itself. It was an interesting challenge, and I enjoyed working on it."

Kane sat down again, continuing, with considerable enthusiasm, "I brought the project home that evening, where I could work on it without distraction. First, I had to typeset the interview; then I had to lay it out newspaper-style. I scanned the old ad for a car dealer and put it on the back side. For the interview, I even morphed the various typefaces with antiqued or 'distressed' fonts so the typesetting wouldn't look too clean; it had to have the appearance of an old letterpress job. Which it did, except for being laser-printed, of course. But no one has an eye *that* good."

He hadn't met Mark Manning.

Grant asked, "When did you deliver the forged—" He stopped, rephrasing, "When did you deliver your work?"

"Monday morning, after my trip to the Chaffee estate with the desk key, I came directly here to campus. I was crossing the plaza, and the guy called my name; he was just coming out of the museum. I was glad he caught me because I was on my way to class. I gave him the project, which he looked at quickly, saying it was great. Then he gave me a hundred dollars in cash and thanked me for putting in the overtime."

"Didn't you find that a little strange?"

"Kind of, I guess. But he said the school preferred to handle overtime out of petty cash in order to avoid some paperwork or something. I don't know how this stuff works. Besides, it was a hundred bucks."

I could understand that Kane might not have a grasp of accounting procedures within a bureaucratic, hierarchical institution, but I was certain he'd been lied to in this respect. It was inconceivable that Glenn Yeats would allow cash payments for his employees' overtime. Further, in my three months at Desert Arts College, I'd met most of the faculty and had no recollection of a Professor Eastman. I asked Kane, "What did he look like?"

"He was older." Kane shrugged. "He wore black."

Great, I thought. Anyone over thirty was "older" in Kane's eyes, and half the faculty wore arty, trendy black.

Kane added, "Both of our meetings were so rushed, he didn't make much of an impression on me."

"Would you know him if you saw him again?"

"Maybe."

Grant had been quiet through much of this conversation, weighing what Kane told us. It was an odd story, to say the least, but no odder than the notion that Kane himself had plotted Stewart Chaffee's demise. Also, the story was consistent with everything we'd already known or heard, including Kane's previous reference to the history display.

Clearly, Grant wanted to believe Kane's explanation of why the clipping was forged. With a note of relief, he said, "Now tell us about that bruise."

Kane hesitated. "You're not gonna like this."

"Then it had nothing to do with a car door?"

"No. It happened Monday morning, when I delivered the key to the estate."

Closing his eyes, Grant asked with restrained composure, "How?"

Kane blew a mouthful of air from his lips, as if expelling something distasteful from his gut. "I drove over there early with the key, arriving shortly after eight. I buzzed the intercom. No one answered, but the gate slid open, and I drove in. When I got to the front door, I rang the bell, and the old guy himself answered it. It took him a while to get to the door; he was in his wheelchair. He offered 'treats,' but I said no and just handed him the key."

So far, Kane's recounting of the incident was consistent with what he'd told us at breakfast on Tuesday. Now the story veered along a different course. "But when I gave him the key," Kane continued, squirming some, "the old man tried to pull me forward, like he wanted to kiss me or something. I'm not sure *what* he wanted, but I didn't feel like sticking around to find out. So I pulled back, naturally. But—this is sort of embarrassing—he didn't let go, and I lost my footing. I fell smack on my ass, banging my arm on the wheelchair as I went down, hard. I was sort of stunned, and that old fart just sat there, laughing at me. I got up, and I got the hell out. I could hear that fucker laughing through the *door*."

"Oh, Kane," said Grant, "I'm so sorry, letting you go there alone. I felt in my *bones* that it was a bad idea. I should have known Stewart would try something. In fact, I felt sure he *would*."

"Hey," said Kane, emerging from the anger that had colored the telling of his story, "no harm was done—except the bruise, and that'll heal." He was an attractive young man, used to occasional pawing, willing to brush it off.

Grant asked, "Why didn't you tell us this before?"

Kane leveled, "I thought it would make you mad."

"Well," Grant admitted with a quiet laugh, "it does. But I'm not angry with *you,* Kane. It was Stewart's transgression, not yours. Monday morning, I had a hunch something had gone wrong. I was *worried* about you, not angry. That's why I tried phoning you here at the museum. When you hadn't arrived by eleven, I decided to visit the estate. I hate to ask, but just where were you?"

"Simple. I was in class. I don't work on Monday mornings. I have a design lab from nine till noon."

I reminded Grant, "Kane told us not five minutes ago that he was crossing College Circle on his way to class when our mysterious man in black called his name and took delivery of the computer-generated newspaper clipping." I hardly needed to add that Kane's class schedule was a matter of record, easily verified.

Kane continued, telling Grant, "Whoever you talked to in the museum office must not have been familiar with my hours."

"Oh, Lord . . . ," said Grant, rising, extending his arms. "Come here."

Kane stood, stepped to Grant, and shared a long hug. After several moments of soppy dialogue (I felt like a voyeur, but had no graceful means of excusing myself), Kane said with a smirk, "Now, then. If you're satisfied I'm not a killer, can I get back to work?"

"Sure. But can't you join us for lunch?"

Kane checked his watch. "It's barely *eleven*. Even so, I've got way too much going on here. Thanks, though."

He, Grant, and I strolled from the gallery to the lobby, where Kane said good-bye and headed back toward the offices. Moving down the corridor, he passed Iesha coming out, who spotted us and signaled for us to wait. Her brass breastplate clanged as she bustled toward us.

Arriving in the lobby, she greeted us, adding, "Didn't mean to seem rude back in the office. There's just so *much* going on."

Grant smiled. "That was quite a huddle you were trapped in."

"With the press conference tonight—and the official opening to-morrow night—there's *more* than enough to huddle over. Kane, by the way, has been a godsend. I think we're actually going to make it *through* all this, but it wouldn't have been possible without his help. He's a good worker, smart too. Sure, Glenn Yeats has given us plenty of support, with Tide and the rest of his staff, but Kane has been indispensable in getting our printed material together. He's a wonderful intern. Thanks for bringing him to our attention."

"He's a great kid," Grant acknowledged, sounding more like a proud dad than a doting lover.

I, too, admired Kane, and though I didn't seriously suspect that he'd had an active connection to Stewart Chaffee's death, I thought it best to confirm a few points with Iesha. Questioning her, I learned that, first, there was no Professor Eastman on the art faculty or museum staff. Second, the museum had been short-staffed on Monday, and someone inexperienced had taken over phone duties that day; this explained why Grant had been told that Kane was late arriving for work when, actually, he was in class, as scheduled. Finally, Iesha reiterated that there had never been plans for a history display relating to the new museum's opening.

As we wrapped up our conversation, into our midst strolled our esteemed college president, D. Glenn Yeats. Entering the lobby, he greeted the cleaning crew like a beneficent monarch, tossing out not coins, but dribs and drabs of textbook Spanish.

"*¡Hola!*" he told us, keeping up the act as he approached.

We wished him a good morning in English.

He asked Iesha, "Everything set for tonight's big event?"

"Yes, sir. Everyone's been notified. The building's in great shape. We'll have a delivery from the printer this afternoon."

"And the exhibit in the main gallery?"

She grimaced. "We put together what we could, but I'm afraid it may seem overwhelmed by the space."

Glenn frowned. "Let's have a look." Turning, he strode from the lobby through the doorway to the gallery, still lit from our meeting there with Kane.

"Good *God*," his voice boomed in the near-empty room as we followed him inside, "don't you think it's looking a bit bare?" He gazed down at the meager Plexiglas display case. Centered among the several objects within it was the ceremonial ring Grant had received at the bank on Tuesday. The rest consisted of a beaded pouch, a feathered doodad of unfathomable purpose, a tattered moccasin, and a few broken clay vessels. "This is pathetic."

Iesha explained, "That's everything from our collection that had been donated by Mr. Chaffee over the years."

Glenn sputtered, "But . . . but what about the bequest? We need something showy as a backdrop for the announcement tonight. It's a photo op, for cry-eye!" His oaths were generally mild.

"To the best of my knowledge," said Iesha, "Mr. Chaffee's collection is still tied up in probate along with the entire estate."

"But the museum is the sole beneficiary. No one has come forward to contest the will. Why can't—"

"I just had a thought," Grant interrupted. "We need to procure something flashy from Stewart's collection, and it may be difficult to get anything out of storage in time for this evening. The house itself, though, is also filled with art, and Stewart was particularly proud of a recent acquisition, a set of some dozen obscure Swedish neo-impressionist works. There's nothing Southwestern about them, but they're newsworthy—and accessible. Stewart had them displayed on easels in his family room."

I updated Grant. "When I was there on Tuesday with your brother, Pea had been doing some organizing and packing. The Swedish paintings were no longer on their easels, but stacked against a wall. I'm not sure if they're still there."

Glenn told us, "I'd like to get them—if only for tonight."

Grant nodded. "Tell you what. Claire and I can pop over to the bank in Indian Wells. Merrit Lloyd is acting as executor of the estate, so he should know the disposition of everything. He's an agreeable sort of guy. Let's see if he can help us arrange to get those paintings quickly."

"It's worth a try," said Iesha.

"Do it," said Glenn.

So Grant and I did it.

Riding to the bank together in Grant's car, we compared notes on that morning's revelations. We both wanted to believe Kane's explanation of how and why he had produced the fake clipping. "Unfortunately," said Grant, eyes on the road, "Kane's story, combined with that bruise, would be found highly suspicious by someone more objective than us." He was referring to someone like a detective, someone like his brother, Larry Knoll.

"I hate to suggest this," I said, "but given Kane's relationship to you, and given your relationship to DMSA, it's conceivable that Kane's forgery would cast *you* in a suspicious light."

Grant's knuckles blanched on the steering wheel. "That worrisome little wrinkle has indeed crossed my mind."

"Grant," I said, touching his arm, "Larry needs to be told this—*all* of this."

With a barely perceptible nod, Grant agreed, "Of course. And soon. But it's a question of when." He pulled the car into the bank's parking lot. It was around eleven-fifteen.

"Our best strategy," I thought aloud, "is to plunge ahead with this evening's press reception. Unless I'm mistaken, the event should be an irresistible lure for Stewart's killer. Larry will be there, and with any luck, he could resolve this on the spot, rendering irrelevant the issue of Kane's forgery." Not only that, I told myself, but a speedy resolution would put the murder behind us and allow my cast to focus on the opening of *Laura*—the hidden, selfish priority behind my involvement in the investigation.

Grant braked the car and cut the engine. "Even when Kane is

exonerated—well, I *hope* that'll be the outcome—it's still reasonable to assume that the forged clipping *is* relevant to the murder. So the mystery boils down to this: Who commissioned the forgery? Who's the man in black?"

"We know he's not who he said he was. We don't even know if he works at the school. It could be *anyone*." Feeling hopelessly adrift, I heaved a sigh of exasperation.

"First things first," said Grant, sounding a more positive note. "Let's check on those Swedish masterpieces." He opened his door.

"*Minor* Swedish neo-impressionist masterpieces," I corrected him smugly as we got out of the car.

When we entered the bank's stylish lobby, the receptionist said, "My, that was fast." We'd phoned on our way over. "I'll inform Mr. Lloyd that you've arrived."

Moments later, Merrit Lloyd's secretary appeared. With a smile and a brisk handshake for each of us, Robin said, "Our quiet morning has turned rather busy. Your brother is here, Mr. Knoll. He arrived a few minutes ago, right after you called."

"Larry's here?" Grant's brow wrinkled.

I thought aloud, "Wonder what he wants."

Robin said, "He's with Mr. Lloyd right now, but they said to send you in."

So she led us back to Merrit's office, announced us at the door, then excused herself to deal with a deskful of work. Merrit's desk of concrete and steel was as sleek and unencumbered as on my previous visits.

Merrit and Larry, seated at the conference table away from the desk, rose as we entered. During our round of greetings, Larry and I made no reference to having seen each other earlier that morning at Bonnie Bahr's home, and Larry showed no surprise that I was now in the company of his brother. This was doubtless no more than simple discretion, but it left me with the uneasy sense that all of us, myself included, were harboring secrets.

Merrit closed his office door and invited everyone to sit. He seemed distracted.

As we settled around the table, Larry told Grant and me, "I felt it was time to bring Merrit up to speed with regard to the clipping. I've just told him that we have reason to suspect that the Stewart Chaffee interview may have been forged."

May have been forged? Although Larry had no knowledge of Kane's involvement, he already knew for a fact that the laser-printed interview was not genuine. Why was his revelation to the banker less than forthright? Perhaps he meant to leave room for discussion, hoping Merrit might float some theories, pro and con. Or perhaps Larry just wanted to soften the news.

If the latter, it didn't work. "This is shocking," Merrit told us flatly, as if his emotions had been numbed. "If word of this got out, it could wreak great damage to the bank's reputation and integrity. News of a possible forgery might even make it appear that *we* had some role in the subterfuge—or, at best, that we'd let our guard down."

Larry said, "Then let's keep this knowledge to ourselves. There's no reason to go public with this angle of the investigation, and in fact, there's considerable reason *not* to. As of right now, we in this room are the only ones who know about the possible forgery."

"And Mark Manning," Grant reminded him.

Larry nodded.

Merrit mulled the name for a moment; then it clicked. "The reporter? Oh, God." He mopped his brow with the back of his hand.

"Don't worry," I told him, "Mark isn't here on assignment."

"So it's important," Larry emphasized, "that this new information not leave this room. Besides, there are several ways a faked clipping could have gotten into Chaffee's safe-deposit box, and they don't necessarily reflect badly on the bank."

"Oh?" asked Merrit, eager for any consolation.

"Sure." Larry took out his notebook and checked a list he'd made. "The way I see it, there are three ways this could have happened. First, Chaffee himself could have forged the clipping, put it in an envelope, then given it to you on Saturday."

Merrit nodded, finding the theory feasible. "But why," he asked, "would Stewart bother with the fabrication?"

He and Larry proceeded to discuss this detail, but I knew they were on the wrong track. Stewart hadn't faked the clipping on Saturday; Kane had done it on Sunday.

"So here's a second possibility," Larry suggested. "Someone *else* forged the clipping and let Stewart unwittingly give it to you on Saturday. Stewart thought there was something else in the envelope, perhaps a homemade will."

"Yeah," said Grant, "why not? Someone in Stewart's household—like Pea or the nurse—could have switched the documents."

They examined this possibility at some length, weighing motives and logistics, but again, I knew they were following a false lead. Kane had not forged the clipping until Sunday, so it could not have been given to Merrit by Stewart on Saturday—unless, good grief, there were two forgeries. My mind was spinning.

"Or," said Larry, "there's a third possibility. Something else was in the envelope on Saturday, presumably a homemade will. Then, later, someone switched the envelopes."

"It was a plain white business envelope," Merrit recalled. "It would be easy to produce an indistinguishable substitute."

Larry checked back through his notes. "When was Chaffee's envelope placed in the vault?"

"On Saturday, early afternoon, after returning to the bank from our morning meeting at the estate."

"Who might have had access to Chaffee's strongbox between Saturday afternoon, when the envelope was deposited, and Tuesday morning, when you opened the envelope and found the clipping?"

Merrit shook his head. "Aside from myself, only Stewart had access. He had the only key outside the bank." Merrit's features brightened as he posited, "Stewart's key could have been duplicated by *anyone*—household help, for instance—or stolen after he was killed."

I asked Larry, "Do we know the whereabouts of Stewart's key?"

"Sorry. The issue wasn't relevant till now."

Trying to inject a lighter note, Merrit told Grant, "You've been awfully quiet. It's a good thing *you* didn't have access to the box. As president of the museum board, you might be seen as a *highly* motivated suspect."

Larry joined Merrit in laughing at this scenario.

Grant and I found no humor in it—other than the grim variety.

Merrit rose from the table, stepped to the door, and opened it. "Robin," he said, "could you get the log of bank customers given access to the vault since last weekend, please?"

A minute later, Robin joined us in the office, placing a leather-bound ledger on the conference table. Merrit turned to the page of vault activity on Saturday, and finding nothing unusual, flipped to Monday, the day of Stewart's death. "Oh," he said, pointing to an entry, "Pea Fertig was in the vault during the noon hour." His in-flection conveyed mild surprise but no overtone of suspicion.

Larry and I exchanged a bug-eyed glance. He asked Merrit, "Don't you find that strange?"

The banker shrugged. "Not at all."

Robin explained, "Mr. Fertig rents a safe-deposit box of his own. He's in and out quite often." She asked her boss, "Anything else, sir?"

"Not right now, Robin. Thank you."

She nodded with a smile, retrieved the vault ledger, and left the room, closing the door behind her.

Though she and Merrit had found nothing remarkable about Pea's visit to the vault on Monday, the rest of us found these circumstances tantalizingly suspicious. Grant mumbled to me, "When we visited the estate on Sunday morning, Pea was wearing black." This com-ment went over Larry's and Merrit's heads, but Grant's meaning was clear to me: a man in black had commissioned the forgery from Kane on Sunday afternoon.

It was tempting to think of Pea as the source of the bogus clipping, but this notion was hampered by some logical inconsistencies. For example, Kane had met Pea on Sunday morning while helping us return the desk, so Kane would surely have recognized Pea later that day on campus. Further, what possible motive might Pea have had for faking the bequest to the museum?

As I pondered this, Grant and Merrit were immersed in an en-ergetic conversation, reviewing the theories that had been floated. Larry rose from the table and paced the room, checking back through his notes. Catching my eye, he signaled for me to join him.

"Yes?" I said, stepping near.

"Earlier today we learned from Chaffee's nurse that Pea had been humiliated by procuring call boys for Chaffee. Now we know that Pea visited the bank vault on Monday, shortly after Chaffee's death. I don't know how any of this adds up, or even *if* it adds up, but now I'm *doubly* eager to have another talk with that guy."

"Did you set up the meeting?"

"We're expected at the estate at one-thirty." He checked his watch. "If you don't have plans, why don't you join me for lunch? Then you can ride over to Rancho Mirage with me. How did you get here?"

"Grant drove me, and—" I stopped short, realizing that Grant and I had completely overlooked the purpose of our visit, sidetracked by Larry's unexpected presence and our discussion of the forgery. "Sorry, Larry. I can't leave yet. Grant and I need to discuss some paintings with Merrit."

"Will it take long?"

"Shouldn't." I stepped to the conference table. "Grant? Aren't we forgetting something?"

He looked up from his conversation with Merrit, blinking as my words sank in. "Good God"—he laughed—"I need to start writing notes to myself and sticking them on my lapels."

"That won't work," I told him dryly. "I've tried it; then I can't remember what the *notes* mean." I wasn't senile, not yet, but now and then my faculties had subtle ways of putting me on notice that the slide had begun.

Understandably, Merrit was perplexed by this exchange. "Is something, uh . . . wrong?"

"Not at all," said Grant. Then he corrected himself. "Well, aside from the murder, the forgery, and the various dead ends, nothing's wrong. Actually, Merrit, the reason Claire and I are here is to ask if the museum could borrow some paintings from Stewart's collection."

Grant and I took turns filling in the details: Glenn Yeats wanted to have something on display at the museum that night during the Chaffee tribute and press conference. Since it was short notice and the estate was tied up in probate and most of the collection was in storage, we were hoping to borrow the set of Swedish neo-impressionist paintings that Chaffee had recently acquired. I assumed they were readily accessible because on Tuesday, I'd seen them stacked against a wall of the great room at the estate.

Merrit followed along, nodding. Then something occurred to him. "The museum event, I forgot about that. Now that the validity of the clipping is in question, doesn't the press conference seem a bit, well, premature at best?"

"Absolutely," I told him. "But Glenn Yeats doesn't know that the clipping was forged, and the museum event was his brainchild. The wheels are in motion. There's no stopping it."

"And besides," Larry spoke up, "I don't *want* to stop it. The press conference and official announcement of the bequest may well lure the killer out into the open. After all, the event is an affirmation of the killer's success. If *I'd* plotted this, *I'd* want to be there."

Grant explained to the banker, "And since you're acting as executor of Stewart's estate, we hoped you could help us arrange to get the paintings—to *borrow* them. They'll be in professional, curatorial hands and fully insured. We need them for tonight only."

Weighing all this, Merrit conceded, "The ploy might work. If you do flush out the killer and we do wrap it up quickly, the bank's reputation would be cleared before the scandal even broke. I like it."

"So do I," said Larry. "How do we make this happen?"

Merrit rose. "We just need to make a few phone calls, make sure the paintings have not yet been moved to storage, and notify Pea that the museum will be picking them up."

Grant rose also. "I'll arrange with the college to send a truck over. How about three or four o'clock?"

"That should be fine. Let me get Robin started with those calls." Merrit stepped to the door and opened it, but found that his secretary was already busy on the phone, typing as she spoke. So Merrit crossed his office to the desk and stared down at his own elaborate, multibuttoned telephone. It had various tiny lights, one of them blinking. With a laugh, he told us, "I *suppose* I can figure out how to work this thing."

"That's not a bad idea," said Larry. "The fewer people in the loop, the better."

"Aaah," said Merrit, "I see what you mean." With a conspiratorial wink, he assured the detective, "I'll make the calls myself."

With our plan in place, Larry, Grant, and I exchanged some parting words with the banker before leaving him to figure out his phone. I was last to file out of his office, closing the door behind me. Robin was still busy at her desk, but she rose briefly, covering the receiver with her hand as she wished us a good day.

Passing through the lobby, we paused outside the bank on the sidewalk. Though noon approached, the sun shone low in the winter sky, slicing between the trunks of date palms that lined the street like a colonnade.

Larry reiterated his earlier invitation. "Join me for lunch, Claire? You too, Grant."

"Sure," I replied. I assumed Grant would be equally agreeable.

But he hesitated. "I think it would be better if I returned to the museum and arranged for the truck."

I suggested, "Can't you handle that by phone?"

"I want to make sure there are no foul-ups."

I found his hedging curious, to say the least. Although Grant had exhibited a hands-on interest in a broad range of human endeavors, trucking was not among them. Besides, it was simply unlike him to squirm out of an invitation to lunch. I'd fully expected him to suggest twenty-dollar salads at the Regal Palms.

Then it dawned on me. Grant felt no urgency to arrange the hauling of the paintings. Grant had no aversion to lunch with me. No, Grant was squeamish about being trapped at table for an hour with his brother. Grant doubtless feared, correctly, that lunching with Larry would compel us to reveal to him that the clipping had been forged by Kane.

It was time to share our knowledge with Larry. It was time to keep everyone honest. "No, Grant," I interrupted his protestations, "do join us for lunch."

"Perhaps some other time, really."

Flatly, I insisted, "We need to have a talk with your brother."

Once Grant realized that he was not to be let off the hook, he groused, "If we're going to do this, we might as well do it in style." So he phoned the Regal Palms from his car, reserving his usual table. Larry followed as we left Indian Wells, driving up valley through Palm Desert to Rancho Mirage, where our little convoy climbed the mountain to the swank hotel in the craggy granite foothills beneath Nirvana.

Larry pulled up behind us under the monumental porte cochere. A crew of parking valets helped us from our cars and drove them away. As we entered the double doors to the lobby, nodding to the natty doormen, Larry leaned to tell me, "A guy could get used to this." We'd lunched at the Regal Palms only two days earlier. Grant strutted ahead as if he owned the place.

The lobby was a buzz of activity as kitchen and decorating staff fussed with the construction of a giant gingerbread house (real gingerbread, you could smell it) under the central chandelier. In its unfinished state, it wasn't clear whether the structure represented a Nativity crèche, a storybook castle, or Santa's workshop. It was surrounded by both palms and pines, camels and reindeer, so go figure. The head decorator flounced about with a pastry bag, frosting the eaves with icicles, the corners with snowdrifts. A florist spruced mounds of white poinsettias and stunning pink amaryllis.

"That's pretty amazing," said Larry as we paused to watch the to-do.

"*Fab*-ulous!" gushed his brother.

"But," I said, sounding a disapproving note, "they should know better."

The brothers Knoll glanced first at each other, then turned to me.

Whirling a hand, I explained, "This cutesy gingerbread hoo-ha—it positively *draws* children."

"Like moths to a flame," Grant agreed before letting out a powerful laugh that drew a disapproving stare from the guy with the icing.

It was barely noon when we three entered the hotel dining room, so we were among the first to arrive. Busboys still tinkered with silver and napery; someone adjusted the long, tasseled drapes, which had been drawn against the morning glare, now framing a pristine desert sky of boundless blue. The host hustled from the far side of the room to greet Grant, then us, walking us to the terrace, where he helped with our chairs as we settled around the table, facing out over the valley.

We all ordered iced tea, then quickly perused the menus, choosing our twenty-dollar salads—today mine would be embellished with chicken, Grant's with shrimp, Larry's with strips of steak. When the tea had arrived and the handsome waiter had left to place our orders (with Grant glancing over his shoulder to watch the young man's retreat), an awkward silence fell over the table.

Grant cleared his throat. "It was good of Merrit Lloyd to be so helpful. I wasn't sure he'd play along and lend us the paintings for tonight."

Larry nodded. "Especially after learning that the museum is very likely *not* the heir to Chaffee's estate."

I said, "Merrit is shrewd enough to recognize the need for damage control. I doubt if he'd have been so quick to lend the paintings if he wasn't so eager to cover the bank's tracks with regard to the *forgery.*" There. I'd said the word—with a tad more emphasis than its context demanded.

Grant's eyes slid toward mine. His features pleaded, Slow down.

Larry blew a silent whistle. "That's still the big unknown in this investigation. If we knew who forged the clipping, all the other pieces would fall into place."

My eyes slid toward Grant's. My features told him, It's now or never.

He sat back in his chair, as if retreating, putting a few more inches between us. He asked his brother, "But that's not necessarily true, is it? I mean, if you knew who fabricated the clipping, you might still be unable to name the killer."

"Okay," Larry conceded, "it's conceivable that the forger and the killer are not the same person. But if not, there's clearly some connection, which means we're dealing with *conspiracy* to commit murder." He summed up, "Name the forger; the rest is easy."

Leaning forward, Grant persisted, "But what if the fabricator was an *unwitting* accomplice? What if he created a facsimile of an old newspaper clipping for someone else, not knowing that its purpose was fraudulent?"

Larry leaned within inches of his brother's face. "Come on, Grant. That's a stretch. How could anyone forge an exacting, aged replica of a bogus interview that carries immense financial implications— and do this for someone else—without suspecting foul play?"

"Trust me." Grant swallowed. "It could happen."

Larry drummed his fingers on the linen tablecloth. "How?"

Grant didn't answer.

Larry turned to me. The twist of his torso revealed a glimpse of the polished leather holster beneath his jacket. "Is there something I haven't been told?"

Finding it difficult to speak, I took a sip of tea, then said, "The answer to that question really needs to come from Grant."

"Okay, Grant. What's up?"

The detective's brother began, "This, uh, didn't come to my attention until this morning. We weren't sure how to tell you, or when."

"You're doing just fine." Larry allowed a smile. "Let's hear it."

Grant paused, then recited without embellishment, "At home this morning, I was checking e-mail on Kane's computer and discovered a file containing the forged interview; Kane did it. Later, Claire and I confronted him at the museum, and he readily admitted that he'd created the document."

"He seemed truly guileless in his admission," I added. "Someone representing himself as a college faculty member commissioned Kane to produce the clipping as part of a history display for the museum's opening. The way Kane told it, it all sounded perfectly feasible—and innocent, at least on Kane's part."

Larry took out his notebook and began recording details of our account. Rotely, he asked, "Did Kane describe the man?"

"Barely," said Grant. "The guy was older, and he wore black."

"How much older?"

I reminded Larry, "Kane is twenty-one. He wouldn't know thirty-five from fifty-five."

With a tone of understatement that verged on sarcasm, Larry noted, "That doesn't give us much to work with."

"Sorry," I said, "it doesn't. And the black clothes don't mean much, either. Many of the faculty do wear black, but we don't even know if this guy is on staff, and in fact, we have reason to suspect that he is not—he gave a false name. Besides, clothes are easily changed."

"Black today, taupe tomorrow," Grant quipped.

Larry underlined something in his notes. He spoke to his pad, not making eye contact with Grant or me. "I know you both believe Kane's story; I want to, too. But I don't need to remind you that I'm responsible for a murder investigation." Then he looked at Grant. "You're my brother, and I know how important Kane is to you, but I'm a cop first. You can't expect me to compromise my objectivity."

Grant slumped in his chair. "I should learn not to compromise my *own* objectivity. I've been blinded by love—God, that sounds trite, but the phrase fits. When Kane entered my life, my world turned upside down and I lost all sense of perspective. Perhaps I did let him rush our relationship, but the truth is, I wanted to be a couple as badly as he did. I would hate to think, now, that he's been harboring motives less loving than mine."

"There's no reason to think that," I told him.

"The clipping. The bruise. Those might be reasons."

Larry asked, "What bruise?"

We told him about Kane's experience at the estate on Monday morning, how he fell against Stewart's wheelchair when fending off an advance, a detail that Kane had failed to mention while talking to the detective on Monday evening.

Larry took notes, staring at the paper as he wrote, his features grave and purposeful. Jabbing his pad with a period, he said, "Whether Kane knew it or not, he was a part of this."

Grant shook his head fiercely, as if shaking off the doubts he had just expressed to us. "Kane *couldn't* have understood what was going on. Maybe I've known him for only three months, but he's not a killer—I'm sure of that much. And he's not a conspirator to murder. He's been framed, Larry. He's been victimized."

"Possibly," said Larry.

Grant thumped the table. "We need to find that man in black."

"I couldn't agree more."

I ventured to ask, "Then you're willing to reserve any judgment—or action—with regard to Kane?"

"Yes," Larry answered, thinking, returning his notes to his jacket, "until tonight. Kane will be at the press reception, won't he?"

Grant nodded. "I imagine so."

"Make sure of it. Whoever commissioned the forgery may be there as well. He just may be the killer. With any luck, Kane may be able to point him out to us."

I noted, "This ought to be quite a night."

Under his breath, Grant added, "Fasten your seat belts."

Larry was about to say something, but our lunch arrived, stifling conversation.

Before long, we were chatting again, but our topic had shifted from murder to extortion. "It's great," Larry admitted, "but twenty dollars for a salad? There ought to be a law."

As Larry and I weren't due to meet Pea Fertig until one-thirty, we took our time, savoring our lunch, the view, and the noontide sun. Shortly after one, we rose from the table, Grant planning to return to his office at Nirvana, where he would phone the college and arrange for a truck to transport the Swedish paintings from the Chaffee estate to the museum.

"I hope Pea doesn't get pissy about this," I told the brothers.

"Frankly," said Larry, "I don't care. Pea can fuss and fret about the paintings all he wants, but he still needs to explain what he was doing in that bank vault on Monday."

The three of us left the terrace, entering the dining room and heading for the hotel lobby. My eyes had not fully adjusted to the dimmer, indoor light as we passed along the banquette of diners facing into the room. A woman's voice said, "Well, hello, Detective. What a nice surprise."

We stopped, and turning, I realized that Dawn Chaffee-Tucker was lunching with Merrit Lloyd—at the very table where, two days earlier, I'd seen Merrit's secretary, Robin. As Merrit was seated in a chair with his back to the room, he hadn't realized that we were passing through until Dawn greeted Larry.

"My, what a coincidence," said Merrit, rising and twisting awkwardly to shake hands, sounding more flustered to see us than surprised. With a tone of embarrassment, he told us, "Mrs. Chaffee-Tucker is staying here at the Regal Palms, and I felt she might appreciate some company. It seems I'm still in the service of her late uncle, a role I'm delighted to perform."

We knew all this; there was no need for Merrit to explain himself. I didn't find it at all remarkable that he would be lunching with his client's niece at her hotel, where he'd arranged her accommodations. What I did find puzzling was that he took such pains to justify their presence.

"I've been made to feel very much at home," Dawn was telling the banker. "Thank you for looking after me." She sat back against the tufted booth, looking decidedly regal.

Larry asked her, "You'll be attending the reception at the museum tonight?"

"Of course." She smiled—perfect teeth, perfect complexion, perfect makeup. "That's why I'm here."

Merrit fidgeted with the large linen napkin in his hands. "In addition to announcing the bequest, the reception will serve as a splendid tribute to Stewart and his philanthropy."

Again, I noted, Merrit was telling us something we already knew, as if struggling to fill voids in our conversation. Why was he so ill at ease? Was his motive for lunching with the woman perhaps something other than stated?

In my several encounters with Merrit Lloyd, I'd seen him squirm only once before. The previous afternoon, when Larry and I visited his office, Merrit had been unable to explain his second visit to the Chaffee estate on Monday morning, claiming first not to recall it, then pleading confusion over the time of an auditors' meeting at the bank.

His current behavior was similarly elusive, his words equally lame.

Was something going on between Merrit Lloyd and Dawn Chaffee-Tucker?

Or was I attempting to connect dots that didn't exist?

21

By one-thirty, Larry and I had arrived at the Chaffee estate in Rancho Mirage. When Larry pressed the intercom button at the gate, Pea Fertig answered—though he did not identify himself, there was no mistaking his vestige of a drawl. Larry announced himself, and Pea signaled the gate to open, telling us curtly, "Go to the back." We drove onto the grounds, circling the house as instructed. As the view of the street disappeared, I wondered if Pea had told us to use the rear entrance as an intentional slight. Was he sending a message that he deemed us too lowly for the front door? Or was he simply busy in the kitchen?

Whatever his attitude, he was in no rush to welcome us. We parked near the garage, which was closed that afternoon, then went to the kitchen door and rang the bell, twice, waiting a minute or two for Pea to answer. When the door at last swung open, he offered no apology, no greeting, simply telling us, "We can talk in the great room," and led the way. He wore a sweatshirt, nylon workout pants, and athletic shoes—all of it black, even the socks.

Nothing had changed much since our Tuesday visit. The grout of the kitchen floor tiles was still stained in front of the refrigerator; the collection of dented cocktail shakers was still haphazardly shoved into a corner of the counter. A half pot of cold coffee sat near the sink, but otherwise, it didn't appear that any cooking had transpired in the last two days.

Christmas decorations still festooned the great room, and I was relieved to note that the Swedish paintings were still draped, stacked against a wall. Pea saw me eyeing them. "So the rush is on," he said cynically.

I pretended not to catch his meaning.

He explained, "I heard from Merrit Lloyd. I understand you plan to truck away the Östman collection. Pretty tacky, if you ask me. It's just plain tasteless of Glenn Yeats to be so quick to claim the museum's windfall and trumpet it to the press."

"That's not his intention at all," I assured Pea, even though his description of Glenn's strategy was on the mark. "The museum simply wants to make the best possible impression when announcing such a generous bequest. It's a tribute to Stewart."

"Oh, please." Pea spun on one heel and plopped on the leather sofa, as if wearied to exhaustion by our bullshit. Sprawling with a leg flung over the arm of the couch, he added, "I have half a mind to lock those away." He jerked his head toward the paintings.

"I wouldn't recommend that," said Larry, sitting in the chair across from the sofa. His tone was conciliatory, not threatening.

But Pea had a taste for confrontation. "Oh, yeah?" He sat up straight, facing Larry squarely. "Why not?"

"Because it would only precipitate ill will, and if word got out, there'd be a public impression of infighting between Stewart's household and his heirs. It would *not* serve his memory well."

"Besides," I added, speaking softly, sitting next to Pea, "the museum will get the paintings eventually, so what would be the point in stalling them?" Both Larry and I now knew, of course, that the museum had no such claim to Stewart's property, but Pea didn't need to know this yet.

"In fact," Larry told him, "I think it would be appropriate for you to attend the event at the museum tonight. You really shouldn't miss it. It may prove to be Stewart's finest hour."

With any luck, it might also prove to be the killer's darkest hour. Larry, truth be told, had little interest in assuaging Pea's grief or helping him with closure; he was still attempting to herd all of the suspects into one room that night.

Pea paused. Then he grumbled, "I'll think about it."

"Good." I patted his arm. "If you missed Stewart's memorial, you'd never forgive yourself." Shame on me. I was not only toying with a man's fragile emotions; I was also guilty of an indefensible linguistic leap. Since when could a media circus, replete with search-lights, be described as a "memorial"?

Larry told Pea, "As I understand it, there'll be a lot of press there tonight, but all of Stewart's friends and associates are welcome to attend as well. Chances are, there'll be a crowd."

Pea's mouth twisted with a smirk. "I suppose Bonnie will be there." His tone conveyed both disgust and resignation.

With a matter-of-fact air, Larry answered, "I suppose so, yes."

Testing the waters, I told Pea, "Dawn will be there as well."

"Who—" he began. Then he recalled, "Stewart's *niece?* She's coming *tonight?*"

"She's already here. She arrived yesterday and spent last night at a hotel."

"What's *she* snooping around for?"

I shrugged. "She's next of kin. Why wouldn't she be here?"

Pea laughed. "Next of kin, like hell. They *never* spent time together. Stewart never even had a civil word to say about her. He couldn't *stand* Dawn."

I nodded, thinking. Pea had just confirmed what Merrit Lloyd had told us—that Stewart, when setting up Monday's appointment with Dawn, had taken pains to arrange it behind Pea's back. So I decided to push further, asking, "Are you sure? We have reason to think that Dawn was here at the estate on Monday morning. She said that Stewart had approached her regarding a reconciliation."

Pea looked genuinely astounded. "Don't you *get* it? If his niece was here on Monday, it was because she was after something, not because Stewart invited her." Pea turned to Larry. "That's *it,* Detective. There's your prime suspect."

Larry made a show of taking out his notebook and writing something. "I'll certainly look into this."

But both Larry and I already knew that Pea's hypothesis was not only wishful thinking, but flawed. We knew for a fact that Stewart had invited Dawn. We'd seen the letter. And there, behind Pea, on a desk mere feet from the sofa, sat the computer on which Stewart had clumsily composed the letter.

Larry continued, "The relationship between Stewart and his

niece—strained, hostile, or indifferent—makes this evening's reception at the museum all the more significant. Can I assume that you'll cooperate when the truck arrives for the paintings later this afternoon?"

With his well-practiced grumble, Pea promised, "I won't make any trouble."

"Thank you. You won't regret taking the high road."

"Yeah, whatever." Pea slapped his knees. "Well, is that it? Is that what you needed to talk to me about—the paintings?" He was itching to see us out.

Before Pea could rise, Larry explained, "No, actually, we're not here because of the paintings. There have been some new developments on the case, and I thought you'd want to know about them. In fact, I'm hoping you can help us with a few more details."

Pea sat back. "I hope so too. We need to find Stewart's killer, right?"

"Right. Find him—and punish him."

Pea nodded. "Great. So what are these 'developments'?"

"Before I get to that"—Larry flipped a few pages of his notes—"I wonder if you could run through Monday morning again with me. Tell me about your comings and goings."

Larry, I figured, wanted to check the consistency of Pea's story. He was also giving Pea an opportunity to mention that he'd gone to the bank vault that day. Pea began recounting the events of that morning, but I'd heard it all before, so my attention drifted. My eye traveled back to the desk, where the computer was set up next to a laser printer.

I had no doubt that this was the equipment that had produced Stewart's letter to Dawn. The more tantalizing thought, the one that didn't quite make sense, was whether this equipment could have convincingly forged a 1954 newspaper clipping. The question seemed moot because I already knew that Kane had produced just such a facsimile on the computer in Grant Knoll's spare bedroom. But the possibility of a second forgery was appealing because it would neatly tie together so many loose threads of a perplexing murder plot. And it would point squarely at the disagreeable little man seated next to me on the sofa.

Pea was telling Larry, "So after the gym, but before I went shopping, I came back to the house to check on Stewart."

"And what time was that?"

"I arrived around nine-thirty. Stewart was sleeping and seemed to be fine, so I left within minutes."

Pea's story was fully consistent with what he'd told us before. Also consistent with his previous telling was the inability to prove when he had *left* the estate—meaning there was no way to verify that he had not been in the house at the time Chaffee died.

Larry asked, "After checking on Stewart, where did you go?"

"I went shopping for clothes and had lunch."

"Is that all?"

"Come on, Detective. You *saw* me return to the house with the shopping bags. I even gave you the receipts."

"Mm-hm. And none of your purchases were made prior to eleven o'clock. Stewart died sometime between ten-thirty and eleven-thirty."

Pea's spine stiffened. He seemed to grow three inches before our eyes. "I must say, I don't care for your tone. You act as if I'm hiding something."

Larry paused. "Mr. Fertig, did you or did you not visit Indian Wells Bank and Trust on Monday?"

Pea froze where he sat. After a moment, he shook his head, blinked, and said, "Damn. You're right. I guess I forgot."

I blurted, "You *forgot?*"

"Sorry. It just didn't seem important."

I was tempted to ask, Not *important?* But there was no point in tipping my hand. Pea did not yet know that the clipping found in Stewart's safe-deposit box was a fake. Pea did not yet understand that the timing of access to the box might prove crucial to naming Stewart's killer. That is, Pea did not grasp these points unless he himself had masterminded the switch.

"All right," said Larry with strained patience, "suppose you tell us about your visit to the bank. When did you go there?"

"After shopping, before lunch. It must have been around noon."

"And why did you go there?"

"Like Stewart, I keep a safe-deposit box at Indian Wells. Over the years, I came to share Stewart's distrust of lawyers, so we've both made a habit of storing important papers in the vault. Since the year is nearly over, I was starting to organize some receipts for taxes. On Monday, when I finished shopping along El Paseo, which isn't far from Indian Wells, I thought I'd pop over to the bank and get a jump on things. I was there for a few minutes, then went to lunch, then came home. Discovering what happened here"—Pea gestured toward the kitchen—"I sorta freaked. The bank slipped my mind. Honest. If you need to know *exactly* when I was there, I think the guard keeps a log of everyone who goes into the vault."

"We're aware of that," said Larry. "So you and Stewart maintained separate boxes in the vault."

"Correct."

"And the boxes have separate keys."

"Naturally."

"Do you know where Stewart kept his key?"

"Well, that's easy. *I'm* the keeper of the keys. Since his stroke, Stewart couldn't drive and generally needed help getting around. He was also more and more forgetful, misplacing things. So I kept his keys to the Rolls, the house keys, and the key to his safe-deposit box. In fact"—Pea got up from the sofa, stepped to the desk, opened the top drawer, pulled out a heavy ring of keys, and tossed it to Larry—"there's everything."

Larry reached up and plucked the keys out of the air as deftly as a cat catching a fly (a guy thing—I guess it's genetic). He looked over the ring, which contained at least a dozen keys, asking Pea, "Did you ever open Stewart's box?"

"Only if he asked for help."

"Did you open it on Monday?"

"Stewart wasn't *with* me on Monday. Of *course* I didn't open his box." Pea's indignant tone suggested he would never stoop to such bad manners—let alone murder. He added, "Why? What's wrong? Is something missing?"

"We're not sure. A document may be missing that could shed light on the crime." Jangling the keys, Larry asked, "Did anyone else have access to these?" He tossed them back.

Catching them, Pea grinned. "You're making this too easy for me, Detective. Bonnie Bahr was here all the time, and I don't generally keep the keys on me; they're too heavy. She could have taken them from the desk just about anytime." He put them back in the drawer and slid it closed. "Sure, Bonnie could have 'borrowed' the keys—then used them or copied them."

Making note of this, Larry looked troubled.

So was I. We had seen the log of vault visitors, and we would surely have noticed if Bonnie's name were on the list. But Bonnie, we knew, was not above using a pseudonym when the situation demanded it. Had she possibly gained access to Stewart's strongbox by assuming the identity of Marjorie Horne, as she had signed her letters to the *Desert Sun* in support of mercy killing? For that matter, she could have concocted any name whatever, at random. What credentials, I wondered, would she have been required to present in order to pass the scrutiny of the guard outside the vault? These frets, however, seemed unwarranted. Merrit Lloyd had reviewed the log with us, assuring us there had been no suspicious activity during the time in question.

Larry turned a page of his notes, telling Pea, "You seem more than a little eager to cast suspicion on Stewart's nurse."

"Damn right. And I make no apologies. I've already told you outright—I always suspected Bonnie's motives in this house. Did you look into those newspaper letters I told you about?"

"We did. The information was useful, but hardly conclusive. In fact, we visited Miss Bahr again this morning."

"And what did that murderous sow have to say for herself?"

Larry closed his notes. "Mr. Fertig, I find your words highly offensive."

"Tough." Pea gave the detective an unflinching stare. "That pig invites mockery. She deserves it."

"It may interest you to know that she gave us a highly reasoned explanation for the letters she wrote to the paper. She became emotional and distraught, though, when the topic turned to you."

Pea leaned toward Larry, bracing his arms on the back of the sofa. "Good."

"Truth is, she sympathized with the dilemma you've felt here in the household all these years—having once been so close to Stewart, reduced to hired help. She had *no* sympathy, however, for some of the more recent duties you'd taken on."

Pea paused. A touch of wariness colored his bravado as he asked, "What the hell are you talking about?"

Ever so slightly, Larry leaned forward in his chair. "I'm talking about pimping, Mr. Fertig."

Pea glared. His mouth pinched. A vein pounded along the side of his neck.

Larry clarified, "Perhaps 'pimping' isn't the precise term, but it's close. I don't mean to suggest that you solicited clients for a prostitute, but you did, it seems, solicit prostitutes for a client—your boss, Stewart Chaffee."

"That . . . *bitch,*" Pea spat at us.

"Bonnie told us that you frequently arranged for young call boys to visit Stewart and perform sexual services here at the estate. I think you may have shocked her puritan sensibilities, Pea. These goings-on did *not* sit well with her. I'm sure she'd swear to this activity, perhaps sign a complaint. She could be very helpful in providing the chronology. Then my department would have no trouble tracing any financial records of your payments."

"Look," said Pea, starting to pace behind the sofa, "you've got the wrong spin on this. I don't know what Bonnie told you, but it sounds like crap. Stewart's special visitors—that's how he preferred to think of them—were *not* prostitutes, and they were *not* underage. They were male escorts, every one of them certified over eighteen. You can find them in any bar rag. Christ, they're even in the Yellow Pages. Point is, they were paid for their *time* here, nothing else."

I suggested, "But if, while they were here, one thing led to another, that was a private matter between consenting adults."

"Absolutely correct. That's how the escort business works. I didn't make the rules."

"You merely took advantage of them," said Larry.

Pea stopped pacing. "*No,* Detective. *Stewart* took advantage of them. I merely set up the appointments and wrote the checks when they had finished."

Mustering an air of sympathy, I shook my head, telling Pea, "That must've been terribly painful for you."

He paused, recalling everything. With a bitter laugh, he asked, "Painful? You don't know the half of it. It was bad enough that I lost Stewart's affections and became his servant. It was bad enough that I wasted—really, truly *wasted*—twenty years of the prime of my life. But when I started arranging for an old man's young tricks, that was *way* beyond the call of duty."

"Then why did you do it?"

"Because he enjoyed it so. You see, down deep, I still loved the man. It even got to the point where I had no problem with the one-nighters—they were just cattle, an expendable commodity. But now and then, one of them would catch his fancy, and I'd hear all about their exploits, in numbing detail, at breakfast the next morning. It was enough to make me gag. So these were the guys he wanted back, and I had to set up the return visits. Now, *that* galled me." The memory colored Pea's face with anger.

Larry reminded him, "Those visits made Bonnie angry as well. It sounds as if you both would have liked to put a stop to the call boys."

He shouted, "Who *gives* a shit what Bonnie did or didn't like? She *worked* here, damn it!"

"So did you."

That parallel slid past Pea. He ranted, "I can't believe it—I just really can't *believe* that Bonnie would divulge such a private matter. She's trash, obviously. Who but trash would use such sordid knowledge to besmirch the memory of her former employer? Stewart was so *good* to her. Then she turns around and pulls *this.*"

Larry said, "She took no pleasure in telling us this background. She must have thought it was relevant to the murder investigation."

"Oh, yeah, I'll *bet* she did. The call boys were 'relevant,' all right. She saw this naughty little wrinkle as a convenient means of casting both Stewart and me in a bad light—while diverting suspicion from herself. How's *that* for relevant? I've said it before, Detective: if you want Stewart's killer, look no further than Bonnie."

Pea had wound himself into such a state, there was little point in protracting the discussion. His emotional reaction to Bonnie's revelation of the call boys made him look far guiltier than she did, though it was easily arguable, in light of the entire investigation, that either the houseman *or* the nurse had had a motive, the means, and the opportunity to kill. I was unable, then and there, to sort through all that we'd learned. Like Larry, I had come to believe that our best chance of clarifying the bigger, blurry picture would be that evening, when all of the interested parties—suspects and bereaved alike— would gather at the museum.

Not wanting to jeopardize either Pea's attendance that night or his cooperation in releasing the paintings that afternoon, Larry told him, simply, "I appreciate your time." Then Larry put away his pen. He rose from his chair. I rose from the sofa.

But Pea wasn't finished. "Stewart's interest in hot young men wasn't limited to call boys, you know." He grinned at us during a meaningful pause.

"I'm sure we've heard enough on that topic," I told him primly while stepping toward the kitchen door, though in truth, I was itching for more details.

Pea supplied them. Sauntering toward Larry and me, he continued, "Yes, Stewart immensely enjoyed the sexual services of the barely legal. He had a habit of getting what—and whom—he wanted. He had recently set his sights on your brother's lover, Detective. What's his name—Kane? Stewart was interested from the moment they met last Sunday. And when the kid offered to bring the desk key back to him the next morning, Stewart was convinced that the attraction was mutual. I mean, I *knew* Stewart was dreaming—a kid like that doesn't drop his pants for an old cripple unless there's cash involved. But Stewart was convinced he had a tryst in the making, and he took great offense when I suggested that he might want to keep a few crisp hundreds in his saddlebag, just in case. 'A kid like that,' I told him, 'would expect nothing less than five.' "

Pea concluded, "That's why I made myself scarce on Monday morning. I smelled trouble, and I didn't want to be around for it."

22

Larry drove me back to campus, where I'd left my car that morning. Talking along the way, we both agreed that Pea's emotional outburst over the issue of call boys had not served him well. "Aside from the thin ice with the law," said Larry, "sex for pay is fraught with dangers. Its practitioners can be disreputable, to say the least. There's no telling what sort of seedy connections Stewart forged as a result of this habit, opening up untold potential for his own demise. Pea should have informed us of this immediately."

"But he was basically in denial," I reasoned. "When the issue surfaced, he blew. Certainly, one of Stewart's tricks could have turned murderous. If not, Pea harbored resentments strong enough that he himself may have done it—exactly as proposed by Bonnie."

We discussed the merits of this scenario, pro and con, agreeing that suspicious details were mounting against both Pea and Bonnie, but there was not yet sufficient evidence to accuse either of the crime.

A detail we were reluctant to discuss was Pea's final revelation that Stewart had not only voiced his carnal interest in Kane, but that the victim-to-be had felt convinced that the attraction was mutual. On the surface, it didn't make sense, easily dismissed as the delusion of a mind turned feeble. What's more, neither Larry nor I cared to entertain a theory that seemed to draw an additional link from Kane—and by implication, from Grant—to Chaffee's murder.

Still, I knew some background regarding Kane and Grant that Larry was unaware of. He knew that his brother and the much younger man were now living together, but I doubted that he knew they were planning a contractual marriage, a legal union promoted largely by Kane. Grant had already been shaken by the discovery of the forged clipping on Kane's computer, sufficiently shaken to question the kid's motive in rushing toward a partnership that would, at a purely material level, enrich Kane far more than Grant.

Kane had met the renowned Stewart Chaffee on Sunday, getting a good look at the wealthy old man's surroundings and witnessing his obvious flirtations. Was it conceivable that Kane had seen in the retired decorator a bigger fish than the one he'd already landed? Was Stewart's wishful contention—that Kane had volunteered to return the desk key as a means for the two of them to meet alone—not so feebleminded after all?

I shared none of these thoughts with Larry as we drove from Rancho Mirage toward the campus of Desert Arts College, but my silence must have clued him that I was pondering Pea's insinuations about Stewart and Kane.

Larry was pondering them as well. Glancing over at me, he said, "After Chaffee was killed and the medical examiner's team arrived on the scene, we made a complete inventory of the effects found on the victim's person. Most conspicuously, there was the nurse's note and the tasseled key, but there were other miscellaneous items found in that pony-skin bag. At the time, I saw no significance in any of those additional items, but now I'm not so sure."

I could have guessed what he was about to say, but remained silent.

"Stewart Chaffee had five new hundred-dollar bills in his purse."

Just as Pea had suggested.

The remaining distance to campus was short, and we traversed it in silence, unwilling to speculate on the meaning of Chaffee's willingness to buy, if necessary, Kane's affections. I couldn't help recalling that when Kane had forged the clipping for the mysterious man in black, he'd been paid a hundred dollars in cash for an evening's work. What, I wondered, would he be willing to do for five hundred— for a task that would take minutes, not hours? Granted, the cash had been found in Stewart's saddlebag, so perhaps the proposition had never been discussed. Or had there been more cash, with five hundred remaining after a deal had been struck?

When Larry dropped me off, he simply asked, "Seven o'clock?" Before closing the car door, I confirmed, "The press reception begins at seven." Gesturing across College Circle toward the museum, I added, "I'll see you there tonight."

I coasted through my dramatic-literature seminar that afternoon, perplexed by this new wrinkle in an investigation that was edging perilously close to home. I tried to keep our discussion focused on the topic delineated by my syllabus—social alienation as a recurring theme of twentieth-century playwrights—but my half dozen students kept steering our discourse back to the murder. Even those not directly involved in the *Laura* production were now well aware that the victim's clock was a centerpiece of the stage setting. One young lady assured me, "*Everyone's* talking about it."

I briefly considered a simple remedy, removing the clock from the stage. Something else—*anything* else—would have to take its place. But then I realized that the clock would become all the more conspicuous by its absence, providing an even greater distraction to audience and cast alike. No, I didn't need a new clock; I needed to solve the larger riddle, naming Stewart's killer and quashing the buzz.

At home, after class, I was fretful and distraught, not caring to eat. When I explained to Tanner what Larry and I hoped to accomplish that night, he offered, "At least let me fix you some soup."

I thanked him with a kiss, managed to down a bowl without tasting it, then primped for that evening's main event, wondering if Larry's gambit to lure the killer to the press conference would pay off. If it didn't and Glenn Yeats announced to the world that the museum was sole heir to Chaffee's estate, which was not true, and if he later found out, as he surely would, that I had kept this information from him and allowed him to make a fool of himself . . . well, I didn't care to contemplate the fallout.

Dressing, I considered several outfits, wintry and sedate, but I ultimately decided, what the hell, wear red. I already knew that I would choose the same hue on Friday evening, just twenty-four hours away, when I would reign at the premiere of my play. Tonight's event, decidedly less festive—even grim—also needed, to my way of thinking, that extra bit of flash and dazzle. Not that I was out to impress anyone at the museum with my vibrant tastes. I simply needed any help I could get in energizing my mind and concentrating my creative energies on the decryption tasks at hand.

As I prepared to leave the condo, Tanner asked, "Do you want me there with you tonight?"

Of course I did. But I asked him, "Would you mind driving yourself? I need to get there early, and to be honest, I'm not sure what the evening may hold. Depending on what unfolds, there's no telling how late I may have to stay." Brightly, I added, "I want you properly rested for the big opening tomorrow."

He readily bought that, agreeing to follow me a while later in his Jeep.

"Wish me luck," I said, latching onto him for a fierce hug.

"Break a leg, Claire."

The December night had fallen. The desert sky was a velvety black as I crossed the valley floor, headed toward campus. I would have no trouble finding my way—klieg lights crisscrossed the heavens, emanating from a spot near the horizon that grew brighter as I drove nearer.

Entering the campus and parking in my reserved space, I noted that College Circle was already aflutter with activity, remarkable on any evening, let alone a Thursday. Lights burned bright in the museum lobby, drawing a crowd from the plaza to the doors. Several television news vans had parked near the entrance, their long antennas poking toward the stars. The searchlights buzzed, burning white-hot in the chilly night. The giant banners wafted with the breeze. If Stewart Chaffee's friends and associates had been expecting a solemn memorial service, they now had ample reason to revise their thinking. If any in the crowd were put off by the hoopla, they hid their indignation well. Without exception, those arriving rushed to the museum like kids to the big top.

I felt my own pace quicken as I crossed the plaza from the faculty garage. Passing my darkened theater, which loomed large but indistinct against the sky, I wondered if tomorrow's opening of *Laura* would generate this kind of excitement. If, twenty-four hours from now, Stewart Chaffee's killer was still unknown and at large, I knew that my premiere would be the focus of too much excitement—for all the wrong reasons.

"Claire," a woman's voice greeted me as I approached the museum.

Glancing over, I saw Dawn Chaffee-Tucker escorted toward the doors by her late uncle's banker. "Dawn, Merrit," I greeted them, "how nice to see you again."

Merrit intoned the obligatory "Even under such unpleasant circumstances."

Dawn halted. "None of that," she said with a smile. "Tonight is the summation of Uncle Stewart's wishes. He led a long, productive life, and now he's leaving behind a genuine legacy."

"Well said," I told her, giving her arm a squeeze. From the side of my mouth, I added, "Let's hope that Glenn Yeats will be equally eloquent and succinct."

With a soft laugh, Merrit suggested, "Ladies, shall we?" And he ushered us through the doors.

The processed interior air, which on previous visits had felt so sterile and bone-chilling, now felt warm and comforting against the night. The whirl and hubbub projected a pleasant conviviality, almost partylike. Tuxedoed waiters (Regal Palms staff—I was beginning to recognize them) passed trays of hors d'oeuvres and offered cocktails, a civilized note amid all the hype and glamour. Television cameras, hoisted on shoulders, recorded snippets of the crowd for the late news.

Merrit spotted his secretary, Robin, in the milling crowd and, needing to have a word with her, excused himself, leading Dawn away with him. As they disappeared, I paused to take stock of who was present.

The media types were largely unknown to me, as I was still new to the area, but this bash was being thrown for their benefit, and there were plenty on hand—reporters, video cameramen, and news-paper photographers representing local media outlets as well as several from Los Angeles. The entire museum staff was working the crowd, of course, including director Iesha Birch. I noticed Kane Richter emerge from an office with a bundle of printed material.

College faculty from all departments had been encouraged to at-tend, and many had—lured more by the food and booze, I gathered, than by an interest in the bequest. Most, I noted, wore black that night. Among them were the composer Lance Caldwell and the painter Atticus, who were engaged in one of their heated discussions of the arts, brandishing tiny chicken kabobs while slurping from oversize glasses of wine—white for Caldwell, red for Atticus. My old friend, Kiki Jasper-Plunkett, did not wear black, not by a long shot. Her penchant for costuming was given free rein that night, and she jangled about in a garish getup best described as that of a Gypsy queen. Our president, Glenn Yeats, and my neighbor, Grant Knoll, huddled near a podium, comparing notes with Glenn's secretary, the amazonian Tide Arden.

Bonnie Bahr, Chaffee's nurse, arrived just then, looking prettier than I'd seen her, done up for the evening in a dressy pantsuit and glittery shawl that were curiously flattering to her heft. A waiter approached her with a tray, and she plucked a dainty stuffed mush-room, placing it on a cocktail napkin as if she did not intend to eat it. A bar was set up along the far wall, and she made her way toward it without pausing to chat; she doubtless knew few among the others attending.

One person whom she knew well, Pea Fertig, arrived after Bonnie had been swallowed by the crowd. He wore black again that night—a good-looking, well-tailored suit, possibly Italian, complementing his buffed but smallish frame. I didn't know whether the dark suit had been chosen as a chic fashion statement or out of deference to the funereal overtones of the event, but I couldn't fault Pea's in-stincts. He presented himself most attractively that evening. I found him rakishly handsome. Devilishly so. A waiter offered appetizers, but he declined with a shake of his head, hotfooting toward the bar.

"Evening, Claire."

I turned to find Mark Manning at my side, studying me with a grin. "Hi, Mark." I gave him a peck. "Sorry if I seem distracted. Lots on my mind."

"The play?" he asked. He held a drink in one hand, vodka on the rocks, and held a padded case in the other, the sort that carries a laptop. "Or is it murder on your mind?"

"Both," I admitted. Eyeing his computer, I asked, "Planning to do some work tonight?"

"Not sure. Am I correct to sniff a story here—I mean, beyond the 'bequest'?" His subtle wink alluded to our shared knowledge that Chaffee's holographic will had been faked.

I leaned to tell him, "I'm *sure* there's a story here. I just don't know whether all the pieces will fall together tonight." Enough of my pothering. I asked, "Is Thad here? I thought you two had set aside this evening for catching up."

"We'll catch up; I merely pushed back our dinner reservation." With a snicker, he added, "No one's going to starve." He jerked his head toward a nearby buffet table, where Thad held his own among a knot of reporters, gorging himself on shrimp the size of lamb chops.

"Mark," I said, touching my fingers to his arm, "I can't thank you enough for alerting us to the forged clipping. I'm still not sure what it means, but my instincts tell me that the forgery is at the crux of Chaffee's murder."

"My instincts tell me you're correct."

Without going into detail, I told him, "We now know who created the forgery, but—those instincts again—they tell me he's not the killer."

Mark sipped his vodka, thinking. "If forgery is at the crux of the murder, but the forger isn't the killer, where does that leave you?"

"Confused," I blurted with a laugh of frustration.

"Then you need to look at every possible aspect of the forgery and compare them to every possible aspect of the murder. The pieces are all there. You just need to make them fit."

I rolled my eyes. "You make it sound baby simple."

"I'm not saying it's easy, but yes, the solution is always, ultimately, simple. You have a field of suspects. Eliminate the ones who could *not* have committed the crime, and you're left with one man standing."

Glancing toward the doors to College Circle, I noticed Detective Larry Knoll enter the museum lobby, talking with Tanner Griffin; they'd apparently run into each other while walking from their cars. I told Mark, "It seems that all the players are now assembled for this evening's little drama. Curtain going up. Enjoy the show."

He assured me, "I intend to." Then, with a courtly nod, Mark excused himself and wandered into the crowd.

Tanner spotted me from across the lobby, hailing me with a wave before slipping over to the bar. Larry saw me as well and headed in my direction.

As I made my way through the crowd to meet him, museum staffers began circulating throughout the room, handing out printed programs of that evening's order of events. Taking one and glancing at it, I noted that its cover was a smaller version of the banner Kane had created, trumpeting in bold letters, THE CHAFFEE LEGACY. The inside pages contained statements from college president Glenn Yeats and museum board president Grant Knoll, as well as a brief bio of the late art collector.

Larry took a program as he stepped up to me. "Is everyone here?"

"I believe so, yes. Though it's impossible to keep an eye on everyone at once." I gazed out over the shifting crowd.

"That's okay." His mouth twisted with a facetious grin. "We've got all evening to piece this together." If he was feeling stressed, he didn't show it.

But I did. Impatiently, I asked, "Any developments?"

"Fingerprints." Though his brief statement sounded promising, he added, "Nothing conclusive, I'm afraid. We've done a thorough study of all the prints found on the premises, comparing them with prints given by individuals known to have been there. As you know, someone—presumably the killer—wiped all fingerprints from the refrigerator handle and from the inside knob of the front door, but not from the outside knob. That knob was covered with layer upon layer of prints, most of them smudged and useless. We did, however, manage to pull one clean thumbprint that seemed relatively fresh and uncontaminated."

"Meaning," I conjectured, "it was left by the last person out."

"Possibly. It's a good theory. Unfortunately, it matches none of the sets given to us since Monday."

"I assume you've run a check on the thumbprint."

"Of course. It's no one with a known criminal past. So it could be anyone—not necessarily the killer—the mailman, for instance." I frowned. "You're right. That's *not* very conclusive."

"Sorry. That's what I've got."

Grant Knoll—the detective's brother, housemate of the young forger of the bogus clipping—rushed over to us. He looked more stressed than I did. "Christ," he said, "I need a drink."

"The bar's open."

"Aarghh"—he shook his head—"not a good idea. Not before a speech. I've never had a qualm about public speaking, never before, not until now."

"It's no big deal," I tried telling him, pointing to the program. "You're simply delivering 'Words of Welcome' here in the lobby. Glenn makes the real speech, later, in the main gallery, when he announces the bequest and—surprise of surprises—unveils the collection of Swedish masterpieces."

He corrected me, "*Minor* neo-impressionist Swedish masterpieces."

I asked, "You managed to get them without incident? No trouble from Pea?"

"I wasn't there. I heard there was a spot of trouble, but not from Pea. It seems the driver sent by the college was given bad directions or the wrong address, so the truck was late. Everything's here now, but the installation of the paintings is still under way." Grant gestured toward the closed double doors of the main gallery, guarded (pretentiously, I thought) by a pair of uniformed security officers, lacking only plumed helmets and broadswords. "Talk about a last-minute rush."

Larry asked, "What's all the fuss? Just hang a bunch of pictures, right?"

"The paintings are hung. And they're already lighted—a big enough project in itself. But then Glenn decided he wanted to do an actual unveiling, so there's a crew in the main gallery rigging the drapery right now."

My features twisted. I recalled, "Yesterday morning, Glenn said there wouldn't be an unveiling."

Grant shrugged. "You know Glenn. He changed his mind—end of discussion. So even the programs had to be reprinted. I'll bet the ink is still wet. Kane has been running full speed, trying to keep up with all this."

I turned a page of the program, and sure enough, Glenn Yeats's appearance was described as "Announcement and Unveiling." Rubbing a finger over the type, I found that the ink did indeed smudge. I asked Grant, "Where *is* Kane?"

"God only knows. He really has his hands full. He must have ducked back into the offices for something."

"But basically," I said, "everything's under control."

Grant answered with a reluctant nod.

The detective asked his brother, "So why the jitters about your welcoming speech?"

Grant exhaled a frustrated sigh. "I guess it's the subterfuge. I mean, we three *know* that the museum isn't Chaffee's true heir, and we also know that Kane—*my* Kane—created the facsimile of the interview." (I noted wryly that Grant did not refer to the clipping as a forgery.) He concluded, "Unless we see some fairly dramatic developments tonight, my world could come crashing down around me."

I had other issues at stake but felt a similar trepidation. I stated the obvious: "Then it's time to wrap this up."

Glenn Yeats, who had been plying the crowd, wooing the press, and strutting about like a movie star, drifted into our midst. He asked anyone, "A splendid occasion, don't you think?"

"As usual," I told him. "You *do* know how to entertain, Glenn."

He pulled me close, told me to smile, and turned us toward a photographer, who snapped a quick candid.

"Yes," said Larry, "it's a wonderful tribute *to Mr. Chaffee*." His implication was that Glenn had lost sight of the evening's purpose.

"Of course," said Glenn, pausing for a dignified moment of silence. Then, breaking this brief spell of reverence, he told us, under his breath, "Frankly, I never could stand the guy, but hey, he handed us this situation, so we might as well work it for all it's worth."

Glenn's secretary, Tide, and the museum director, Iesha, hustled toward us. Iesha said, "They've finished in the gallery, Mr. Yeats." Tide overlapped, "We can begin the program whenever you're ready."

"Excellent!" said Glenn, raring to go. "Grant? Do you have your welcoming speech prepared?"

"Yes, Glenn." Grant paused, then reminded him, "You wrote it."

Glenn laughed. "Ah! So I did."

Within a few minutes, the lobby lights had dimmed and the crowd, numbering perhaps a hundred, had clustered around the podium near the doors to the main gallery. The security guards squinted into the glare of a spotlight as Grant stepped to the microphone.

"On behalf of the Desert Museum of Southwestern Arts, I wish to welcome you to this evening's special tribute, titled 'The Chaffee Legacy.' My name is Grant Knoll, and I'm privileged to serve as president of the museum's board of directors. Stewart Chaffee, who died so suddenly and tragically this past Monday, was a longtime acquaintance of mine, a man I was proud to call a friend—an honor shared by so many of you present tonight. I also want to welcome the many representatives of the press who have come to share this evening with us.

"Tonight's event, you see, serves three purposes. First, it is the grand opening of the new museum building itself. Second, we have chosen to dedicate this occasion to the memory of Stewart Chaffee, whose lifelong commitment to the arts has enriched our community beyond measure. And third, well, that's not for me to say—except to tell you that D. Glenn Yeats, founder and president of Desert Arts College, will make a very special announcement this evening. I know there's been widespread speculation regarding the tenor of this announcement. I can assure you that this speculation will end tonight on a happy note indeed.

"And so, ladies and gentlemen—without, as they say, further ado—I invite you to enter the museum's main gallery and to hear the words of our esteemed college president. Welcome, one and all."

To a smattering of applause, Grant signaled the guards, who made a show of unlocking the huge gallery doors and swinging them wide open. Simultaneously, recorded music swelled through the lobby, a sort of electronic fanfare, surely the work of Lance Caldwell. It almost worked, the pomp and ballyhoo, but to my jaded eye, the entire doings came across as trumped-up and artificial. Then again, I was one of only a few present who understood that the premise for these festivities was false to the core.

Larry and I, with everyone else, herded through the doors and entered the gallery. After all the buildup—the speech, the guards, the fanfare—the gray, quiet space within seemed distinctly anticlimactic.

The floor still contained clusters of display cubes, and as before, only one of them displayed anything—the Plexiglas case containing the ring and other primitive whatnot. The wall at the far end of the room was now draped with some dozen swags of burgundy velvet. Looping through them was a long golden cord that ended in a huge tassel of green silk hanging near the podium where Glenn Yeats awaited the arrival of his audience.

The color scheme of this drapery—burgundy, gold, and green— lent a vaguely Christmassy note, appropriate enough to December, but the seasonal theme was probably happenstance, as the museum crew had scrambled to rig the unveiling apparatus even as the first guests were arriving in the lobby. The green tassel seemed especially out of place as a finial for the gold cord; it was doubtless used solely because it was at hand when needed. Save for its operatic proportions, it reminded me of the little green tassel that decorated the key to Chaffee's antique Biedermeier desk.

The lighting in the gallery was generally dim, except for a floodlight on the podium and a dozen pin spots on the velvet swags. Voices rose and fell as the crowd worked its way into the room, settled into the new surroundings, and wondered aloud what was concealed by the drapes.

"Come in, everyone," Glenn said from the dais, his voice booming from unseen loudspeakers. Someone scurried to adjust the amplification; then Glenn repeated, sounding less gargantuan, "Please, come in and get comfortable."

The crowd drew near him. As previously arranged, the press gathered in a roped-off section that afforded the best view for the unveiling. Larry and I stepped aside, where we could best observe not Glenn or the draped paintings, but the other onlookers.

Prominent among them was Dawn Chaffee-Tucker, the bereaved niece, looking more Jackie-esque than ever; all that was missing was a black lace chapel veil. Merrit Lloyd, banker of the deceased, stood by her side as escort and surrogate uncle. Recalling their lunch at the Royal Palms, I wondered again if Merrit harbored more intimate interests in the arty woman from Santa Barbara.

Merrit's secretary, Robin, stood several feet away with Chaffee's nurse, Bonnie. The out-of-work caregiver looked misty-eyed and contemplative, at odds with her spangled holiday outfit. Was her mood the result of genuine sorrow, I wondered, or guilt? Robin leaned close, offering the big woman a hug, saying something to boost her uncertain spirits.

Pea Fertig, the victim's erstwhile houseman, stood alone in the crowd in his smart black suit, staring at the swags beyond the podium. His hard features hid thoughts I couldn't fathom. Was he mourning the loss of a long-ago lover? Or was he gloating over the accomplishment of a deadly revenge that had simmered for twenty years?

Lance Caldwell and Atticus caught my attention. They still hung together, elbowing their way toward the front of the assembly, still blathering and boasting. The two great egos—music and art—grunted at each other and postured for anyone who would look at them.

Looking at them from the press corps was Mark Manning, who'd flashed his credentials to enter the cordoned-off area near the draped paintings. Then Mark glanced about as if he'd lost track of something. His eyes traveled toward the lobby doors. His features brightened as he spotted his nephew Thad, who had just entered the gallery—chomping on one last giant shrimp. Thad paused to wipe a smear of cocktail sauce from his chin.

Also near the door, slipping in from the lobby, were Kiki and Tanner, who must have met at the bar. Both carried concoctions in martini glasses—Kiki's was pink, Tanner's clear—moving slowly into the crowd, careful not to spill.

Grant stood just outside the door. Though I would have expected him to appear relieved that his welcoming speech was finished (by now there should have been a drink in his hand), he looked even more flummoxed than before. Keeping an ear on the activity in the gallery, he stepped back and glanced about the lobby, as if, like Mark Manning, he had lost track of someone. Of course, I reasoned—Kane. Where was he?

". . . this most generous and unexpected bequest."

A hearty round of applause nipped my thoughts. Absorbed as I was with the to and fro of the crowd, I'd managed to miss the opening of Glenn Yeats's speech, which was now in full swing. He'd already announced the terms of the alleged will. As he paused to acknowledge the applause, the room blinked with strobe lights from photographers who captured the moment.

"Well," said Larry Knoll, standing at my side, clapping halfheartedly, "it's a matter of public record now."

"Too bad it's all bogus. When the truth gets out, Glenn's going to have egg on his face."

The detective puckered and blew a low whistle.

Glenn continued, "Stewart Chaffee dedicated his life to the decorative arts, and later, to the fine arts. His collection grew to proportions rivaled by few others in Southern California, private *or* public. Pending final clearance of probate—a mere formality, I'm told—stewardship of this marvelous art trove will pass to the Desert Museum of Southwestern Arts."

Glenn turned. Fingering the green tassel that hung at his side, he continued, "We've arranged, through the executor of Mr. Chaffee's estate, to preview a small sampling of the vast body of works that constitute the museum's new legacy . . ."

As Glenn's words flowed, extolling a benefactor he didn't like and a gift he didn't want, my attention was riveted to his hand on the tassel. Again I recalled the dainty green silk tassel that had adorned the key to the Biedermeier desk. Keys, I realized, had played a role throughout the developing circumstances of Chaffee's death. The desk key had been returned by Kane on the morning of the murder; the same key was found on Chaffee's dead body. Later, when the forgery of the clipping was discovered and access to Chaffee's safe-deposit box became an issue, Pea had shown us the key to the box, among many others attached to his key ring. He'd even looked after Chaffee's car keys. "I'm the keeper of the keys," Pea had said.

"And so," said Glenn, pausing dramatically with his hand gripping the tasseled rope, "I'm highly honored to unveil for you one of Stewart Chaffee's most prized and recent acquisitions, a rare collection of works never before publicly displayed. I present to you"— he yanked the cord—"paintings by the Swedish neo-impressionist master, Per-Olof Östman."

The swags of velvet drapery fell, revealing the twelve little landscapes. Cameras flashed as the crowd broke into hearty, sustained applause. Their clapping was underlaid by gasps of approval and excited chatter. The delicate, colorful paintings, now exhibited in a proper gallery setting, perfectly lit, were indeed breathtaking, and I suspected that even Glenn Yeats would grudgingly acknowledge that Stewart Chaffee's final acquisition had lent profound distinction to his lifelong efforts of collecting.

Glenn quelled the applause, telling his onlookers, "I'd now be happy to take any questions you may have." As he said this, Tide and Iesha appeared from the shadows behind the podium, bearing cordless microphones. They began circulating among the guests, who suddenly took on the appearance of a daytime TV talk-show audience. This impression was made all the more vivid by the television cameras that now panned the crowd from the press pool.

Someone raised his hand; Iesha rushed to him with a microphone. He asked Glenn, "Can you give us some background on the artist?"

With an apologetic laugh, the computer magnate acknowledged, "Unfortunately, art history, especially that of Östman's period, is not my forte. However, we've garnered some essentials from the collection's certified provenance, and we're preparing a printed handout, which should be available shortly."

Bonnie, I noticed, was now openly crying. Robin seemed at a loss to console her. Pea approached the nurse through the crowd and said something quietly into her ear. I recalled, once more, that he was the keeper of the keys.

Atticus raised his hand. Both Iesha and Tide started toward him with their microphones, but Iesha was closer, so Tide dropped back. "Glenn," said Atticus, grabbing the mike like a lounge singer, "let me be the first to congratulate both the college and the museum on its acquisition of this fine collection. What a marvelous surprise. These Östman works are delightful." The crowd seconded his appraisal with a quick round of applause. "However," said Atticus, puffing his chest, "aren't these works rather far afield from the museum's artistic mission?"

Glenn bluffed an answer, stopping short of conceding that most of Chaffee's collection would end up in storage.

Many of the assembled reporters held tape recorders over their heads, capturing these exchanges. Others scribbled notes. Mark Manning had sat down on one of the display cubes, taken out his laptop, and begun typing. The computer sprouted a little antenna that looked like a black pinkie finger—he was on-line with a newsroom somewhere. I recalled our earlier conversation. He had asked me, "If forgery is at the crux of the murder, but the forger isn't the killer, where does that leave you?"

Pea and Bonnie were now conversing, and I was surprised to note no apparent hostility in their manner. Robin stepped away from them and sidled through the crowd toward Atticus. She touched her fingertips to his forearm—a gesture I recalled from Tuesday, when happening upon their romantic luncheon at the Regal Palms. She now looked him in the eye again and spoke to him with the same quiet intensity. Was she cautioning him against challenging the powerful Glenn Yeats, his employer, in so public a setting?

Someone near Larry and me raised his hand, and Tide bounded toward him on her muscular brown legs, thrusting the microphone toward his mouth. The squirrelly-looking professor—a potter, I believe—first cleared his throat, then got down to business, generously lacing his convoluted words with academic gibberish. Glenn, never one to back away from bull, took his time in responding, relishing the sound of his own voice, layering clause upon dependent clause.

During this drone, Merrit Lloyd stepped away from Dawn Chaffee-Tucker, slipping through the crowd toward the back of the room, where he found Grant Knoll near the doorway. Framed by the light from the lobby, they leaned together in conversation. Dawn, niece of the deceased, was left alone near the front of the assembled guests. She stood ramrod stiff, staring at the paintings, dismayed.

"I'm the keeper of the keys," Pea had said.

"Forgery is at the crux of the murder, but the forger isn't the killer," Mark had said.

Kane appeared in the doorway from the lobby carrying a stack of papers.

"My God," I blurted.

Larry turned to me. "What is it, Claire?"

But I had already rushed to Dawn's side. Larry followed. Dawn still stared at the paintings, unblinking. I leaned close and asked, "What's wrong?"

She shook her head as if emerging from a fog, then turned to me and gave the answer I expected.

I turned to Larry, asking, "You know what this means?"

"Not . . . exactly . . ."

Glenn, at the podium, was making wrap-up noises. There was no time to explain; within moments, the crowd would disperse.

I stepped forward to a clearing in the crowd and raised my hand, calling, *"Glenn?"* Tide had her microphone in my face before the word had left my mouth.

"Ah!" said Glenn. "Always a pleasure, my dear." He told the crowd, "Ladies and gentlemen, the illustrious Claire Gray." Television cameras swung in my direction. "I'm sure Claire wants to remind us all that her production of *Laura* will open tomorrow at—"

"Glenn," I interrupted, "don't you think it's time to let everyone in on our little secret?"

Rarely had I seen Glenn Yeats at a loss for words, but now he was. He stood looking at me with a quizzical expression, mouth sagging open, unable to formulate a question. Whispers rose from the crowd.

"The *plan*," I said with a sharp nod, a visual nudge, as if to tell him, Play along.

"Of course," he said uncertainly, "the . . . uh, plan." His eyes pleaded for help.

I told the crowd, "We apologize for calling everyone here this evening on a specious pretext, but it was part of a necessary ruse, designed to solve a murder. Stewart Chaffee, you see, did *not* bequest his estate to the museum."

Instantly, the room broke into a swirl of hushed conversation. The press was now on full alert. Glenn looked downright stupefied. "Uh, Claire?" he asked.

"So it goes without saying," I continued, speaking to everyone, "that the paintings unveiled here tonight are not the property of the museum. In fact, they were not even painted by Östman. They're frauds."

Gasps of disbelief rose from the chatter as Merrit Lloyd rushed forward from the back of the gallery. "That's *impossible*," he called, approaching me.

Tide and her microphone followed as I stepped to Dawn. I told the crowd, "This is Dawn Chaffee-Tucker, niece of Stewart Chaffee and a noted art scholar in her own right." I asked Dawn, "How can you be so sure that these paintings are not the work of Per-Olof Östman?" Tide flipped the microphone in Dawn's direction.

Without hesitation, Dawn explained, "Because there is no such painter as Per-Olof Östman, and to the best of my knowledge, there never was. What's more, there was never a neo-impressionist movement active in Sweden. The paintings, I must say, are exquisite; the technique is extraordinary; the compositions are masterful. But I have no idea when, where, or by whom they were painted."

By now, Merrit had arrived at my side. As he opened his mouth to speak, Tide was ready with her microphone. With a calming gesture of both hands, Merrit said, "I'm so sorry to contradict you, Dawn, but you must surely be mistaken in this matter. Indian Wells

Bank and Trust fully backs the authenticity of the Östman collection, which we arranged for Mr. Chaffee to acquire. My assistant, Robin Jones, researched and certified the provenances." He looked across the gallery. "Isn't that right, Robin?"

"Yes, sir," her voice came quietly from the crowd. As Iesha stepped toward Robin with a microphone, I recalled Saturday morning, when Merrit had first introduced his secretary as Robin Jones. Now, something else made sense to me.

I told the banker, "Actually, Merrit, it is you, not Dawn Chaffee-Tucker, who is mistaken with regard to the authenticity of the Östman canvases. They were painted not in Sweden, not in the 1890s, but right here, quite recently, by a master of many styles, Atticus Jones. The forgeries were authenticated by your secretary, Robin Jones, who I now presume is the painter's daughter. And it was Robin, by the way, who killed Stewart Chaffee."

After a moment of stunned silence, the room erupted with conversation. Larry Knoll moved in the direction of Robin and Atticus, where the crowd instinctively pulled back, except for Iesha with her microphone. Cameras swung from me to the accused.

From the clearing in the crowd, Atticus bellowed, "Don't be preposterous, Claire. How could you say something so slanderous and unfounded—in public, no less? Is this the thanks I get for contributing my sumptuous portrait of Laura to your stage play?"

I asked firmly, "Is Robin your daughter—or perhaps a niece or a young cousin?" Their age difference, which had appeared so unflattering in the context of romance, now made perfect sense, as did their shared last name, their red hair, their common interest in art, and their penchant for fraud.

Atticus hugged the young lady's shoulders. "Yes, of *course* she is my daughter. What of it?"

I quoted Mark Manning's earlier words: "Forgery is at the crux of the murder, but the forger isn't the killer."

Atticus laughed, telling the crowd, "The woman speaks in riddles."

Recalling Pea Fertig's earlier words, I asked Robin, "And you were the keeper of the keys, were you not?"

Atticus blustered, "Again the riddles!"

I told him sharply, *"I was speaking to Robin."*

She said quietly, "I'm afraid I don't know what you mean, Claire."

"I mean," I explained, "you've been more than just a secretary to Merrit Lloyd. You've been his executive assistant in every sense of the word. You organized his schedule, handled his papers, carried his briefcase, even dialed his phone. Most important, you kept his keys—both the keys to his car and the keys to the bank's safe-deposit boxes."

"Yes," she said uncertainly, "I try to be helpful."

"Helpful?" I laughed. "You took advantage of your employer, and you defrauded his most important client. Then, when circumstances threatened to reveal your scheming, you stooped to kill."

"Really, Miss Gray." Robin sounded flustered and panicky. "This is all rather far-fetched."

"Is it?" As the cameras swung back in my direction, I told everyone present, "Consider this scenario: A painter of considerable renown and great stylistic flexibility, Atticus conspired with his daughter, Robin, to defraud a wealthy art collector, Stewart Chaffee, whose business affairs were handled at the bank where Robin is employed in a position of trust. Working as a team, Atticus forged the Östman collection and Robin faked its provenances. They had likely done this before, with Stewart as their main 'client.' " I paused, recalling that Glenn Yeats had frequently questioned the quality of Stewart's art collection. Glenn's criticism, I now understood, had been based upon more insight than I'd been willing to acknowledge.

I continued, "Robin and Atticus knew that, to prevent discovery of their crime, it was crucial for the forged works to remain out of circulation. When Stewart asked his banker, Merrit Lloyd, to set up a meeting with his niece, Dawn, the task fell to Robin, who reasoned that the purpose of the meeting was reconciliation. Robin's hunch was reinforced last Saturday, when, in my presence, Stewart gave Merrit a plain white envelope, saying that it would make his intentions clear regarding the disposition of his estate. Merrit gave the envelope to Robin, who put it in Merrit's briefcase.

"Later that Saturday at the bank, Robin was entrusted to put the envelope in Stewart's safe-deposit box; she was keeper of the key and had full access to the vault. Instead of depositing the envelope, however, she opened it, discovering that Stewart had indeed written a homemade will, which may have named Dawn as heir to the Östman paintings. Robin understood that Dawn was a knowledgeable art dealer and would readily recognize the paintings as fraudulent. Since Stewart was scheduled to meet with Dawn on Monday morning, Robin and Atticus had to devise some preemptive action.

"So they hit upon a plan that involved yet another forgery—an interview supposedly published in an untraceable issue of a defunct newspaper, in which Stewart would state that everything he owns would be left to this museum. Atticus reasoned that since his forgeries did not fit the artistic mission of the museum—a point he raised just this evening—the paintings would be forever hidden in storage with DMSA's inactive collection.

"Atticus himself took charge of having the fake clipping produced, paying a museum intern to create the facsimile, which would purportedly be used as part of a history display. The clipping was commissioned on Sunday, produced that evening, and delivered on Monday morning. Atticus gave it to his daughter, who called upon her own forgery skills, adding marginal notes and Stewart's signature, copied from bank documents, before sealing the clipping in a fresh white envelope and depositing it in Stewart's vault box.

"It was a good plan, but its success still depended on two prerequisites. First, Stewart could not keep his appointment with Dawn, which would reveal the true intentions of his homemade will. And second, in order to effect the stipulations of the new, bogus will, Stewart had to die.

"On Monday morning, Robin was working against a deadline of eleven o'clock, the time she'd arranged for Dawn to visit Stewart at his estate. At ten o'clock, Merrit Lloyd entered a lengthy auditors' meeting at the bank. Robin would later fudge her boss's records of this meeting, convincing him that it had begun an hour later—yet another forgery. She couldn't let him know that, shortly after ten that morning, she'd taken his keys and driven his car to the estate, passing through the gate at ten-fifteen.

"Robin knew the security code, and she may even have had a key to the house. Stewart had been dozing most of the morning in his wheelchair; he was probably still asleep when Robin arrived. She woke him, perhaps explaining her presence on some banking pretext while calculating a way to forestall the eleven o'clock appointment. Robin and Stewart conversed for a while, and Stewart may have still been drowsy, but he became alert when he discovered a note left in his lap by his nurse. She had made a batch of pink fluff, his favorite treat, and had left it in the refrigerator for him.

"Sometime after ten-thirty, Stewart wheeled himself from the living room, through the great room, and into the kitchen, followed by Robin. He beelined for the refrigerator, but Robin froze in her tracks at the sight of the twelve Östman paintings displayed on easels in the great room. Now there was no doubt—Dawn Chaffee-Tucker could *not* be admitted to the house that morning. The mere sight of the paintings would raise her suspicions. Robin had to act fast, and she saw her opportunity as Stewart began tugging at the refrigerator door.

"With ruthless premeditation, Robin walked to the kitchen and, in the guise of friendly assistance, pulled upon the door for Stewart, swung it wide, then toppled the refrigerator onto his wheelchair, crushing but not immediately killing him. In the precious seconds when he still might have been saved from an agonizing death, Robin paused only to wipe her fingerprints from the chrome door handle. Then she fled.

"Some minutes later, Stewart's niece arrived at the estate, keeping her appointment of reconciliation with the uncle she had never known. But no one answered the door that morning, so she turned around, got back into her car, and returned to Santa Barbara."

In the hush of the crowded gallery, I turned to the press corps, summarizing, "And *that's* how Stewart Chaffee died."

Larry Knoll's footsteps grated on the stone floor as he approached Atticus and Robin, then stopped. "Well?" he asked, placing his hands on his hips. His suit jacket flapped open, revealing a glimpse of his leather shoulder holster.

Atticus aped the detective's posture. "Well, what? Surely you don't take any of this speculation seriously. Miss Gray has a fine sense of drama—I'll hand her that—but her story is nothing but bombastic nonsense."

I turned toward the double doors to the lobby. *"Kane,"* I called, "could you come here, please?"

Heads turned as the intern paused to set down his stack of papers (the freshly printed handouts detailing the fictive background of Per-Olof Östman were of no use now), then made his way around the perimeter of the gallery to where I stood.

I pointed to the clearing in the crowd, asking, "Do you recognize anyone?"

"Yeah. The old guy. The old guy in black. That's the man who asked me to make up the newspaper clipping. He paid me a hundred bucks. He said his name was Professor Eastman." It was lost on no one that the names Eastman and Östman were embarrassingly similar.

"Like hell, Detective," growled Atticus. "That kid's a liar, plain and simple. Isn't it obvious? You can't trust *that* sort. He's boyfriends with the museum-board president. *They're* behind this."

Larry looked Atticus in the eye. It was a steely gaze, quiet, but full of contempt. "That kid you're talking about? His name is Kane. He's boyfriends with my brother."

Atticus, at last, shut up.

Robin attempted a rescue, telling Larry, "I do hope you'll forgive my father's surly manner. It's easy jumping to wrong conclusions when you're under pressure." With a simper of a laugh, she tossed her head, brushing aside her china-doll bangs. "It seems this evening hasn't developed the way *any* of us planned."

She certainly hadn't planned to find twelve forged paintings hanging in the main gallery that night. Neither had Atticus.

Larry said, "Let me get this straight, Miss Jones. You're telling me that your father is wrong. You're telling me that neither Kane nor my brother was behind what happened to Stewart Chaffee."

She wriggled, "Well, I hope they weren't."

"Were *you?* Were you behind it?"

"Of course not, Detective. How could anyone possibly think—"

"Robin," I interrupted, "before you go too far with that denial, you should know about a crucial development in the investigation."

Larry's eyes slid toward me, wondering what I was up to.

I forged ahead, telling Robin, "The crime scene, obviously, was checked thoroughly for fingerprints. As you know, the killer cleaned the refrigerator handle before leaving, not only concealing her identity, but proving foul play. She also cleaned the prints from the inside knob of the front door when leaving, proving her escape route."

With a smirk, Robin noted, "Then you have nothing."

"Ah, but we do. It seems the killer was rushed or distracted when leaving the house, and she neglected to clean the *outside* doorknob."

Robin's smirk faded.

I wasn't sure how much latitude Larry might be allowed in fudging the facts to coax a confession, but I was bound by no such restrictions, so I felt no compunction in telling Robin, "The killer, the last person to use that door, left a full, clean set of fingerprints on the outside knob, including a beautiful thumbprint recognized by experts as that of a female. Prints have been taken from everyone known to be at the house on Monday, and the mysterious thumbprint has no match. Which means, we have abundant knowledge of who did *not* kill Stewart Chaffee. Since you claim to be innocent, Robin, I assume you'll be more than eager to volunteer a set of your prints."

Silence reigned for a moment as the young woman considered her options. Her fingers curled into fists; she dared not look at her hands.

When she opened her mouth, Atticus told her, "Don't, Robin. It's a trick."

"No, Dad." She shook her head. "I'm afraid this is it. It's over."

Atticus seemed to wither before our eyes. A talented artist, perhaps a genius, had fallen from greatness, weighted down by his own ego, damned by his pride.

Robin watched as her father buried his head in his hands. Then she turned to Larry and spoke softly. "Yes, Detective, I think you'll find that the unknown thumbprint is mine. I was there that day, in Mr. Lloyd's car, as suggested by Miss Gray. The rest, well—now that it's out, you'll have no trouble tracing the forgery of the paintings or the false certification of the provenances."

Larry nodded. "And Mr. Chaffee's death?"

Robin sighed, began to speak, then hesitated. Regaining a touch of her spunk, she said, "I don't intend to make this easy for you, Detective. You've got a lot of circumstantial evidence. But did I kill Stewart Chaffee? You'll have to prove it."

"I intend to, Miss Jones. And it won't be difficult."

With that, in front of a roomful of witnesses and a battalion of reporters, Larry Knoll arrested Robin for murder and Atticus for complicity; numerous counts of fraud would doubtless be added to their litany of woe. He handcuffed both, recited their rights, and led them from the gallery while phoning for backup.

The mum crowd parted, as if to let lepers pass.

They had no sooner left the room when the grim silence gave way to jolly pandemonium. The dramatic arrest had been far more entertaining than the dreary press conference to which the guests had presumably been invited. The crowd gabbed and laughed, comparing notes. Some rushed out to the lobby to watch the killers being hauled away—and to have another drink.

Most of the reporters left as well, scurrying to capture the scene outside the building. Others stayed behind, including Mark Manning, who still typed diligently at his laptop, pausing to glance at me, smile, and salute me with a thumbs-up. One of the television crews was clustered near the podium, interviewing Glenn Yeats. The microphone was still on. He told the reporters, ". . . so we saw our duty, and we never hesitated to assist the sheriff's department in this crime-solving effort. It's *so* gratifying to know that we played a small role in seeing justice done."

Grant and Kane strolled up to me, again the happy couple, secure in the knowledge that their relationship had not been undermined by scheming, greed, or murder. Grant gave me a hug. "Congratulations, doll. You did it again."

"Nonsense. Haven't you heard? This was *all* Glenn's doing."

We shared a laugh. Then Grant and Kane spotted Iesha and, needing to talk to her, excused themselves.

"Miss Gray?"

I turned to find Pea standing behind me with Bonnie. My eyes surely bugged at the sight of the little man in black with his arm around the big nurse in spangles.

"We wanted to thank you," said Pea, "for straightening this out."

Bonnie nodded. "The shock of Stewart's death was hard on everyone. He was a difficult man, but I did love him, and I know that Pea did, too."

Pea bowed his head. "We've both said and done some terrible things."

"That was anger talking," I assured him. "And the loss."

"But that's no excuse," said Bonnie. "Our feuding was no help to the investigation. I'm real sorry."

"So am I," echoed Pea.

"Claire!" said Merrit Lloyd, striding toward me with Dawn Chaffee-Tucker. "What a night, eh? Who'd have thought—a murderess in my own office. I'm mortified." He didn't sound mortified; he sounded tickled pink.

With a soft smile, Dawn told him, "Just be thankful it's over." She looked as composed and elegant as ever, utterly unruffled by the turn of events.

Merrit shuddered. "But the forged paintings, and the forged will, and the security breach." Sounding less giddy, he repeated, "I'm mortified."

I told them, "I just had a thought. This all began when Dawn received a badly typed letter from her uncle. I assume that letter was written on the home computer at the estate sometime during Pea's absence. We're reasonably sure that Stewart delivered a homemade will to Merrit, the one in the original white envelope, destroyed by Robin. I'll bet Stewart wrote his will on that same computer. Since it's now evident that Stewart's intentions were not those expressed in the fake newspaper column, what *did* he intend? If I were you"—I looked from face to face, from Merrit to Dawn to Pea to Bonnie—

"I'd search those computer files and figure out the true disposition of Stewart's estate."

They gaped at each other, having overlooked this promising angle. Pea, the keeper of the keys, jangled them, telling the others, "I'll open the house. Let's get going."

And with words of thanks, they left.

Tanner and Kiki were making their way through the crowd, laughing at something, bearing fresh drinks from the bar. Tanner carried an extra martini, and seeing it, I realized that I needed it badly—I'd been doing *far* too much talking that evening.

"Claire! *Darling!*" gushed Kiki as they approached. "You were a *triumph,* my dear. An unmitigated triumph."

"Thank you," I cooed, hugging her tight. With a wink, I took the glass from Tanner's hand and sipped behind Kiki's back. It was icy, stiff, and wonderful.

"My turn," said Tanner, wrapping his arms around me, managing not to spill either his or my cocktail. With an offhand tone, he asked, "Have I ever mentioned that I love you?"

I smiled wryly. "I can't say I recall." My God, he'd said the word. Would I utter it as well?

Before I could speak, Kiki interrupted at the decisive moment. "They really *are* charming, aren't they?"

"Hmm?"

"The *paintings,* dear"—she wagged a bracelet-clad arm toward the wall of faked Swedish masterpieces—"the Östmans or the Atticuses or whatever the hell you call them. Despite their shady pedigree, they're quite delightful." She sipped the pink liquid from her bird-bath, adding, "Simply enchanting."

I eyed the canvases. They were, in a word, captivating. One in particular, that little landscape at evening featuring a crude draw-bridge over a stream, drew me into its bucolic charm and its evocation of simpler times. Its lively palette was even more appealing than before. Nice frame too.

Why, it would look just dandy on one of my bare living-room walls.

To whom, I wondered, did the Östman collection now belong?

Tanner said the word again that night, after we returned to my condo, and again on Friday morning, as we tangled the sheets before rising.

Did I tell him, in turn, that I loved him? It seems hopelessly scatterbrained to claim that I cannot remember, but remember I cannot. I had flirted with the simple declaration for months, while weighing a schizophrenic mix of relief and resentment that Tanner, too, had felt no rush to label our emotions. So on Friday morning, during a moment of high rapture, when the word again rolled from his lips, it may at last have rolled from mine as well.

If I didn't speak it, I felt it. And I communicated my love with a physical intensity that delighted Tanner and amazed even me.

"Wow," he said, catching his breath when we had finished. "I mean, *wow.*"

I needed a cigarette. But I had quit on the day when I had moved to California. Still, a trace of telltale tobacco huskiness colored my voice as I told Tanner, deadpan, "You weren't so bad yourself."

Springing from the bed, he informed me, "I'll get the coffee going." Then he bounded down to the kitchen, taking the stairs by twos. I heard the latch of the front door as he opened it to grab the paper. "Hey!" he called. "You made page one."

I flopped back on the pillows, heaving a big sigh, as if bored by it all.

We had slept late for a weekday, till nine or so, a just reward for my exploits the previous evening. Besides, our production of *Laura* was to open that night, and I wanted Tanner well rested for the long-awaited debut. By nine-thirty that morning, we had thrown on some clothes and headed out to the pool terrace bearing a tray loaded with coffee, the paper, and Tanner's protein slop (his regimen usually struck me as superfluous, but that morning, following our vigorous romp, I silently conceded that he might be due for a booster).

The overnight chill had lifted, and we settled comfortably at the round glass table, dismissing any need to light the firepot. Abundant sunshine slanted through surrounding palms and pines, dancing on the placid surface of the pool.

"Morning, doll!" called Grant, spotting us from the French doors of his neighboring condo. "How's the lady of the hour?" he asked, slipping out to join us with an oversize mug of coffee. Dressed for his day at the office and fresh from his twenty-minute shave, he made me feel like a feckless sloven. Arriving at the table, he set down his cup and leaned to give me a kiss.

"What about me?" asked Tanner wryly.

Grant circled behind him with a menacing growl, then chastely pecked the top of Tanner's head, pausing a moment to savor the touch and scent of sandy, bed-rumpled hair. "Hmm," Grant sounded an accusing note. "I smell sex."

"Stop that." Behind my playful reprimand, I wondered if Grant had made a good guess—or were his senses truly that well honed?

"*Well,* now," he said, sitting across from me, tapping the newspaper on the table, "milady will have a tough time of it tonight, topping last night's performance."

"Not at all," I assured him. "Last night was merely a diversion, an improvisation. But *tonight*—that performance has been fully rehearsed and polished. Besides, my work is done. It's Tanner's turn to shine." I reached over the table and rubbed the back of his hand.

"I'll do my best," he told me, flashing a smile that would, I was certain, make any audience wilt.

I asked Grant, "Where's Kane this morning?"

"Up and out already. The museum crew will have their hands full today. 'The Chaffee Legacy' is now history, the figment of a fake newspaper clipping. So it's back to plan A, and the kachina exhibit returns to the main gallery in time for the opening of your play tonight."

"Claire!" hollered my other neighbor, Kiki, from somewhere unseen, probably the center courtyard, near the fountain. "Where are you?"

Tanner called, "We're by the pool."

Footfalls raced through the courtyard, crunching sand on the terra-cotta tiles. Appearing at the terrace gate, Kiki announced, "You made the *Times*, Claire."

"*What?*" I had no doubt that the *Times* she waved was the one from New York, as Los Angeles had not yet registered on Kiki's radar.

She banged the gate and bustled toward the table, fluttering the newspaper, jangling her bracelets (though the day was young, she never left the house less than fully accessorized). Plopping the paper on the table, she said, "And Mark Manning wrote it."

Sure enough, there on page three, above the fold, was Mark's bylined story, which had been picked up by wire, apparently running in numerous papers that day. The *Times* headline proclaimed, FLAIR FOR DRAMA, followed by an italic subhead, *Claire Gray, toast of Broadway, snares killer, art swindler at museum opening in California.*

The story, which I read aloud, recounted the events of the previous evening with Mark's typical precision, insight, and charm—there was no mistaking his style. He'd gotten some good quotes from Detective Larry Knoll as well as D. Glenn Yeats, who basically took credit for aiding police in setting the trap. Mark spared no ink, however, in describing me as "the undisputed hero in untangling a most heinous crime." He even plugged the opening of my play. Setting down the paper, I shook my head, telling the others, "This is far too flattering."

"Nonsense, doll." Grant beaded me with a stare. "You *love* it."

"Yes," I admitted with a grin, "I *do*."

Kiki joined us at the table, sitting next to me. With a pensive sigh, she asked, "Why would he do it? Atticus, I mean. Robin's crime was terrible, but there's no mystery to her motive; the murder was a cover-up, an attempt to hide other transgressions. But Atticus—what made *him* tick? Did he really think he could get away with such an outrageous forgery scheme?"

Tanner reminded her, "He damn near did."

Repeating Kiki's question, Grant asked rhetorically, "Why would he do it?" Then he answered, "For the money. It was greed, pure and simple."

"I'm not so sure," I thought aloud. "Atticus had great talent—and an enormous ego. I think he undertook the forgery scheme simply to see if he could pull it off. When he succeeded, the secret must have driven him wild. After all, what's the *point* of a stupendous hoax if it's known to no one? Ultimately, he was brought down by his own pride, the classic flaw of theatrical tragedy."

"And he brought down his daughter with him," said Kiki. With a shudder, she added, "It's like a sordid twist on *Oedipus*."

Shrugging off this sobering observation, Grant told me, "At least you got his portrait of Laura."

Kiki perked up. "That's right! My *God,* think of the buzz. It's now known that Atticus forged the work of an obscure painter who was entirely fictitious, much as he created the fictitious Stuart Jacoby's portrait of Laura. So the play's set is graced by *two* remarkable artifacts: a murder victim's clock, and a portrait painted by the father of the killer. Oooh, how delicious."

With a start, I realized that Kiki was right. I had hoped, by solving the murder, that I would put an end to the hype and allow my cast and their audience to focus on the play itself, without the distraction of the recent crime. Instead, I had generated more headlines and cranked up the noise.

"Claire, *darling,*" Kiki reminded me with an elaborate flourish, "sell the sizzle!"

I laughed. Whom, pray tell, was I kidding? Certainly not myself, not anymore. The clock, the portrait—remnants of murder—they were sensational additions to our show, adding to a staged mystery some real-life sizzle that I couldn't have bought at any price. I now understood that my motive for getting involved with the investigation had had nothing to do with protecting the integrity of my production.

No, I realized, I had simply enjoyed the challenge of another twisted plot. I also enjoyed the satisfaction of knowing I was up to the challenge; in fact, I was good at it.

Tanner was saying, "I have nothing but positive vibes about tonight's opening. The murder is behind us, the cast is ready, and the curtain is ready to rise."

With a slow, exaggerated nod, Kiki intoned the words of the bard: " 'The play's the thing.' "

"I couldn't agree more," I said firmly, dismissing the real world and its woes, gladly shifting my attention to mayhem of the scripted sort. I told my well-rehearsed heartthrob of a sleuth, "Don't forget, Tanner—important guests in the audience tonight."

"Forget? I can think of little else. Knowing that both Hector Bosch and Spencer Wallace will be out there in the dark, watching, I can feel the butterflies already."

"Perfectly natural," I assured him. "That's the adrenaline working. Don't fear it; use it. Harness those jitters, and they'll give you your edge."

"Pearls of wisdom," said Grant. "At such an ungodly, early hour." He slurped his coffee.

I confessed, "The pep talk was meant for me as much as for Tanner. Truth is, I'm nervous about seeing Hector again. We parted on shaky terms when I left New York."

"Nonsense," said Kiki. "Hector has *always* carried a torch for you."

"That's what has me worried."

"Hello?" asked a voice. "Anybody home?"

Grant rose and looked over the wall into the courtyard. "Yes? May I help you?"

"We have a delivery for Miss Claire Gray."

"Ah. She's here with us. Just use the gate, please." Grant motioned toward it.

The rest of us exchanged a round of quizzical glances.

A moment later, the deliveryman and a young helper entered the terrace bearing gifts from a local florist. Grant signed for them as the kid aligned three arrangements near the edge of the pool. There was a small one, a bud vase with some carnations. The second vase, a tasteful crystal cylinder, contained a dozen red roses, a few long black twigs, and no greenery, conveying urban sophistication. The third was an opulent arrangement of callas and white roses, easily fifty stems, suggesting not only price-is-no-object extravagance, but overtones of (God help me) matrimony.

I felt reasonably sure of who had sent the first and the third, but the one in the middle left me guessing.

Sitting again, Grant quipped, "Who died?"

The kid asked me, "Would you like the cards?"

"Please."

So he plucked the little envelopes from each of the bouquets and placed them in order on the table in front of me. Then he and his partner left.

I sipped my coffee.

The others stared at me, waiting. Grant finally offered, "If you'd prefer to be alone . . ."

"Of course not." I grinned, then opened the first card. "Aww," I said, reading it privately, "I thought so. Thank you, Tanner." He'd used that word again. I rose from my chair, stepped to his, and leaned to kiss him. Holding his face in my hands, I told him, awkwardly but deliberately, "I, uh . . . I love you too." He smiled; predictably, my knees went weak. Steadying myself, I plucked one of the carnations from his vase, then sat again.

"Let's see," I said, fingering the third envelope, "any guesses?"

With a snort, Kiki said, "Judging from the proportions of that overgrown nosegay, I'd say the sender is fairly obvious." She added, "Not that it wasn't thoughtful of him."

"Glenn can be very generous." The understatement left my lips before my fingers had extracted the card from its envelope. Reading the inscription, I confirmed that our speculation was dead-on. I told the others, "Get this: 'Dearest Claire, once again it seems congratulations are in order, but perhaps it would be prudent to limit your future triumphs to those of the theatrical ilk. Break a leg tonight! All my love, Glenn.' "

No one breathed a word.

"Well, now," I said, tossing the card aside, "who do you suppose sent the red roses in the middle?" I eyed Grant, wondering, Was it he? Perhaps his brother, Larry? Or even the banker, Merrit Lloyd?

Hearing no guesses, I slit open the envelope, pulled out the card, and gasped. "Oh, Lord," I muttered, "they're from *Hector.*"

"See?" said Kiki. "His torch is still aflicker."

"Oh, *please.*" I read aloud, " 'Brava, dear lady. Despite your abandonment of our fair city, you are still making headlines in the *Times.* I am leaving for the airport now and will soon be winging my way west to see you once more. Till this evening, my darling!' And it's signed, 'Hector Bosch'—as if I might know more than one Hector." I tossed the card on top of Glenn's, lifted Tanner's carnation from my lap, and sniffed its clean, unaffected scent.

"How terribly sweet of Hector," said Grant with a crooked smile.

"I just hope he likes the play," I worried aloud.

"Of *course* he will." Kiki's chair scraped the pavement as she rose. "If everyone will excuse me, I really *must* put myself together for the day." She looked thoroughly put-together already, but I refrained from commenting. There was no telling how many costume changes her day would see.

Tanner rose as well. "I need to get going too. I've got some business on campus and a few errands to run."

I told him, "Good idea to keep your mind occupied today. Don't stew over the play. Eight o'clock will come soon enough."

He leaned to give me a kiss, then lifted our tray of breakfast things. Kiki gabbed some pleasantries in parting. Within a few moments, Grant and I were left alone at the table.

"He really does suit you," said Grant. "Tanner and you are looking very . . . domestic."

Wistfully, I admitted, "I hope so. I mean, God, I'm not sure *what* I want. Do I dare to think this can actually *work?*"

"Why not, Claire? Live your dreams. I'm living *mine* with Kane. This weekend, we'll decorate our first Christmas tree. You know the old bromide: life is *not* a dress rehearsal."

"I've heard *that* once or twice." Looking Grant in the eye, I told him, "What scares me is this: What if I decide that Tanner and I *are* right for each other, and then I lose him? He'll find someone younger, or his career will take off, or—"

"Listen, Claire. You can't control what you can't control. You can only do what's right for *you*. If all the other pieces fit, fabulous. If not, at least you tried."

I twirled the flower in my hands, mentioning, "I may need a bigger place."

Offhandedly, Grant suggested, "Move in with Glenn. He's all but proposed it. He'd *love* to have you. And his digs are spectacular."

"Stop that. You know what I mean. I may need a bigger place for the *two* of us, Tanner and me." A hummingbird darted from a nearby arbor and began exploring Hector's red roses.

Grant reminded me, "I'm a real-estate broker. Anytime you're ready . . ." He paused, drumming his fingers on his chin. "Come to think of it, I've got a listing that's *perfect* for you."

Footfalls passed through the courtyard. Then Larry Knoll appeared at the gate. "I *thought* I might find you back here."

"He's so clever," said Grant. "My brother, the detective."

"Good morning, Larry," I called to him. "Come on in."

He crossed the terrace, greeting both Grant and me, then sat at the table with us. With a broad smile, he shook his head, saying, "I've got to hand it to you, Claire—you really pulled it off. I have no idea how you pieced everything together when you did, but your timing was impeccable."

"Must be due to my theatrical training." I primped. "It was nothing."

Grant asked his brother, "And how are the deadly duo this morning?"

"Haven't seen them today. But they were feisty as hell last night. The fraud charges are a done deal; we'll have no trouble picking up the money trail."

"And the murder charges?" I asked.

"Robin played it smug until we took her fingerprints. I gave her one last chance to level with me, dangling the carrot of leniency. Your gambit worked, Claire. She believed your story about the incriminating 'female' thumbprint. We got a complete confession."

I shrugged. "Happy to help."

Grant said to Larry, "You mentioned a money trail. Where *is* all the cash they swindled out of Stewart? Neither Robin nor Atticus seemed to be flashing it around, living beyond their means."

"They managed to hide it, invest it, or plant it somewhere off-shore. Robin is well acquainted with the ins and outs of banking; she's a pro. Chances are, their scam would never have come to light if it hadn't been for the murder. Now, though, tracing the money will be a breeze."

I flipped my hands. "Neat and easy. You must have been tucked in by ten last night."

Larry laughed. "Actually, no."

Grant and I turned to each other with an inquisitive look.

Larry explained, "Apparently you suggested that several interested parties should check the victim's home computer. No sooner had I finished up with Robin and Atticus than I got a phone call from the banker, Merrit Lloyd. He was at the estate, and they'd found a file on the computer, claiming it spelled out Chaffee's last wishes."

"Ahhh." I sat back in my chair. "Then we were right all along. The envelope that Stewart gave to Merrit last Saturday *did* contain a homemade will."

"It would seem so, yes. And that's why Merrit phoned. He wanted to instantly alert someone in an official capacity that the file had been found, presumably to forestall any future claims that the electronic document was a fraud. So I went right over there, taking with me a computer specialist from the department. Everything seems to check out. The document was created in Stewart's directory late last week."

Grant asked, "Can I presume, then, that the Desert Museum of Southwestern Arts is *not* Stewart's true heir?"

"Correct. He left a few minor items to the museum, stuff that fits its collection, but most of his estate goes elsewhere." Larry crossed his arms.

I had to ask, *"Well?"*

"Let's just say that when I arrived last night, I was greeted by some very happy people. First of all, Stewart willed the house, many of the antiques, and several other real-estate holdings to his longtime companion, Makepeace Fertig. Second, he left the bulk of his art collection to his niece, Dawn Chaffee-Tucker. And finally, he left a sizable cash remembrance to his nurse, Bonnie Bahr." With a grin, Larry added, "Among those parties, there was a consensus that everyone had been treated fairly. The will named Merrit Lloyd executor of the estate, and the banker was greatly relieved that probate battles now seem unlikely."

Grant swirled some tepid coffee in the bottom of his mug. "And thus ends a colorful chapter in the history and lore of Palm Springs decorating." He tossed the coffee along the roots of a nearby hedge.

Larry stood. "Forgery and murder—yes, I'd call that fairly colorful."

I stood as well, offering Larry a farewell hug. "Forgery . . . ," I echoed as he was about to leave. "I wonder what will become of the Per-Olof Östman paintings faked by Atticus. I suppose, with all the other art, they'll go to Stewart's niece."

Larry laughed heartily.

I turned to Grant, who sat there with a blank expression, looking as mystified as I was. So I asked the detective, "What am I missing?"

Still chortling, he said, "I thought you'd *never* get around to asking about those."

"Okay, okay," said Grant, "we're asking: Did Dawn inherit the Östmans?"

"No, Grant." Larry stuffed his hands in his pockets. He paused. "You did."

Grant and I shared a dumbstruck, jaw-dropping glance. Then he rose, asking his brother, *"Me?"*

"Yup. Chaffee was explicit. It seems he had truly admired you over the years, and he was especially pleased that you'd now taken over at the museum. He claimed that acquiring the Östman collection was his crowning accomplishment. The paintings are yours."

"I'm . . . stunned."

"And you'd be rich—if they were real."

"Yeah." Grant turned to me, hand to hip. "Did you have to be *quite* so quick in exposing this artistic chicanery?"

"Sorry." I hugged him. "Easy come, easy go."

He sighed. "The story of my life."

"Get over it."

Larry said, "Gotta run. Thanks again, Claire. I'll see you tonight at the theater. And, Grant—congratulations." With an exaggerated wink, the detective left.

When his footfalls had receded and tapered off to nothing, the glorious desert morning seemed suddenly quiet. Even the birds hushed, as if an angel of silence had passed through the trees.

"Grant," I said, taking his arm, strolling him across the terrace, "I need to have a word with you."

"Yes, doll?"

"Regarding a bridge."

"Hm?"

"A drawbridge. A rustic drawbridge captured at sunset in a neo-impressionist masterpiece."

He stopped in his tracks, correcting me, "*Minor* Swedish neo-impressionist masterpiece."

I further corrected, "Fake, *worthless* minor masterpiece."

"Ah, yes," he said, tapping his noggin, "*that* one. I recall it well, a bucolic treasure. Milady isn't . . . *interested,* is she?"

"Possibly, Grant. Possibly."

We pattered on in this affable manner, ambling together along the apron of the pool.

The hummingbird, having needle-nosed its fill from Hector's roses, shot across the water, then flirted with the towering orange finger of an ocotillo flower before skirring to the heavens.

I watched, breathless, as the iridescent speck disappeared in a vast, blue December sky.